# Praise for Anna Larner's

### *Highland Whirl*

"I loved this so much! It had every conflict, angst, cute moments, hell, you could ever want for a perfect rom com!...Everything about the story was just so perfect and I know my review cannot do it justice. *Highland Whirl* is one of those AMAZING stories that you just have to experience for yourself."—*LESBIreviewed*

"*Highland Whirl* by Anna Larner is the third book I've read by this particular author and I've loved every one. Although this is a follow up to *Highland Fling*, there is no need to have read the previous story as it works as a standalone too...The writing was beautifully descriptive and one could almost imagine being in the Highlands with them. The setting was perfect and the characters exceptionally well imagined. Anna Larner writes in a gentle, kind and loving way, and I look forward to every book she brings out. A wonderful story."—*Kitty Kat's Book Review Blog*

### *Highland Fling*

"[This book] just kept surprising me at every turn! I had a few moments of 'Really did I just read that?' and 'Did she just say that?' I love when a book does this because you feel the writer is writing outside the box...All in all, I loved *Highland Fling* and think Anna Larner will definitely be an author I'll be watching out for."—*Les Rêveur*

"Take a day off, curl up and lose yourself in this lovely lesbian romance by debut novelist Anna Larner."—*DIVA*

"[T]his is one of those books that breathes 'good reading.' The author Larner has the perfect ear for a certain type of LGBT space, and weaves a convincing queer & lesbian psychogeography into the narrative, and her own experiences and previous work with archiving and creating space for LGBT history to be shared gives this book an authentic feel, not just in tone, geography and accent but also the emotional honesty that marks this book out as such a charming read."
—*Gscene Magazine*

## *Love's Portrait*

"Author Anna Larner combines a satisfying mix of humor, bittersweet revelations, family and workplace dynamics, drama, opposites attract romance, and history."—*Omnivore Bibliosaur*

"This story was absolutely wonderful. The characters were dynamic and engaging, the flashbacks moved the story forward instead of dragging it down, the romance was sweet and awesome and perfectly paced. Just all around a great book, I enjoyed every second of it."—*Elisa Reviews and Ramblings*

"This book pulled me in so amazingly fast I'm pretty sure I got reading whiplash. It was awesome…What was most impressive about this novel was the emotion throughout the book, the whole novel seemed to vibrate with all sorts of different emotions. Especially the stuff that was set in the 1800s, which I loved. It was an amazing book, complex and compelling."—*From Bella to YLVA*

"I mean it as the utmost compliment that at times I felt I was reading a compelling C19th novel that just happened to be set in C21st Leicester with lesbians. It's not too much of a leap to say that, if Jane Austen was writing lesbian romance fiction today, she might have come up with something akin to *Love's Portrait*!"—*Sam O'Nions, Kenric Newsletter*

"Beautifully Romantic! I just got so lost in the romance inside the romance that I was genuinely in love with the story and blown away by the end. This is only the second story I have read by Anna Larner but I am in awe of her ability to capture such passion, longing, and love as she has with *Love's Portrait*. It was truly beautiful, even the more tragic elements, and I longed to learn that there was happiness and there was. I adored every second and became fully immersed in the story to the point I just couldn't put it down."—*LESBIreviewed*

"*Love's Portrait* is a perfect mixture of love, romance and belonging. Anna Larner's writing has a gentle beauty to it, an engaging tone throughout. Her characters feel real to me and she makes me want to know more about them. This is the second book I have read by this author and I must admit she has become a favourite of mine. A lovely story."—*Kitty Kat's Book Review Blog*

**By the Author**

Highland Fling

Love's Portrait

Highland Whirl

Invisible

Visit us at www.boldstrokesbooks.com

# INVISIBLE

*by*
Anna Larner

2023

**INVISIBLE**
© 2023 BY ANNA LARNER. ALL RIGHTS RESERVED.

ISBN 13: 978-1-63679-469-3

THIS TRADE PAPERBACK ORIGINAL IS PUBLISHED BY
BOLD STROKES BOOKS, INC.
P.O. BOX 249
VALLEY FALLS, NY 12185

FIRST EDITION: DECEMBER 2023

THIS IS A WORK OF FICTION. NAMES, CHARACTERS, PLACES, AND INCIDENTS ARE THE PRODUCT OF THE AUTHOR'S IMAGINATION OR ARE USED FICTITIOUSLY. ANY RESEMBLANCE TO ACTUAL PERSONS, LIVING OR DEAD, BUSINESS ESTABLISHMENTS, EVENTS, OR LOCALES IS ENTIRELY COINCIDENTAL.

THIS BOOK, OR PARTS THEREOF, MAY NOT BE REPRODUCED IN ANY FORM WITHOUT PERMISSION.

**CREDITS**
EDITOR: RUTH STERNGLANTZ
PRODUCTION DESIGN: STACIA SEAMAN
COVER DESIGN BY INKSPIRAL DESIGN

# Acknowledgments

A heartfelt thank you to the BSB team, in particular, Len Barot, Sandy Lowe, and Ruth Sternglantz.

To my awesome beta readers—thank you from the bottom of my heart for your amazing support—it means the world.

And to the fabulous Alison Child—thank you for bringing the world of the drag king alive for me.

To my wonderful partner, family, and friends—thank you, as ever, for your love.

To readers—a huge thank you for choosing *Invisible*—and welcome to Unwin's Emporium, where imagination and inspiration await you.

To all the rebel women past and present.

## Chapter One

"Charge!" Violet Unwin launched herself from behind the embattled trenches of the shop counter and into the blood and smoke and violence of outright war. She leaped over the landmines of unexploded cushions and swerved just in time to miss the certain devastation of falling shells. How narrowly she missed the sting of bullets whistling past her head. And oh—please, no—don't let the fearsome airplanes stalking above spot her through the clouds.

"Take cover!" Violet landed flat on her stomach with a winding thump. Maybe she should have taken into account the unforgiving solid concrete floor, but under the pressure of warfare there was zero time to think or, for that matter, feel. So what if her palms smarted from having grazed against the thin layer of scratchy green felt carpet? For these were the hazards of engagement and she was more than up for the fight. Oh yes.

Undeterred, pressing her helmet tight against her head, she propelled herself ever forward. At the same time, she brandished her bayonet rifle at the surprised enemy.

"Surrender your arms, and I will spare your life." She poked the bayonet into the chest of her ambushed foe. The dressing-up mannequin rocked back on its pedestal with each press of her weapon. "Don't resist. You know it's futile." The mannequin's Lord Nelson style hat slipped down over its eyes. Violet lifted it back into place with the tip of her bayonet. "Denial is pointless. We have reserve battalions gathering at the base of that hill." Violet turned and pointed to the bottom of the stairs located through a small doorway in the corner of the room. They were, after all, the wooden hill to her accommodation that she climbed every evening after a busy day's work at her uncle's costume shop.

She rested her rifle against the chair outside the dressing room and stood to take a moment's breath. She found herself staring at the doorway and at the short run of steps that angled away to the right and disappeared into the darkness. Her thoughts strayed from the heat and urgency of battle to the comfort and familiarity of her daily routines. What simple pleasure she found in the unhurried sequences at the beginning and end of the working day.

Like clockwork, she would shut the shop at five, flip the sign to *Closed*, and turn the key in the lock. But first she would step out onto the street and glance up and down at the hustle of passers-by and reassure herself that there were no customers rushing to catch the shop before it closed. How many times had she been hailed a lifesaver by a harried office worker who'd hoped against hope that the shop would still be open? Why had they left organising their party outfit to the day before, they would say.

And each time, without fail, they would gape in confusion at the rails of hanging costumes and look to Violet for help. Did she think the gorilla outfit would be too hot? Or the maid's uniform too saucy? Maybe they could go as a 1920s flapper girl? No, maybe not. And weren't clowns the most frightening of things? *Perhaps Wonder Woman?* Violet would suggest. Their eyes would light up. Violet was never sure whether it was the boots or the corset-style top that won them over. They would emerge from the dressing room, spinning and brandishing their lasso with empowered delight.

Violet loved to witness their transformation from tired and flustered to kick-ass glamourous heroes. For the men it was a cowboy. Always a cowboy. And for her? These were not just costumes—they were escape. Escape from a world where she didn't fit. Escape from a world where, more often than not, her encounters left her feeling lonely and utterly invisible.

Every costume offered Violet a world of adventure, whether as a swashbuckling pirate terrorising the high seas, a globetrotting megastar entertaining a stadium of fans, or even an astronaut blasting to space. She could travel wherever the outfit sparked her imagination. For Unwin's Emporium was not just a costume shop—it was freedom.

It was *everything*.

And today, where would she go? Into the fury of battle. Violet turned to face the dressing room mirror. Her cheeks were tinged pink with effort, and her eyes sparkled with the thrill of it all. She lifted the bowl-shaped metal shrapnel helmet from her head and tucked it under her arm. Then she puffed at her fringe before giving a sharp salute. Her heart sank at the sight of a torn shoulder strap on her khaki World War One infantryman's jacket. It must have happened in the hard landing. That would not do. Any sign of imperfection would be noticed by the enemy. She spotted the figure of the mannequin sheepishly reflected to the side of her. Espionage.

"Right. Don't say I didn't warn you. Hand-to-hand combat it is." Violet cast her hat aside and, without warning, gripped her arms around the mannequin's waist and wrestled it to the floor. There she struggled with it until one of its arms fell off in her hand. There was no dignity in defeat—that was for sure.

A scrape of keys in the lock followed by the shrill ring of the brass doorbell announced the arrival of an unexpected visitor. Before Violet had the chance to untangle herself from the mannequin, the door swung open and a cold breeze swept in, accompanied by the looming figure of her cousin, Carl Unwin.

"What the hell are you doing, Violet?" Carl narrowed his eyes and fixed a wounding stare upon her. It was an expression of utter disbelief combined with enough disgust to leave Violet feeling beyond worthless.

"Nothing." Violet quickly stood and brushed at her jeans. She held the stray arm of the mannequin behind her.

"You do know you're ridiculous?"

Violet followed Carl's incredulous gaze from scattered cushions to discarded helmet to the criss-cross barricades of fabric on rolls pressed up against the counter.

"It's a fortified front line," Violet mumbled, more as an apology than an explanation.

"It's a freak show. That's what it is."

"I was just messing around."

"You're eighteen. Not five. Get a life and grow up."

Violet pinched her lips together as tears stung her eyes. She would not cry in front of him. If he was an example of adulthood, then never let her age another day.

"Stupid bloody shop…" With cheeks colouring to a deep shade of puce, Carl pushed in frustration to close the door behind him. It took several hearty shoves to force the door to fit flush. The glass shook in its frame, and the doorbell rang out with each push. "How on earth do customers actually get in and out of this place?"

How could Violet tell Carl that no one else found the door a struggle but him. Not to mention that it was a Wednesday, and this meant early closing. Telling Carl anything was so awful that Violet spent as little time in his company as possible. You could say he was less a man and more of a mood. And a foul one at that. Just the sound of his voice, whiny with disdain and frothy with anger, pressed tight in her chest. Even the sight of him made her feel sick. She knew he was all talk and no action, but he still frightened her anyway. It had been such a relief when he had left for London some three years ago to become a banker.

She took a deep nervous breath to ask, "What are you doing here?"

If Carl heard her, he ignored her. Instead, he made his way behind the counter and began clumsily to open drawers and rifle through their contents.

Violet stood frozen on the spot. "What are you looking for?"

He stopped and looked up at her. Her mouth became instantly dry. She tightened her grip on the mannequin's arm. Carl turned away only to give up with a growl. "The accounts. Where are the ledgers, Violet?"

"For which years?"

"For which years?" Carl repeated mockingly. And with a tone of deliberate condescension he added, "This year to the fifth of April and last year to the fifth of April."

"They're in the drawer underneath the till." Violet kept immaculate accounts. She could have gone on to tell Carl the income and expenditure figures. She wanted to point out the profits rising year on year. She wanted to tell him to stick his sarcasm up his—

Carl pulled the slim leather-bound volumes free and tugged a cloth tote bag from the collection hanging up for sale. He shoved the ledgers into it and paused as if examining the logo. *Unwin's Emporium. A family business since 1898.* He gave a scoff. Without even bothering to close the drawer behind him, he made for the front door. His foot kicked at the infantryman's helmet as he pushed past Violet.

"Wait. What do you need the accounts for?"

Once again, Carl struggled with the door. "Open this shitting thing."

"Not until you tell me what you want the accounts for." Violet winced inside.

He turned and looked at her with all the menace and venom of a cornered rattlesnake. The rattlesnake had more charm and could have worn Carl's expensive suit with more style.

Carl all but foamed at the mouth with fury. "Do *you* own this shop?"

"No. But Uncle Walter has left me in charge. You *know* that."

Everyone knew that. Those in the trade looked to her, and the shop's customers had valued the natural continuity that came with Violet taking the reins. When her uncle unexpectedly retired due to ill-health, some six months ago now, it had been agreed, in principle at least, that Violet would take care of the Emporium on his behalf. On the very morning that he left, with tears in his eyes, her uncle had said, *I take great heart, Violet, that I am leaving Unwin's Emporium knowing that it's safe in your hands.* Her uncle had assured her that he would keep in touch regularly and that together they would develop a longer-term plan to secure the future of the Emporium.

With a vein bulging at his temple, Carl replied, "What I *know* is that my father Walter has asked *me* to handle the future of the shop."

"You?" That couldn't be true, could it? That wasn't the plan. But then, despite her uncle's reassurance, a long-term plan had yet to be put in place. In fact, her uncle's calls had become more infrequent and eventually stopped. When Violet had rung for him, concerned, her aunt had answered and told her that Walter's health had deteriorated, and she wasn't to disturb him with shop business. Violet's question—*You will let me know when he's better?*—seemed to fall on deaf ears. Violet had been waiting ever since for a call that never came. It had worried her, but she told herself that her uncle would be better soon and that it didn't mean anything. Turned out she had every reason to be worried.

Struck rigid with the fear of the possibility, Violet asked, "What do you mean by that?"

"I mean…" Carl took a step towards Violet. His bulky frame cast a cold shadow over her. "Open. This. Door. Is what I mean."

The message was clear. Carl now considered the shop to be his. And Violet, well, she might as well be invisible.

Violet reached around him and opened the door with the lightest of effort.

Without waiting another second, Carl Unwin left, and only the faint smell of his cheap aftershave lingered. Violet wafted the door open and closed until there was no trace of her cousin. If only that was all it took.

❖

Phoebe Frink was a loser. That's what everyone thought about her, wasn't it? There was nothing else to say. She was a loser *and* a failure. No. A loser, a failure, *and* a disappointment.

"Hey, watch it!" A cyclist swerved and wobbled as he narrowly missed her. Phoebe stepped back up from the edge of the road and onto the pavement. Note to self—walking into a main road without looking is not cool. The cyclist pulled up in the gutter and awkwardly repositioned the large Deliveroo bag on his back. That was someone's dinner sloshed about and with sauce where it shouldn't be. He'd get bad feedback from the customer and no tip. Two evenings ruined because of her. Good job, Frink.

"Sorry! My fault." Of course it was her fault. A loser, a failure, a disappointment, *and* a general hazard to society.

The cyclist muttered something expletive that ended in *airhead*. She'd leave that one off her list. Instead, she would add honestly: *I haven't got a Scooby what to do next with my life.* Clueless—perfect. A loser, a failure, a disappointment, a general hazard, *and* clueless. That was her in a nutshell.

So that left her with only one option, and that was to put one foot in front of the other. It was a simple plan that Phoebe found always helped. She pulled her coat closer around her and set off again on her daily walk.

This wasn't just any walk in her adopted city of Leicester. This was thirty minutes of highly customised time. She'd perfected her route over several weeks. It must have a hill to raise her heartrate. And it must have a bit of greenery for mindful well-being. And there must be a spot of motivational window shopping for *If I had the money I would buy*. And to finish, a bit of city buzz to get her ready for her shift at The Banana Bar. On this particular late afternoon on a Wednesday, the city buzz was all about Christmas. Because everyone knew that Christmas begins in November.

A further ten minutes of determined walking led her to the halfway point of her route. This was marked by her arrival at the Haymarket Memorial Clock Tower. Located in the heart of the city, it was the perfect spot to pause and catch her breath. Each time she would stare up at the tip of the tower and note the direction points of the compass rose. And then she would check the time displayed on one of the four clock faces. In that moment she would know precisely when and where she was, despite the fact she had no idea *who* she was any more.

She remembered the first time she'd seen the Clock Tower. It was the university open day, and she had wandered around with her parents to see what she thought of the city. She'd loved it straight away. Diverse, packed with history, and thrumming with life, she knew this was the place for her. And today was no exception. A crowd had gathered by the Clock Tower to watch a huge Christmas tree being hoisted into place. The majestic spruce dangled helplessly in the air above them. A slim man wearing a high-vis vest and an expression of someone who'd had a late night squinted up at the tree and beckoned it down to the ground. The hoist operator divided his attention between his phone and his colleague. Both seemed oblivious to the plume of diesel fumes from their rumbling truck enveloping the crowd. The poor tree was trussed up in netting, which quite frankly looked cruel. How many years had it taken it to grow that big, to be felled and netted in a matter of minutes? What relief the tree would feel when the net was cut and its branches spread free again. Before its pine needles fell off, that was. Before it stood there naked but for its tinsel and lights.

The memory of her mum hoovering up the fallen needles from their family Christmas tree came brightly to mind. *Next year we are having an artificial tree* her mum would say to Phoebe and her dad. But come the next year, it was always a real tree with tinsel and decorations and lights. For they were a family of three who each adored Christmas. They knew the words to all the carols, and never missed the monarch's speech, and wore their Christmas cracker hats all afternoon and into the evening. Together they made it such a special time. Without question, Christmas meant joy. That was up until this Christmas, when she would have no choice but to tell them the truth. That Phoebe Frink, the apple of their eye, was…dropping out.

The thought pinched at Phoebe's heart and made her feel sick. How had everything gone so wrong, so quickly? Everything had been so certain. Her future had been mapped out and her life trajectory was set in the direction for success. Straight A-stars at A-level combined with immaculate references had set her on her path to medical school. In five years she would graduate as Dr. P. Frink. Her parents would be so proud. For the last nineteen years, she had been their clever girl. She could simply do no wrong in their eyes. All their years of unshakable pride and faith in her would culminate in that moment when she would toss her graduation cap into the air. What a moment that would be—or would have been. Phoebe looked up into the dusky amber of the setting winter sky. Not a falling cap in sight.

She hadn't meant to just give up. She wasn't someone who gave up on things. For as long as she could remember she had dreamed of being a doctor. She excelled at science at school and had a natural curiosity for how things worked. As a young child, she remembered asking her mum *How does your heart beat?* Her mum had cupped her chin and replied *It beats with the power of love*. Her father had laughed and added *With plumbing and electrics, Phoebe*. For several years after, whenever she saw a plumber's van or an advert for an electrician, she thought about how many hearts they were mending. And if she came across something or someone injured, she felt a compulsion to help and to make them better. So, as hard as she was finding university, she hung in there and completed the first year and passed her exams. *I hung in there.* But it was all too much. Too much work and, more to the point, too much scrutiny.

One of the things she treasured more than anything was the freedom to be her. Leaving home had made this need to claim and create her own identity even stronger, to have every colour she wanted dyed in her hair and bright clothes that spoke of sunshine and life. There was not a single item of clothing in her wardrobe that was plain or formal. Yet, day by day she began to feel the expectations reshaping her and directing her away from who she felt she was, the girl of colour, sunshine, and freedom, and absorbing her into the person the profession needed her to be—formal, procedural, and restrained. It frightened and overwhelmed her.

And then one day, less than two weeks into her second year, she was sitting in a lecture listening to the tutor. Nothing he said was going in. Everyone around her was tapping away at keyboards or scribbling notes in earnest. Everyone but her. What had she been thinking to presume she could do this? Why on earth had she imagined she had what it took to be a doctor? Whatever confidence had taken her through her first year seemed to dissolve in an instant. All of a sudden, an all-consuming urge to run away flooded in upon her and threatened to drown her. She couldn't breathe. She walked out and just kept walking and walking and walking. It was only her blistered feet that made her stop.

The memory of it all triggered her heart to ache so much so it stole her breath. She looked up once more at the compass rose. *You're okay, Frink.* What did Dee say? *Chin up, Frinky Boots. Don't know will know.* What would she have done without Dee and The Banana Bar?

On that day, with her heels bleeding and tears dripping salty on her cheeks, her walking led her to the one place she felt safest in the city—The Banana Bar. She'd sat on the pavement sobbing her heart out. With uncanny timing, Mr. Duke had appeared in the doorway. *I'd rather you didn't cry outside my bar, kiddo. Not to mention you're eight hours early for your shift. I mean, completely understand you can't wait to see me again but to cry about it—a little too keen.* It had made her laugh. Mr. Duke was infuriating like that.

She remembered the first time she'd seen Mr. Duke. It was freshers' week, and there was a hushed whisper in her halls of residence about a drag bar in town that was looking for bar staff. She'd pretended to be uninterested and then went straight there the next day and signed up. Mr. Duke was onstage practising for that night's gig. Looking in every way the debonair cad about town dressed in a dinner suit and pencil-thin moustache, Mr. Duke was probably the most handsome person she'd ever seen and, without doubt, the most cocky. From that moment, she hadn't looked back. When she wasn't at uni, she was at The Banana either working behind the bar or hanging out. There was no question about it—she had found her family away from home.

As well as a glass of Coke and a plaster for her blisters, Mr. Duke had given her board and lodging that day. *Just to be clear, this is in lieu of pay. I know I look like a heavenly saint but I ain't.* Phoebe hadn't needed divine intervention. What she'd needed was a safe place in the city away from uni and from her halls of residence. Being at The Banana gave her a chance to work out what to do and what on earth she would say to her parents. What could she possibly say to them? She was going to break their hearts. And not to mention her own.

The bell of The Clock Tower struck five times. Crap, she was going to be late.

"Right. Get a grip, Frink." She rushed away from her memories and headed for the soft greenery of City Walk and on to the lifeline that was The Banana. And with each step, she wore away at her worries, pushing them to the background. At least for now.

## Chapter Two

Saturdays were always such a busy day at the Emporium, and this Saturday was no exception.

"Hi. I don't know if it was you I spoke to earlier?" The woman approaching the counter managed to look at Violet without looking at her. Or rather without seeing her.

Every time someone who had met her had no memory of their meeting, Violet wondered what it was about her that was so forgettable. The stab of loneliness it triggered would steal her breath just for a second, until she could rally herself to muster a polite reply.

"Yes, Mrs. Allen. I remember. And you called in last Saturday too. I helped you with your husband's strongman outfit." Violet lifted her name badge. "I'm Violet. Violet Unwin."

Mrs. Allen double blinked. Was she remembering? "It's the leotard. It's too…" She was looking at Violet as if she would know what came next.

"Oh, okay. Too…?" Should she say too small or too large?

"It's pinching."

"Got it. We have other sizes—"

"I've brought it back." Mrs. Allen disappeared below the counter and began rummaging in her shopping bags.

At that moment, a young woman emerged from the dressing room, spinning on the spot and whirling a gold lasso. Her delighted friend, who had been waiting patiently, scrolling on her phone, squealed in delight. "*O-M-G*, those boots!"

Wonder Woman turned to face the mirror and proceeded to tuck her shoulder-length blond hair under the wig. "I'm *so* getting laid tonight."

This news seemed to attract the attention of Mrs. Allen, for she bobbed up remarkably quickly and stared at the excited scene.

"Would Mr. Allen consider Superman as an alternative?" Violet offered. "Just a thought."

Mrs. Allen's eyes grew wide and glinted at the potential of Violet's suggestion. "Mr. Allen would be delighted."

"Great. I'll just grab that costume for you. One moment." Violet went straight to the superheroes section. If the leotard pinched, then something generous. Extra-large Superman it was.

"Here we go." Violet returned to Mrs. Allen to find that her attention had drifted to the expansive rail of costumes that lined both sides of the long and narrow room. Mrs. Allen's gaze had settled upon the section featuring the Victorian era.

"Such a formal and yet elegant period in history," Mrs. Allen said. Her wistful tone matched her entranced demeanour as she stared up at the shelf where upturned top hats with fine white gloves draped over their edges rested alongside hand tied bow ties and starched collars. "I always think of the past in black and white," she continued. "Isn't that funny? As if colour is a modern thing."

"I know what you mean," Violet said. "As if the sun didn't shine and the sky wasn't blue."

Mrs. Allen smiled at her. "Yes. Oh, I mustn't forget Superman."

"Just a straight swap." Violet dutifully exchanged the leotard for Mr. Allen's new outfit.

"Thank you for your help…?" Mrs. Allen then gave a small frown, as if trying to remember something or someone. That someone was her, wasn't it?

"Violet."

"Violet. Of course. Will next Saturday be okay for me to return it?"

"Yes, no problem. See you then."

"Excuse me. Can I rent this?" Wonder Woman's face beamed with excitement. "And the boots too, please?"

"Enjoy your evening, girls," Mrs. Allen said to Wonder Woman and her companion as she left the shop. The doorbell dinged with her departure.

"Yes, of course, I'll get that sorted for you." Violet carefully folded the bodice with its attaching pleated skirt and gently slipped it with the wig into a large paper bag. She curled up the lasso and eased it in alongside. "Please take care with the lasso. We accept no responsibility for damage to persons or property through its use."

"You bet. Only minor injuries. Got it."

"Maybe *no* injuries," Violet said with a giggle.

The doorbell rang out as a new customer entered. Violet glanced up towards the door. The new arrival was dressed in a crumpled tan raincoat and had a mop of hair that curled in all directions. He paid particular attention to closing the door properly behind him. Then he removed his glasses and began wiping them, taking meticulous care with the task. He was definitely new to her. She tended to recognise customers who had been to the shop before. Over the years, she'd developed a method of assigning their identity to the costumes they rented. Mrs. Allen would now be known as Lois Lane.

Violet quickly returned her to attention to Wonder Woman. "Here are your boots. We're just missing your forearm guards—they should have been with the rest of the costume."

Wonder Woman pointed to the dressing room. "Sorry. I must have left them in there. I'd be dead pissed off to have forgotten them. Thanks." She held her wrists in the air and crossed them over each other in a Wonder Woman stance.

"No problem. I'll fetch them for you."

"You're a star."

Violet liked the thought of being somebody's star. Not the famous sort. But the one that shines and blinks in the night sky. The one that someone wishes upon. How amazing would that be?

As Violet collected the forearm guards, she took the opportunity to glance in the dressing room mirror and discreetly check out her new customer. He was squinting through round black spectacles at the mannequin dressed in the infantryman's jacket and shrapnel helmet. Violet could imagine him standing in the conscription queue, holding tightly in his hand the form that excused him from the front line on grounds of poor eyesight.

"Won't be a minute, sir," Violet said to him, with a smile she hoped would say *Welcome to Unwin's Emporium. We are here to help.* He looked up at her and nodded.

Violet returned to the counter. In her brief absence, Wonder Woman's companion had unearthed a large feather fan from the performing arts section. She fanned herself coquettishly. Wonder Woman leaned against the counter in stitches.

"Do people rent this?" The girl looked directly at Violet and at the same time fluttered her fan.

Violet's cheeks flashed hot and tingled. She quickly looked away. "Yep. Burlesque is super popular." Had the girl noticed her blush? She shrank into herself a little with the thought. But then people never noticed her, did they? No, it was fine. Everything was fine. "So, that will be twenty pounds, please. And twenty pounds deposit. Cash or card?"

Wonder Woman waved her card at Violet. "You don't still use that thing, do you?" she asked, gesturing to the vintage cash register.

"Yes, for cash transactions. It's fun." Violet lifted the card reader towards her.

Wonder Woman flicked her card over it without taking her eyes off the unusual till, or bizarre relic, as Violet felt sure she would describe it in later conversations with her friends.

"It's kind of weird," Wonder Woman said. "No offence."

Violet knew it was weird to use something that was so impractical and that incurred twice the work of modern technology. But it was not just a piece of ornate metal—it was so much part of the history of the shop itself. Violet printed off a receipt and handed it to Wonder Woman.

"You'll need to bring this with you for your deposit."

"Will do. Thanks."

Wonder Woman's companion reluctantly parted with her feathery fan, and the pair left full of plans for their night out.

Violet checked her watch. It was lunchtime. She wandered over to the door and replaced the *Open* sign to *Closed for lunch, see you at two.*

The man stood up abruptly from where he had taken a seat outside the changing room. "Do you need me to go?"

"No. You're fine. How can I help?"

"It's a long story."

Violet's stomach rumbled. "Sorry. It's been non-stop, and breakfast was a long time ago."

"The short version, then," he said with an apologetic smile. "I'm a university teacher. And my colleague is retiring and some smart alec suggested a fancy dress leaving party."

"Right. Is there a theme?"

"Science. Someone said I should go as a mad scientist." He glanced at the costume rails. "Do you have that outfit?"

People could be cruel. All he would need for Violet to do was to hand him a white lab coat and a clipboard. She knew how it felt to be him. The butt of the joke. She had no idea either how to be anything other than herself. And the world could not have made it clearer that being herself was not cool. From a very young age, the relentless teasing, and then the relentless ignoring, left her wanting to hide away. And now all she felt was hidden. In fact, she found it hard to convince herself that she wasn't invisible. Some days, the loneliest days, often when the shop was closed, she would even wonder whether she was a figment of her own imagination.

"So do you have that outfit?" the man asked, with a kind tone that gently brought her back to him.

"I have something even better. Fancy going to the moon?" Violet headed for the section marked *Occupations*. She lifted a white NASA space suit free from the costumes of a chef and a policeman that nestled next to it. She handed it to the man. He looked surprised—in a good way. Then she rummaged underneath the costume rail and brought out a large plastic dome complete with a rubber neck surround. "Now the helmet gets hot inside, so you'll need to take breaks from wearing it. But there are plenty of air holes, so you won't suffocate." Violet demonstrated by slipping it over her head. Speaking with a slightly muffled voice, she added, "It doubles for our deep-sea diver, but matched with the spacesuit—ta-da!—astronaut!" Violet moonwalked a step or two, and the man laughed.

"A space scientist. It's wonderful," he said. "I always wanted to go into space."

Violet lifted the helmet from her head. "Me too. But then maybe it might make you feel odd. Like the world is too small or that you'd prefer to stay in space and not return. Like you've been an alien all along."

The man looked at her with an expression that suggested empathy.

"We don't have the boots, sorry. But I reckon if you got shoe boxes, painted them white, and strapped them to your shoes it could work. Would you like to try the suit on? My guess is that it will fit you well."

"Well then, I'll just take it. And let you have your lunch."

"Oh okay. If you're sure."

"I am. And I'll pay cash to see you open that till of yours." The man followed Violet to the counter.

"It's a National and dates from 1905."

"It's really great you have it."

Violet punched at the large numbers standing erect on the vintage till. Paper number cards lifted up to be displayed in the glass section on the top. Violet pressed *Sale*, and the drawer popped open. "That's—"

"Twenty pounds. And twenty pounds deposit." He handed Violet the cash. "And for your receipt, my name is Jack."

Violet wrote down his details and tore off his slip from the duplicate receipt book. "Here you go. I hope you have a lovely party, Jack."

"And I hope you have a lovely lunch"—Jack leaned in a little and squinted at her name badge—"Violet Unwin of Unwin's Emporium."

As the doorbell rang with Jack's departure, Violet stood for a moment replaying his words on her lips. That was her in a nutshell. She was Violet Unwin of Unwin's Emporium. That's who she was and all she'd ever wanted to be.

❖

"Dee! Our Christmas leaflets have arrived!" Phoebe heaved the cardboard box from the doorstep and carried it against her chest to the bar. She slid the box onto the countertop and clapped her hands in delight.

"Seriously, don't shout. And as for clapping just...don't." Dee sat hunched on a bar stool nursing a coffee and a hangover. She was wearing what Phoebe recognised as the *I'm feeling sensitive, leave me alone* jumper. Its thick dark grey wool always seemed to mirror her shaded mood, and the holes at the elbows betrayed the frayed nature of her feelings. Phoebe had a favourite jumper too that she tended to reach for on those days when life overwhelmed her. It was a washed-out blue striped hooded top with bobbles on its sleeves and front from repeated wear. It was a fabric hug. Come to think of it, she'd worn it a lot recently.

"Sorry." Phoebe peeled off the tape sealing the box and peeked inside. Two stacks of folded A5 leaflets were packed tightly together and bound with elastic bands. An image of a Christmas tree, sparkling with rainbow-coloured lights, shone out from the front page. A smiling yellow banana, complete with a Santa hat, replaced the traditional fairy on top. A night sky of gold stars twinkled in the inky blue background. And, as the finishing flourish, a looping garland of baubles and fir tree needles spelled out the heading: *A Christmas Extravaganza of Events.* "Oh my God. They look fab!"

Dee turned towards her and briefly inched her sunglasses slightly down the bridge of her nose. Her pained expression needed no interpretation.

"Sorry for shouting. Again." Phoebe reached into the box and excitedly freed a leaflet from its stack. She then climbed up on a stool next to Dee and proceeded to study each slim folded page. "I adore the cover. And I just love that each event is listed within its own gold star. I'm proper pleased. Very Hollywood glitz. Can you see?"

Dee's dark glasses made it impossible to tell where she was looking or indeed whether her eyes were actually open. It didn't help that her response was a barely discernible nod.

"Erm, so, inside"—Phoebe softened her voice to just above a whisper—"inside is a little more detail about each event. I've listed everything by date. In the end I opted for Sunday the eleventh for Turkey Twizzler Bingo, and on the two Wednesdays we have A Crafty Christmas, make your own cards and crackers. Craft is always a crowd magnet. Friday the sixteenth was a no-brainer for Karaoke Christmas Carols. It was so popular last year. Are you sure I can't persuade you to be Bing Crosby again for the night?"

Dee's stony silence spoke volumes.

"No. Fair enough. And then on Saturday the seventeenth there is the return of the Mince Pie Eating Challenge. The twenty-third is Pin the Beard on Santa. Winner gets a bottle of Irish Mist. And not forgetting our awesome, night of all nights, The Festive Rebellion Banana Ball on Christmas Eve. Yes, it's all here. No spelling mistakes that I can see. On the back is a bit about The Banana Bar and contact details. What do you think?"

Dee released a groan.

"You know, we can always do this later, if you want—"

"Yes," Dee said, deadpan.

"Oh. Okay, then." Phoebe folded the leaflet closed.

"Wait. I *want* to do this later. But we *need* to check them now." Dee took a shaky sip of her coffee, then gestured towards the leaflet with her cup. "I like that you've given the ball the biggest star. Headline event and all that."

"It's great, isn't it. And here is the inside section with the details for the ball. Just there." Phoebe nudged the leaflet closer to Dee.

Dee cleared her throat and began to read aloud. "Christmas Eve, Saturday twenty-fourth of December. Eight till late. Calling all rebels for The Festive Rebellion Banana Ball. Come dressed as your favourite rebel. Tickets in advance £10, £15 on the door. Buffet, competitions, disco until late." Dee gave a sharp nod of approval and then immediately winced. "You've done an awesome job, Pheebs. Much appreciated."

"My pleasure. Everyone's going to be so excited by our plans." Phoebe jumped down from the stool and collected an armful of empty glasses left over from the night before. She proceeded to load them, as quietly as she could, into the dishwasher behind the bar.

Dee sighed. "Let's hope so. If only every month could be a December. And then I could stop eating baked beans for every meal."

Phoebe laughed and then stopped herself. "Things aren't that bad, are they? I mean, Bonfire Cocktail Night was a winner. And with only one singed eyebrow from the sparklers, I think we can say that's a success. We were packed out for Halloween. And let's not forget the Summer Beach Party was a total hit. And—hello—what about our regular favourite, Sundays Are a Drag? That night is totally the highlight for people's weekend."

"I know that. But we can't survive on highlight events alone. Midweek, it's quieter than a sponsored silence. I'm wondering whether we should close Monday to Thursday—"

Phoebe gripped Dee's arm. "*No.* You can't do that."

Dee raised her eyebrows in an unmistakable reaction of *I'm the boss*.

Phoebe let go of her arm. "I mean, of course you can. But it's just, we both know that we're not just a bar—we're home to some people. Family, even."

"It's not like I want to. And nothing's decided yet."

"There's got to be another way. There has to be."

Dee shrugged. "We've tried reducing costs. Not even blocking off access to the Saloon has been enough. So, right now, I can't think of one. We need to keep all options on the table. I'll speak to the bank, of course, but I don't hold out much hope of a loan. Don't get upset, kiddo. You'll keep your place here for as long as you need it. On the plus side, with less shifts, it'll give you a bit more time to work out what you want to do going forward. Look at it like that."

That's the last way Phoebe wanted to look at it. In fact, it was the last thing Phoebe wanted to think about, let alone look at. "What would I have done if you hadn't taken me in? There's no way I could have hung around in halls, having to see my course mates every day. And the thought of going home…I can't."

"Your parents would have understood. They *will* understand."

"They won't. They have no idea anything's wrong. As far as they're concerned, I'm a grade-A student acing my course. Acing life."

"And even grade-A students are allowed to take time out. Look, I'm sure they're very proud of you. But ultimately a parent's job is to understand."

"I can't hurt them with the truth."

"By protecting them, you're hurting yourself, Pheebs. You do know that, don't you?" Dee drained her coffee cup dry. "What have the uni said?"

"I'll need to give them an answer either way by Christmas so I don't fall too far behind. At least that's what my tutor said when I first told her." Phoebe hung her head and stared at the black and white floor tiles, cracked and tarnished by years of wear. There was no doubt about it—time was ticking like an unexploded bomb. "What am I going to do?"

Dee carefully lifted her sunglasses free from her face and rested them on the counter. She then pinched at the bridge of her nose. "It's a classic case of *don't know, will know*. Just the same as our situation here at The Banana. And in the short term, I suggest you get the costumes for the ball sorted for the bar temps and for us. And in the immediate term, like right now, get me a paracetamol and a full fat Coke."

"Oh, right. Sure thing. Thanks, Dee. I'm very grateful. For everything."

"And I'll be very grateful when you get me pain relief."

"Oh yeah. Coming up." Phoebe hunted in her bag tucked under the bar. "I always carry some. Aha, here we go." She squeezed out two tablets into Dee's palm, filled a half-pint glass with Coke, and watched as Dee pretty much drank it down in one.

"I'm sorry you're in pain."

Setting her glass aside, Dee replied, "Serves me right. I need to learn to say no to people buying me drinks. You would think, after all these years, I could muster *thanks, but no thanks*. I just know they're going to look at me like I've turned down their marriage proposal."

Phoebe laughed. "I imagine that's probably actually happened to you."

"Marriage proposals? I won't lie, there's been a few over the years."

"How many have you had?"

"Four, maybe five. Serious ones. They were all in love with the idea of me rather than me. And the proposals were from both men and women, and I might add not all of them were single at the time."

"And I'm just guessing you said yes to each one."

"Every time. Luckily, they mostly had no memory of it in the morning. And it's always possible to find a kind way to say no if need be. And then of course there's my *actual* marriage proposal from Mrs. Dee. An entirely different matter. I couldn't wait to say *I do*." Dee closed her eyes before slipping on her sunglasses once more.

Dee rarely spoke of her late wife. Phoebe wanted to ask her about how Suzie proposed, but she didn't like to pry.

"And here I am," Dee said, after a moment. "With a head that any minute will burst over the pork scratchings and drip all over the salted peanuts."

Sure enough the subject had been swiftly changed. "Thanks for that. That's an image I won't get rid of quickly."

"Unwin's Emporium."

And thankfully changed again. "Sorry?"

"The costume shop that will be able to help you with the outfits for the ball. It's on Duke Street."

"Unwin's Emporium? Now you mention it, I think I've seen it. It's always got a mannequin in the window dressed amazingly."

"That's the one."

"I can't believe I've never been in it."

"Well, a treat awaits you, Frinky Boots. Unwin's Emporium is not just any costume shop. No sirree. It is the place where you can instantly transform into who you've always wanted to be. It transports you from yourself to somewhere wonderful. Honestly, it's just like the TV show *Mr. Benn*."

"Mr. Benn?"

"It's an animated TV series from the seventies. You need it in your life. Basically, a man dressed in a suit and a bowler hat, Mr. Benn, goes on adventures in a costume shop with the help of a fez-wearing shopkeeper. It's out there. You'll adore it."

"Sounds fun. I'll check it out."

"Fun? It's a cult classic. Just like Unwin's Emporium. Honestly, that place is a piece of the city's history. It's been in the Unwin family *literally* for generations."

"I love places steeped in history like that."

"Then wait till you see it. Stepping inside is like time has stood still. It's quirkier than quirky and cooler than cool. I've been going there for years. In fact, it was the first place where I dared to try on a gentleman's dinner jacket."

"Really?"

"Everything changed for me from then. Mr. Duke was born in their dressing room."

"That's amazing."

Dee stared absently ahead. "It was. That jacket fit me like it was made for me." Dee shook her head slowly. "Strangest thing. I've always thought that there's something about that shop. Something sort of..."

"Magical?"

"Maybe. I can't quite put my finger on it. I'd be interested to see what you think, and for that matter what outfits you choose. I expect to be dashing."

"Definitely."

"Great." Dee slipped down from the stool, placed her hands on her hips and looked about the bar. "There's no question, Friday nights are for fighting. Look at this place." Stools were lying on the floor and glasses littered every tabletop. Darts were pinned everywhere but on the dart board. And not one picture hung straight. It was a scene of jubilant devastation.

Phoebe placed her hand lightly on Dee's shoulder. "We can make every night a Friday night. We're in this together."

Dee's cheeks flushed pink against her grey pallor, and she quickly looked away. Her voice then faltered a little when she replied, "Good to know. The toilets are all yours."

"No, I didn't mean…"

Dee walked away laughing softly to herself.

Damn her. She always had an answer. Please, let her always have an answer.

## Chapter Three

"The end." Violet closed her book with a satisfied sigh and returned it to her bedside table.

How she loved to read cuddled up in her bed, day or night. It was the ultimate comfort in what could often feel like a comfortless world. And to be tucked away in her room was where she'd always felt the safest. For it was more than a bedroom. It was her sanctuary within her precious retreat of the Emporium, and the only space she had dared to think of and to claim as her own.

Violet knew it helped that no one else had wanted her room. It had once been a storage space for those items that her aunt and uncle either did not want or did not know what to do with. Violet had told herself that wasn't the reason she had been put there, and it was simply the spare room. But when she was fifteen and Carl moved out, there was no talk of her moving to the larger, sunnier, quieter room he'd vacated. But then, there was rarely talk of her at all.

Violet came to understand that people don't always tell you outright what they think of you, but no words were needed for her to know that her aunt resented her. Why her husband had felt obliged to take in his troubled late sister's little girl was beyond her aunt's comprehension. Carl was their beloved child, after all, and Violet was someone else's unplanned mistake they seemed to be paying for. Why was it suddenly their problem that Walter's fragile sister chose to end her life with the same lack of regard she gave to contraception? It wasn't so much that her aunt wished Violet dead, but rather that she had not been born. For as far as her aunt was concerned, Violet was not only an inconvenience but a threat to the order of things. Uncle Walter was kinder, but clueless as to what to do with the lost skinny kid who turned up on his doorstep with no more than a suitcase and a library card. In fairness, he had tried to engage with her, particularly when Violet showed an early interest in the shop, but this seemed to anger her aunt and cousin. It was clear there was an unspoken rule that any attention belonged to them and them alone. Perhaps it had just been easier for her uncle to give in to them, or maybe they left him with no choice.

Either way, communication with her uncle subtly shifted to shop-related matters only. He stopped asking how she was or what she wanted, and what she might need never seemed to enter his head. So they had fed her and clothed her and given her shelter, and then done their best to forget about her. They had fulfilled their duty. Their sense of obligation clearly didn't extend to love. But what they had given her, even if by default, was the most precious of gifts—the wonder of the Emporium and the sanctity of her own room.

Violet pulled the blanket up around her and gazed about her precious space. It had never mattered to her that it was the box room. She had simply always thought of it as cosy and imagined it like a nest high in the trees above the world. And its simplicity was calming when compared with the fullness and busyness of the shop beneath. Her furniture, a chest of drawers and wardrobe and bedside table, was modest and functional. And to fit in the compact space, her single bed was tucked into one corner of the room. To combat the cold walls, Violet had piled cushions where bed met plaster. Over the years she had squirreled blankets and discarded rugs from other rooms and eventually had created the comfiest of spaces in the world. To mark her sixteenth birthday, Violet had saved up for a tin of dark blue paint. She'd waited until her uncle and aunt were away, and then over the course of a day, she'd transformed her ceiling into a night sky complete with a dozen gold stars. Other than to comment on the lingering smell of paint, her uncle and aunt did not even step inside Violet's room to stare up and admire her work.

Violet sat up a little in her bed and moved her fingers through the beams of setting sunlight that had spilled like an accident across her floor and walls. Winter light was so fragile that she held her breath and stared at her fingers, lit and glowing. Any minute the delicate sunbeams would disappear…

"Violet!"

Violet released her breath and caught it quickly again in a gasp of fear. Carl's angry growl from the street outside her window was as distinctive as the howl of a wolf and as chilling. It was Sunday afternoon. What was he doing here? Why was he shouting up to her? He must have forgotten his keys.

A hard dull thump on the front door made it clear that she must hurry before his temper damaged the poor door he seemed so intent on battering down.

She clambered from her bed and ran down the steep stairs. As she let Carl in, he all but knocked her over as he barged past.

"Why would you put the snib on, Violet? I couldn't get in. What a stupid thing to do."

"I didn't...I'm careful with the snib. I know how to use it."

He pointed at her and angrily stabbed out the words into the air. "You know nothing. That's perfectly clear. I guess there's no point me asking you where the deeds are to this place." Carl made his way to behind the counter. He paused at the large oak cabinet of shop drawers and scratched his head. "Turn the lights on, for God's sake. It's always so gloomy in here. I hate this place."

"It's dusk outside, that's all. It's not gloomy normally."

"I don't care. Where are they? Be some use and help me find them."

"Why do you need the deeds?"

"Why do *you* need to know? Huh? Or have you already forgotten our last conversation?"

It wasn't a conversation Violet was going to forget in a hurry. "I remember it."

"Good." Carl pulled at the vintage drawers. Each one frustrated and resisted his efforts. Beads of sweat glinted on his forehead. He kicked at the base, leaving a dusty mark on the old wood.

"Wait. Please. They're here." Violet went to the drawer under the till. She lifted out a roll of parchment, part sealed with the remnants of a red stamp of wax. Reluctantly she handed them to Carl. "Have you finished with the accounts?"

"No." Carl unfolded the roll and stared at the handwritten legal text. "Are these even valid?"

"Yes. Completely. They're the originals. Please take care with them."

Carl stuffed them into the pocket of his jacket. As if from nowhere, a gust of wind from the street rattled the front door and caused the bell to ring. "This place gives me the creeps."

*You give me the creeps. Creep.* "Tell me why you need the deeds. Please."

Carl gave a heavy sigh. To her surprise, he reached forward and held her by the arms. His small bloodshot eyes fixed on hers. It was impossible to look away. "Don't you want a change, Violet. To be free of this place?"

Violet felt every muscle in her body shrink under his touch. Why was he asking her that? "No."

He let go of her and seemed to hold himself stiff as if he was just on the edge of a tantrum. With sweaty cheeks flushed with anger, he said, "Well the thing is, I do. I've always hated it. And the fact is, we're closing it. It can't come soon enough."

No. "What? You're closing the shop? You can't."

"It's done."

"It can't be—"

"You have a month. Then the shop will close for good. You need to make preparations." Carl pointed to the cabinet of drawers behind him. "Sort all this old crap out. And get on with it. The buyer won't wait."

"There's a buyer? You've sold it already? Without telling me?"

Carl shrugged and began to move for the door. Violet reached for his arm. Carl roughly pulled it away. "Why would I?"

"Because this is my home. It's where I work. It's my *future*."

"Why would you think that? This has never been your home. No one wanted you." Carl took a deep breath. "And as for your future, er, newsflash—no one cares. One month. Okay?"

Violet's legs began to buckle, and she reached for the counter to steady herself. "What about Uncle Walter? There's no way he'd agree to this. Does he actually know what you've done?"

"Of course he does. I told him prices are good. Now is the time to sell. There was nothing left to say."

"There's plenty to say. It's been in the Unwin family for generations. It's not just a shop—it's an inheritance."

"It's an embarrassment."

"But it's a profitable business. I'm going to ring Uncle Walter—"

"Don't you dare. The last thing my father needs is to be upset by you."

"But he'd want to know if I was okay. He'd wonder what I was going to do without the Emporium."

"I told him you were fine, Violet."

"Why would you say that? I'm not fine. That's a lie."

Carl snapped, "You're not our responsibility any more." Violet could hear her aunt's words in Carl's anger. With a new weariness to his tone, he then added, "For God's sake, Violet, which bit of *It's done* don't you understand?"

Violet hung her head. "I don't understand any of this."

"Your stupidity's not my problem." He reached the door and turned back to Violet. "There will be post about the sale addressed to me. I've instructed my solicitors, Sharp and Co., to handle it. I'll collect it at some point." Carl yanked at the door, which opened with unexpected ease. He staggered back to regain his balance. "Bastard shop." Carl slammed the door after him. The glass rattled in its frame, and the bell dinged, and that was seemingly that.

Violet held her hand over her stomach, stifling a pressing urge to be sick. Why had no one even asked for her opinion—or forewarned her, at least? Why hadn't they paused for just a moment to consider her? But then the person they always listened to and considered was Carl. Had he bullied Uncle Walter to the point where there was nothing left for him to say? Was Uncle Walter just too ill to defend the shop? She should ring him and ignore Carl's warning. Perhaps she could even suggest Uncle Walter reconsider for her sake? But would he stand up for her against Carl? Had he ever? And what if Carl was right and her ringing would make her uncle even sicker? That was the last thing she wanted to do.

She pressed her hand against her face in the vain hope that she could hold back her tears. "What am I going to do?"

A twinkle of Christmas lights turned on in the street and drew her attention to outside. At exactly the same time, a figure moved away from the window. Had someone been watching her from the street? No, of course not. If anything, they would just have been looking at the costumes. After all, who looked at her? Who thought about her? No one.

Anger wasn't an emotion Violet knew what to do with. Indulging it never made her feel better, and she never understood what angry people gained from hurting others by discharging their anger onto them. Over the years she'd taught herself to control it, but never had it been harder than right then to stop it bubbling in her blood and raging through her veins. Her head throbbed with fury as she paced up and down the shop, re-enacting her conversation with Carl, and rehearsing all the things she should have said to him and, moreover, all the things she should have said in her life. *How could all of you disregard me all these years? How can you live with yourselves? I am alive, don't you know?* Violet shouted into the room, "I exist!"

The only thing Violet could think to do next was to walk, just walk until her head cleared and her angry hurting heart stilled.

Pulling her coat from the rack in the corner of the room, she flicked off the light switch and made for the street. As Violet stepped out onto the pavement, she all but collided with an equally surprised young woman.

"Oops, sorry," the woman said. "My fault." She pressed at her bright yellow bobble hat, rearranging it to fit more squarely on her head, then stuffed her hands into the pockets of her multicoloured patchwork coat.

Reeling from the emotional distress of her run-in with Carl, Violet couldn't think what to say or what to do. Her feet wouldn't move, and her brain couldn't find any words.

"I was just checking when you were open." The woman pointed to the opening times pinned to the side of the door. She then gave a small shrug and smiled.

Her tender, warm smile felt just like the sun in Violet's room a few minutes before.

"I hope you don't mind me saying, it's just…I couldn't help but notice…" The woman glanced to inside the shop. "I promise I wasn't being nosy, but are you all right? The man who was with you, well, he seemed very cross—"

*She saw us arguing?* "He's my cousin. He gets himself worked up over nothing. Nothing at all."

The woman replied with an uncertain, "Okay." She searched Violet's face as if she would find another answer there.

*She would surely see that Violet had been crying. What on earth* would this woman think of her, of them? "Honestly, it was nothing at all." Before the woman had a chance to comment further, Violet intervened with, "And, I'm afraid we're not open today. It's Sunday."

"Oh yes. I wasn't sure. I tried to check your hours of business online, but you don't seem to have a website or anything, so I was passing and thought I'd check you out. The shop, I mean. Not you." The young woman looked down at the pavement, clearly embarrassed. "Obviously."

Violet followed her gaze to the floor. "I was going to get us online, but, well..." All that was gone now, wasn't it. The shop's future was over and surely so was hers. She needed to walk or else she would cry again right then and there. Violet locked the door and moved to leave.

"I'm thinking I'll call back tomorrow." The young woman was smiling again.

There was something sincere and personal in this stranger's smile. She seemed genuinely lovely. "Sure. We'll be open from ten till five."

"Great. It'll be in the afternoon. I like to have a walk at about four, half four each day. It somehow helps to clear my head before work. So I'll pop in then."

"I like to walk too. Pretty much every day, if I can." Violet wasn't quite sure why she'd just confessed that. Come to think of it, she couldn't actually remember the last time she confessed anything to anyone. But then you had to have someone to confess to in the first place.

"Cool. I'm Phoebe, by the way." Phoebe briefly raised her hand in a small wave of hello. "I work at The Banana Bar."

Phoebe? Her name couldn't have suited her more. And The Banana Bar? Violet occasionally passed the bar on her daily walk. The bar's sign in the shape of a banana with a smiling face and holding a rainbow flag always made her smile. She liked that it seemed different from all the other places in the city. But as tempting as it was to just see what it was like, she never went in. Even though Violet knew she was different, she understood that she was not different *cool* but different *weird*, different *strange*. If her time at school had taught Violet anything, then it was that. "Right."

Phoebe seemed to wait a beat or two as if expecting more. But Violet found that no more words came.

"So, anyway," Phoebe said, with a breezy tone, "we've got a fancy dress ball coming up, and we need some costumes. We've chosen the theme of rebels."

"Rebels? Sounds fun. I can definitely help you with that."

Phoebe beamed an even deeper smile at Violet. "Fab—thank you so much. See you tomorrow. I'm looking forward to it."

"Yep." Violet turned away and began to walk off towards the soft green of the city's park. Her breath seemed harder to catch, and an urge to run made her walk at pace. But what was she running from? Carl had gone. She could sense that Phoebe hadn't moved from where they'd stood together. Was she watching her leave? Why? What had Phoebe found so interesting in her? The thought was so exposing. Or was she imagining everything and overthinking an encounter that meant nothing to the lovely woman in the yellow hat? Of course she was. Phoebe wasn't still there looking at her. If today had shown her anything, as far as anyone was concerned, when it came to Violet Unwin, there was nothing to consider. And if there was nothing to consider, then it followed that there was nothing to notice and therefore nothing to see.

"See you later!"

What? Violet turned back to find Phoebe waving at her. Violet's heart swelled in an aching rush. She was shaken and beyond delighted in equal measure. Who knew that there was nothing more revealing and perplexing than being seen?

She needed to get a grip. *Stop being weird and say goodbye.* "Bye!"

Phoebe gave a last wave, zipped up her coat to beneath her chin, and strode off into the twinkling Christmas-lit streets.

Violet watched her until she disappeared out of sight. Had she just imagined Phoebe? Had she dreamed her into being? For surely, the coolest person in the world that she could possibly conceive of hadn't just been waiting on her doorstep. That was someone else's life. Someone *with* a life. Someone *with* a future. And that someone was not her.

So no, she would not look forward to tomorrow because tomorrow had never been the answer to anything. It was just another day of being alone. Another day of being Violet Unwin.

## Chapter Four

Phoebe pressed the receiver close to her ear and put her finger in her other ear. Lady Gaga singing "Born This Way" at full blast all but outcompeted the quiet voice at the other end of the line.

"Yes," Phoebe said, raising her voice to almost a shout, "that's right Sundays Are a Drag is on tonight. Yes, Mr. Duke is this evening's act—"

"Oh, I *love* Mr. Duke." Reggie the Regular, as everyone in The Banana knew her, made no secret of her long-held affection. Rumour had it, Reggie was one of the first people to see Mr. Duke perform. She had lost her heart at the sight and had held a fluttering candle for him ever since. It turned out, she would not be the last to suffer such a fate. "Don't let him start without me. Tell him I'm coming."

"I'll be sure to pass that message on. Just to let you know, things kick off at eight."

"Eight? I've not put my face on yet. And I'm not one for hurrying. Last time I hurried, I aggravated my dropped arch. And I can't go out as I am. You see, I've had a moth in my wardrobe, and now I've more holes than clothes. If you could see me, Phoebe love, you'd have a fit."

"You always look fab, Reggie. So we'll see you soon then."

"Bless you, you're a little smasher, that's what you are. Would you believe I can see one of those blighters now. Brazen as anything on my nets."

Phoebe waited and listened to muffled fumbling. "Reggie? Reg? Are you still there? So, I'm going to hang up now, see you later!" She ended the call, knowing that Reggie had not phoned about that night's entertainment but because she needed to hear the reassuring sound of a familiar voice. If proof was ever required, it was right there—The Banana was not just a bar. To its loyal patrons it was a lifeline, and the answer in those dark moments to their question *Is anyone there?*

Mr. Duke stuck his head round the corner from his office where he had been getting ready. His white dress shirt was partly unbuttoned, and his neck flushed pink against his vest. The loops of his sparkling braces lay against his hips, and his bow tie dangled loose from his shoulders. "I take it that was Reg. Is she okay?"

"I think so. She's got moths ravaging everything in sight. But she's told me to tell you that she's coming tonight and you're not to start without her."

"She needs to get some lavender bags and a move on. This crowd won't wait."

They both stared out to the bar heaving with revellers all waiting to be wooed to breathless peaks of excitement. The seating around the small stage was full, and every stool was taken at the bar. With only a few tables by the window left unoccupied, it would soon be standing room only.

"You should *so* add another Mr. Duke night in the week," Phoebe said.

"Honestly, I don't think I've got it in me. I leave it all out there on the stage. It takes me all week just to build myself up again."

"I get that."

"I can't even get my moustache on for this one." Mr. Duke pressed and pressed at the fur strip above his lip with growing frustration.

"You can always go on clean-shaven."

"And break the girls' hearts? Never. I need more glue."

"Is that wise? You had your moustache for a fortnight last time you double-dipped it in the glue pot."

"I'll take my chances. What's life if you're not living it on the edge, kiddo?"

Mr. Duke retreated to his office. Phoebe continued serving the stream of excited customers until the music went off and the lights went down. Any last unsettled patrons found their seats or leaning posts, and a hush of quivering anticipation fell upon the bar.

"This one goes out to all the ladies." Mr. Duke swaggered into the room like he owned not only the bar but the street and the city and every fair maiden in it.

A roar of applause and wolf whistles and cries of pained adoration erupted and filled the space in a molten fervour of craving.

A momentary cooling breeze blew in from the briefly opened door and was followed by a heavily breathing Reggie to Phoebe's side. "Am I too late?"

Phoebe gave Reggie a hug. "Perfect timing. And here's your white wine spritzer. Easy on the spritz. Just how you like it."

"You're a lifesaver. I'll brace myself against the counter. For my legs will surely buckle at the sight of my beloved."

"Good plan." They both then stood in silent awe as Mr. Duke began his routine.

Somehow, Phoebe always felt nervous for Mr. Duke, and yet every time she wondered why. Over the years, he'd honed a winning performance, which he had down to a tee. Dressed in a smart dinner suit, with swept-back hair, he'd begin with a flurry of flirtatious compliments that everyone felt was for them. The audience would all stare up at him with pleading eyes that begged him to rest his gaze upon them. And then he would sing a song with his lips pressed softly against the microphone as if its surface was the nape of a neck just exposed. It would be a smooth melody, smoky with blues-filled late-night longing. Without fail, he would always end with a blown kiss for a girl in the crowd. And right there another heart would be lost and another candle lit to never go out.

Frankly, he could probably just stand there without saying a word or singing a note or performing at all. Because all the crowds wanted was him and to be bathed in the honey-sweet glow of his charisma.

With his set completed, Mr. Duke left the stage, masterfully dodging flung knickers and the hazard of a tossed bra.

Phoebe looked across to Reggie. Her expression seemed fixed in wonder. She held the straw of her drink between her lips and sucked in a daze at an empty glass. And then she drifted away in a state of silent rapture.

Reggie wasn't the only one left dazed by the night's capers. Sunday evenings always flew by in an exhausting rush of high emotion.

When Dee eventually returned to Phoebe's side, she slumped onto the bar top as if her life was about to expire. "They're animals. Each and every one of them."

Phoebe laughed. "And you love it. Don't dare deny it."

Dee smiled broadly and nodded as she teased, "No way. You're kidding, right? What masochist endures assault by underwear?"

"Rock stars, just like you."

"When you put it that way. Get me a Coke, will you? And make it caffeine-free or I'll be up all night." Dee rallied herself to climb up on a stool. Her hair was loose about her face again, and she'd changed into red tracksuit bottoms accompanied by a white cotton T-shirt. With the exception of his moustache, all signs of Mr. Duke were gone.

The last of the revellers shouted, "Goodnight!" over to them as they made their way to the exit and home. The silence that followed was always a bit strange, and Phoebe knew to expect the ringing in her ears to last for the next twenty-four hours at least. This didn't stop her adoring every minute of it.

"Here you go." Phoebe handed Dee a glass of Coke, climbed up on a stool, and rested her own drink in front of her. They clinked their Cokes together. "Cheers."

"Cheers." Dee wiped the Coke fizz from her moustache.

Phoebe carefully asked, "Is it?"

"Stuck on forever? Yes. Before you say anything, I know you warned me."

"I could try pulling it—"

"*No.* And it's as itchy as hell." Dee scratched at her whole face to make the point.

"Isn't your appointment with the bank tomorrow?"

"Tuesday. But worry not, for I have a plan."

"Knew you would."

"No you didn't. You hoped I would."

"*No.*"

"*Yes.* Anyway, I shall go as Mr. Duke. What better way to explain our offer to customers that has them returning each and every week. And I will take one of these with me." Dee lifted the Christmas events leaflet from the scattered pile on the counter and waved it in the air. "Winner winner chicken dinner."

"How could they say no?"

"Precisely."

A deflated silence followed. It was hard not to believe that the actual answer to her question was *quite easily.* But the Christmas events had attracted a lot of attention. Dee could report in all honesty to the bank that ticket sales had begun to trickle steadily in, particularly for the ball. Thoughts of the ball returned Phoebe in an instant to that afternoon and the horrid man, and then to the most intriguing person she had ever met. "I had a bit of an odd encounter earlier."

"Really? Good odd or bad odd?"

"Kind of both. I was going to tell you earlier, but you were getting ready for tonight and I didn't want to disturb you."

"That doesn't sound good. Look, if ever there's a problem, Pheebs, I'm never too busy. Got it?"

"Got it."

"So what happened?"

"I called by Unwin's Emporium this afternoon to see when they were open."

"Okay. Good plan."

"What wasn't in my plan was to witness a really mean man intimidating the girl from the shop."

Dee sat up straight. "Go on."

"Even though the shop was closed, the light was on, so I had a little peek to see what costumes they might have. This tall bully of a bloke came into view. He was leaning over the girl, and she was obviously trying to reason with him. At one point she reached for his arm, and he shoved her off."

"What the…?"

"And then the man burst out of the door, nearly knocking me flying. He didn't even apologise. His whole face was bright red with anger. And he was wearing this really strong-smelling cologne that literally made me cough."

"Carl Unwin, I bet you anything. Angry dickhead, stinky aftershave, it was him for sure. Was he dressed in an ill-fitting suit?"

"Come to think of it, yes. It was a shiny blue thing, and he had these tan suede loafers. I trod on his foot by accident when he collided with me. He immediately started brushing at his shoe in panic. I thought he was going to burst something. Do you know him?"

"Let's just say, I know of him. He's the son of the owner of the Emporium, Walter Unwin. I get on with Walter, but his son is something else. Carl is a walking warning to all parents who spoil their children. Aggressive, selfish, and a total self-obsessed cock. He came here one night with a group of losers. He heckled all through my act. I wanted to pull out my"—Dee gestured to her crotch—"*banana* and shove it in his mouthy gob."

"You didn't."

"No, I gave him a restrained middle finger and told him that people weren't laughing *with* him."

"Good for you."

"To be honest, I'm not sure I would have been so confident as Dee. He's certainly intimidating. Poor Violet."

"Violet? Is that the name of the girl? It's just, I met her too. At least I think it was her."

"Small-framed, with saucer-wide dark eyes and jet-black hair?"

"Yes, that's her. She's beautiful, isn't she?" Phoebe knew she'd stared a bit too much. What must Violet have thought when she'd called her back just to see her face once more. Who did that? She must have thought *Oh no, I've got to see that weirdo again tomorrow*. Who could blame her?

"Yes, she is," Dee said, bringing Phoebe back to her with a nudge of her knee. "A real cutie." Dee's expression had shifted from concern to amused and intrigued, and she was wearing a knowing kind of smile.

Phoebe's cheeks tingled, and she took an extra-long slug of her Coke.

"Not that I suspect Violet would realise it." Dee shook her head. "I don't think the kid's had that great a life, to be honest. I remember Walter introducing her to me. He explained that she was his niece and the daughter of his late sister. She always struck me as a really sweet, kind girl. Walter seemed proud of her at first, but I don't know, I can't help thinking that Violet hasn't had that much love."

"That's awful."

"So as you met her, did that mean you checked on her after Carl's rant?"

"Yes, I lingered a bit after he'd gone. I was worried about her and took another quick peek through the window. She looked more like a shadow in the half-light than a person. I was so drawn to watching her." Phoebe caught Dee's eye, and her cheeks tingled once more. "She was clearly distressed and wound up. She was pacing up and down, and then I'm pretty sure she began to cry."

Dee gripped at her glass. "That fucking arsehole. I bet he gets a kick out of hurting people. Sorry, Pheebs, go on."

"And then I think she must have sensed me watching her because she looked up straight at me. I ducked out of sight. But then the next thing I knew, the shop door opened and there she was. I'm not sure which of us was more surprised to see the other."

"Did you ask if she was all right?"

"Yes. I confessed to her that I'd seen that the man seemed angry."

"What did she say?"

"She played it down like it was nothing at all."

"That's how arseholes get away with it. Even though there's not much you could have done, it was good you were there, by the sound of things."

"I guess. It felt a bit awkward at first, to be honest. She didn't seem very comfortable with a stranger poking her nose in, but then, who would? We had a nice chat actually in the end. She likes to walk each day, just like me."

"Freaks."

Phoebe laughed. "And she's going to help with the costumes for the ball."

"That's great. You're in good hands. For a shy girl, Violet's a natural at her job. It'll be fun. And I reckon, Frinky Boots, just what you need. A bit of company from someone your own age."

"Yeah. I mean no, not that you're old—"

"It's all right, don't sweat it."

"You know, I'm really looking forward to sorting the costumes."

"And spending time with a beautiful girl can't hurt, eh?"

Phoebe's cheeks hurt with all the blushing. "You're embarrassing me."

"It's my job."

"The plan is I'm meeting her at the shop tomorrow afternoon."

"Make sure you choose something wonderful for me. Remember, something dashing or maybe even rock star."

"You can count on it."

Dee slipped off her stool. "I'm off to bed. I'm beyond knackered. Let's clear up in the morning."

As Phoebe switched off the lights behind the bar, she turned to Dee. "I wish there was something we could do about Carl."

Dee replied through a yawn, "We're a bit late to drown him at birth. You never know, there's a chance it was just a flying visit. The last I heard, until today, was that he'd gone to London to be a wanker—sorry, banker—or something."

"So he might be gone again already?"

"Let's hope so. He never made any secret of hating the shop and Leicester."

"But then why come back?"

"He missed bullying his family?"

"That's a horrible thought."

"So let's not think about him. Goodnight." Dee left for her room, leaving Phoebe staring into space.

Not thinking about Carl was easier said than done when all Phoebe could think about was his cousin. How could anyone hurt her? How could anyone not love her? Why did the world make no sense at all?

## Chapter Five

"Holding her steady at 14,000 feet." Violet tapped at the circular dial drawn in black marker pen. "Oh, mechanical hitch." She bent forward and adjusted the cardboard arch of the instrument panel, re-straightening the bend in the card that had once formed the box she had repurposed. "Heading north to north-east, wind speed thirty knots and gathering." She carefully eased her yoke to the left with both hands gripped tightly around the lever. The handle of the wooden spoon had never been put to such good use, and her cockpit formed of cushions was just perfect for this groundbreaking flight. "Conditions icy, with strong north winds. Visibility moderate to poor." How the press would greet her. The first woman to complete a solo crossing of the Atlantic. Fear was no match for her ambition, no sir.

Violet mimicked the noise of an engine straining and stuttering. "Damn it, smoke. I'm leaking fuel." There was no way she would make Paris. An unscheduled landing was her only option. "Mayday. Mayday. Mayday." She tightened the chin straps of her aviator's hat and rubbed at the lenses of her swimming goggles to clear the mist formed from her excitement and concentration. "Brace yourself, Ireland, I'm paying you a visit." She pushed forward at her yoke to send the craft towards the ground. Where could she land? There! That field would do. Rough and ready, but it would do. "Mind out, cows. Mind out! Moo! Moo!"

This wouldn't be easy. But she was Amelia Earhart, and what did she always say? *Fears are paper tigers. You can do anything you decide to do. Anything.* "Steady now, steady. Two hundred feet. One hundred. Fifty feet. Brace! Wheels down!" Violet bounced up and down as her wheels hit the ground and her plane bumped its way along the field to a grinding halt.

With a long exhale of breath, she lay flat on her cushions and pulled down her goggles to rest at her neck. "Phew. That was close." She unclipped the chin straps of her aviator's hat and slipped it from her head to rest in her lap. "What a ride—"

"Hello!"

Violet looked over at the open letter box and the blinking eyes of the man shouting in through the slim horizontal gap.

"I'm from the building society, Global Local Inc. I have been instructed to call and undertake a valuation on behalf of the prospective buyer of this building. Hello?"

Who? What? Violet scrambled to her feet and opened the door. She was greeted by a small man dressed immaculately in a grey suit and clasping a slim leather A4 wallet to his side. He pushed his glasses back in place on his nose. "I did knock, but I don't think you heard me. I'm Mr. Burrows." The man's eyes lingered for a moment on her goggles. "Am I speaking to Ms. Violet Unwin?"

Violet glanced down at her tan-coloured decorator's overalls, which had been the closest thing she could find to a pilot's outfit. "Amelia Earhart."

"Sorry?" Mr. Burrows frowned, unzipped his wallet, and stared at his notes. "So you're not Ms. Unwin?"

"No. I mean, yes, I am."

"Right. Excellent. May I come in?"

"I wasn't expecting you."

"Oh. I understood from"—Mr. Burrows checked his notes once more—"Mr. Carl Unwin that I would be expected."

Was this her life now—expecting the unexpected? What was the point of protest? "I must have forgotten."

"So may I come in? This hopefully won't take long." Mr. Burrows looked over Violet's shoulder and was clearly attempting to assess the space in one glance from the doorstep. The remnants, strewn about the floor, of a record-breaking flight across the Atlantic might not have been helping.

Violet glanced at her watch. Half-past nine. "The thing is, we open in half an hour. And I've got to prepare the shop for customers."

"Like I said, hopefully it won't take long. And I've already received most of the information I need from Mr. Unwin."
What did Carl know about the shop? What possible information did he have to impart? How much could he really *know* when he didn't care? But then he had the accounts and the deeds, the cold bottom line and the legal rights. All that omitted her from existence.

Violet gave a reluctant, "Okay." She stepped aside, and Mr. Burrows gave a polite nod as he entered.

He paused just inside the threshold and took a sweeping glance at the space. "I'll let you know if I have any questions."

Violet kept a discreet eye on Mr. Burrows as he began his survey. He started taking measurements by pointing a reader with a red light at each wall. He then stared up at the ceiling, glancing along its edges. His gaze stopped at an area of light cracks on the hinge side of the front door. Violet always thought of them as the laughter lines of a long life well-lived. The small groan Mr. Burrows emitted suggested he didn't think anything was funny. Violet caught his eye. Quickly looking away, she continued to busy herself, tidying up the cushions from the floor and preparing the till with the day's float. Then she went to the window, bringing with her the cardboard replica of the instrument panel along with a black-and-white photograph of Amelia with her plane. Together, these would form the perfect backdrop for her display. With the scene set, she then climbed up on to the sill and hung a red painted polystyrene plane from the ceiling of the window bay. Even if she said so herself, it was coming together well. She finished by placing her goggles and aviator's hat on the mannequin. Once Mr. Burrows had left, she would add the final flourish with the addition of the overalls and neck scarf that she was wearing. She checked her watch again. It was quarter to ten.

Mr. Burrows joined her at the window. He tapped at the plane, making it move slightly. "Lockheed Vega 5B. May 20–21, 1932, fourteen hours, fifty-six minutes," he said, staring at the swaying aircraft until it stopped moving.

Violet couldn't decide whether to be impressed or freaked out by this sudden burst of unexpected knowledge. "Yes. I can't imagine how scary it must have been to cross the Atlantic on your own. How did you know?"

"You introduced yourself earlier as Amelia Earhart. I'm an enthusiast."

"Really? Of pioneering women?"

"Of planes."

"Oh yes, of course." Violet hung her head. She couldn't have felt more foolish.

"And pioneering women. I have two daughters who impress me every day. Not to mention my wife, who is very much my better half."

Wow. Violet had never heard a man speak in such a way.

Mr. Burrows returned his attention to his notes. "Your brother—"

"Cousin."

"My apologies. Your cousin said there was a two bedroom flat above?"

"Three bedroom, if you count my room."

Mr. Burrows flicked over a few pages to a basic plan of the building's layout. "You mean the storeroom at the front?"

Violet didn't know what to say.

"So it's been repurposed as a bedroom?" His gaze settled on Violet for a brief moment. There was something about his expression that made her throat thicken with the impulse to cry.

Violet nodded. Words would not come.

"I'll need to see the flat," he said, with a note of apology to his voice.

"Yes. But"—she glanced away to the front door—"I've got to open the shop in a moment."

He acknowledged her comment with another small nod and proceeded to rattle a window catch.

"Before I go upstairs," he said, gesturing with his pen to the far end of the long space towards the counter and the drawers and stacked boxes behind, "I need to take a quick look at the area at the back there."

"Yes. But it's just boxes and drawers—"

"Freestanding?"

"How do you mean?" Violet followed after Mr. Burrows as he made his way to the counter.

"My valuation will just include fixtures and fittings. Nothing that can be removed by the seller."

"What about the costumes?" Violet had shut out the thought of losing the costumes, and now the notion banged open, bruising her heart with the blow. "Does that mean you won't be including them in your valuation?"

Mr. Burrows had stopped at the vintage cabinet of drawers. "You'll need to talk to your cousin about them. I am able to confirm that the shop's stock is not included in the sale."

"But what will happen to them?"

"I'm sorry, Ms. Unwin, that is a question for your cousin to answer."

Violet knew without asking Carl what his answer would be. And it wouldn't involve keeping them. She doubted he could be bothered to even sell them. But to throw them away? She looked at the mannequin in the window. *No.*

"Goodness, there is no moving this old girl. At least not without a lot of effort." Mr. Burrows patted the cabinet's surface and then seemed to step over something. From where Violet stood on the other side of the counter, she couldn't see what it was. "My guess is that she's been here from the get-go," he said, lifting one of the tote bags hanging from a drawer knob and reading aloud. "Since 1898."

"The shop's been in our family for a really long time." Violet swallowed down the pressing urge to cry.

"That's quite something." Mr. Burrows's warm smile underlined further that he understood the significance of what she was saying. He rested the bag gently back in place.

It *was* quite something. A wash of pride soothed Violet's aching heart. She was an Unwin, and it was her grandparents and not just Carl's who had owned the business before Uncle Walter. And did they think it hadn't occurred to Violet that her mother, as the older child, should by all things fair have inherited the Emporium? Had they dismissed her mum as incapable? Or was it simply they gave preference to the male line, and Walter's future entitlement was decided at his birth? Unwin's Emporium was morally in every way *her* inheritance and not just Carl's.

Mr. Burrows's attention lingered on the cabinet. "This is an excellent late Victorian example of an oak cabinet of shop drawers. It has real value."

"I love it. And the counter." Violet drifted her hand along its bevelled front edge, rubbed smooth by the years of customers leaning against it. "It's just when I stand behind it, I can feel the generations of Unwins standing here with me. Serving customers each day just like I do. Making sure that each person is served with care. I even hope that they leave feeling better for having been here. It's more than just a costume shop, Mr. Burrows. To me, at least."

Mr. Burrows gave a sympathetic sigh. "I can see that. I often feel sorry when I cannot set a price to what a place means to someone."

"You do?"

"Young lady, this may not be any consolation to you, but what makes a place, or in this case a business, and where the value lies, is not bricks and mortar or price per square meter—it is the heart of the people who love it. And that is not for sale." Without dropping a beat, he then continued dispassionately, "Is that the door to the flat?" His focus had moved on to the door tucked in the corner and the accommodation beyond.

"Yes, you can go straight up. It's open."

"Thank you. Oops, nearly tripped…" He stepped over the same something again and left the room for upstairs.

Violet stared after Mr. Burrows. They both knew he could not help with action, but that hadn't stopped him helping her with words. Carl could not take from her that which would never be for sale. He could not claim and discard her memories, or her feelings, or her moral right to her inheritance.

A figure passing in front of the window reminded her to ready herself for customers. She went behind the counter and all but hit her leg on an open drawer from the bottom row of the cabinet. So that's what Mr. Burrows had been obliged to step over.

"Odd."

Each drawer had a small rectangular brass frame for a label just above its handle and an ornate keyhole beneath. The keys were a matter of folklore, rather than fact, for they had been lost so many years before. Most of the drawers in the cabinet opened without a key, except for the bottom row, which could not easily be prised open and were therefore assumed locked. As the contents were not needed for the general running of the shop, the urgency to open them was not there. Curiosity was not enough reason to risk damaging the cabinet or paying for the locksmith's time. At least that was what a curious young Violet had been told.

"What are you doing open?" Violet bent to read the label on the drawer. "1900–1914." Carl must have forced it, looking for the deeds.

It would be like him not to bother closing it again. But then why hadn't she noticed it before? You literally couldn't miss it, let alone avoid it.

As tempting as it was to explore its contents, for now at least, she needed to try to close it. The drawer was heavy and awkward. It took a jiggle and a firm push to relocate it on the runner that allowed her to eventually slide it back into place. A pulse of anxiety gripped her stomach at the thought that she would soon need to go through *all* these drawers and sort out the contents. What would she do with everything? *Sort all this old crap out. And get on with it.* That was what Carl had said. That was his plan. This *crap* was her history. She would sort it and find a way to keep it. But first she had to find a way to live. How on earth would she do that?

Mr. Burrows arrived back into the shop from upstairs.

"That's everything I need," he said. "Thank you for your help and time, Ms. Unwin." He held out his hand and Violet shook it.

"Thank you…for listening to me, Mr. Burrows."

"It has been my pleasure. Every good wish for your move." He turned to make for the door.

"What happens now?"

He stopped and pushed his glasses to sit more squarely on his nose. "I will prepare my valuation report. If everything is to our satisfaction, then subject to the usual process, the sale should be completed by the end of December, give or take."

"December?"

"Yes. Well, I'll leave you to it. Thank you again." With this Mr. Burrows left.

December? That was only just over a month away. So it wasn't just a threat when Carl had said they were done.

She quickly brushed away an embarrassing tear on her cheek. A terrible sense of helplessness overwhelmed her. Necessity had meant that she'd got used to being alone. But then she'd always had the shop. The reality of being alone in the world now took on a whole new meaning and triggered a sense of dread. "It'll be okay," she said repeatedly into the room. "Please let it be okay. You see, I don't know what to do. What do I do?"

The red plane rocking in the window bay prompted her to look up and stare at it in puzzlement. Why wasn't it stopping? It was sent rocking by Mr. Burrows's leaving. It was nothing. She went to the window and paused the plane's movement with the lightest touch of her finger.

"It'll be okay." Maybe if she said it enough, it would be true. She took a deep breath, unzipped the decorator's overalls, and slipped them off revealing her jeans and T-shirt underneath. Then she unlooped the scarf from her neck and finished the mannequin's outfit with the final flourish it offered. How brave Amelia Earhart had been. Could she be as brave? Her own life ahead was so unknown it was like the vast Atlantic Ocean. But she was no Amelia Earhart. She was Violet Unwin, and her fears were not paper tigers. They were real and clawing at her frightened heart.

"It'll be okay. Please let it be okay."

❖

*That's so clever.* Phoebe lifted the cuff of her coat and rubbed the drizzle of rain from the patch of window she was gazing through. She loved the display window of Unwin's Emporium. There was always something to admire or be amazed by. *I wonder if that hat's original?* "Go away, rain." Phoebe squinted into the sky, blinking away the light drips that were now becoming heavy raindrops. She rummaged in her bag for her umbrella and quickly put it up. Then she returned her attention to the display. A black-and-white image had been blown up and placed in the bay of the window. It showed a smiling woman in a flying suit standing on her plane surrounded by people cheering. The first words of the text under the picture read *Amelia Earhart.*

*How cool is that.* Moreover, how cool was Violet for having the imagination to create such a display. Phoebe had fallen asleep last night thinking about what Dee had said about Violet's life. That Dee suspected Violet never had much love. And to have lost her mum must have been awful. She kept thinking how alone in the world Violet must feel without someone loving her, and how frightening that must be. Phoebe herself felt afraid of the future, but she had Dee by her side. And even though she didn't feel she could speak freely and honestly with her parents about her struggles, she knew deep down they would be there for her. A surge of dread at the thought of the conversation with her parents she had in front of her formed a twisted ball in the pit of Phoebe's stomach. She wasn't ready to talk to them. Not yet. Not ever. She felt embarrassed by how self-indulgent that sounded, given that Violet would no doubt give anything to talk to her mum. Self-indulgent, that's what she was. A loser, a failure, a disappointment, a general hazard, clueless, *and* self-indulgent. *Stop.* Phoebe dropped her umbrella to her side and held her head back to feel the cool rain on her face. When negative thoughts gripped her, she knew she needed a distraction to break the cycle of self-hate. She needed to be taken out of herself. She needed to be here. Lifting the umbrella over herself once more, she checked her watch. It had just turned four. A flutter of nerves played in her stomach. What did she have to be nervous about? Aside, of course, from having looked like a weirdo in front of Violet yesterday. *Stop it. Stop hurting yourself, Frink.* She must occupy her brain, otherwise it would occupy itself, and that was never good. Costumes. She must concentrate on the costumes and preparations for the ball.

Phoebe peered through the shop's window further in beyond the display. All seemed suspiciously dark and quiet inside. If she didn't know better, she would say the shop was closed. But she could have sworn that Violet had said they were open ten till five.

Phoebe made her way from the window to the front door. Sure enough the sign was flipped over to read *Closed*. Her heart sank.

"Phoebe?"

Phoebe turned to find Violet standing behind her. Wide dark eyes blinked at Phoebe from within the shelter of Violet's hood. Mists of wet had gathered on her cheeks and neck. She was properly beautiful. "Yes. Hi!"

"Hi."

"Sorry, here." Phoebe held her umbrella over Violet. "Crappy rain."

Violet visibly blushed at Phoebe's gesture. She seemed to blush even more when Phoebe stood closer to her so they could share the shelter from the rain.

"Thank you," Violet said, staring up at the struts of the umbrella. "Actually, I like the rain as it happens."

"*Yes*, yes. So do I. Just not the..." How could she put it?

"Wet bit," Violet offered with a shrug.

"Exactly. Not keen on that particular element." They shared a self-conscious smile.

"So you'd prefer dry rain?" Violet's expression definitely had elements of playful amusement tinged with reserved bafflement.

Phoebe laughed. "Yes, I would. Although not dry sandy rain like you get in sandstorms. I'm very particular. Come to think of it, I like the beach but not the sand. And I like a breeze but not a draught. And I don't like biscuits that have gone soft, but I like soft biscuits in that I like to dunk. I like silence but I don't like being alone. And I like ice cream, but I don't like ice cubes. I like weeping at films but I don't like to cry. I like history but I don't like to look back. And happy people often make me feel sad. I have no idea where all that came from. Sorry. I'm being weird. I'm a little nervous." *Oh my God, what was that?*

Violet looked at the ground. "Then I'm weird too. Because I totally get what you just said. Particularly the happy people thing." Violet swallowed. She cleared her throat. "I like hot drinks when they've gone cold."

"Yeah, you're on your own there." They laughed until giggles became contented sighs, and then they stood under the umbrella for a moment longer without speaking, just smiling at each other. Phoebe could have stood there all day in the rain with the sweetest of strangers, not talking, not caring about getting wet or being late for work. Wait. Work. Dee would have a field day if Phoebe returned having never even made it into the shop because she was so distracted by Violet.

"So, can I come in and see the costumes?"

"Yes, of course." Violet shook her head. "What was I thinking, leaving you on the doorstep?" She awkwardly pulled her key from her pocket. "I haven't been feeling that great today, so I closed a bit earlier to take a walk. But I didn't forget that you were coming." Violet looked away as if embarrassed by that last statement.

"I've been looking forward to today." There, they could be embarrassed together. "We can do this another time, though, if you're not feeling well."

"*No.* I mean. It's fine." Violet led the way inside.

Phoebe shook her brolly free of rain before entering and resting it, along with her bag, on the mat just inside the door.

"Wow, this place is amazing." Phoebe stared in unabashed wonder at the interior of Unwin's Emporium as a child might gaze open-mouthed on entering a toy shop. She struggled to take everything in, for there was almost too much to see. Costumes of every description, and on every theme you could imagine, filled two long rails which ran either side along the length of the space. At the end was a counter with a vintage-style till and behind that a large antique-looking cabinet of drawers. Dee had got it spot on when she'd commented that stepping inside was like time had stood still. To her left was a curtained changing room with a small seat outside it. Any moment, just like Dee had said, Phoebe expected the shopkeeper from Mr. Benn to appear wearing his waistcoat, bow tie, his little moustache, glasses, and trademark purple fez-style hat. Unwin's Emporium was truly surreal. And truly amazing.

"Dee was right," Phoebe said. "She told me this place was cooler than cool and that I was in for a treat."

"Dee?" Violet closed the door.

"Dee from The Banana. She's a regular of yours. You might know her as Mr. Duke."

"Oh yes, I remember. My uncle used to always be very particular about serving her—him, rather."

"Used to? Your uncle doesn't work here any longer?"

Violet shook her head. "He took early retirement. Nearly six months ago now. He moved with my aunt to the seaside." She briefly turned away and moved to the far end of the shop where she slipped off her coat and hung it up. Violet looked so sweet as she tucked a stray edge of her shirt neatly back into her jeans. Making her way back to Phoebe, she added, "It's just me here…at the moment."

"So your cousin…?"

"Oh no. He's not interested in the shop."

"It must be hard being on your own. Dealing with all this."

"I just get on with it. Even though we're often very busy, I've never found it stressful being here. I enjoy it."

Phoebe nodded and glanced around the space once more. "I bet. I'd never be out of the costumes. The customers wouldn't get a look in."

"You like dressing up?"

"I *love* dressing up."

"Me too." They shared a smile.

"No way, is that a Coldstream Guard's outfit?" Phoebe rushed over and lifted the sleeve of a red ceremonial tunic hanging up alongside a pair of black trousers complete with a red stripe down their legs. She stared up at the shelf above. "You've even got the bearskin hat."

"Do you want to try the outfit on?"

"Can I?"

Violet smiled broadly. "Of course." She unhooked the tunic and trousers from their hanger, lifted the bearskin carefully from the shelf, and handed them to Phoebe. "The changing room's there. Obviously. Here you go."

"Thank you. This is so fab. One sec." Phoebe dropped her coat to the floor where she stood and then bent to unzip her boots, and rather than kick them off, she took great care to ease them from her feet and leave them in an orderly way. For they were no ordinary boots. Fashioned in black leather, they rose, skin-tight, to just under the knee. Decorative laces ran along their length and were threaded together like a corset. Every time Phoebe looked at them, they thrilled her.

"I love your boots," Violet said. "They're really edgy."

"They're my favourites. I have too many boots, to be honest. Every time I find myself in a charity shop, which is often, I can't resist the shoe rail. It's fair to say that I'm a bit obsessed." Phoebe gave an unapologetic shrug, pulled off her jumper, all but taking her T-shirt with it, and then took the outfit from Violet and made for the dressing room.

Once inside, she released a small squeal of delight. She had loved dressing up as a kid. The worries of adulthood could take a hike—this was childhood fantasy at full volume. She yanked off her jeans and climbed into the trousers. She couldn't wait to see what she looked like with them on. Perfect! That was it—she was never taking them off. "I love the trousers," she called out.

Violet called back, "They're fun, aren't they?"

Phoebe then dipped her arms into the cold, smooth fabric of the sleeves of the tunic and shrugged it onto her torso. The tunic was a little big, but this didn't diminish the off-the-scale delight of the effect it created. She pressed her fingers to the mirror as if touching to see if the experience was real. It was magical. She then hurriedly buttoned up each brass button. "I've always wanted to be a guardsman at the palace. You know—in those guard boxes."

"Yes, I know what you mean," Violet called through the curtain. "How do they stand there so still for so long?"

"I've absolutely no idea. I'd be forever fainting. Okay, here goes the hat." Phoebe placed the bearskin carefully on her head, and everything went dark as the fur tickled her eyelashes. "How do they parade in this? I can't see a thing." Phoebe fumbled for the curtain and emerged walking more like a zombie than a soldier. "Violet?"

"I'm here." Violet lifted the bearskin gently away from Phoebe's eyes to sit a little further back on her head. "Hello, Guardsman," Violet said with a smile that sent Phoebe's stomach fluttering.

Her cheeks tingled as she asked, "What do you think? Do I pass muster?" She saluted gingerly at the same time as trying to balance the hat on her head.

"Almost. Your bottom button's a bit…" Violet nodded to the bottom of the tunic where one end was longer than the other.

"Oh, tricky. Can you?"

"Yep." Violet unbuttoned and rebuttoned, straightening the tunic. Phoebe held her breath. She watched Violet's delicate fingers work their way effortlessly in and out of the buttonholes. "There."

"Thanks."

Violet saluted in return. "Inspection complete. You can stand down, soldier."

Phoebe laughed. "I can't believe you do this all day."

"I don't normally play with my customers, to be honest." They both giggled.

"Well, I feel very honoured." Phoebe rested the bearskin hat on the chair and ruffled her hair into place. "So, am I the only soldier today?"

"Yes." Violet perched herself on the windowsill. "I had a Pope, a fairy princess, a vampire, a clown, a headmistress, Dolly Parton, and a dalmatian."

"A dalmatian?"

"Yep."

Phoebe laughed and then laughed some more. "You have such an odd job. In a good way."

"I know. I love it." Violet swallowed several times before staring down at the floor with an expression newly shadowed in sadness.

"Are you okay?"

"Yes, I'm just, like I said, having a bit of a rough day. But this is fun. Thanks."

"*No*, thank you. For giving me your time when you're feeling icky. Even when you love your job, keeping going is super hard when you're not feeling well. I mean, your window display alone must have taken you ages. I love it, by the way."

Violet's expression brightened. She looked up to the mannequin just behind her. "Amelia Earhart. She's a hero of mine."

"She was so brave and adventurous. She died tragically young, didn't she?"

"Yes, she went missing just three weeks before her fortieth birthday." Violet straightened the cardboard backdrop. "She was trying to fly round the world." Violet's voice was so full of sorrow. It was like she was talking about a friend.

"But then at least she was doing something she loved," Phoebe offered with a cheery tone.

Violet's cheeks blanched. "Yes."

Okay, that didn't help. Phoebe wasn't sure what she'd accidentally said to upset Violet. Could she ask? No, maybe not. "I should say, I love all of your displays."

The faintest of smiles flickered in Violet's eyes. "Thanks."

"Do you have a favourite?"

"I've never really thought about it. Can I say all of them?"

"Of course. It must be impossible to choose. I mean, come to think of it, I also loved your last display of the World War I infantrymen. They were really brave men to sacrifice their lives, weren't they?" Phoebe looked at the Coldstream Guardsman's bearskin resting on the chair.

"Yes. And women. Not just men. Women tried to sign up, often disguising themselves as men. But they tended to be sent home. Some did fight, though. The Serbians particularly let women fight on the front line. I've been reading about it."

"That's awesome. I love that you know that."

Violet blushed and folded her arms.

"Sorry, I didn't mean to embarrass you. I have a tendency to be too enthusiastic."

"It's fine. I'm just not used to people noticing stuff about the shop or, erm, about me." There it was again, that cloud of sadness shadowing her face. "Anyway"—Violet gave a small shake of her head, as if dispelling the clouds herself—"all through history, actually, women have made great warriors and fighters. You just don't hear about them much."

"That's totally crap, isn't it."

"Yep. Which is why I like to feature awesome, courageous women from history in my displays whenever I can."

"Good for you, retelling things in that way."

"It's not much."

"It's more than I do. And more than many do. Just saying. I'm guessing you aced history at school."

"Not really. I left after GCSEs. I didn't like school very much. I preferred to be here." Violet shrugged, as if to say no big deal. But from the upset in her voice it clearly was.

"Violet—"

"So mostly I just read books from the library or stuff online. How 'bout you?" Violet asked the question with a tone that Phoebe understood to mean *Please, I'm fine*.

"I don't really read much," Phoebe said, matching Violet's shrug with her own. "I liked science at school."

"Is that what you study at uni?"

How did Violet know she went to university?

As if she'd read Phoebe's thoughts, Violet added, "Your brolly." She nodded to Phoebe's umbrella by the door. "It has the uni emblem on."

"Oh, okay. My dad bought me the brolly." Phoebe took a deep breath to steady her emotions. Her father had been so proud when she'd been accepted into university. The last thing Phoebe wanted to talk about in that moment was how she had thrown it all away. "At least he said it was for me, but I think he had in mind to borrow it for golf." It was the truth even if it wasn't the answer to Violet's question.

Thankfully, Violet smiled and didn't press the subject any more.

A heavy silence fell upon them both. In the quiet the shop seemed to breathe in and out with each creak of its rafters. Phoebe stared up at the ceiling, listening.

Violet eventually said, "I love stories of people who are brave." She fiddled with the base of the mannequin. "I never feel that brave."

"No, me neither."

"You seem pretty confident, though," Violet said, a note of surprise in her voice.

"All bluff really. I'm someone who needs to keep busy, to be honest. If I have too much time to think, then I can find it hard sometimes to keep the negative thoughts at bay, and then I lose my confidence. Sorry, that's a bit deep. I've only just met you and I'm blurting all this out."

"It's fine, I'm enjoying chatting. I don't get to talk to many people. I mean, properly. Work and everything."

Phoebe's heart ached for Violet. She might not think she was brave, but Phoebe hadn't met anyone braver. "Oh God. Is that clock right?" Phoebe looked at the brass clock above the door in the corner.

"Yes, it's quarter past five."

"Sorry I've got to go. I'll be late for work." Phoebe rushed back into the changing room and hurried out of her costume and into her jeans. She emerged breathless and asked, "Can I come back tomorrow? Same time? I promise I'll try not to talk you to death. I will actually concentrate on the costumes for the ball."

"That's okay." Violet handed Phoebe her jumper and coat. "Same time tomorrow. I'll be here."

"Great," Phoebe said, pulling on her boots. A fizz of excitement tingled on her skin at the thought of returning. "Thank you."

"No problem. Oh, before you go, was there anything on the theme of rebels in particular you had in mind? I could get some ideas going. Fetch out some costumes."

"That would be awesome. We need, let me think, three for bar staff including me, and then there's Dee's outfit. It might be a good idea to have a couple more just in case some of our regulars need help with costumes. Dee is hoping for something rock star or anything that makes Mr. Duke look dashing."

"Okay. What about you?"

"Confession time again. I've always fancied being a pirate. All that swashbuckling." Phoebe giggled with the suggestion that delighted her. "I mean, don't all girls?"

Violet blushed, as if the confession had been hers. "I didn't think other girls thought that."

"Believe me. They do." Phoebe didn't mean to hold Violet's intrigued gaze for as long as she did. And she certainly didn't mean to feel so unsteady as a result. "I better…"

Violet nodded and looked away to the door. "I'll see you out."

Phoebe in turn rallied to gather her brolly and her bag. "Thank you. And I hope you feel better soon. And, really, if the costumes are too much—"

"They won't be. We'll sort them. Don't worry."

"I won't. I've got you. To help me, I mean." *I've got you?* What did she say that for?

With an embarrassed chuckle, Violet replied, "Yes. See you tomorrow, Guardsman."

Phoebe stood to attention and saluted. She turned sharply and marched out of the shop, calling out, "See you soon!" as the door closed.

It took all of Phoebe's small supply of self-restraint not to burst back in the shop and announce that she'd skip work and *Let's do the costumes now.* But a glance over her shoulder showed that Violet had turned off the lights in the shop. Unwin's Emporium and all the wonder that went with it was now closed.

*Okay, Phoebe Frink, how fast can you run? Because you are already late.* Phoebe began to move from a walk to a jog to a sprint. With each step she tried to think of what she would tell Dee. She could say that Unwin's Emporium was closed. Technically true. But then what had she been doing all this time? Violet was unwell. Again, this was in fact true. Yes, that's what she would say. She had no costumes because of her concern for Violet. She knew before she even arrived back at The Banana what Dee would say. *Would that be your concern for the* beautiful *Violet?*

Could she say yes?

## Chapter Six

"No!" Violet woke herself up with a start. She blinked into the darkness of her bedroom. Was she awake? She reached across to her lamp and switched it on. The light hurt her eyes, and she squinted to read the time on her phone. It was six fifteen. She rested back under her covers and lay there motionless. Her heart thumped incessantly in her chest, and her hair clung to the nape of her damp neck. "It was a dream, nothing to worry about, just a silly dream."

Nightmares were nothing new for Violet. When she'd first moved in, she could barely sleep. She would wake at three in the morning regular as clockwork and worry. Her aunt clearly hated her, and her cousin frightened her, and no doubt soon they would ask her to leave, and where would she go?

She would dream that she was wandering the streets, trying each door that she came across and finding each one locked. And people would walk through her and talk about her as if she wasn't there. The most disturbing of dreams was her mum calling for her through a thick grey fog and Violet trying to answer and her mum not hearing. After those dreams, whenever she ate her breakfast with her new family, her aunt and Carl would glare at her and her uncle wouldn't look at her. She'd worked out that she'd been calling her mum's name out loud in her sleep and disturbing them. And they'd hated her for making them pity a lost child missing her mum.

And then the dreams settled as she made her room a little fortress of rugs and blankets, and she carved for herself a space of her own within the shelter of the Emporium. Even when her aunt and uncle moved out, she found she could sleep, albeit lighter and with worries gathering on the horizon yet to arrive. But then Carl's announcement out of the blue changed everything, and sleep these last two nights had become fitful and weird. Really weird.

They were not dreams or even nightmares—they were something else. Violet lifted her hands from under the covers, stared at her bare fingers, then turned them slowly to reveal her pink palms. As she slept last night, it felt as if her hands were in navy suede gloves that were soft and smelt of leather. She was crying into them, and when she dropped her hands from her face she'd looked down at her embroidered skirt, full with deep pleats and wet with her tears. She was in the Emporium sitting on the chair by the dressing room. She'd been reading something and it had upset her. Violet couldn't now remember what it was. With every moment of being awake, the clarity of the night became muddled and distant. She knew one thing—that whoever she was in her dream, it wasn't her, and yet it was her. It was so strange.

Violet couldn't bring herself to turn off her lamp. Perhaps a glass of water would help. She pulled on her dressing gown and made for the kitchen. Off the landing, just across from her room, the door to the spare room that was once Carl's was ajar. She'd always taken great pleasure in keeping it firmly shut. Mr. Burrows had obviously left it open. Just as she was about to close it, a pinch of curiosity urged her to take a look. She gently pushed the door half open and peered inside. Lit just by the moon shining through the open curtains, the room had the feeling of someone having only just left it.

Violet stepped a little further inside. The bed had been stripped to its mattress, and the lamp had lost its shade. The small dressing table stool had fallen on its side. Violet went to it and lifted it back into place. A sense of something or someone made her turn to look back to the landing. There didn't seem to be anything unusual. She was still half asleep and full of her strange dream. That was it. It was the unsettling dream lingering and setting her imagination on high alert. This was her home. This was the Emporium and the place that had always kept her safe. There was nothing to fear here. If she knew nothing else, she knew that.

She took one last look at the room, letting her gaze fall for a moment upon the large dark wood wardrobe that stood opposite the dressing table. One door was ajar, and a tiny silver-coloured key was in place in its lock. A deep woody darkness could be glimpsed within. It could have been used for a production of *The Lion, The Witch, and The Wardrobe*, for it was less furniture and more fantasy. Carl had hated what he called the musty, ugly relics in his room. And if Mr. Burrows excluded them from the sale, what would happen to these pieces that time had forgotten? There was nothing Violet could do except hope that the new buyer would keep them and love them as much as she did.

She returned to the landing and pulled the door to the spare room closed. She filled a plastic tumbler from the kitchen tap and made her way back to her room. A strange sound from the shop below made her pause. If she didn't know better, it was like someone was rifling through the costumes, causing the metal hangers to clink together. Over the years she had become accustomed to the creaks and groans and thumps and bumps of the Emporium. But this was something different. She stood holding her breath and listening. All was quiet. But then a discernible rattling noise began. It came in several short bursts, which sounded like someone trying the shop door. Violet couldn't move. *Please don't let me hear glass smashing.* All fell silent again. She knew she would not sleep if she did not check the shop.

"Hello!" Violet called out as she inched her way down the stairs, repeating the greeting several times. Reaching the final step, she flicked on the light. Everything in the shop looked in place. Slowly, she went to the door, checking all about her as she went. She tugged at the door handle, which remained securely locked. Whoever had tried to get in had obviously given up. On inspection, all the shop windows were also undisturbed. Violet released a long sigh of relief. Before returning upstairs, she went to the till just to check that there was nothing amiss. As she did so her foot kicked at something, which slid with a hiss along the floor and disappeared underneath the cabinet. She couldn't remember dropping anything yesterday. She could leave it, but then, what if it was important?

Violet glanced about the shop one last time. Whatever it was that went under the cabinet couldn't have gone in far. Getting down on the floor, she lay on her stomach and reached through the slim gap. *Please don't let there be any spiders.* The tips of her fingers could feel a piece of card. With a last squeeze of effort, she managed to tease the card out from its hiding place.

She sat with her back against the cabinet and stared at the dusty postcard she had rescued. On one side, framed in an oval portrait surround, was a black-and-white photograph of a woman that Violet half recognised. The woman's face had a certain serenity about it and a quiet resolve. Yet there was a heaviness in her expression too, which spoke of something sad or endured.

Violet's curiosity drifted to the text underneath the portrait. *Mrs. Pankhurst, Hon. Secretary, Women's Social & Political Union, 4, Clement's Inn, W.C.*

"I remember you. You were the leader of the suffragette movement." It was one of the few lessons from school that had amazed Violet, how her country had such a proud history of brave campaigners for women to have the right to vote. She was fascinated by these women. She still was. This was the most incredible find, and in the shop too.

Violet flipped the postcard over. There was no stamp or full address, suggesting that perhaps the postcard had been hand-delivered. All there was on the left-hand side was a handwritten line that looked rushed or dashed off on impulse. The ink was smudged here and there in places.

"No way." Violet gripped the edges of the card, as she read:

*FAO Vi Unwin, Unwin's Emporium. 4 April 1911*
*Vi. Just for one night I needed to be invisible. I thought, no, I hoped you of all people, would understand. Harry.*

"Vi Unwin? Did Vi stand for Violet? Violet Unwin? Could that really be?" The revelation that Violet might share her name with someone was just amazing and sent shivers and goosebumps prickling over her skin.

Violet stared entranced at the postcard as questions raced through her head. So if Vi Unwin lived here in Unwin's Emporium as the postcard suggested, then it was highly likely she was Violet's direct ancestor. If that was the case, then Vi could possibly be her great-great-grandmother and an Unwin through marriage. How incredible was that? But then who was Harry? Her husband? And why would Harry send Vi a postcard with an image of the leader of the suffragettes? And what had happened for Harry to need to be invisible? And why hadn't Vi understood? Did the date 4 April 1911 offer any clues?

Hold on. Violet moved on impulse to the drawer marked 1900–

1914 that only yesterday she had strangely found open and then struggled to close. Had this postcard come from that drawer? To her surprise, it slid open easily. Violet leafed gently through the top layers of papers. Letters and ledgers showed the signatures of the Emporium's founders, Violet and Robert Unwin. It was fascinating. This was *her* history.

A further deeper rummage revealed a slim leaflet dated December 1910. It seemed to be a shop brochure, and on its cover was a photograph of a couple standing by the very counter still in use. To their right, a large Christmas tree, its branches decorated with ornate baubles and ribbons, spoke of celebrations and seasonal delight. In the photograph, the man of the couple stood beside the till smiling proudly. He was portly and dressed in a suit that seemed a little tight. He reminded Violet of a tailor, as a measuring tape was tucked in his breast pocket. Behind the man was a row of shelves laden with a whole variety of headwear, from the plumes of feathers a dancing girl would wear, to top hats, to berets, to police helmets, to animal heads. A crown even sat on a cushion accompanied with long white gloves. It was magical. It was the Emporium through and through.

To the man's left, to the side of the counter, stood a woman wearing an ankle-length floral patterned dress with a broad belt, finishing just above black heeled shoes. A wide-brimmed hat cast a soft shadow over her face, and a fur coat was draped over her arm. She looked like she was on her way out and had been caught by chance by the photographer. There was a hint of a smile on her lips, and her distant expression suggested that her thoughts lay elsewhere beyond the shop. She was captivating to look at. There was no question about that.

Violet strained to read the faded ink title beside the image. *Mr. and Mrs. Robert Unwin welcome customers to the Emporium to select their outfits for the Christmas season.*

Violet's heart pinched at the thought that there would be no more Christmases here at the Emporium, no more welcome to customers to celebrate the season with outfits from the shop. They were the first and she was the last. Had they ever thought of the shop's future? How it might all end? It was strangely consoling and enthralling to see the shop more than a century earlier looking remarkably unchanged. Cruel time and conflicts seemed to have spared her beloved Emporium. Their city retained so many of its late Victorian and Edwardian buildings that

Vi would still likely recognise her home now. It was a mind-blowing thought.

Violet let the strangeness of it all linger before returning her concentration to Robert. Was he good to Vi? Did he treat her well? Did he know about Harry?

She tried to remember all that she'd been told or rather gleaned from half-heard conversations. There was that one time when she was eleven. She had been sent home early from school one afternoon bruised and feeling upset, having had a run-in with the mean girls who had teased her about her name. She'd tried to say that evening at dinner that no one else she knew was called Violet. Her unusual name had made her feel isolated and alone. There was no mention at the time of Violet being a family name. Her aunt had chipped in with the fact that apparently the Unwin girls all seemed to have a reputation for trouble. At the time Violet had understood that to be a jibe about her and likely her mum—unmarried, unwell, unsettled, without a career, alone, and struggling to be a mother. Violet had wondered at the time how that made her mum *trouble*. Hadn't that meant she just needed a bit of support? And what trouble had Violet caused her aunt, apart of course from being born?

But maybe her aunt's comment was actually about other Unwin women throughout the generations. What had she heard from the family grapevine, passed down over the years? Was Violet's namesake trouble too? Violet stared at Vi's image. Could it have something to do with Harry? Violet turned the postcard over to the image of Mrs. Pankhurst. Or maybe even…did she support the suffragettes? Otherwise why would Harry choose that card? Could she even have been a suffragette? How amazing that would be.

Could the answer be somewhere in these drawers or in the many boxes stored at the back of the shop, gathering years of dust? It was possible. Possible but daunting. Before Violet had the chance to dwell on how overwhelmed she felt by the work ahead of her to sort through everything and pack up the shop, with a flood of giddy pleasure she remembered that in a matter of hours she would see Phoebe again—hands down, the coolest human in the world. Just in that moment, with thoughts of Vi and Phoebe, Violet no longer felt quite so alone.

She pushed the drawer closed once more. With her discoveries tenderly held in her hand, Violet returned to her room and placed the postcard and brochure on her bedside table. Just like her, they would be safe in this room. She turned off her lamp and snuggled down beneath her covers. Images of Phoebe drifted like a spring breeze into her tired brain. There she was in her guardsman uniform looking so excited and full of life and wonder. She was simply lovely in every way. Violet never even dared to imagine that such a person existed in the world. And Phoebe had wanted to chat with her, and they'd laughed together and shared unhurried smiles that lingered and stayed with Violet still. Had they stayed with Phoebe too? What's more, Phoebe seemed to be genuinely impressed, and not only with the window displays. When she looked at Violet, she *really* looked at her. There was interest and genuine concern in her eyes.

Had anyone ever really taken the time to look at her, let alone care? She would cherish her time with Phoebe, even if it was only for one more day for the costumes to be sorted. Because everything about Phoebe felt like an unexpected gift. How lucky the person was who got to be with her every day. Imagine having her in your life. Wow. Imagine that. Violet closed her eyes, and thoughts of Phoebe stayed there with her until a peaceful sleep eventually found her once more.

❖

Phoebe found herself running to the Emporium for her meeting with Violet. She knew it was ridiculous, but walking seemed too slow when all she wanted to do was arrive as soon as possible. Thank God that, for once, she was wearing trainers. What was wrong with her? Where on earth were these feelings of urgency coming from? She needed to slow down and find a moment to breathe. If she arrived all rushed and flustered, she would gabble away and embarrass herself as she did yesterday.

She found a spot on the street corner opposite the shop and took a moment to compose herself. Phoebe's urgent sense of excitement, however, soon deserted her, and in its place was the embarrassment of not being able to move. She stared at the shop, the lights within, and the shadows of customers moving inside. What on earth was she now feeling nervous about? She was meeting Violet in her magical shop. She couldn't think of anywhere else she'd rather be.

She checked her phone. It was four fifteen. *Shift it, Frink.*

Forcing herself to get a grip, Phoebe crossed the road and opened the shop door, to find Violet politely refusing a tip from a customer holding a goldfish bowl under his arm.

"No, really, I couldn't," Violet said, cheeks tinged pink with evident embarrassment. "But thank you, Jack."

"I absolutely must insist. Thanks to you I had the most wonderful of evenings. Most notably, I am not now the mad scientist but the spaceman. My social status has never been so impressive. And I have you to thank."

Violet's cheeks deepened a further shade of red when she glanced over to the door and clocked Phoebe's arrival. The customer turned to look at what had caused Violet to become distracted from his pleading.

Phoebe waved and pointed to the dressing room chair, where she took her place to wait for Violet to become free. She slipped off her coat and rested it over the back of the seat. It was wonderful to be in this amazing place again surrounded by costumes, where playing make-believe and having a break from being you was what it was all about. A glimpse of the red tunic of the guardsman hanging on its rail made her smile. She only wished she'd visited the shop sooner, but at least she'd found it now. It was a thought that filled her with warmth and joy. She stole a glance at Violet.

"Really," Violet said, raising her hands in a gesture of small surrender, "I was just doing my job."

"Yes. But you do it well. So please, spend this on yourself. Buy something nice or go somewhere special." He turned back and glanced at Phoebe. "Take a friend with you."

"Really, I can't."

"Yes, you can. I am giving you no choice." The man pressed the twenty-pound note with his finger as if fixing it into the counter.

"Then…thank you."

"Good. Next time I need an outfit," he added, "I know where to come."

Violet seemed to hesitate, as if she wasn't sure what to say. Her eventual reply of, "It's been lovely meeting you, Jack," seemed a bit odd in that it had a strange finality to it. It was like *goodbye* rather than *see you soon*.

Even Jack looked a little puzzled. "Yes, you too. Thank you again,

Violet Unwin of Unwin's Emporium." He rested the goldfish bowl on the counter. "Goodbye."

Phoebe couldn't help but notice that Violet's voice broke a little as she replied, "Bye. Take care." With a polite nod, Jack turned away towards the door, sparing a moment to smile kindly at Phoebe as he left.

Violet looked so fragile in that moment. Maybe she was still feeling unwell. Or was she simply overwhelmed by Jack's gratitude? Whatever the reason, it was clear that Violet needed her to be full of positive energy. *Come on, Frink.* "What will you spend the money on?" Phoebe asked with a broad smile as Violet approached.

"Oh. I've honestly no idea." Violet glanced back at the door. "I shouldn't really have said yes to him."

"From what I heard, you didn't get a choice. You obviously helped him a lot."

Violet shrugged, adding modestly, "I guess."

"No guessing about it. You are his total hero."

Violet looked down and folded her arms. *Great, well done, Frink.* Phoebe felt instantly dreadful. She'd been there less than thirty seconds and she'd embarrassed Violet already. She could have just said hello, like a normal person, not battered her with unwanted compliments. She didn't like them yesterday, so why would Violet want them today? *Just say hello.*

"Hi, by the way." Phoebe tried to adopt a tone and demeanour she hoped said *Don't worry, I am here for business*. "Thanks for today. It'll be great to get the costumes sorted. I promise not to chew your ear off."

Violet unfolded her arms and tucked her hands into the front pockets of her trousers. As she looked up, she gave an unexpectedly impish smile. "Chew away," she said, with amusement bubbling in her voice.

Now it was Phoebe's turn to feel embarrassed. "Maybe just a small bite."

They both laughed. It was a self-conscious yet heartfelt laughter that tingled all the way to Phoebe's toes.

"So." Violet cleared her throat. "As promised, I've begun to pull together some costume ideas." She swept back the dressing room curtain and gestured to a collection of outfits hanging together from a series of three hooks set into a slim wooden board. A handwritten label with the words *The Banana Ball* was stuck to the board with Blu-Tack.

Phoebe leaped from her chair. "Sounds so exciting. Honestly, it feels like Christmas has come early."

Violet's beautiful eyes sparkled with her task at hand. "To be honest, there are so many awesome rebels to choose from, and I hate missing out any of them. But I had to start somewhere. So, I was thinking about how you said you loved pirates."

"I do." Phoebe covered one eye and adopted her best pirate accent. "Shiver me timbers, me hearties!"

Violet laughed. "You're really silly."

Phoebe dropped her hand from her face. How effortlessly she could embarrass herself. "Sorry."

A look of concern passed over Violet's face. "*No.* In a good way, I mean. You're fun is what I'm trying to say."

Phoebe heart's thrilled in her chest at the compliment. "You're fun too."

Violet blushed so deeply it spread across her cheeks down to her neck. She looked away to the outfits and reached up to unhook the first costume. She held out a long-sleeved emerald-green dress with a corseted bodice and full skirt. It wasn't quite what Phoebe expected for a pirate's costume.

"I'd remembered reading about an amazing Irish woman called Grace O'Malley." Violet levelled up the ribbons on the bodice. "Not many people have heard of her. She was around in the 1500s, and not only was she an infamous queen and clan chieftain at that time, she was a fearless pirate to boot."

"A pirate *and* a queen?"

"Yep. She was totally kick-ass. She was fierce and fearless and protected her land and sea from invaders, particularly the English."

"Good for her."

"Yep. And she was certainly very much a rebel for her time. As a young woman she wanted to join her father and go to sea but was told that girls couldn't be sailors."

"Yeah, I bet."

"So rather than give up, Grace cut her hair and dressed in boys' clothes and proved them all wrong."

"Yay! Go, Grace. A rebel pirate queen is totally on theme for the ball."

"That was my thinking. Here you go. Try it on by all means."

"Thanks." Phoebe took the dress from Violet and rested it against herself, pressing the waist into hers. "I could so rock this."

Violet nodded enthusiastically. "Definitely. It will be okay to wear all night as well. It doesn't have the hoop I would add if it was more formal wear. Grace needed to be able to fight, so fussy dresses wouldn't have worked. But then she was also a queen, so a formal-ish dress works well for that. That reminds me, would you believe that she actually met Queen Elizabeth I, who thought she was awesome."

"From what you've told me, I'm not surprised. I bet Queen Elizabeth met her match. FYI, Elizabeth I was also amazing."

"FYI, couldn't agree more. In fact, I'll add her to our options. What I love most about her is that she outwitted the plotting men around her and completely defied expectations. That gives her a rebellion big tick."

Violet mimed the big tick action. Her passion shone out and brightened the dusk of the day. "And I bet they thought they could control her because she was a woman."

"I reckon she knew they underestimated her and used it to her advantage."

"More women need to do that."

"More *people* need to do that. The world would have fewer bullies."

Violet stared at the floor and said with a heartfelt tone, "I hate bullies."

"Me too. I bet Grace would have made them walk the plank."

Violet looked up. "Yes. She would have held a swashbuckling sword to their throats and forced their surrender."

"Sword, eh. I don't suppose—"

"Oh yes. One sec." Violet dashed over to a large wicker basket and returned with a plastic cutlass and a small plywood dagger. "Here. Choose your weapon, you scoundrel of the sea."

Phoebe thought her heart would burst with excitement. She set the dress carefully on the chair and turned with a flourish. "It has to be the dagger for the surprise attack." Phoebe reached dramatically for the dagger in Violet's hand. She held it aloft and shouted, "Be gone from my lands, you English invader! I am Grace O'Malley, and you are soon to be defeated."

"Best you not underestimate me, for I am the Queen of England." Violet dipped down to a bag on the dressing room floor beneath the outfits. She pulled out a vibrant auburn wig and placed it on her head.

Phoebe struggled to keep a straight face. Violet adopted a very strict expression, which only made keeping the laughter at bay harder.

"Wait, is that the Spanish Armada?" Phoebe pointed to the door and skipped past Violet. "Aha, fooled you!"

"That's what you think." Violet matched Phoebe's skilful footwork, and the two duelled, leaping around the shop with unrestrained delight. With dagger pressed to heart and sword swept in turn to cheek, they bravely fought until they collapsed onto the floor in breathless defeat.

Violet rested up on her elbow and straightened her wig. "Shall we call it a truce, for now?"

Phoebe sat up and looked back at her. "Can you be trusted?"

"Can you?"

"Er…no. I'm a pirate." Phoebe stood and held out her hand to Violet.

Violet looked at it for a second. "Then I will trust you because you're honest about being untrustworthy." She took Phoebe's hand and stood up with a jump.

Still holding Violet's hand, Phoebe gave a low bow. Violet bowed to her in turn.

"We are each other's equal," Violet said. "Queens of our lands." Her hand felt so warm and soft in Phoebe's. Phoebe could have held it all day, and it seemed in that moment that Violet might have let her.

The handle on the front door rattled, and the bell struck a single ring. Violet dropped Phoebe's hand, and pulling off her wig, she went to the door. "The snib's not on. It's not locked, so they should be able to come in." Violet opened the door with surprising ease to find a woman with her child standing there, looking put out.

"Are you open?" the woman asked in a scolding tone.

Phoebe stepped forward. Before she had chance to say *You were hardly kept waiting*, Violet gestured for the woman to enter.

"I'm very sorry," Violet said, with a conciliatory tone. "Our door can be a little…temperamental at times. How can I help?"

"My son has a party." The woman pushed her son forward into the shop. "He wants to go as a ghost."

"No problem." Violet smiled at the boy who was staring at the long rails of costumes. "What kind of ghost would you like to be?"

"He wants to be the one who explodes in *Ghostbusters*," his mother said. "The marshmallow man. I've told him it's impossible."

"I love the Ghostbuster films. Particularly the latest." Violet turned briefly to Phoebe, and they shared a smile that said without words *totally kick-ass*. Violet returned her attention to the little boy and said, "And Stay Puft's my favourite ghost too. I'm sure we can help. Let me think." Violet went to the section marked *Christmas*. "We could maybe use this snowman costume as a base. I'm sure we could source some white thermals or stretchy sportswear to go underneath. Then I can sew in some inflatable swimming arm bands for the arms and legs. And then…" Violet brought out a sailor's outfit from the *Military* section. "Yes, we could borrow both this flap collar and the cap from our sailor suit. A little bit of face make-up. It could work."

Violet glanced at Phoebe, who gave a thumbs-up. She was beyond impressed.

"I'm not sure," the woman said. "I was thinking bed sheet with holes for the eyes."

Her son sank a little into himself.

"We can do that too." Violet turned to the boy. "One of my customers at Halloween put his phone in his pocket under his costume and played monster sounds from YouTube. It was really scary." The boy's eyes lit up. The mother's silence spoke volumes.

"When would you like the outfit by?" Violet asked, with a breezy tone that left little room for the woman's scowling.

"Now, please. The party's in an hour." The woman seemed to make a point of checking her watch. How did Violet keep her composure when faced with such rudeness, Phoebe wondered. Even the drunkest of customers at The Banana seemed to understand where the line was drawn.

Violet cast an apologetic look in Phoebe's direction.

Phoebe mouthed, "It's okay."

Violet didn't seem convinced and moved to Phoebe and spoke softly. "Are you sure? I understand completely if you need to leave. I don't want to make you late for work."

Phoebe looked at the clock in the corner. It read two minutes to five. If she ran, she could be at The Banana in five minutes, ten minutes max. If she was a little late, Dee would understand. But then Dee had been to her appointment with the bank that afternoon. She should probably go now. Except nothing about her felt ready to leave. "I can wait. No problem."

"Great," Violet said. "Try on the other costumes hanging up, if you like. One's an outfit for Anne Lister, complete with her barometer. Then we have Mary Anning, the trailblazing nineteenth-century fossil hunter. Oh, and the stuffed toy is her pet dog Tray. There's also a suffragette outfit representing the incredibly brave Emmeline Pankhurst."

"That's so cool, Violet. Thank you."

"No probs. Won't be a mo." Violet returned her attention to the lady and her son. "Thank you for your patience." Violet went to the costume section marked *Halloween* and selected a couple of generic ghost costumes for the boy to choose from. His mother seemed pleased. "If you'd like to follow me to the counter."

Giddy with everything Violet was suggesting, Phoebe took a moment to gather herself and to wander along the long lines of outfits. She paused at the section marked *Musicians*. She drifted her fingers along the shoulders of the costumes. *Hold on. Is that?* Phoebe inched out a pair of gold lamé hot pants. She read the label looped with a piece of string from the hook. "No way."

Violet looked across to her. Phoebe mouthed, "Kylie?"

Violet gave a broad smile and nodded.

Phoebe gave an audible gasp. "*O-M-G*."

Violet laughed, only for her expression to return to professional seriousness when the woman looked at her watch again.

With the hot pants held feverishly tight in her grasp and unhooking the accompanying satin vest top from the hanger, Phoebe went into the dressing room and swept the curtain shut behind her. It had to be done. For one night only she would be the Princess of Pop herself…Ms. Kylie Minogue. Oh yes.

Pulling off her trainers, Phoebe stripped down to her underwear and stepped into the skimpy shorts. She slipped on the vest, noting but not caring that the backless top did nothing to cover her bra strap. It was almost impossible not to squeal with delight. The material around the bust was a little loose, but other than that it fitted her perfectly. The little bit of bottom cheeks showing made her feel daring and super sexy. She adored Kylie and to be her for a few moments…There were simply no words as she stood and stared in disbelief at the pop star in the mirror. The ding of the front door's bell surprised her back to the moment. Had that awful woman left? She stood still and strained to listen.

"Here, try these." Violet's voice was such a welcome sound. She'd slipped two strappy gold high heels under the curtain. "I borrowed them from the Tina Turner outfit."

"I love them." Phoebe slipped her feet into the sandals and bent to fix the straps. "Thank you." Dared she strut her stuff beyond the dressing room? How could she not? "Ta-da." She swept back the curtain, and without waiting a beat, she launched into the disco routine for "Spinning Around," accompanying her moves with a passionate rendition of the song.

Through teary laughter and delight, Violet said, "Wait, I've got an idea." She grabbed the mannequin from the window, and Violet and Amelia Earhart joined Phoebe as her enthusiastic backing dancers.

The stadium full of adoring fans couldn't get enough of them. Even the gathering crowd at the Emporium's window lent a kind of authenticity to the moment. It was utterly embarrassing and completely wonderful all at once. Phoebe couldn't remember the last time she had felt so free or so happy.

"That was so much fun," Phoebe said, lifting her hand towards Violet in a high five gesture.

Violet returned the high five and gave a breathless, "You're a brilliant dancer."

"*Kylie's* a brilliant dancer. I think we should add her to our choices for the ball. I love that she's been such an ally of the gay community. She totally gets a rebel big tick for me for standing against prejudice and discrimination."

"Definitely. Couldn't agree more."

"And I won't lie. I feel super hot in this outfit."

"You look super hot." Violet couldn't have blushed a deeper shade of pink. "I mean…it suits you." She looked down at her shoes. She was so cute.

"Thank you. I'm very flattered. Oh no." The clock caught her eye.

It was half past five. Where on earth did that half an hour go? Phoebe rummaged for her phone in the pockets of her coat. "I've just got to ring Dee. Let her know I'm on my way."

Violet's cheeks blanched a little, and she looked a bit disorientated. It clearly wasn't just Phoebe who'd lost track of, well, everything. "Of course."

The number for The Banana Bar just rang out. "I'd best go."

"I'll let you get changed." Violet lifted Amelia back into the window, returning her to her important job of inspiring the young women of the city to reach for the sky.

Back in the dressing room, Phoebe untangled herself from the hot pants wonder of Kylie. She pulled on her jeans and jumper and pushed her feet back into her trainers. Gone were the high-heeled sparkling gold sandals, and in their place the reality of her life returned.

"I've left the outfit hanging up," Phoebe said as she emerged from the dressing room. "I'll leave the sandals here on the chair."

"Thanks." Violet shoved her hands in the pockets of her jeans.

"I feel sorry to have to go. It's been great. Thank you."

"No problem." Violet looked as sad as Phoebe felt. "What would you like to do about the costumes?"

"Come back again tomorrow?" Was she asking too much? "Unless—"

"*Yes.* I'd like that. It's Wednesday early closing tomorrow, but that's still fine with me."

"Great. I could come earlier. Say, two?"

"Perfect. I mean, that would work."

They stood there smiling at each other as if time didn't matter and Phoebe had nowhere particular to be.

"Oh, sorry." Violet was the first to come round to the reality of the moment. She shook her head. "I'm stopping you from leaving. Here." She opened the door for Phoebe.

Just as she stepped out, Phoebe asked, "Do you like cake?"

"I love cake."

"I'll bring some with me tomorrow. Anything you don't like?"

"Is that a trick question?"

Phoebe laughed. "See you then."

Phoebe knew she was skipping rather than walking away. But the pavement felt like the air, and the sparkling Christmas lights in the street might as well have been the stage lit up, ready for Kylie and her crew. When Phoebe glanced back to the Emporium, this time Violet had remained in the doorway. They exchanged a goodbye wave.

Tomorrow couldn't come soon enough. And when Phoebe began to run back to The Banana, she knew she was running not to make time slow down so she wouldn't be quite so late for work but in the simple hope of making tomorrow come faster.

## Chapter Seven

"Morning." Phoebe joined Dee at the breakfast table. "Have you finished with the milk?"

"Help yourself."

"Thanks." Phoebe poured out a bowl of Rice Krispies and added a tsunami of milk. She leaned in to listen to the sound of the snap, crackle, and pop.

"What's it this time?" Dee said, with a decidedly grumpy tone.

"'Jingle Bells'?"

"Cynic. It's breakfast mindfulness."

"If you say so."

"I do." Phoebe eventually lifted her head and began to eat her cereal. Dee sipped at her coffee. Phoebe couldn't decide whether Dee's pained expression was a hangover or disappointment following yesterday's meeting with the bank. She decided it was likely both.

When she'd arrived back at The Banana yesterday afternoon full of apologies, Dee had simply shrugged and said, "Don't worry about it." Dee had then sloped off, and this was the first time Phoebe had seen her since. It didn't take a genius to see that it wasn't good news.

"Your moustache finally came away then?" It was as good a place as any to conjure conversation.

"It literally fell off in my lap yesterday while I was talking to Mr. Risk Averse at the bank."

"It didn't."

"It did. We both pretended otherwise, of course."

"So by Mr. Risk Averse you mean…"

"No loan for The Banana."

"I'm sorry, Dee."

"So am I, kiddo."

"Did he give a reason? Something we could work on maybe?"

"He rambled on about global market pressures and the general downward trend of the high street and of the high risk nature of the hospitality sector. None of which of course we have any control over."

"Oh."

"He suggested they would be more inclined to lend on capital projects with a finite period to them and for specific measurable business development aims rather than core ongoing funding."

"Did you show him our Christmas leaflet?"

Dee nodded.

"Oh."

"Yes, Pheebs, *oh* is about right."

It was heartbreaking to see Dee so down and, for the first time since they'd met, so defeated. What was the point of asking her what they were going to do? Closing during the week, maybe even closing altogether, was the answer she didn't want to hear. Right now all she could do to help was talk of something practical and positive.

"The costume choices for the ball are coming on well."

"That's something good, then."

"Yes. We have Anne Lister."

"Ooh, Gentleman Jack. She'll be popular."

"That's what I thought. We also have Queen Elizabeth I and Grace O'Malley—"

"Who?"

"Exactly. Fearless Irish pirate from the Elizabethan period. Faced off with Queen Elizabeth and everything."

"Have you and the beautiful Violet been smoking grass?"

Phoebe laughed. "The beautiful Violet is a *genius*."

Dee gave the broadest of smiles. "Told you. So, what else?"

"Mary Anning, the fossil hunter. Violet said she was trailblazing. I don't know much about her, to be honest. Apart from the fact that Kate Winslet played her."

"I'm not sure you could call that a history fact, Pheebs. Mary Anning, I'll have you know, was a total hero for doing her thing in spite of poverty *and* misogyny. And then—surprise, surprise—her achievements were forgotten about until the recent past. But at least we know she existed, eh?"

"I'm impressed you know so much about her."

"You could sound less surprised. I know the odd thing or two. Although, to be fair, I wouldn't have known about her if it wasn't for Suzie." Dee's expression drifted a little. "She loved science and people who discover things. Female pioneers in particular. I remember Mary Anning really struck a chord with her."

Phoebe was amazed to hear Dee speak of Suzie in such a way. "Was she a keen fossil hunter?"

"Hum? No. They shared the same fate. Cancer screwed them both over." Dee stood up, dropped her bowl into the sink, and watched it disappear into the suds just like their hope.

"I'm sorry, Dee."

Dee shrugged. Sometimes there are no words.

*Dee needs you to keep going, Frink.* "And then we also have a suffragette costume."

Dee turned around and leaned against the sink. It was hard not to notice that her eyes were red-rimmed. She cleared her throat to say, "Rebellious women with an important cause. It all sounds great. Good work."

"Oh, I nearly forgot we also have Kylie Minogue's hot pants."

A hint of a smile returned to Dee's lips. "We do? Goodness. Just as well that we have more discreet options with our other costumes. Showing so much...*leg* might be a bit much for some of our regulars. I'm impressed."

"It's all Violet's doing. She's so talented."

"Remember, it takes two to create something good. *Don't* sing the song."

"What, this one?" She lifted her spoon, poised to sing into it, mustering her best Cher impression before thinking better of it at the sight of Dee's glare.

"You can drown someone in an inch of sink water, you know."

Phoebe laughed. "Anyway, I'm going back to the Emporium today around two to finalise everything."

Dee frowned. "Isn't the Emporium closed on a Wednesday afternoon?"

"Usually. But Violet's making an exception and opening especially."

"That's very kind of her." Dee's tone carried the obvious question. Phoebe pretended she hadn't noticed. "I'll come with you."

What? "Sorry?"

"To the Emporium. To choose my outfit. Don't get me wrong, I'm loving everything I'm hearing—it's just Mr. Duke will need something with a certain *twist* to it."

"Okay." It was not okay. This was *her* time with Violet. She was bringing her cake. It wasn't a party for three.

"It'll be a bit later than two, though."

"Great." Oops, that came out wrong. "I mean, great that you'll be able to find the right outfit."

"Uh-huh. Give Violet the heads-up, will you? I'll need her help for certain." Dee gave the heaviest of sighs.

"Will do. And thanks for the tip about going to the Emporium, by the way. It's an amazing place."

"I had a feeling you'd love it. And I'm looking forward to catching up with Walter."

"Oh, he's not there any more. He's retired."

"Really? When?"

"I think Violet said six months ago."

"I didn't know. Is Violet managing the shop on her own?"

"I guess so."

"Good for her. I admire that ambition. Walter's lucky to have her take the shop on."

"Definitely. Right. I've got to go and choose cake."

"Cake?"

"I'm taking Violet and me some. I think I'm going with lemon and poppyseed."

"I see. A cake date."

"Yes, and I'm very much looking forward to it. I'll save you a slice."

"No need, I'm watching my weight. From a distance with my eyes shut."

They both laughed. Phoebe moved to leave.

"Pheebs."

"Yeah."

"Maybe take care with Violet."

"How do you mean?"

"The impression I've always got is that she is a sensitive girl. Maybe a little lacking in worldliness."

"Worldliness? Honestly, she knows loads about everything. History in particular."

"I'm guessing from books. Not from life."

"I'm not sure I understand what you're getting at."

"If Violet is as taken with you as you clearly are by her, then I worry that her heart might be more tender than most."

"Her heart? We've literally just met."

"And ever since, you've been the happiest I've seen. Your face brightens with the mention of her name. And it takes a matter of moments to fall for someone."

"It's fun being with her, and it's just cake." Phoebe knew it wasn't just cake. The cake was the excuse to extend their time together and to move from customer to friend and then…was she hoping for something more? Could she honestly say she wasn't? "In any case, I'd never hurt Violet."

"Look, I know that you won't mean to hurt her. Honestly, you're hands down the kindest kid I know. But you're not in the best headspace, what with uni and everything…"

"What you mean is, who would want to be with a dropout like me, don't you?"

"No, that's not—"

"See you later."

"Pheebs. Wait. I didn't mean to upset you—"

Phoebe left the kitchen without waiting to hear more wisdom. She'd heard enough. Dee was wrong to steal her excitement from her. Yes, she was messing up. Yes, her future looked…non-existent. But it belonged to her. And she would think of it what she wanted to. And right now, she wanted to think of it with the Emporium in it. With Kylie and Grace and Queen Elizabeth I and Amelia Earhart in it. But most of all, she wanted to think of it with Violet Unwin in it. And if Dee was right and Violet felt the same, then that would be just the most amazing thing and, if possible, even more magical than the Emporium itself.

## Chapter Eight

"Damn the biting cold gnawing at my bones like a hungry dog." Sitting cross-legged on a cushion on the shop floor, Violet tugged the brown sheepskin rug thrown over her shoulders ever closer to her neck. "I give thanks to the Old Gods of the forest for this fire." She held out her palms in front of a pile of stones in a variety of sizes and shapes that had been arranged into a circle of sorts. Nestled amongst them were pieces of cardboard cut to the shape of flames and coloured in yellow, orange, and red crayon.

How she missed the tender warmth of the long summer. And now all that remained in its place was a coldness like no other, freezing her perilous route north. What would she face ahead of her? Violet glanced across to the window. A large piece of card rested underneath the sill, and on it a landscape had been drawn in black pen, depicting a long, high wall sketched like a range of cliffs, holding at bay an ocean of white. The single image of a deathly figure on a horse with a spear raised in the air was silhouetted in the foreground. She would not be afraid. No. For she was Arya Stark, and she would avenge her family and return to Winterfell, for there was an even greater battle ahead.

Violet looked down at the plastic bow and the quiver full of toy arrows resting to her side. She must be vigilant at all times. For the dangers at every turn were as much unseen as seen, unknown as known. Leaping to her feet, she reached for her sword at her hip and slid it from her belt. Moving with the stealth of a cat, just as Syrio had shown her, she darted to the dressing room and stopped to stare for a moment at the warrior assassin reflected back at her. Wearing her leather tunic fit for battle, she was not a lady waiting to marry a lord, oh no, she was a fighter intent on revenge. Violet closed her eyes, breathed in deeply, and raised her sword.

She must remember the names of her enemies, list them one by one. "Cersei, every last Frey…" Violet paused, squeezing her eyes ever tighter shut. Who or what would be on *her* list? "My aunt. Cousin Carl. Cruelty. Anger. Fear. Loneliness." She dropped her sword to her side, turned sharply around, and held her breath as she stared towards the counter. She had the same feeling that she had the other night, of not being alone. She'd unsettled herself with her make-believe, hadn't she? That's all it was. How silly she felt. Who behaved like that? What was she doing? What would Carl say? *Get a life and grow up.* That was what she needed to do, wasn't it? The time for make-believe was over. She had to prepare the Emporium to close for good and work out how to be in the world without this place.

But her world *was* the Emporium.

A stone rolled from the pile and stopped at her feet. As she picked it up, its smooth surface felt oddly warm, as if it had been held in someone else's hand before hers. That couldn't be, surely? It was her imagination, wasn't it? She was just upset and making everything feel strange. As if the world wasn't strange enough already.

Violet went to the window, where that morning she had removed one remarkable person to make way for another. She placed the stone where the fire would be and glanced at the clock in the corner of the room. It was half past one. If she got on with it, she could have the window display recreating Arya's world of embattled kingdoms and brave heroines in place for Phoebe's arrival. But she must hurry and move as fast as her beating heart, which was gathering pace just at the thought of seeing Phoebe again.

She had just finished resting the bow and arrow on the mannequin's lap and was turning her attention to securing the cardboard backdrop when an excited Phoebe knocked on the window and waved.

Violet's heart was beating so fast it hurt. Had anyone's heart ever exploded just at the sight of someone they were so excited to see? Her wave in reply was met by Phoebe's beaming smile.

"I love it!" Phoebe's shout was soon lost in the traffic noise. She puffed out a warm burst of air which steamed a patch of mist on the window. She wrote a big tick in the moisture.

Violet climbed down from the windowsill and opened the front door for Phoebe, who all but bounced into the shop.

"Honestly, you're so clever, Violet." Phoebe untangled her scarf from her neck and pulled off her woolly hat. Her blow-away blond hair was dyed pink and silver. If it was even possible, she looked more lovely than Violet remembered. "You've captured *Game of Thrones* so well. And as for Arya Stark—I just love her."

"Me too. I was thinking we could add her to our options for the ball. I remembered your passion for swashbuckling heroines."

"*Yes.* Thank you so much for thinking of me."

"Of course." *I think about you all the time.*

"Sorry, hi, by the way."

"Hi." Violet didn't quite know what to do with herself.

"As promised, I've brought cake with me. Well, pastries actually." Phoebe slipped a floral-patterned bag off her shoulder, rummaged inside, and pulled out a brown paper bag. "I went with a cream horn because it made me laugh when the lady next to me in the queue ordered it. It's got apple with cinnamon inside. I hope that's okay."

"It's more than okay." Phoebe was the first person to give her something without it being a birthday or a Christmas or an obligation. "Thank you so much."

"My pleasure." There they were, smiling again at each other. It felt so, so good. Phoebe's smile was what Violet imagined a heartfelt hug to be like, a human touch full of love and care. A stab of pain in her chest came with the thought that their reason to meet would soon be over. Would it have been easier not to have met Phoebe and not to have felt her smile?

"You okay, Violet? You disappeared on me then for a moment. Were you thinking about the pastries?"

Violet laughed and nodded. "Caught out. Can we eat them now?"

"I was hoping you'd suggest that." Phoebe shrugged off her coat and rested it on the chair along with her hat and scarf. The sight of Phoebe pulling off a fur-lined pair of suede boots made her smile. She loved the thought of her delight in discovering them in a charity shop. She was just so hip and trendy.

"I'll make us a brew to go with them," Violet said. "I won't be a sec. Try anything on you want."

"Don't encourage me."

Violet called over her shoulder, "It's my job to," as she rushed up the steps to the small kitchen. She'd already filled the kettle. And last night before bed she'd laid out the tray with a teapot, milk jug, two mugs, and two side plates. None of them matched, but they were pretty and felt just right. Two neatly folded triangles of kitchen roll sat underneath the plates. She should have felt nervous hosting someone for the first time, but it just felt so natural, as if this was what she and Phoebe always did on a Wednesday afternoon. If only that could be true.

"So, here we go." Violet carried the tray with the utmost care as she negotiated the bend in the stairs and the last few steps. "I'll just put the tea here on the counter."

Phoebe emerged from the dressing room. She was wearing the suffragette outfit. "I remembered that you'd set this aside for me. What do you think? I can't seem to stop looking at myself."

And Violet too couldn't draw her eyes away from Phoebe. Words seemed to fail her.

Phoebe turned to face the mirror. She lifted the sash, which had slipped slightly from her shoulder, taking care to position the words *Votes for Women* to be central and seen. She couldn't have suited the long-sleeved white blouse and matching full-length skirt more. It was like it had been made for her.

"The hat might need to be pinned to be worn for the ball." Phoebe repositioned the wide-brimmed white hat, complete with a black ribbon trim, so it sat a little further back on her head. Brushing at her skirt, she added, "Of all the amazing outfit choices, this is the one that feels the most, I don't know, right for me? Does that make sense?"

Violet nodded.

"Can you help me with this flower? I don't want to put a hole in the blouse."

"What flower?" Violet moved to Phoebe.

"This one. You put it inside the hat." Phoebe stepped briefly back into the dressing room and emerged holding a purple, white, and green flower made from ribbons gathered into loops. Underneath was a pin sewn in such a way that it held the flower together. It was intricate and beautiful and Violet had never seen it before. "Did you make it?" Phoebe asked with a tone that suggested she was as intrigued as Violet.

"No."

"So where shall I pin it?" Phoebe gave a small laugh. "Earth to Violet."

"Hmm?"

"Collar or chest?"

"Sorry. Collar. Let me help you."

Violet took the flower from Phoebe and unclipped the pin. She lifted the collar of the blouse and slipped the thin metal pin into the buttonhole. She could sense Phoebe's eyes upon her. She clipped the pin closed and stood back as Phoebe pressed the ribbon petals into place, then took a moment to admire her outfit in the mirror.

"It really suits you," Violet said. Weirdly, it was as if Violet had seen Phoebe in the outfit before. Even though this was impossible and made no sense.

"Thanks." Phoebe turned to Violet. "I feel really emotional wearing this, and I've absolutely no idea why. I know from school what the suffragettes went through. So maybe that's it. This is going to sound strange, but it's like I can actually feel their defiance and their fight." Phoebe pressed her hand against her heart. "In here. It's what I'm going to wear to the ball. I'm decided."

Violet couldn't seem to find the words to reply.

"Oh, Violet, our tea."

"Here's hoping it's still hot." Violet went to the counter followed by Phoebe. She poured the tea and added the milk while Phoebe placed the cream horns on plates.

Violet watched as Phoebe tucked her napkin into the collar of her blouse.

"I'll be careful," Phoebe said. "Are you ready? One, two, three."

On three they both took huge bites and giggled as the cream covered the tips of their noses and the pastry crumbs coated their lips.

Violet's taste buds exploded. "That's so tasty."

Phoebe licked her lips. "Is it your first?"

"Yes, but hopefully not my last." They couldn't stop smiling. For this wasn't just apple and cinnamon—it was far sweeter and far more intoxicating, pure unmistakable happiness. Violet had often heard people speak about it, but up until that moment she had never felt it. Even if many times she had tried to imagine it—waltzing round the shop with the mannequin, make-believing it was that someone special in her arms, or lying on her bed looking up at the stars on her ceiling and turning her head to the figment of the girl at her side and kissing her. How many lonely nights had she pressed her body against the soft, giving pillow until sleep stole the moment from her? It was always a young woman just like her, and it had felt so natural that Violet had never questioned it as one never questions the setting sun. And here was Phoebe, smiling at her, laughing with her, vividly real and unimaginably wonderful.

A strong and persistent knock on the door made them both jump. A shadowy figure lingered on the doorstep. Was it Carl? *Please God, don't let it be Carl.* Violet froze on the spot. She felt Phoebe's warm hand cover hers.

"It's okay, it's Dee. I'm sorry, I meant to say she was coming over. You've gone really pale."

"I'm okay." Violet looked down at Phoebe's hand covering hers.

Phoebe gave her hand a quick squeeze and then went to the door. "Hi."

"Hey, kiddo." Dee rubbed her gloved hands together. "Oh, nice outfit. Suffragettes, right?" Before Phoebe had a chance to reply, Dee continued, "Look, sorry about before. I was in a mood, and I shouldn't have said what I said about you and Violet—oh hi, Violet."

"Hi."

"Do you remember me?" Dee squeezed past Phoebe and stepped inside. "Your uncle Walter used to help me with outfits. Phoebe says he's retired now."

Violet not only remembered Dee, she remembered her every visit. After all, not every customer worked their way through the section of suits from every era. And not every customer wore them so well. Even Uncle Walter couldn't take his eyes off Dee. "Yes, that's right. He's gone to live on the south coast. And I remember you, Dee. Welcome back to the Emporium."

"Thank you. I'm delighted to be back." Pulling off her gloves finger by finger, and tucking them into her pocket, Dee made her way over to the coat rack, then hung up her leather jacket with an assured demeanour of someone who had been there many times. "And lucky old Walter. I'm off to somewhere hot and shameless when I retire."

"You could just put the heating on in The Banana," Phoebe offered, closing the door.

"Did you know Phoebe was a comedian, Violet? Laugh a minute, this one."

Given that Dee's comment was entirely sarcastic it felt like a trap, not a question. There definitely seemed to be a bit of a rub between them. What had Dee said that might have upset Phoebe and how did it involve her?

"All righty," Dee said, holding out her hands, raring to go. "What have you got for me?"

"Erm…" One minute Violet was drinking tea, devouring pastries, and feeling so happy in the company of the loveliest person in the world, and the next she was back at work on duty. She felt anything but prepared.

"Why do I get the impression you weren't expecting me?" Dee glanced at Phoebe, who had returned to the counter and, having set her hat aside, had taken another bite of her pastry.

Talking through her mouthful, Phoebe said, "I forgot to mention you were coming today. Sorry."

Dee stared at Phoebe, who gave a shrug.

"Well, I'm here now," said Dee, with a deep sigh, "and I'm sorry for disturbing your tea, Violet."

"No problem. Phoebe mentioned to me a couple of days ago the kind of outfits you wanted."

"Great." Dee began to explore the long line of costumes a little further down from Violet. "I figured all musicians are rebels, aren't they?" Dee flicked through the costumes clinking the hangers together as she went. "Because you have to break the mould to create something new, something unheard before."

Violet nodded. "Did you have someone in mind?"

"I kind of want showmanship, glamour, and decadence—oh, I've always loved this suit." Dee had paused at the section marked *1920s*. She pulled free a grey pinstriped suit complete with trilby hat and spats. With a flourish she dropped the hat on her head. "Now we're talking. Gangster groove."

"Gangsters? Don't we want the ball to celebrate rebellion as something positive?" Phoebe wiped her lips with a napkin. "As I see it, breaking or challenging the law when the motive is purely for personal gain isn't true rebellion."

"Point taken," Dee said, her attention divided between Phoebe and the spats she was trying on.

"*However*," Phoebe continued, "if you're challenging a law or calling into question a status quo that is clearly wrong or unjust or unequal, then you're not a criminal, you're a rebel with a cause." Phoebe looked down at her sash. "And a brave one at that."

Violet's chest swelled with the sentiments expressed so eloquently by Phoebe. Violet's thoughts returned to the postcard sent to Vi with the image of Emmeline Pankhurst. She glanced to the stairs that led to her room and her bedside table, where the postcard and brochure rested. Phoebe caught her eye and smiled. She looked so radiant in her outfit, and her expression carried the sparkle of the defiance she spoke of.

"Oh hello, what have we here?" Dee had returned the suit and hat to their place and unearthed instead another item. This time, it wasn't a glamorous suit but a rich chocolate-coloured fur coat. Without wasting a moment, Dee went to the dressing room mirror and slipped the coat on. She turned to Violet and Phoebe and struck the pose of someone languidly smoking a cigarette. With a German accent she then said, "I am at heart a gentleman."

Violet looked at Phoebe, who returned her gaze with a frown and shake of her head.

"Seriously? Nothing? Marlene Dietrich. Famous Hollywood actress who had a penchant for fur, suits, and ladies, I might add. And men. And glamour. For Hollywood, groundbreaking stuff. She certainly helped to expand the notion of womanhood to include the whole self, unconfined by gender expectations. Rebel with a capital *R*. Add her to the options, would you, Violet. But for me, my fans will be hoping for Mr. Duke–style rebellion. Let me think."

"I like the sound of Marlene," Phoebe said. "I'm not sure about her choice of fur, though." She moved to Dee and lightly touched at the sleeve. "Is this real? I'm more a faux-fur fan."

"Oddly, I'm not sure I've seen it before." Violet stood beside Phoebe and watched as Phoebe's fingers stroked the fur. "Today's been really weird. I thought I knew this shop inside out."

"Stop fiddling with my arm." Dee ushered them away. "Give Marlene some space. Wait. I've got it. Freddie Mercury. I'm certain Queen were inspired by an image of Marlene looking up with her fingers lightly pressed to her cheeks and her face lit from below"—Dee struck the pose—"and borrowed it for their video of 'Bohemian Rhapsody.' And Freddie loved a fur coat too. It could definitely work."

"I like Freddie," Phoebe said. "I'm just still not sure about the fur…"

"*You* don't have to be sure. It's my choice. Would I buy a fur coat now? No. Do I think the fur trade's okay? No. Would I rule out something gorgeous and vintage? No. My work here is done." Dee shrugged the coat free and handed it to Violet.

Violet rested the coat over her arm. "I'll set it aside for you."

"You are a superstar, Violet." Dee collected her own coat from the rack. "I'll set up the bar tonight, Pheebs. Take your time."

"Really? Thank you."

Dee squeezed Phoebe's shoulder. "Sorry again that I upset you earlier."

"Forgotten."

"Thanks, kiddo."

With that Dee swept out, leaving the room with the sense that a whirlwind had passed through.

"Dee's fun," Violet said, smiling. "I always enjoy her visits."

"She certainly owns her space. Sometimes she can be a bit forthright, but I know it comes from a good place."

"Have you known her for long?"

"Kind of. I met her last year when I started working shifts at The Banana. It feels like I've known her longer than that, though."

"I get that. You have an easy way with each other."

"We hit it off straight away. Dee's been a really good friend and she's a big softy at heart—but don't tell her I said that. She helps me when I don't know what to do." Phoebe's expression drifted off to somewhere distant for a moment. "Anyway"—Phoebe fanned out her skirt—"I best get changed."

"Okay." There was clearly more to it, but it was none of Violet's business. It didn't stop her wondering, however. Not that she would ever have occasion to know more.

Phoebe went to the dressing room, and Violet moved behind the counter and rested the fur coat on her stool. The silky lining felt so luxurious, and the fur was softer than soft to touch. It spoke of a very different age and of very different lives gone by. What kind of person had first owned this coat? Maybe they had worn it to a ball too? It had been an afternoon of unanswered questions.

As Violet turned her attention to the crockery from their afternoon tea, Phoebe called out from behind the curtain, "I love being here."

Violet gripped the plates in her hand. No one had ever said that. People had complimented the shop but not in a way that sounded so personal. Could she say in reply *I love you being here*? Surely not. But then, why not? It was the truth. But, "Good," was all she could eventually manage. After all, Phoebe hadn't actually said I love being *with you*.

Phoebe swept back the curtain and pulled on her jumper as she walked to the counter. Her warm smile definitely carried a tinge of embarrassment.

"It slipped out. It was meant to be a thought. Sorry." Phoebe pulled a face of contrition.

"It's all right." It was more than all right. "It was kind of you to say."

"I wasn't being kind—I was being honest, to be honest." They laughed. Phoebe's laugh ended with a heavy sigh. "So, I guess that's the costumes pretty much sorted. I won't steal your plates, by the way."

"What?"

Phoebe nodded to the side plates Violet was holding against her. She must have looked such a fool, gripping on to the crockery for dear life. She quickly set them aside.

"Yes." Violet did her best to muster composure. "I think we're there with the costumes. I'll mark them as reserved for The Banana. You can collect them whenever it suits. There you go." Violet handed Phoebe her receipt. "I've given you a multiple item discount."

"That's brill," Phoebe said in a tone that didn't match her statement. She sounded sad. "Every little helps, doesn't it."

"Yep. You can pay whenever. No pressure. And don't worry about the deposit—after all, I know where to find you." They once again shared a warm tender smile.

"You should come and see us. You'll love The Banana." Phoebe paused, and she softened her voice to say, "It's where I found my tribe." Her tribe? Could it be that she was trying to tell Violet that she was a girl to stare at stars with? It looked like Phoebe had in mind to say something more. Her eyes flitted over Violet's face, but then she seemed to change her mind and added, "We're open in the evenings, sixish to elevenish. Last orders ten thirty."

"Oh...erm." Deep-set fear barrelled in, knocking Violet off her stride. She wanted to see Phoebe again more than anything she'd ever wanted, what felt like more than life itself. But to go to The Banana Bar? She wouldn't cope. It would be awful, and Phoebe would see it and regret asking her. "I'm quite busy at the moment what with Christmas and everything." Everything really was *everything*. That would be preparing for the Emporium to close and trying to survive without it. In fact, she should ask when the ball was. What if the shop had already closed? Why hadn't she thought about that before?

Phoebe hung her head. "If you get a moment, then."

"Yes, I'll keep it in mind. When is the ball?"

Phoebe looked up with eyes bright with hope. "*Yes*, do come. It's the best night of the year. I can get you a ticket. It's on Christmas Eve. It kicks off at eight. In fact, you don't need a ticket, you know. Just come on the night. I'll sneak you in."

Here was the most amazing person, all but begging her to come to The Banana. And yet *yes* felt like the most impossible thing to say.

Phoebe held her palms in the air. "Of course, you don't have to decide now. I'm pressuring you. Sorry. You must think I'm desperate to sell tickets. Well, I kind of am. So, anyway, thanks again"—Phoebe collected her belongings from the chair—"for everything. It really has been a blast."

Violet stood there, not able to say what she most needed to—*don't go*. All she had as her default was the language of costumes. "Would you like me to add some flowers to Emmeline's hat? I could use the colours of the suffragettes, purple, white, and green." Violet lifted the hat and gestured to the brim. "Along the edges. Maybe even a border of them. I think it would look good." Violet heard her voice break.

"Yes," Phoebe said, her expression lit with excitement. "And I could help you make the flowers. I don't sew, but you could show me. I'm a quick learner."

Violet nodded. "Would Sunday work for you?"

"Absolutely. Same time? Two?"

"Yep." It was incredible how much being here meant to someone else other than her. How could she tell her that in a matter of weeks all this would be gone?

Phoebe tried the door, and it wouldn't open. She flicked the snib up and down, and it made no difference.

Violet went to her and tried the door for herself. "I'm sorry—I can't seem to open it either."

"Someone wants me to stay." They laughed. It was such a silly notion. She loved being silly with Phoebe.

"I think you're right." Violet turned into the room and said, "She has to go to work. We have to let her go."

They laughed some more.

"I'm now too frightened to try the door." Phoebe chuckled. She closed her eyes and tried the door again. Violet watched as the door swung freely open and the cold wind blew into them. Phoebe opened her eyes, turned back to the room, and said, "Thank you."

Violet laughed. "Free at last. See you Sunday."

"I will amaze you with my craft skills."

Could Violet say *I am already amazed with everything about you*? "I'm looking forward to it."

"Me too." And with that Phoebe stepped out into the street.

Violet closed the door behind her and glanced about the room. All was quiet and still. Not that the same could be said about the thrumming beat of her excited heart.

## Chapter Nine

"Pheebs?" Dee switched on the lights behind the bar. Phoebe was sitting on a bar stool leaning on the counter with her head propped up in one palm. She was fiddling with the edge of a large BubbleWrap envelope.

"Ouch." Phoebe winced at the painful burst of sudden light.

"Sorry." Dee squinted at her. "I went to the loo and saw that your bedroom door was open."

"Yeah, I haven't made it to bed yet."

"I can see that." Dee climbed up on the bar stool beside Phoebe and tugged her dressing gown cord ever tighter about her. "It's midnight and you're sitting in the dark in an empty bar. Either the dearly departed of The Banana are having a lock-in, or you're not doing so good."

"I'm all right. I just couldn't sleep."

Dee looked at the envelope and frowned. "I think we need a nightcap. Two shots of Bell's please, bartender."

Phoebe scrunched her nose. "I don't really like spirits."

"Who said the second was for you?"

"Oh."

"Just kidding. It'll help you sleep."

Phoebe gave an uncertain, "Okay." She moved half-heartedly from her seat to behind the bar, reached for two whisky glasses, and proceeded to dispense a shot in each from the bar's optic.

"Here you go." She slid Dee's across the counter to her.

"Cheers, Frinky Boots."

"Cheers." Phoebe took a sip and coughed. She pressed her hand against her throat. "It burns."

"Exactly. Now you can't feel your heartache for the pain in your throat. It's officially how it works."

Phoebe couldn't help but smile. "I'd always wondered."

"They may try and tell you something different at med school. But now you know better."

"Med school? What—the very course I've dropped out of?"

"The very course you're just taking a breather from."

"Why would you say that? I'm not taking a breather. I can't do it. I've dropped out. You *know* that." Phoebe's cheek stung with the angry heartbroken emotions churning in her stomach.

Dee held her palms aloft. "I know that when a person is certain of their decision, they don't agonise over it on a daily basis."

"What, so I'm not meant to be upset that I'm letting everyone down? I'm not meant to feel *crap* that my parents have sent me a uni care package?" Phoebe gestured to the envelope in front of her.

"Just talk to them, Pheebs."

Phoebe shook her head furiously. "I can't. I've told you—they won't understand."

"Then at least talk to someone. A careers adviser, or better still a student counsellor. I'm surprised they haven't been in touch with you, to be honest."

"They have." Phoebe pushed a pile of unopened letters into view. "I think one of these might be from them."

"How long have you had *them*?"

Phoebe winced at the fib she was about to tell. "Not long."

Dee gave a sceptical, "Not long? That's a lot of letters for not long."

"I can't face going to halls to collect my post, *okay*."

"*Okay*."

"I've asked one of my course mates to keep an eye on my pigeonhole for me. We've agreed that when it's full, she'll drop off any post here in exchange for a pint."

"Maybe you could talk to her?"

"*No*. She's got loads on, and in any case it's private."

"Fair enough." Dee took a large swig of her whisky. "You never know, there might be some positive news in those letters."

"I doubt it. They'll just say *Where is your answer? We need a refund of this amount. Don't apply again.*"

"How on earth do you know that? When you haven't even opened them?"

"I can't. Please don't ask me to."

"*Okay.* I get it. Really, I do. So, what about the package?"

"What about it?"

"That's different, right? It could have money in it. Or...*chocolate.*"

"Fine. You open it."

Dee made short work of ripping it open before tipping it upside down.

"Steady on," Phoebe said, gathering the spilled contents into a pile. She stared at the voucher card for the university's bookshop, along with a credit note for her mobile phone. Was that a hint for her to both study and ring home more?

"Oh, Pheebs, now we're talking." Dee pushed aside a set of new pencils and a crisp notebook to make way for a large bar of Dairy Milk Caramel. "Gotta love your parents."

"I do. It's just...I don't know."

"Oh, there's a note."

"I'll read it later."

"We both know you won't. Tell you what, I'll take a peek and report back."

"They should have addressed the package to you."

"Just what I was thinking. Although"—Dee frowned as she read the note—"I'm not sure I'd like the pressure."

"Why? What does it say?"

"Just that they know you're doing brilliantly and how proud they are of you."

Phoebe choked back the emotion thickening in her throat. "That's why I can't tell them."

Dee shoved everything back into the envelope, except for the chocolate. "You know, there's a very thin line between encouraging someone and placing undue pressure on them. Don't take this the wrong way, but I think at least some of what's happening to you, your crisis of confidence if you like, comes from the weight of your parents' expectations upon you."

"It's not their fault."

"Are you sure? No one likes to let their loved ones down.

Particularly when you're the only child. You're so petrified of letting yours down, Pheebs, that just like all fears, it has become self-fulfilling."

"You think?"

Dee nodded. "That's my guess, for what it's worth."

"It's worth a lot."

Dee gave Phoebe's shoulder a squeeze. "You need to talk to them."

Phoebe shook her head. "Not yet."

"When you feel ready, then. In the meantime, you've got chocolate."

"Absolutely." Phoebe couldn't help but smile as she stared down at the bar of Caramel. "I might take this with me to the Emporium on Sunday."

"The Emporium?"

"Yes. We're just adding a few finishing touches to my outfit."

"Ah, gotcha. It looked great on you, by the way."

"It felt really good to wear. In fact, it felt sort of great but also, I don't know, a bit strange maybe."

Dee finished her whisky. She gestured to Phoebe's glass. "Want that?"

Phoebe pushed her drink towards Dee. "Help yourself."

"Thanks. Strange in what way?"

"This is going to sound bananas."

"You're in the right place."

Phoebe smiled and shook her head. "I could feel her."

"Who. Violet?"

"*No.* I'm serious."

"Sorry. Go on."

"Emmeline. At least, I could feel *someone*. I could definitely sense anger and frustration. And a heavy feeling, sort of like sadness. And it was definitely more than just acting out the role. I know that sounds weird."

"It doesn't sound weird. It says to me that you're the right person for that outfit."

"*Yes.* I really believe that too. Like really deep down."

"Good for you. They were fearless chicks. Perfect rebel role models."

"Do you think we would have been suffragettes?"

"I'd like to think so. I'd like to think I would be brave enough."

"You run a gay bar and perform as a drag king. That's pretty brave."

"It doesn't even register anywhere close."

"I disagree. You're the most fearless person I know. And the reason I don't need a counsellor. FYI."

"God help you if a cynical old sod like me with a business on the rocks is your guiding light."

"You say that, but surely the last person you want advice from is someone leading a perfect life. Rubbing your nose in it. No way. I mean, what are they going to know about struggling, in any case?"

"Good point. Do you know, *you* should be giving advice. What kind of person gives advice? Oh, that's right…a *doctor*."

"I take that all back."

Dee laughed. "Get yourself to bed, kiddo. I'll turn the lights out. And don't forget your letters. FYI—not opening them won't make them go away."

Phoebe nodded. What could she say to that? "Would putting them in the bin work?"

"Are you still talking?" Dee plunged them into darkness. "And if you fall up the stairs, I take no responsibility. Got it?"

Phoebe stared out into the darkness. "Got it." She couldn't see anything beyond the suggestion of light from the upstairs landing window. Still, on the immediate bright side, it was more than she could see of her future.

Dee flicked the light back on.

Phoebe said quickly, "I'm going, I'm going." If only her future was that easy. One flick of a light switch and she would see the way forward. She dashed up the stairs and into her room. She closed the door behind her and listened to Dee yawn and close her door as well. And then she heard Dee say, "Goodnight, Suzie. Miss you."

Poor Dee, she must think that her worries were nothing compared to the loss she felt. That's it. She would sort her post in the morning and try not to feel so defeated. She would concentrate on the positives in her life. She pulled off her clothes and replaced them with her pyjamas and climbed into bed.

Closing her eyes, Phoebe took a deep slow breath. She would focus on the things that made her happy. She would think of Sunday and of sewing flowers with Violet.

❖

Violet twitched in her bed. She knew she was dreaming, but it felt so much more like drowning, as every time she reached the surface of wakefulness her dreams dragged her under in a swirling riptide of dislocated images, voices, and feelings.

"Don't go! Please, wait." Violet pulled at the shop door. It wouldn't budge. She pulled again. "No. Please don't leave. Please." She rested her forehead against the cold square of glass. It was pointless. It was too late. The woman was gone.

A double click behind her made her turn. "Mr. Burrows?" Mr. Burrows was pressing at his pen and making notes. He was dressed as a 1920s gangster in a pinstriped suit and spats. The jacket was too big for him, but he didn't seem to care. He just kept making notes and clicking his pen. Every so often he broke off from writing and lifted a costume from the rail to inspect it. What was he doing?

"I thought they weren't part of the sale? Mr. Burrows?" He seemed to ignore her or not hear her.

She went to move to him but found she couldn't. As much as she tried, her body wouldn't work. She watched helplessly as he made his way to the counter. He lifted the fur coat from the stool. "*No*, you can't take the coat."

Mr. Burrows rested it on the counter and then reached into each pocket in turn. From the left-hand pocket he pulled out a sheet of paper, unfolded it, and stood reading it. What was the piece of paper? What did it say that was so absorbing? He then looked up and stared straight through her. He couldn't see her, could he? She was invisible to him. But they'd chatted and he'd been so kind. Surely he would notice her? His expression changed from absent concentration to one of concern. What had he seen? Violet turned behind her. There standing on the sill of the window was Arya Stark with her bow drawn back and the arrow pointing straight at her. Arya let the arrow go. Violet screamed out, "No!"

"Violet?"

"Phoebe? Is that you?" Phoebe was looking down at her, dressed in a satin vest and gold lamé hot pants lit up and shimmering under disco lights. Violet gasped as arousal flooded in and stole her breath.

Everything in her ached with need as she watched Phoebe spin slowly around, smiling, laughing. She looked so hot. She always looked so hot.

"Yes, it's me." Phoebe reached out to her and squeezed her hand. "Someone wants me to stay."

"*I* want you to stay."

"You've gone really pale."

"I'm okay. You see, it doesn't hurt too badly." Violet's chest felt damp. "I can take it out." Violet tried to move the arrow. Every time she tried, the blood circle that surrounded it expanded. "My heart hurts."

"Mine too."

"Where are you going? Don't go! Please!" Violet was at the door again with her head pressed once more against the glass. Her hair felt damp against her forehead. "Don't go." She shouted out, "What do I do?"

Violet woke with a start to the sound of her own shout. Gripping her bed sheet, she took a guarded glance about her. She blinked several times, taking in as much of the reality as she could and grounding herself in the familiarity of the here and now. There was her wardrobe and her side table, and the surface of her chest of drawers lit by the moonlight shining through a gap in her curtains. She felt at her chest and found no arrow to account for her aching heart.

She spoke into the empty room. "It was just a dream. Nothing more than a dream."

Violet pulled back the covers and sat for a moment on the edge of her bed. The cold night air chilled her skin and caused her to shiver. She reached for her dressing gown and, heavy headed with her dream, made her way to the bathroom. As she stood at the sink, she caught her reflection in the mirror. Her face was a hazy blur of skin, hair, and eyes. She pressed her finger against the glass to where her chin was. *Am I real?* It felt like her dream had crossed the divide and followed her into the waking real world. And if she stepped out onto the landing, Arya Stark would be waiting to take aim once more. She risked a nervous glance beyond the bathroom. She could see the top of the stairs. She waited, for what exactly she didn't know. Nothing. Of course there was nothing.

With a determined resolve to sleep, she left the bathroom, taking care not to indulge the pressing urge to look towards the spare room or the stairs. And no, she would not listen expectantly for an unexplained rattle or scrape or creak. It was not these phantoms of her imagination that meant her harm. It was the reality of her situation that was truly frightening.

Violet's resolve stayed with her throughout the next day, and the next night she slept without dreaming. Saturday morning was as busy as usual, with customers arriving to return their costumes or with the hope of finding just the right one. Violet loved to be busy, especially when it meant that there was no time to think or, for that matter, to worry. That was, until lunchtime when the post arrived.

"One to sign for, love." The postman handed Violet a bundle of letters. The one at the top had a red slip along one edge marked *tracked and signed for*. The letter plate read *Sharp & Co.* It was addressed to *Mr. C. Unwin c/o Unwin's Emporium*. Violet's body seemed to drain itself of blood and she felt instantly sick. "So, if you sign your name here, please." The postman thrust a digital handset towards Violet.

Violet made a distracted mark on the screen. What did the letter say? Was everything done and dusted? Was the shop sold already?

"Vi Unwin? Is that right?" The postman looked at Violet and held the screen towards her.

Vi? Why had she written Vi? She could have sworn she wrote her name in full.

"Yes, my name's Violet Unwin."

The postman left in the hurried manner in which he had arrived. Violet placed the letter next to the till and did her best to continue with her day.

Except that throughout the afternoon, in between serving customers, Violet kept stealing glances at the letter. It wasn't just the question of the contents that began to eat into her. It was the thought of when Carl would turn up to collect it. He never announced his arrival, and it always came in an unexpected storm of anger and resentment. And Violet was always in the eye of it. She seemed to embody everything he hated. And he embodied everything she feared. He would see that she had not started on the work to prepare the shop for its sale. He would assume she was defying his instructions. How angry he would be then. Her time was running out.

Violet turned the key in the front door and flipped the sign to *Closed*. It was quarter to five, and her last customer had left ten minutes earlier. It broke the rule she had set herself to never close early unless she was unwell. But her rules now seemed oddly pointless, and she felt embarrassed to have cared so much to have set them in the first place. Carl had done far more than close the shop, for he had belittled all that she cared for and in one swift action deemed it worthless.

Violet could taste the salt of her tears gathering at her lips. She brushed them away with the cuff of her jumper and moved to the counter. Here were the cabinet of drawers and boxes that needed sorting. Her head spun at the overwhelming impossibility of everything. She reached for her stool to find the fur coat resting on it just where she had left it. As she lifted it up to place it on the counter, her strange dream came flooding back to her. The words on waking from her dream—*What do I do?*—came to her lips.

Without pausing to wonder why, she slipped her hand into the left-hand pocket of the coat, expecting to feel the silky cold material, and instead she felt the crisp smoothness of paper. She quickly pulled her hand out and stepped back. It was a coincidence. So many people read far too much into coincidences. It'll be a dry cleaning receipt or a cloakroom ticket from a night out. Violet took hesitant steps back to the coat and reached inside the pocket to retrieve the paper.

She rested the paper on the counter. It was folded in half and much larger than a ticket, closer to a leaflet in size. She carefully opened it fully and smoothed it flat. How long had it been there? It had aged to a light caramel colour, and it was almost crumbly to touch. Rippled lines of white here and there revealed that it had been folded in various different ways before. How many people had touched the paper before her?

Violet focused to take in every detail, just as Mr. Burrows had done in her dream. She said absently, "So this was what he found so interesting." It was a form with preset typed sentences and blank spaces where each personal and unique detail could be added by hand. Although the handwritten entries were hard to read, the typed portions were clear. The title in particular was perfectly legible: *Metropolitan Police.*

Violet traced her finger along the lines of text and began to read the contents out loud, line by line. "*B division. Canon Row Station. Take notice that you Miss Harriet Frink are bound in the sum of two pounds to appear at the Westminster Police Court.*" Violet looked up for a moment to digest what she was reading. "It's a bail form." Violet flicked her eyes down to the year the form was signed and to the detail of the crime committed. Did that say *1909* or was it *1907*? And was that *July* or shorthand for *February*? To understand the handwritten scrawl was a process of deducing more than reading. It didn't help that the paper had been folded through the date to attend court for likely the last century or more, rendering it illegible. And were those words *Disorderly conduct & resisting police*? So, who was Harriet Frink? And moreover, what was her bail form doing in the coat pocket of a fur in the stock of the Emporium?

Violet stared at the form for a moment longer, willing answers to fill the space left by questions. And then, with a small shake of her head, she refolded the paper and tucked it into the pocket where she had found it. She would not let herself dwell on what part the dream had played or how strange everything felt.

It didn't help that there was also something a little odd, at least at first, about the fur coat. When Dee had pulled it out, Violet couldn't immediately place it. Sure, the shop had several vintage coats for customers to choose from, and this fur could easily be overlooked amongst them. But there was definitely something unfamiliar about it, which didn't answer the question as to why no one had found the bail form before.

Violet took her seat on her stool and stared at the coat. *Think.* She must remember the coat in some way. Wait. *This dead thing.* That was it, wasn't it? The only explanation could be found in a half memory of a fuss her aunt had made about a coat that had got mixed up with her belongings. *Remove this dead thing from my sight* were her exact words to Uncle Walter. Following Carl's departure, her aunt had stored her coats and excess clothes in the wardrobe in the newly vacated room. She had an effortless knack of colonising everything. And when she was packing to leave, the fur must have got caught up and dragged out with her clothes. Understandably, no one had thought that Carl would claim the coat as his. So naturally it would have found its way into the shop's stock in as swift a manner as possible and without much close inspection so as not to aggravate her aunt further. No one had chosen to rent it in these last few months. Until Dee. The thought made her smile. Mr. Duke would look so good as Freddie Mercury. Dee looked good in it as Dee. There was no doubt—it was a coat you would look good in. Whoever you were.

Maybe she could try it on? Violet lifted the coat, and as she prepared to slip it on, she noticed a label. The gold lettering was worn away, and there was just the suggestion of a glamorous designer or boutique. Violet felt a pinch of disappointment. Imagine if it been Harrods or Selfridges. She lifted the label in the hope that the back had survived the ravages of time, make-up, and perfume a little better. Her heart skipped a beat at the handwritten name inscribed on the reverse: *Mrs. V. Unwin.*

Violet gripped the coat. "It's your coat." Without thinking, Violet hugged it to her chest and closed her eyes. "It's your coat." An image came instantly to her of the postman holding out the handset towards her and asking: *Vi Unwin?*

Violet opened her eyes. She slipped an arm into the coat and then pulled it over her shoulders, feeling the weight of it against her. She reached for the sleeve for her other arm and gathered the front of the coat together. She settled the collar flat against her neck. The action felt so natural and familiar as if she did it each day and as if the coat had been hers for years. Because it had been. Hadn't it?

Violet took a deep breath and moved to the dressing room mirror. She stood before it wrapped in the fur and stared and stared until her own face began to be foreign to her, *other* to her.

Every sense heightened and gathered behind the question on her lips that she needed so desperately to ask. Fear gripped at her heart. But she was not afraid of Vi, she knew that much. She was afraid that she had imagined the woman in front of her when she needed her to be real. She needed it more than anything. In one hurried rush, she asked, "Are you Vi?"

In reply, the face looking back at her remained neutral and still.

And then Violet watched her lips move with hers as she said, "We have the same name. I'm Violet too. I'm Violet Unwin."

## Chapter Ten

When Phoebe arrived at the Emporium on the dot of two, she found the door slightly ajar. Violet was nowhere in sight. A pile of cushions gathered on the floor by the dressing room caught Phoebe's eye. Circles of green felt, along with strips of silky fabric in purple, green, and white, had been laid out next to them. A Perspex craft box, filled to its rim with cotton reels, scissors, pin cushions, and the like, sat on the dressing-room chair. The ribbon flower that had been pinned to Emmeline's outfit rested on one of the cushions and was no doubt to be used as a template. It was a craft enthusiast's heaven right there.

"Hey." A clink of crockery announced Violet's arrival down the stairs into the shop. She was carrying a tray complete with a teapot, a milk jug, and two mugs. A packet of Rich Tea biscuits rolled around on the tray as she rested it on the counter.

"Hi," Phoebe said. "I hope you don't mind—I let myself in."

"Not at all, I left the door open for you." Violet held the Rich Tea in the air. "For dunking. Just how you like it."

"You remembered? That's a terrible thought. Please forget that rambling on. In fact"—Phoebe joined Violet at the counter and rested a teaspoon against each of her temples and made a buzzing noise—"there. All memory of that has been officially zapped."

"Who are you?" Violet said, deadpan. They both laughed.

"I'm Phoebe the loser." Violet double blinked. "Sorry, I'm having a wobbly self-pitying day. But nothing that tea and craft and lovely company won't sort."

Violet blushed. "Take a seat. I'll bring your brew over."

"Great. Thanks." This time, somehow, she found she didn't care if she had embarrassed Violet. After all, she meant every word, and why shouldn't Violet know that she was lovely? Why shouldn't someone make a fuss of her? Phoebe shrugged off her coat, rested it over the back of the dressing room chair, and hung her bag at its side. She then nestled herself on a cushion and picked up a length of purple material. "This must have been expensive."

Violet passed Phoebe her mug of tea. "Nope. You're looking at the remnants of a belly dancer's purple trousers, a Christmas angel's white satin skirt, a mermaid's emerald tail, and an elf's felt hat."

"Oh no, how sad. Won't you need them?" Phoebe's question seemed to catch Violet off guard.

"Erm." Violet frowned and then glumly shook her head and sat down, tucking her knees up to her chin. "No." There was something so forlorn in her tone. What was that about? Whatever it was, she would not draw attention to it and make her sadder. She wanted to be someone who made Violet happy.

"So, what do I do?" Phoebe clapped her hands together.

"Okay, I thought we could use the flower we've got as a guide." Violet reached for the ribbon flower and turned it over. "We have a base circle of stiff material to which each loop of ribbon has been attached with a series of simple stitches. I propose to shortcut this by using a stapler where we can." Violet lifted a small stapler free from under a square of the poor elf's hat. "For our base I thought we could use card and then glue a circle of felt to it."

Phoebe nodded as she took a sip of her tea. "Good plan."

"To save time, I've already done these for us. I've also pre-cut the strips of ribbon to what I think will be the right length to form the correct size of loop."

"Even better plan."

"I'm glad you approve. The green ribbons would have been added first to be the outside layer." Violet held the flower towards Phoebe and eased the individual loops slightly apart to reveal the intricacies of their combined beauty. "If you see, there are six green loops in total."

They leaned forward together, and as they did Violet's ruffled fringe brushed against Phoebe's forehead. Neither moved their heads away.

"Oh yes. And six white and then…" Phoebe felt Violet move away, just a touch. She could sense that Violet was now looking at her, prompting Phoebe to glance up straight into Violet's beautiful eyes.

Violet gave a self-conscious smile. Then, without breaking their exchange, Violet said, "Twelve purple. Overlapped a little more."

Without looking at the flower, Phoebe gave a distracted, "Yes." Phoebe's gaze travelled to Violet's parted lips. They were soft and shapely and perfect…

Violet sat back on her cushion and looked down.

Okay, that was intense. Surely they had both felt it for it to feel so strong? Or was it all in her head?

It was difficult to read Violet, except for those moments when sadness clearly weighed upon her. *You keep so much in, don't you, Violet Unwin.*

Violet simply continued, "With each ribbon attached, we can then fix another felt circle in the centre." She lifted a piece of green felt and smoothed it flat. "I was thinking we could write something like *Votes for Women* on it."

"Yes, I love that idea," Phoebe said. "Just perfect." Violet didn't look up.

"And then on the back we can attach a safety pin. Again, it might be easiest to try to staple it on somehow. We can see how we go."

"Cool. I'm excited."

"Great. Let's make a start." Violet reached for the ribbons and began looping and stapling effortlessly, creating the rudiments of the flower in no time.

Phoebe hadn't meant to sit utterly mesmerised, watching her work. Eventually she managed to draw her focus away and said, "Oh, so I don't forget, I've brought you something." Phoebe stood and went to the chair. "To say thank you for today."

Violet looked up at her. Her expression was a mixture of puzzlement and delight. "You didn't have to. And technically you're helping me."

"It's just something small." Phoebe rummaged in her bag and pulled out the chocolate bar. She headed back to Violet.

"Oh, you've dropped something." Violet pointed to a white envelope.

Phoebe turned quickly and picked up the letter emblazoned with the university's emblem. Every time, the image caught her breath and filled her with feelings of dread and shame.

"You okay?"

"Me. Totally." Phoebe stuffed the letter back into her bag. She'd told Dee that her backlog of post was all sorted, but instead she had shoved the letters in her bag and now it bulged with mail, and she all but looked like a postman. She couldn't have felt more pathetic as she returned to her cushion. She held out the chocolate bar to Violet. "Here you go."

"*Yum.* Thanks so much." Violet's smile spoke of her pleasure and surprise.

"I have a confession—I was given the chocolate by my parents as part of a care package they sent me. But I thought of you immediately when I saw it."

Violet gave an embarrassed nod. "That's very honest of you to say."

But she wasn't being honest with Violet. Anything but.

"Your parents sound lovely," Violet said. "Where do they live?"

"Cornwall."

Violet swallowed, and the sparkle of pleasure instantly disappeared from her eyes. "That's a good distance from here."

"It depends on the traffic, but yes, my life at home feels a long way away." Not that Phoebe minded. She had come to cherish the independence she'd claimed for herself.

"I imagine your parents worry about you studying so far away at uni."

"Yes, I guess so." How could she keep lying? And to Violet of all people. Phoebe reached for her ribbons and looped the first and stapled it to the felt just as Violet had shown her. "Actually, that's not quite true."

Violet paused from writing *Votes for Women* on a felt circle. "How do you mean?"

"I mean, you deserve to know...I've dropped out of uni."

Violet looked at Phoebe with the kindest of expressions. "You're not obliged to tell me anything."

"I don't feel obliged. I hate lying to you." She instinctively trusted Violet, and she wanted Violet to trust her in turn. Dee had wanted her to talk to someone, and Violet felt in every way that special person she felt able to share things with. "I hate lying, full stop. The thing is, I can't face telling my parents, and the deceit makes me feel sick." Phoebe tucked her hands into the front pocket of her hooded top. "Thank God for Dee, who took me in because I couldn't bear the thought of having to be around my classmates. I have no clue about anything, and I have no idea what I'm doing any more."

"University isn't right for everyone," Violet said with a shrug.

"Yes. I did want to go, though. I was studying medicine, you see." Phoebe looked at Violet who gave no reaction either way. "I wanted to help people."

"I get that," Violet said, with a small nod. "I can see that in you."

"It's just, if I'm honest, I'm not sure now if I ever believed I was truly good enough to be a doctor. You have to be brave, and I seem to have lost all my courage. If I had any in the first place, that is." Phoebe's voice broke. She quickly cleared her throat. "Dee thinks I still want to be a doctor and this is just me taking a breather."

"You know each other well. So maybe she's right?"

"I don't know. She also has this notion that I'm feeling the pressure of my parents' expectations. She keeps telling me to speak to them. I don't think they'd understand. They have this fixed idea of me as their perfect daughter who always achieves. I know it seems ridiculous that I can't just say *Hey, I'm not doing so well*. But failure isn't an option to them, let alone a possibility. And here I am, failing. I can't even open my post."

"If it's any consolation, I don't like getting post either." Phoebe watched Violet glance over to the counter. "If you want, we can open it together. When you're ready to and if you think it might help."

What a thoughtful offer. Phoebe nodded. But would she ever be ready? "Thank you. I appreciate it."

"And it's not true what you said earlier, that you have no clue about anything. You know how to make suffragette flowers. And you know the moves to Kylie's songs."

Phoebe felt herself smile. "Maybe." Violet was so sweet.

Violet took a deep breath. "Not maybe, definitely. And what's more, you know how to light up a room and to make my day by just being you. That officially makes you the loveliest person in the world." Violet's cheeks tinged pink.

*The loveliest person? Just being me?* This was more than empathy—these were healing words with more power than years of therapy and every drug that anyone could invent. Without another thought, Phoebe leaned forward and hugged Violet. In response, she felt Violet wrap her arms around her and the warmth of her cheek and ear tucked against her face. She smelt like spring and felt like heaven. Phoebe whispered in Violet's ear, "And you're so cool. Everything about you. Never forget that."

In that instant, a soft thud could be heard above them. They released each other and both looked up to the ceiling at the same time.

Phoebe looked to Violet. "Did you hear that?"

Violet gave a slow nod as she stared up to the ceiling. They sat in silence for a moment, waiting to see whether there would be any further noise.

"It might have been the traffic," Violet said, with her gaze still fixed to the ceiling. "Maybe a lorry going over a pothole in the road, and it just sounded like it was upstairs."

"Maybe." The noise came from upstairs—Phoebe was certain of that. "Is that one of the rooms in your flat? Where the noise might have come from if it isn't traffic?"

"Yep." Violet frowned slightly. "The landing or my bedroom."

If it was her, and she lived alone and she heard that noise come from her bedroom, Phoebe would be up there in a flash with something you could hit someone with, but Violet seemed sort of curious rather than alarmed. She had even now returned to the flower she was working on.

"I'm just going to glue this felt circle on top. It will take a little while to dry, but I don't think a staple will work as well." Violet set the completed flower gently aside and gathered the next set of ribbons.

"How many do you think we'll need?" Phoebe asked, trying to gauge how many flowers the pile of ribbons would make.

"I'm not sure. I'll fetch the hat. And we can measure them out."

"And I'll have a look online to see if there are any pictures of suffragettes in their hats to give us an idea of how many to put on."

"Good idea." Violet stood up and Phoebe saw her look to the ceiling again before she made her way to the counter.

"You know, I could have sworn the hat was with Emmeline's costume." Violet was bent under the counter. "Is it over there with you somewhere?" She came into view again and laid out onto the countertop the costumes Phoebe recognised as the ones set aside for The Banana.

The hat was nowhere to be seen, either by the dressing room or where they had been sitting. "Sorry," Phoebe said. "Not over here either, I'm afraid."

Violet held her chin and frowned. Her gaze had fallen to the stool at her side. She looked utterly lost in thought, probably trying to remember where on earth she'd put Emmeline's hat.

As Phoebe had promised, she searched for examples of suffragette hats online. "This is really cool. There's a page dedicated to the suffragettes on the history website belonging to the city council. There are all sorts of images on it. Amazingly there is a photo of a procession of suffragettes, marching through the streets carrying a large banner—dated May 1911. I recognise exactly where they are. It's so awesome. It could be you and me marching, Violet. It could be today." Phoebe glanced up at Violet, who remained completely distracted.

"Violet?"

Violet looked up. "Yes, that's a mind-blowing thought, isn't it?"

So Violet had been listening to her?

"They're all dressed so smartly," Phoebe continued, "and they're all united in wearing white blouses and skirts and jackets. Their hats are slightly different from one another. There's one—my favourite—which has flowers dotted all over the top of the hat as well as the brim. If we have enough ribbon, we could maybe do that. What do you think?" Phoebe brought her phone to Violet. "It's this one on the right. The woman's also got the smartest little bow tie. I think I might wear a bow tie with my costume. What do you reckon?"

Violet looked to where Phoebe pointed at the image. Violet gave a broad smile. "She looks really fab." And then just as Violet was about to look away, she stopped and stared intently at the page. It was difficult to tell what had caught her eye. Whatever it was, she made no comment about it.

"I love their logo on the banner. I might adopt it. Can you see?" Phoebe pointed to the motto. "*Always and always facing toward the light.*"

An even louder unmistakable thud, this time from the ceiling a little further across from the first sound, could be heard the moment Phoebe finished reading the motto.

Rather than look up to the ceiling, Violet was now staring at Dee's fur coat resting on the stool.

Phoebe held her chest in fright. "Seriously, Violet, if you don't check upstairs, I will. It's not traffic noise, okay? I know a thud when I hear it."

"Okay." Violet shook her head as if ridding herself of her thoughts. "Sorry, wait here. I won't be a sec."

"I'm coming with you. Hold on, we need these." Phoebe fetched a plastic sword and a spear from the basket and hurried up the stairs after Violet.

She gripped the sword ever tighter as she took a tense glance about. There was a narrow galley kitchen immediately to the left of the stairs. A placemat for one was set out on a small kitchen table with a drop-down leaf. How many meals had Violet eaten alone? Next to the kitchen was an empty room with a fireplace, which Phoebe guessed might once have been the sitting room. Next to that was a bedroom defined by two bedside wall lights. Just like the sitting room, it had been stripped of its furniture, and just the shape of where it once stood could be seen outlined in the wear of the carpet. Both the sitting room and the bedroom had views over the back of the building to an empty yard. It was noticeably quieter back here away from the city streets. But not in a calm way—in a bleak way.

How could Violet's family have left her in such an empty flat? The inhumanity of it was simply staggering.

"Violet?"

"I'm in here." Phoebe followed Violet's voice past the bathroom to a bedroom, which this time contained its furniture. Violet was staring at a stool which had fallen on its side. "Our thud," she said, without any particular alarm.

"Have you been burgled?" Phoebe immediately realised how stupid that sounded, as quite frankly what was there to burgle?

Violet lifted the stool back in place. "No, it's fine." She then turned to the wardrobe on the opposite wall and stood for a moment with her hand on the handle of its open door. "I should have brought it up here and put it back in place."

"Sorry? Put what back in place?"

Violet looked at Phoebe as if she'd forgotten she was there. "Oh, an item of clothing that belongs in this wardrobe."

"Okay."

"Let's go back down and finish the flowers." Violet closed the wardrobe door and turned the ornate small key in its lock.

"What about the first noise?" Phoebe looked out across the landing to the only remaining room—Violet's. She could sense Violet's eyes upon her.

"I'll check," Violet said. "But I don't think there'll be anything amiss."

Once again, Phoebe followed after Violet. Violet paused at the threshold of her room. "It's not a big space," she said, with a self-conscious apology in her tone.

"Bigger's rarely better. It's just bigger." Phoebe shrugged. "Dee made the mistake of letting me paint my room when I moved in. I was so low that I brought black paint. I feel a bit silly now."

"You painted it black?"

"Yes. Every wall and the ceiling. Dee calls my room The Darkness and not in an admiring way. She was horrified and encouraged me to paint stars as a symbol of hope. I add a star now and then when I'm feeling particularly happy. I painted one the other day with a little trail of gold to make it a shooting star."

"That's fab. I have stars too."

"I've got a feeling I'm going to love your room."

Violet pushed the door fully open, and they stepped inside. It couldn't have been more different from the starkness and emptiness of the rest of the flat. It was full of fabric and colour and life. Violet's single bed was all but covered in bright cushions. A striped mat was joyful at their feet, and sure enough a ceiling of stars set against an inky-blue night sky made the tiny room feel voluminous and on the very edge of the universe.

Phoebe perched on Violet's bed and set down her sword and spear. "It's magical, Violet."

"It's my special place."

"I bet."

Phoebe watched Violet cast her eye over her furniture and towards her window.

"So, nothing amiss," Violet said. "Just one of those things."

"Okay." Phoebe still wasn't quite convinced, but Violet seemed reassured that all was fine.

As Phoebe stood to leave, a postcard resting on the bedside table caught her eye. "No way, is that…?" Phoebe stared in wonder at the image on the card. She looked to the text beneath for confirmation. *Mrs. Pankhurst, Hon. Secretary, Women's Social & Political Union, 4, Clement's Inn, W.C.* She looked up at Violet who stood leaning against the door frame with her arms crossed. "This is amazing. I mean *really* amazing. Can I take a closer look?"

Violet looked at the postcard, and an anxious, uncertain expression washed over her face. Everyone had lines in life, and Phoebe had the distinct sense that this postcard was one Violet did not want her to cross.

"I'm sorry, Violet. I didn't mean to be nosy."

"It's okay. To be honest, I've only just come across it myself. I found it on the floor in the shop just the other day." Violet stared at the card. "It was just randomly there."

"You'd never seen it before?"

Violet shook her head. "I think it might have come out of one of the archive drawers when my cousin was…" Violet hesitated. "I'm still letting everything sink in about it."

Everything? "Look, I shouldn't have asked."

Violet picked up the postcard and handed it to Phoebe. "It's fine. Really. I'd like to share it with you."

She would? "Thank you, that means a lot. I'll be careful. I promise." Phoebe returned to her seat on Violet's bed. She stared down at the postcard and tried to take in what she was looking at, as the incredible Emmeline Pankhurst stared out from the card into the distance beyond. Phoebe gazed at the high ruffled white collar brushing at Emmeline's neck. An academic-style gown was draped over her shoulders, conveying a sense of her intelligence and wisdom. "She looks so dignified, doesn't she? It's the maddest thing—she seems so familiar to me. Like I've met her before. I obviously paid more attention to history at school than I thought I did."

The postcard felt so precious and fragile. She couldn't help but notice that it was a little dog-eared at its edges, and a patina of imprinted dust dulled the whiteness of the surround to the oval portrait. In the bottom right-hand corner, there was a fingerprint of grease from where many fingers had probably held the postcard and stared, just like she was now, at Emmeline's haunting expression. It made Phoebe wonder whether it could be an original from the time of the suffragettes. It couldn't. Could it?

"Can I?" Phoebe gestured to her wish to turn the postcard over.

Violet nodded, adding, a little dreamily, "She has my name."

Who had Violet's name? Phoebe turned the postcard over. She strained slightly to read the handwritten words.

*FAO Vi Unwin, Unwin's Emporium. 4 April 1911*
*Vi. Just for one night I needed to be invisible. I thought, no, I hoped you of all people, would understand. Harry.*

Every nerve in Phoebe's body tingled with the strangest sense of recognition. She'd read these words before. She was certain of it—it was as if she'd written them herself just a moment ago. But that was impossible. Why was everything connected to the suffragettes feeling so familiar and resonating so deeply with her? What's more, if this was how she felt reading this, what on earth was Violet feeling?

She looked at Violet. "Vi Unwin?"

"Yes. Turns out, by my reckoning, she's likely to be my great-great-grandmother."

"Really? Violet, that's just so cool. Did you know about her before?"

Violet shook her head. "It's a bit of a revelation for me."

"I can imagine." Phoebe returned her focus to the postcard. "And does that really say 1911?"

"It's a bit scruffily written, but yes, that's what I read too. When I saw the date, my first thought was to go to the cabinet of drawers, you know, by the counter in the shop." Phoebe nodded. She remembered in that moment the first time she stepped inside the Emporium. How she'd marvelled at the amazing shop furniture. Violet continued, "I went to the drawer marked 1900–1914 to see if there was anything that might tell me a bit more about who Vi Unwin was."

"Makes sense."

"The oddest thing is, I don't think I would have immediately thought of that drawer—in fact, I believed it was locked—but it had recently just opened randomly. Almost like it opened on its own. Which, of course, it hadn't, but your brain can play tricks on you can't it."

"I guess. It does sound spooky, though." Maybe she shouldn't have said that. "But, as you say, common sense and all that."

"It somehow didn't feel spooky as such, just sort of...unexpected." Violet lifted a leaflet which had been partly obscured by the postcard. "I discovered this in the drawer." Violet joined Phoebe and sat with her on the bed. "It's an advertising brochure." Violet held the slim document between them. "The inside pages list the costumes for hire. Although the party wear is more elegant evening dress and feathered mask for a masquerade ball."

Phoebe was transfixed. She was sitting with the past in front of her as if it was the present, and as if time dissolved and no distance existed between then and now. It was thrilling and kind of weird at the same time.

"On the reverse side"—Violet turned the leaflet over—"are the contact details and costume order form."

Even the reverse side had beautiful tendrils of flowers decorating each corner. It had been produced with such care.

"*Mr. Robert and Mrs. Violet Unwin*," Phoebe read aloud, "*Proprietors, Unwin's Emporium, Duke Street, Leicester.*" Phoebe smiled at Violet. "Mrs. Violet Unwin?"

"Yep. It's still sinking in that I have a namesake. I've always thought…"

"What?"

Violet's eyes misted over. "That I was alone. You see…my mum passed away when I was young."

"I'm sorry, Violet. That must have been so hard."

"The thing I struggled with the most was the fear I would lose my memory of her. I don't even have a photo."

Phoebe's heart ached to hear something so truly heartbreaking. "Oh, Violet. And, just so you know, you're not alone. Okay?"

Violet bit her lip and nodded. She looked away from Phoebe. Phoebe could never tell whether her words simply upset Violet more. Violet's focus returned to the leaflet as she flipped it over to its front page.

"Finding out about my great-great-grandmother, it's a lot to take in." Violet tapped at the image of a woman wearing a long floral dress and a large hat. "And that's her." She was standing by the shop counter, and her upright demeanour and dignified presence were more owner than shop worker. The fur draped over her arm reminded Phoebe of the coat Dee selected for the ball. Mrs. Violet Unwin was most certainly glamourous.

Phoebe stared and stared at her. She was looking back at Phoebe with eyes that said, *It's me, Vi.*

"Vi." Her name spilled out of Phoebe's lips. Phoebe reached to the page and brushed her finger lightly over Vi's face. An overwhelming affection for her swelled in Phoebe's heart.

Violet shifted in her seat. "She's got quite a haunting expression, hasn't she?" Violet offered, almost as an apology.

Phoebe looked at Violet. "I *know* her. And not like Emmeline Pankhurst where I simply feel I've met her. I *know* Vi and that we know each other. That if she walked in now, she would know me too."

Violet quickly turned and glanced to the hall. Phoebe could sense the tension in her.

"Have you seen something?" Phoebe asked, turning herself to see.

"*No.* No one." Violet looked back at Phoebe, her eyes wide with something behind them. Intrigue? Recognition?

"I know how impossible and irrational that sounds." Phoebe shook her head. But then how else could she explain it. Unless…"*Of course.* It's you."

Violet swallowed. "How do you mean?"

Phoebe gently lifted the brochure from Violet's hand and held it up at the height of Violet's head. Her eyes flitted from Violet's face to the brochure and back. "She looks like you."

"Like me?" Violet laughed. "We look nothing like each other."

"That's not true. Yes, she's not in jeans and a T-shirt, and her hair is longer. But you have her eyes. Can you see? It's the first thing I noticed about you. You have the most beautiful, intense eyes. And so has she."

"I do?"

Phoebe smiled into those eyes, so deep and intoxicating. "You are the beautiful Violet Unwin." There, she said it. She held her breath, expecting Violet to blush and shrink away with the pain of embarrassment, but instead she held her gaze. It was Phoebe who lost her breath first with the intensity of their exchange. She looked away to catch her balance, and her eyes fell upon the brochure once more. This time the magnificent Christmas tree to the right of Robert caught her attention. Although the scene was in black and white, the image of the ribbons seemed to shine out from the page. It was just perfect.

"I love the tree," Phoebe said. "I feel really inspired by it. In fact, I will steal a few of the ideas for the tree at The Banana. The ribbons in particular are a total winner. I can't wait for the first of December when Dee has promised to let me go wild." Phoebe's smile was matched by Violet's. "When will you decorate the shop?"

Violet's smile faded and she gave a small shrug. "I'm not sure."

"If you need a hand, I can hold your baubles." She and Violet released a spluttered guffaw.

Violet went bright pink, clearly as much with embarrassment as laughter. "No one's said that to me before."

"Well, what can I say, the offer's on the table. Seriously, though, anything you need. Just ask."

"Thanks."

"I mean it. Just look how useful I've been with the flowers." Phoebe rested her palm over her face. She'd not even completed one. She looked at her watch. And now she needed to head back to The Banana to set up for Sundays Are a Drag. "And I've got to go now. I'm sorry. But I can come back tomorrow. Oh no, I can't make tomorrow. Let me think…"

"I'd forgotten all about the flowers." Violet gathered the postcard and brochure and placed them on the bedside table with great care. "I'll finish them for us." Violet smiled. "No worries."

Phoebe winced at the rejection that came with Violet's offer. For Phoebe it had never been about the flowers. It was about being with Violet. "You don't want me to finish them with you?" *Oh my God, Frink, needy much?* "Sorry. You can finish them in a flash without me. Of course."

"*No*, it's not that. It's just…"

Just what? "There's no rush for them, is there?" Phoebe asked. "The ball's not until Christmas Eve."

"No, no rush." Violet didn't sound quite sure. "But I think it's best I finish The Banana's order today or tomorrow. You never know what the future will bring."

What did that mean? "No, I suppose not. Will you let me know when you've done the hat, so I can see it all finished?" Phoebe dug in her pocket for her phone. "Would you like my number?"

Violet blushed. "Yes. Although"—Violet glanced at her bedside table—"I don't know where my phone is. Probably downstairs or possibly the kitchen. To be honest, I don't use it very often. When I do, it's for looking things up rather than social stuff."

"So you don't have anyone regularly keeping in touch or saying hi or...I mean, not that that's, you know." She might as well have said *Have you got no friends?* "I'm sorry. I'm being really nosy."

Violet shrugged. "It's okay. To be honest, less so recently. I had a best friend at school called Billy. His mum would invite me to tea and take us to the cinema. We were called the hillbillies at school by the mean kids even though we both lived in the city."

Poor Billy and Violet. Kids could be so cruel.

"For some reason, my aunt took a dislike to him, and then the invites stopped. In any case, I left after GCSEs, and Billy did his A levels and now he's at uni. He keeps in touch now and then and has invited me to visit. But it's clear he's pretty much moved on, and I get the impression, unsurprisingly, that I remind him of a time in his life he'd rather forget."

"I'm sorry."

"Don't be. He needed to get away."

"And, not to worry, because you have this awesome place."

"Uh-huh." Violet's cheeks blanched. "And, erm, other than that, every so often I get an email from my book group. Funnily enough, I was replying to one just before you arrived."

"A book group sounds fun."

"Yes, we meet online every month or so. There's talk of meeting up in person. They're a bit older than me and always seem frazzled from family life. But they're nice."

"Cool. And no worries. You can just add your number in my phone, if you want to. And then I'll text you mine."

Violet nodded, carefully tapped her number into Phoebe's phone and handed it back to Phoebe with the most adorable of smiles.

"I'm so jealous that you don't use your phone that much. I honestly hate this thing," Phoebe said, shoving her phone back into the pocket of her jeans. "Obviously, it's useful for contacting people, but otherwise I hate it. I feel the pressure to be on social media, but it doesn't feel healthy or good for me. In fact, it makes me feel sad."

"I thought I was the only one who felt that way."

"Seriously, you're not the only one who feels the way you do about things. And anyway, being different is definitely far cooler than blending in. Far, far cooler. That's what I've always loved about The Banana. Everyone has their own thing going on. Tell you what, if you wanted, would you like to join me and Dee putting up the Christmas decorations at The Banana? How about Wednesday afternoon? It's literally the day before the first, so Dee can't possibly complain it's too early. And we'll be closed to customers until six. Come at two maybe? Or half two if that's easier? After all, it's definitely my turn to make the tea."

Violet couldn't have looked more uncertain. But then, what did Phoebe expect? Violet hadn't seemed keen to go to The Banana before. She was wrong to ask again, wasn't she? But this time The Banana would be closed. Surely that would make it easier if Violet felt shy. The Banana was everything to her, just as much as the Emporium was to Violet. *Please say yes, Violet.*

Violet was staring at her feet. She was going to say no, wasn't she.

"Wednesday afternoon?" She glanced up at Phoebe. "Can I think about it?"

"Yes." That sounded desperate. "And just turn up and ring the bell and maybe bang on the door as well, just to be sure. No need to ring ahead or anything. We'll be there. I'll be there." Could she say *please come*? No. She should leave it there, shouldn't she? "Right, I'll get my coat." Phoebe stood and brushed at her jeans. Just as she was wondering how to leave with her dignity intact, to her delight and surprise Violet moved to her and hugged her goodbye. Phoebe held her tight and whispered in her ear. "Hope to see you soon."

Phoebe's heart skipped with relief and delight when Violet gave a nod, and the sentiment *yes* shone out from those beautiful, beautiful eyes.

## Chapter Eleven

"There, all done." Violet sat back on her cushion and admired the collection of ribbon flowers that sat on the carpet in front of her. She picked up a few stray pins from the floor and secured them once more, before returning them to the craft box. She gathered the material into a more orderly pile and restacked the cardboard for reuse on another window display. Although, how many more displays would there be? Were these flowers the last work on the shop's costumes she would need to do?

Violet had returned to the flowers immediately after Phoebe had left, and with determined concentration, and before she knew it, she had completed twenty in total. This, she reckoned, allowed for about ten around the brim, and then the remaining would fill the crown of the hat. This was the pattern that Phoebe had admired in the image of the marching suffragettes. It was important to Violet that Phoebe had the hat she had chosen. She would not let her down. Perhaps she should recheck the image.

She moved to the counter and retrieved her phone from where she'd remembered leaving it after all, in the drawer under the till. She noticed the symbol for a message on the screen and opened the text. It was from Phoebe. Violet gripped the phone and read, *Hey, Violet. This is my number. Hope to see you soon, Phoebe x*

Violet stared at the *x*. Why were her hands shaking? It was just a courtesy sign-off, nothing more. How she wanted it to mean more, to mean *I am sending you a kiss blown from my virtual lips to yours. This x marks where my heart aches with the hope of seeing you soon.* Violet shook her head at how ridiculous her thoughts were. Like Phoebe meant that. Like life would suddenly change for her and gift her someone to love. And while Phoebe said she'd found her tribe at The Banana, did that actually mean for certain that she fancied women or, for that matter, a scrawny girl like her? Anyway, would she even know how to love Phoebe? She knew nothing about love or about dating or how to reply to a text from a girl sending an *x*. She hovered her finger over the box to reply. What would she say? She typed a hesitant, *Hi, this is Violet. Thank you x*, then quickly pressed send before she had chance to retype it.

She must now concentrate on finishing the hat. That was easier said than done. She allowed herself one more look at Phoebe's text before she retrieved the same webpage Phoebe had found a few hours earlier. Violet stared at the smartly dressed women gathered together and poised to campaign with their banner held high. They all faced forward to the camera, looking directly at the viewer. They did not smile but adopted instead a steady gaze of determination. The sentiment was clear—this was a protest march, not a springtime stroll. No wonder Phoebe had been so captivated by them. They embodied female power and agency. They were not empty rioters or troublemakers but respectable citizens bravely asserting their right to equality under the law. Violet felt the emotion of their cause swell in her chest. Would she have been brave enough to join them? Certainly not on her own. How bonded these women must have been in their shared fight for justice. Given what they risked for one another, they would probably have been inseparable. What stories they could tell of their time together, and yet each face captured in the photographer's lens would remain forever inscrutable.

The woman on the right of the image caught Violet's attention just as she had captured Phoebe's. She drew the eye more than any of the others. Her bow tie, that Phoebe had loved so much, was so smart and suited her perfectly. She wore it with an uncomplicated ease. Her face, Violet decided, was more handsome than pretty, and she carried in her eyes a certain wariness and suspicion. "You didn't trust the photographer, did you? I bet you didn't quite trust the world, and who could blame you? I don't trust it either."

Violet's gaze flitted to the street outside and back again to the image. It was intriguing that the captivating woman had the most floral hat of them all. The blend of masculine and feminine was utterly beguiling. Violet took a long look at the arrangement of the flowers that covered her hat. Yes, she knew where everything would go. Even if she still hadn't come across the hat they were meant to go on. It would turn up just as lost things did where you left them without remembering. The hat wasn't the only reason Violet wanted to revisit the webpage, in any case. No, there was something else she'd seen.

Violet scrolled down to reveal the inset photo of a bail form. The form belonged to the local suffragette hero, Alice Hawkins. It was the same format, and from the same station, as the one she had found in Vi's coat. There was no question, was there? Harriet Frink was without doubt a suffragette and a brave one at that. Was she marching with these women? Maybe she was the captivating woman in the floral hat? Yes, she liked to think so. Violet looked at the fur resting on the stool. What did all this say about Vi? Did she know about these marches? Violet scanned every face that she could but recognised none of them as her great-great-grandmother. What about Harriet? On impulse, Violet asked into the room, "Who was Harriet to you, Vi?"

Violet looked up at the sound of the same thud on the same part of the ceiling that had sent her and Phoebe running upstairs just a few hours earlier. "I know that's you," Violet said. "It is, isn't it?"

Violet pushed her phone into her pocket, lifted the fur coat into her arms, and made her way upstairs. She wasn't frightened. If it was Vi, she wouldn't hurt her. Violet knew that with every inch of herself. She pushed the door to the spare room open, took a deep breath, and stepped inside. Just as she expected, the dressing table stool had fallen once more. "Clumsy much?" she said, with an affectionate tone. "I've brought your coat. It belongs in this room, doesn't it?" Violet stood still and listened. "I'm just going to put this in your wardrobe. Don't worry, I won't let anyone rent it." Violet listened again. Nothing. "Okay. Just wanted you to know." She turned to the wardrobe and stopped short to find its door unlocked and ajar. "Lock picker, hey? Hold on." Violet put her hands on her hips and faced the dressing table mirror. She pointed at her own reflection. "Do you mess with the shop's front door? You do, don't you? Wait, did you try to keep Carl out the other day and then make him fall over?" Violet laughed. "I approve. I don't like him either. You must have hated him in your room. I hated that he was in the Emporium at all. I hate him even when he's not here. He's coming back to collect his letter. But then you know that, don't you? Have you been here all along? Why haven't I been aware of you before?" There were so many questions and, as always, so few answers.

Violet turned back to the wardrobe, opened it fully, and hung the coat into place. "No way. I've been looking for this." Violet reached for Emmeline's hat on the thin shelf at the top of the wardrobe. It couldn't be Vi's—could it? Violet turned the hat upside down, lifted the inside edge of the rim, and fed it through her fingers until an ink mark made her stop. The initials spoke for themselves *V. U.* "I didn't know."

Violet placed the hat on the dressing table, turned the stool upright, and took her place upon it.

She stared at her reflection. She remembered Phoebe's words: *You have her eyes.* "Vi?" Violet stared and stared and stared until her own face became a blur and all that she could see was a sense of someone in the mirror. "I'm sorry, please believe me, I didn't know the hat was yours. It's just always been in the shop. At least I think it has." What was real any more? "The thing is, Phoebe loves that hat. She has her heart set on wearing it for the ball. We've made flowers for it. But then you know that too, don't you? Wait, the flower Phoebe found, was that yours? Did you leave that for her? Did you want her to wear it? But not your hat? Is that what you're trying to tell me?" Violet's face unblurred, and she was left staring once again at herself in the mirror.

She moved from the stool and returned the hat to the shelf. Then Violet glanced briefly to the mirror. "Will you find a way to tell me one day who Harriet was? Only if you want to, of course." With this, she closed the wardrobe door once more. "I won't lock it. And I'll find another hat. Phoebe won't mind."

Violet stopped at the door and turned back to the room once more. "I'm glad you're here." And with that, Violet gently closed the door, then paused and opened it again, leaving it ajar. She walked across the hallway to her room and collapsed onto her bed. She stared up at the stars on her ceiling and imagined Phoebe staring up at hers. Phoebe had opened up to her and trusted her with the things she was struggling with. It had made Violet feel wanted and needed. She'd never dared dream that anyone would ever need her as Phoebe seemed to. Or that anyone would look at her the way Phoebe did. Almost as if she wanted more from her. Like she wanted to be closer to her. Closer than a friend? Or was she imagining it, hopelessly hoping again for the happiness belonging to others.

And where on earth had she found the nerve to tell Phoebe that she lit up the room and that she was the loveliest person in the world? The words had rushed out of her as if her feelings were in such a hurry to come out into the open and be seen. It was a moment of unguarded impulse, yet Phoebe hadn't minded. Instead, she'd hugged her. *You're so cool. Never forget that.* That's what she'd said to her. Violet turned on to her side and pressed her pillow into her chest. She closed her eyes and called to mind the sensation of Phoebe in her arms. She could still feel the brush of her soft skin against her face and the warmth of her body pressed against hers. Could she tell that Violet didn't want to let go and that she didn't want to be just friends?

What must Phoebe *really* think of her? She'd looked so shocked by the bareness of the flat. Violet had seen that same expression of discomfort in Mr. Burrows's face when he'd finished surveying. It was part pity, part horror, and complete amazement that anyone would live as she was doing. But then, what else was she supposed to do? Where else was she supposed to go? With the emotions of the day crashing in upon her, Violet burst into tears. She cried out, "I don't know what to do."

A creak in the hallway made her look towards her door. She sat up and swallowed down her tears to ask, "Vi?" The silence that followed was not empty. It was full of stillness and comfort. Was she here with her? Violet wiped at her tears. The words *Always and always facing toward the light* found their way to Violet's lips. There was always light wasn't there, and even when all seemed dark and unknown. The suffragettes must have despaired, but against the odds they won their fight. "So will I be okay if I face towards the light? But which way is that?" Thoughts of Phoebe came instantly to mind. *You light up the room.* "Phoebe." She would accept Phoebe's invite to The Banana on Wednesday. "I'll go to The Banana." Violet wasn't sure if Vi was still there, but it somehow made it real to say it aloud. She pulled her phone from her pocket and typed the message, *See you at The Banana Bar 2.30pm on Wednesday. Violet x*

No sooner had she sent it than Phoebe replied, *x*

Another creak in the hall made Violet turn to her door. "Goodnight then, Vi. And thank you."

Violet lay back down on her bed, and if she was not mistaken the stars above her seemed to shine even brighter.

## Chapter Twelve

Phoebe stared in dismay at the threadbare tree which could barely hold its own weight, let alone a bauble. She could have sworn Dee had said she was fetching the majestic spruce from the loft. Everything in her wanted to say *Is this it?*

Dee dropped a battered box marked *Xmas Decs & Other Shit* next to the tree on the stage, and a festive tinkle of bells could be heard from within. Dee groaned. "I can't believe I've got that noise for the next four weeks."

"Five, at least." Phoebe tried to resuscitate the tree by spreading out each spindly wire branch to its maximum and fluffing its fake needles. "We can't take the decs down before New Year. It's bad luck."

Dee headed to the counter. "Is it too early for a drink?"

"Yes." Phoebe pulled her phone from the back pocket of her jeans. She took a picture of the tree and then composed a text: *SOS. Tree. No vital signs.* She added the photo and Violet's number and pressed send. "There. Not to worry Mr. Tree, help is on its way."

"So what time can we expect the beautiful Violet then?" Dee handed Phoebe a glass of lemonade.

Phoebe climbed up on a bar stool. "Thanks. In"—she glanced at her watch—"half an hour. Which gives me time to finish my scones. Oh no, I meant to get clotted cream." She took uncomfortably large swallows of her fizzy drink. "I'll need to get a move on."

"Take it easy. You'll give yourself indigestion."

"I want everything to be nice for her."

"Violet won't care if the scones have cream or not."

"She *will*."

"She *won't*. Violet has come to see you, not your scones. And my bet is she won't come again if she thinks she has caused you to be stressed."

"You don't think she'll come again?"

"Oh my Lord—"

"Sorry. You're right. Absolutely. Although, it wasn't that easy to get her to come over, actually."

"Makes sense. Gay bars can be intimidating places, even those with a smiling banana on the sign outside. And if you're a shy girl whose whole world is a costume shop…"

"You don't know that."

"Phoebe, come on, we both know that."

Dee was right. Violet Unwin and Unwin's Emporium were one and the same. Where one went the other did, and where one didn't go…"So that's why I want to make it as nice as I can for her. So that she knows there's another space where she can feel happy and safe and wanted and—"

"Fancied?" Dee pointed her finger at Phoebe. "Don't pull that face. It's the truth."

Phoebe gasped. "You don't know that."

Dee tilted her head.

"Anyway, what does it matter if I do like her?" Who was she kidding? It mattered more than a lot.

"It doesn't. You pair are the sweetest kids I know. Despite my initial…overprotectiveness, I'm glad you found each other."

"Thanks. Although, we haven't. I mean, I don't know how Violet feels. What if the reason she was reticent about coming over is because she doesn't think she belongs here because she's not…like us."

"What, hip and trendy?"

"You know what I mean."

"Nope. And there's a flaw in your theory."

"Yeah, maybe you're right. The people she admires so much are all women, and sometimes I catch her looking at me, particularly when we were last together, like—"

"She wants to snog your face off."

"*No*. Well, maybe, but—"

Dee put her hand up as if stopping the traffic flowing from Phoebe's mouth.

"If I can get a word in edgeways, the flaw in your theory of her not wanting to come over is that she's coming over in"—Dee tapped at her empty wrist where a watch would go—"twenty-five minutes. She didn't have to if she didn't want to. And believe me, after seeing for myself the way that girl looks at you, my initial assessment stands. Violet Unwin *wants* to come over because she's smitten."

Phoebe's cheeks stung with unabashed joy. Violet was coming over. It was the most wonderful thought in the world.

"Earth to Phoebe. Oh, is that Violet knocking?"

Phoebe looked to the door.

"Fooled ya."

"Very funny. Oh, before I go, can I ask you a question?"

"Like you have time to chat more. But go on, then, if you have to."

"Do you believe in ghosts?"

"Not the question I was expecting. I'm nervous to ask why you want to know."

"When I was at the Emporium last Sunday, I, we, heard a bump from the flat above, where Violet lives."

"A bump?"

Phoebe nodded. She expected Dee to make fun of her, but she didn't. She seemed genuinely interested, but then Phoebe remembered that Dee herself had said that there was something about the place she couldn't quite put her finger on.

"And you think it was a ghost?"

"By a process of elimination, yes. You see, when we went upstairs to check, there was no sign that anyone had broken in, and yet a stool had been knocked over in one of the rooms without there being a reasonable explanation."

"Sounds a bit odd, but then not everything in life can be explained. What did Violet think?"

"That's the thing, she didn't seem overly alarmed. She went a bit distracted, but that's about it." Phoebe glanced towards the door. "I think it might be nothing new to her."

"You mean Violet's used to having a friendly ghost wandering around? Could be." Dee shrugged.

"Do friendly ghosts knock over stools or, for that matter, stop people leaving?"

Dee sat up a little. "How do you mean?"

"The time before last that I was there, I was saying goodbye to Violet, and the shop door wouldn't open. Even Violet couldn't open it. We jokingly pretended to speak to the phantom door fiddler and then—lo and behold!—the door opened. We laughed it off, but that didn't stop it being weird. And not only that, Violet mentioned that a drawer in the shop has been randomly opening. She said she was curious about it rather than thinking it was spooky, but for her to mention it to me, she must have been a bit freaked out."

"That does seem kind of strange. And a bit like a ghost making their presence felt."

"*Exactly.* Then shouldn't we help Violet?"

"I'm not saying ghosts exist or don't exist, but it is likely that there will be a logical explanation for it all. It could be a faulty doorknob, or a stool with a wonky leg, or simply a loose drawer. In any case, if you say Violet's not concerned, then you don't want to frighten her by making a big deal of it. That's the last thing that girl needs."

Dee was right, wasn't she? "I guess so."

"But what Violet does *need* is for her host to be ready for her arrival."

"Oh crap." Phoebe scrambled off her stool. "You'll listen out for Violet for me, won't you. Tell her I won't be a sec."

"Will do."

"Great."

"And, Pheebs—she's coming to see you, that's all. So breathe."

Breathe. That was easier to say than to do when the girl you thought about pretty much all the time was coming over. Breathing was the last thing on her mind. Not making a complete twit of herself was surely more important. *Be cool, Phoebe Frink. Be cool.*

❖

*SOS. Tree. No vital signs.* Violet chuckled as she read Phoebe's message. She had just finished getting ready to visit her when the emergency text came in.

Violet enlarged the image of the tree. She always saw the potential in the most modest of things, and it always brought her so much pleasure to see the transformation in something, although this would need a Christmas miracle.

Her first thought was to share some of the shop's decorations to help bring the poor tree to life. Yes, that would be a good start. Tinsel would be key to giving a little more volume and body to the tree, and shiny baubles were a must to distract the eye and delight. And hadn't Phoebe mentioned her wish to have ribbons? She would find some material for her. All Violet wanted to do was to make Phoebe happy. She stared again at the tree so in need of Christmas spirit. Something else would be required as well, wouldn't it. What made Christmas magical? "I know," Violet said. "Snow."

Violet hoped that a light dusting from her can of Christmas snow spray would work wonders and disguise the odd bald patch here and there. Thoughts of Christmas frosting, as she liked to call it, took her back in an instant to the memory of her and Uncle Walter spraying the white dust to form triangles on the inside corners of the shop's window. It was their tradition that when the window was finished he would turn to her and say, *Happy Christmas, Violet*. His eyes, without fail, would fill with tears. She always wondered what he thought about in that moment, but it never seemed to be thoughts of joyful festive cheer. *Happy Christmas, Uncle Walter*, she'd reply, but he never held her gaze or let the sentiment sit upon him for too long. It was not the fault of Christmas, Violet had decided long ago, and so she loved the season in spite of those around her.

The Emporium's decorations were stored at the back of the shop amongst the many boxes. It was time, in any case, for her to bring the boxes out and sort through them. Maybe this was the push she needed. But for today, she wouldn't be late, so she rummaged in a targeted way towards the boxes marked with pen drawings of holly, stars, and angels with their wings out wide.

"Ah, found them." Thankfully the boxes, three in total, had been stored towards the front. She stared at the other boxes stacked against the back wall, several rows deep. Was each row a generation of stored items and forgotten memories?

Violet lifted the box marked *Tree* onto the counter. She opened it and couldn't help but smile at the sparkle of the tinsel and the glint of the baubles that greeted her each year. "I don't think we need you." Violet pulled out a disgruntled looking angel for whom Christmas had clearly lost its allure many years before. Each year, Violet's aunt would insist on Carl putting the finishing touch to the tree that Violet and her uncle had decorated. Carl hated anything joyful and stuffed the angel on the top in a slapdash way to make the point. Uncle Walter would tell him to take care, which only made him rougher with the poor thing. Violet had taken to looking away. When it came to Carl, it was always best to look away. Violet sighed. It was so hard to muster festive cheer this year, or any cheer for that matter. But she must, if only for Phoebe's sake.

Violet quickly rallied and dug around in the other two boxes to retrieve the can of snow. While rummaging, she came across a neatly tied loop of multicoloured tree lights. What was a Christmas tree without illumination? So she added them, along with the spray snow, to the box marked *Tree* that she would take to The Banana. Phoebe could then choose the items she needed, and Violet would bring back the remainder.

Inside one of the other boxes, Violet found her Christmas stocking. She released a heavy sigh at the sight of it. She'd made it for herself and told no one. And she had pretended that Santa had come and filled it with Christmas craft items she had made. How silly that sounded now, and how sad it made her feel. The material was red and silky—perfect for ribbons and just perfect for Phoebe's tree. It took Violet no time to fashion ribbons from the material, cutting V shapes into the end of each strip. Violet smiled at the pleasure they would bring Phoebe, and the thought filled her heart with joy. She just couldn't wait to see Phoebe again.

With everything she wanted to take gathered in the box, she pressed the lid closed and placed the box by the door. She then reached for her phone once more, now always at hand, and texted Phoebe. *On my way. Have resus items for tree x*

No sooner had Violet sent her text than Phoebe replied, *Thanks so much! See you soon. PS. Have made scones x*

How could she be so happy and yet so troubled at the same time. How could anyone feel so much and be okay? Was she foolish to care the way she did for Phoebe? Was she expecting too much from her? But then what was she hoping for? Love?

"Who's ever going to love me?" Violet asked into the room.

A sense of movement drew her eye to the bottom of the stairs to the flat.

"Vi?" Violet stood still and listened as was her habit now when she wondered if Vi was with her.

She held her breath for a moment waiting, for what she wasn't sure. She then released her breath with a sigh and made her way to the dressing room mirror. She glanced up and down at the outfit she had chosen for her visit to The Banana. It had taken her a while to decide upon the right clothes to wear. Not that she had much to choose from. She'd settled on jeans and her yellow sweatshirt. It would have been all too easy to put on her usual brown or black jumper just as it was all too easy to feel sad. Violet knew that since they had met, Phoebe had seen her get upset, and she must have seemed so miserable to Phoebe at times. Who wanted to be in the company of someone like that? That's not how she wanted Phoebe to think of her. And Phoebe had confessed how low she had been feeling too, so Violet wanted to dress brightly for her. She wanted to dress brightly for them both.

Her gaze eventually settled upon her face and, more particularly, her eyes. "So what do you think? Do I look okay?" Was Vi with her? She watched her lips form the words. "I want to look nice for her, for Phoebe, I mean." On this occasion, all Violet could feel was herself. Her face was her face and her presence her own. "Anyway, I'll be late." Violet turned away from the mirror, and her heart ached in her chest. She wanted Vi to tell her she looked good. She wanted Vi to care about her and to tell her to be polite and to remember to thank Dee for having her and to compliment Phoebe on her scones. More than ever before, she needed Vi. But there was no one there, was there. It was all in her head.

She took a deep shaky breath. Everything would be okay. She just needed to be brave. Violet pulled on her coat and reached for the box of decorations waiting at her door. She could have sworn she had closed the lid. But then she could have sworn many things that it turned out she'd just imagined all along. Phoebe was real, though, wasn't she? Violet dug out her phone from her pocket and reread Phoebe's last text. She was real and wanted to see her. Violet would not hesitate for a moment longer.

## Chapter Thirteen

Violet reached The Banana Bar in no time. She'd been so engrossed by thoughts of Phoebe and of what The Banana would be like that she'd given almost no regard to the awkwardness of the box or to the people on the street who had moved to avoid colliding with her. The anticipation that any moment she would feel the tender warmth of Phoebe's smile upon her was simply magical. And would they hug, leaving the smell of Phoebe's delicate perfume to linger on her collar? Would Phoebe show her her room with the ceiling full of stars? Or were the stars for someone else to see, for someone else to lie under them with Phoebe's body pressed to theirs and wonder at how lucky they were? Nerves pressed at her stomach. So much was unknown.

Violet stared up at the image of a cute happy banana waving a rainbow flag. She placed the box on the doorstep and took a deep breath. *You can do this. Be brave.* The solid front door was closed, and Violet rang the bell as Phoebe had suggested. When no one answered, she remembered that Phoebe had told her to knock as well. She was just about to raise her fist to politely bang a few times, when to her surprise the door swung open.

"Miss Violet Unwin. Welcome to The Banana." Dee was dressed from the waist up in a black shirt and partly tied tie. From the waist down she was in sweatpants and bare feet. "Come in, kiddo. Don't mind me. I'm trying on a few outfits for our drag night on Sunday. You'd love it. Awesome costumes and even more awesome performers."

Violet lifted the box into her arms once more. "Sounds fun."

"Oh, it is." Dee gave Violet a wink.

Violet felt every inch of her blush.

"Here, let me." Dee took the box from Violet. "I'm guessing the contents have something to do with Phoebe's tree disappointment. Honestly, you should have seen her face. It was like I was The Grinch and I'd stolen Christmas."

Violet smiled. "Yes, it's just a few Christmas bits. And no worries. We'll sort it."

"Thanks." Dee put her arm around Violet and squeezed both Violet and the box at the same time. "It's good to have you here. Come through."

Violet glanced about her as she trailed after Dee. It struck her that The Banana was more compact and intimate than she had imagined. A quick glance to her right revealed an upright piano positioned against an ornately frosted set of doors with the word *Saloon* engraved on them. The Saloon was in darkness, and she had the feeling it wasn't used. In the main bar, there was just a small selection of round tables—ten, maybe twelve maximum—with partly burnt candles on each. It definitely had something of a cabaret about it. The bar itself ran the width of the room and had several stools dotted along it. A wide mirror ran along the back of the bar reflecting the coloured bottles and bouncing light around the otherwise muted space. If the walls of this bar could talk, Violet wondered what on earth they would say. The space had an atmosphere of a party just finished, with the emotions of the last partygoer lingering like tobacco in the air in the days when everyone smoked and nobody cared.

Dee headed across the room to a small stage and set down the box next to a forlorn looking tree.

"Pheebs won't be long," Dee said, with a small groan at the effort of bending. "She's upstairs panicking over scones and cream and worrying she won't impress you."

Phoebe wanted to impress her? "She doesn't have to impress me."

Dee turned and smiled at Violet. There was an affection and an understanding behind her smile. But an understanding of what? "That's what I told her." She then glanced to a door just to the right of the stage marked *Private* before heading off again, this time towards the bar. "Between me and you, kiddo, Pheebs is quite taken with you."

"She is?"

"Yes, indeed. Although, maybe don't tell her I said anything. And

I would offer you a drink," Dee said, gesturing to the optics, "but I'm pretty sure you'll eventually be offered a cup of tea."

Phoebe was taken with her? Was Dee actually saying Phoebe fancied her? That she too had lost her heart with each shared smile, stolen glance, and precious touch? That, just like her, she longed for more and, just maybe, maybe, dared to imagine where her desire might lead?

"You okay, Violet?"

"Hmm? Yes, totally fine." Violet made her way to Dee. "Sorry, what was the question?"

Dee laughed. "I don't recall asking a question. Give me two secs. I need to change my trousers. Then come and take a pew with me in my office while you wait." Dee disappeared into a small room tucked away to the side of the bar.

Before Violet had chance to let Dee's comment about Phoebe sink in fully, Dee called out from her room, "So, what do you think?"

What did she think? Was Dee actually asking her outright if she fancied Phoebe in turn? Violet poked her head around the corner. Dee was standing behind her desk with her back towards her, buttoning up a waistcoat.

Violet did her best to steady her breathing. Dee knew Phoebe well. So if Phoebe did feel the same, then wasn't it okay for Violet to confess how she felt? "I...I feel the same as Phoebe."

Dee turned around. Her newly moustached lip quirked, and then a broad smile spread across Mr. Duke's face. "That's good to hear, Violet. Although, I meant what do you think about my outfit."

*Oh God.* Violet stepped a little further into the room, and at the same time she stumbled over her words, to say, "Great. Mr. Duke always looks great."

"Please, have a seat." Mr. Duke gestured to the wooden chair in front of his desk. Violet took her place and watched as he lifted an emerald-green velvet jacket from the back of his chair and slipped it on to complete his attire of smart black trousers, black shirt, and silver waistcoat. He proceeded to fix the black tie that hung about his neck into a tight knot.

He then held out his hands in an open gesture. "What is it that you think works particularly well? And what could I do better? I need an expert opinion."

Violet did her best to concentrate on Mr. Duke's questions and not on her confession. She took a long-considered look at his outfit. Everything seemed in perfect order. Violet wasn't sure how she could help. "I'm not really an expert."

Mr. Duke strolled languidly around to the front of his desk. He moved some papers aside and sat upon the desk with his arms crossed and his long legs spread out in front of him. He smoothed his finger over his moustache and rested a steady gaze upon her.

"You are the goddess of costumes and imagination, Violet. Phoebe and I worship at the altar of your creativity."

Violet chuckled but Mr. Duke remained straight-faced. He was serious. "Oh, okay. Erm, let me think. Shoes, for example"—Violet gestured to Mr. Duke's bare feet—"are really important. The wrong choice of shoe undermines an outfit's full effect."

Mr. Duke nodded towards a rack of shoes tucked underneath a freestanding rail of suits. "Which pair should I choose?"

Violet cast her gaze over black patent oxfords, tan brogues, blue suede derbies, a spats-style brogue with a black upper and white sole, and a surprise addition of fluffy pink slippers. "The oxfords. Perfect dress shoes," Violet said, "for this formal outfit. And I particularly love your black shirt. White shirts are usually a sound go-to option, but I think the black really sets off the emerald green of your jacket. And the silver waistcoat shines and pops and is wonderful and classic in its design."

Mr. Duke nodded and gave a small tug at the bottom of the waistcoat. "That means a lot coming from you. Thank you. And I'm glad you said classic because that's my thing. Classic always says to me"—Mr. Duke gestured in the air as if pointing to a Hollywood billboard—"timeless allure rising above the fickle whims of small-minded control and opinion. Small minds crush spirits, Violet, and damn souls to wither in hopelessness because they once dared to hope for more or, God forbid, to be different. I want to be free of all that. When I'm on stage, I embrace my masculine swagger and unapologetic ego. I shrug off gender expectations." Mr. Duke rolled his shoulders. "Mr. Duke is my freedom."

Violet had never seen that serious expression of quiet resolve that came over Mr. Duke. It suited him just as much as the swagger and bravado. It struck her that his sincerity carried with it just as much authority and power. Violet understood immediately that Mr. Duke was so much more than dressing up. "I like the idea of Mr. Duke making you feel free," she said in a thoughtful way.

Mr. Duke nodded and held Violet's gaze. And then his serious expression softened, and the glint in Mr. Duke's eye returned. "So, no top tips for improvement?"

"You could…"

"Yes?"

"Add a trilby. Nothing ostentatious but a sleek finish. The one you tried on when you visited the Emporium really suited you."

Mr. Duke's eyes widened and he raised a finger in the air. "I have one." He bent down and reached underneath his desk and pulled out a laundry style bag. "Aha. Bingo. Quick, heads-up." He tossed the hat as if it was a Frisbee for Violet to catch. "Try it on."

"Me?"

"Yes, in fact…" Mr. Duke rifled through his bag again and this time pulled out a small tin. He opened it and stared at Violet's face and in particular her mouth. It was disconcerting to say the least.

Violet looked out of the office and across the bar towards the stage and the door marked *Private*. Where was Phoebe?

"Here. Hold still." Mr. Duke pressed a strip of fur to her upper lip. He then took the hat Violet was gripping and placed it on her head, tipping it to a slight angle. "Damn, Violet Unwin. You look how I always hope to. Check yourself out." Mr. Duke beckoned Violet over to a mirror. He turned on the surround of light bulbs around the frame of the mirror that you'd expect to find in a theatre. But then Mr. Duke was a performer, after all.

"Come on." Mr. Duke led Violet by the sleeve from her seat. "I promise you look fab. What have you got on underneath your sweatshirt?"

Underneath her sweatshirt? "A T-shirt. Why?"

"Perfect. Take your jumper off."

What? "You want me to take it off?"

"*Yes*. What are you waiting for?"

"Nothing." Violet had no idea why she didn't seem to be able to say no. Although it was kind of fun in a *What was happening to her?* kind of way. She took off her hat and handed it to Mr. Duke, then pulled off her sweatshirt.

"Here." Mr. Duke unhooked a waistcoat from a hanger and held it up for Violet to put her arms through. He placed the hat back on her head. He then stood back and folded his arms. "Boom."

Violet looked in the mirror. "Wow." It was her, but her turned-up on full beam. That was the only way she could describe how it felt to see herself with a moustache and a cool waistcoat and a trilby hat set at a jaunty angle. It was thrilling to look and feel so different, and yet be herself. "I'm used to dressing up, but this feels completely new."

"You look awesome. Wouldn't you agree, Pheebs?"

*Phoebe?* Violet spun round to see Phoebe standing in the doorway carrying a tray and staring open-mouthed.

"Shall I take that tray for you before you drop it?" Mr. Duke was smiling with the same smile he'd given Violet when she confessed her feelings for Phoebe.

Phoebe seemed to almost not notice when Mr. Duke lifted the tray from her. "Violet, you look amazing," she said breathlessly. "You look so…handsome and beautiful at the same time."

She did? "I feel a bit self-conscious."

Phoebe came over to her, took her hand, and gave it a squeeze as if it was the most natural thing for her to do. "Well, you don't look it." Then she blushed as she said, "You look really hot."

The sensation of Phoebe's hand in hers was beyond wonderful. "You think?"

"Right. My work here is clearly done," Mr. Duke said, looking out to the bar. "I'll pop your tray on the table nearest the stage. Unless you want to have afternoon tea in my office?" If Phoebe heard Mr. Duke, she didn't react, for her focus seemed to be entirely fixed upon Violet. "No? Didn't think so." Mr. Duke turned and left the room.

Violet looked down at her hand held tightly in Phoebe's. Phoebe seemed as disinclined as she was to let go.

Speaking softly, Violet said, "It's good to see you. Thanks for inviting me over."

Phoebe squeezed Violet's hand once more.

Mr. Duke gave a cough from the doorway.

"Sorry." Phoebe let go of Violet's hand. "We're going."

Mr. Duke gestured into the bar. "Enjoy. And save me a scone."

"Will do." Phoebe skipped past Mr. Duke who shook his head affectionately at her.

Mr. Duke strolled back into his office. "Thanks for the outfit advice, Violet."

"I'm not sure I was much help." Violet slipped off the waistcoat and carefully peeled off her moustache. She placed them on the desk, along with the trilby.

Mr. Duke handed back her jumper, holding it with Violet for a brief moment. "Just in case you hadn't realised, you're helping far more than you know." Mr. Duke looked out to Phoebe, who was busy spooning jam onto scones.

Violet nodded. "She helps me too. Very much." There was so much more she could say. How just the thought of Phoebe was keeping her going, but she could tell that Mr. Duke somehow knew. "And thank you for…" Violet glanced at the items on the table. "It was fun."

"Good. On both accounts. Now, go do wonders with my tree."

Violet laughed. "I'll try." She made her way out into the bar.

Mr. Duke called after her, "That's all anyone can ask of anyone." And with that he closed his office door.

Phoebe was smiling so broadly it was utterly infectious, and Violet could not help but smile with her in complete delight. "There you go," Phoebe said, as she pulled out a seat from the table in the flamboyant manner of a waiter. "Your seat, madam."

"Thank you." She made a point of resting her napkin on her lap with a flourish.

Phoebe placed a scone on her plate and her mug of tea next to it. "They should still be warm as they're not long out of the oven. I managed to burn the first batch, hence why I was late. Sorry."

"You've nothing to apologise for. This is just amazing. Thank you for taking the trouble for me."

"I wanted to."

Violet's cheeks stung.

"Oh, the candle. I love candlelight." Phoebe dashed behind the counter and returned with a lighter. She lit the candle in the centre of the table. "There. Perfect. Table for two."

Violet stared into the flickering light. This was all so new and so incredible. One minute she was alone, and the next she was eating scones with the loveliest girl in the world in one of the hippest bars in town. How did that happen?

Violet bit into her scone. "Oh my God. Lush."

"Actually, they are good." Phoebe seemed genuinely surprised. "My scones can be a bit heavy. I think I overwork them. Looks like not having time to overthink and to faff with them has worked."

Talking through a mouthful, Violet said. "Totally." They both laughed.

"You've got cream on your lip." Phoebe leaned forward and brushed the cream away with her thumb. Her fingertips lightly touched the side of Violet's cheek in the process. "You looked so cool in your moustache."

Violet placed her hand over her face. "I felt a bit silly, to be honest. I'm not *exactly* Mr. Duke."

"I think one Mr. Duke is enough. And you were *exactly* you. Handsome and beautiful, just like I said." Phoebe licked jam from her fingers. "Even though you felt a bit self-conscious, did you enjoy dressing in drag?"

Violet nodded. "It was fun. Actually, it was more than that, it was empowering."

Phoebe smiled, with warmth and understanding shining in her eyes. "Drag suits you, then."

Violet wiped at her mouth with her napkin and set it aside. "Mr. Duke was telling me about how performing was his freedom. He really hates the judgement from small-minded people, doesn't he?"

"He loathes it. He can't stand the thought of someone's full potential being squashed by other people's fear and hatred." Phoebe looked about them. "That's why Dee set up this place, so there was a space for people to be themselves in all the wonderful rainbow shades of difference."

Phoebe was so smart. "Rainbow shades of difference. I love that!"

"It's the truth. Just by existing, this place challenges ignorance. I remember one time, after Mr. Duke had performed, and Dee was dressed again as Dee and having a post-show nightcap like she does, a customer came up to her and asked her why she performed as a man and wasn't she a lesbian in any case and didn't lesbians hate men."

"Really?"

"Really. The woman was on a hen do. And she'd wolf-whistled at Mr. Duke the whole night. Of course, Mr. Duke played up to it and flirted with her shamelessly." They both giggled. "The woman wasn't being mean as such, more curious than anything. Dee was not remotely offended and just said *I am a lesbian and I am a drag king. I am me.* And that she didn't hate men, she hated dickheads, male or female. Then she brought her a drink. Before the woman had the chance to enjoy it, her friends dragged her off." Phoebe shrugged and finished her tea.

"Wow." Violet looked across at the closed office door.

"Not all drag kings identify in the same way as Dee."

Violet turned back to Phoebe, who was looking at her intently.

Phoebe continued, "Every drag king is uniquely themself. Some identify as non-binary, and some won't be drawn into any definition, and why should they? What unites them all is their dedication to their performance and the fact that they are awesome."

Could she ask Phoebe about herself? "You've never been tempted to dress in drag?"

"Not something I've thought about for me, really."

"Why do you think Mr. Duke encouraged me to?"

"My guess, for what it's worth, is that Mr. Duke must have seen something of him in you. Maybe he wanted you to embrace your inner swagger."

Violet took a deep breath. Could she speak aloud what she held so privately in her heart? "I am like Mr. Duke." She could feel herself shaking. "I…"

Phoebe stood up and bent down at her side and rested her hand at her back. "It's okay, you don't have to say—"

"I'm a lesbian."

"I wondered. Me too. And very proudly so." Phoebe kissed Violet on her cheek. It was a kiss that said *We are the same.*

Violet pressed her hand to where Phoebe had kissed. "Why did you wonder about me?"

"I guess it was the way you made me feel."

"How did I make you feel?"

"Entranced."

"Tree's looking great, girls." Dee dropped a letter on the table. "Sorry, Pheebs, meant to give you this earlier. I found it on our doormat this morning. Got to give it to your uni buddy—she makes a great postman."

"Yeah, definitely. Thanks." Phoebe stood up and shoved the letter in her pocket. She seemed to do her best to avoid Dee's scrutinous gaze at the sight of the letter being tucked out of sight. "Violet and I were just talking."

"Okay. Great. How are you doing, Violet? You look a little flushed."

Violet stood and tucked her chair under the table. "Good, thank you." Violet patted her stomach. "Full of scone."

"I bet…"

Phoebe placed her hands on her hips. "Before you say anything rude, they were surprisingly light."

"Well, I'm not going to take your word for it, obviously." Dee grabbed a scone and bit into it. "I've got good teeth, Violet, don't worry."

Despite the intensity of her chat with Phoebe, Violet struggled to hold in the urge to laugh. Her feelings were all over the place. Dee raised her eyebrows and nodded in approval as she munched.

"*Anyway*," Phoebe said, mock scowling at Dee, "we best get stuck in." Phoebe went over to the stage and patted the tree. "Poor thing. Fear not." Phoebe rummaged in the box Dee had brought down from the loft. She pulled out an Easter chick, a partially deflated beach ball, a recorder, a fur banana, and a chipped bone china plate commemorating a royal anniversary. She frowned. "Which one of these items says Christmas to you? Oh no, sorry—wait." Phoebe lifted some plastic holly in the air.

"There you go." As Dee spoke the single red berry fell to the floor. "Oh. But we can stick it back on—can't we, Violet?"

"Uh-huh. Yep." It might be the most pre-Christmas merriment Violet had ever had. Phoebe looked less delighted.

"We definitely heard Christmas bells when we got the box from the loft." Phoebe dug deeper with even more determined gusto. A jingling noise prompted short-lived optimism as Phoebe lifted out a strap-on harness for a dildo.

"Oh, that's where that went. Thanks, Pheebs." Dee leaned forward and lifted the harness away from an open-mouthed Phoebe, then proceeded to try it on over her trousers.

"Why has it got bells on it?" Violet watched captivated as Dee tightened the straps around her hips. Phoebe shot her a look that said *Seriously, you're asking her that?* "Actually, no answer needed."

"Duh, it's festive," Dee replied.

"*No.*" Phoebe held her palm up towards Dee. "Before you say Suzie, chimney, and Santa bells in the same sentence. Just, no. I currently enjoy the thought of Christmas greatly, and I'd like it to stay that way."

"So it's not going on the tree, then?" Dee asked with a mischievous smile.

Violet laughed and laughed. Wiping at her eyes, she said, "I don't think Phoebe's keen."

Dee stepped out of the harness and looped it over her shoulder like a holster for a gun. "I'm sensing that too, Violet."

"Hold on, I take it all back. I think we might have tree lights." Phoebe lifted out a tangled mess of green wire and teardrop bulbs. She rushed behind the bar and plugged them in. They lit up first time. The three of them stood in silent wonder.

Dee cleared her throat. "See. No idea what the drama was about. That said, Violet, if you maybe have some tinsel up your sleeve, we'd appreciate it."

Phoebe unplugged the lights and placed them carefully on the stage. "We'll need an extension cable and some gaffer tape to secure it to the floor."

"I'm on it," Dee said, as she headed off to her office.

"Can I see in your box? Not a word, Dee."

Dee held her arms out wide.

Violet nodded. "Of course. I brought lights, but I can just take back what you don't need. No probs."

Phoebe opened the box with childlike excitement on her face. "It's like Christmas has arrived early. Oh, Violet, did you make it specially?"

"There's tinsel, and yes, I made you some ribbons."

Phoebe held up a golden star, which twinkled in the candlelight. "I love the glitter. You're so clever."

*What?* She had no memory of a star. She remembered excluding Carl's angel, but she was sure she hadn't added anything in its place. It must have been in the box all along, and she simply missed it. But how?

"It's just perfect. It's going to look so good on the tree. Violet?"

Violet nodded. "Yes. Good idea."

Please let her recognise the other items inside, otherwise she was surely going mad. Violet lifted out the lights and then the ribbons, tinsel, and baubles in turn and placed them on the stage. Rolling around at the bottom of the box, the spray can of snow was thankfully the last of the items. Violet picked up the can and gave it a small shake. "I thought we could cheer up the tree and maybe the windows with some spray-on snow."

"Oh my God, y*es*." Phoebe set down the star carefully by the tree. "That's inspired. Thanks for bringing all this over. I hope we've left you with enough decorations for the Emporium."

The Emporium. How long could she keep its imminent closure from Phoebe? Yet nothing in Violet felt ready to tell her. Not yet. "No worries. The decorations were just at the back of the shop. And as it happens, I need to do some sorting there anyhow, so this was a good kick-start for me." Violet hadn't meant to give such a heavy sigh.

"Stocktakes are the worst, aren't they?" Phoebe gave Violet a consoling rub of her arm. "Dee and I do this place's inventory together. In fact, I could help you, if you like."

Having Phoebe with her would make all the difference. What harm was there if she thought it was for a stocktake? And in some ways wasn't that what it was? An inventory of everything she was losing. "Would you?"

"Of course, anything you need. You know that."

Violet nodded. She never even dreamed that anyone would care enough about her to make such an offer and to clearly mean it. "I can't tell you how much I appreciate it. Thank you."

Phoebe's kind eyes sparkled as she blushed a little in reply. "My pleasure."

How could she show Phoebe in deeds and not just words how much she meant to her? Maybe there was some way she could help Phoebe in return? "How about, and only if you want, I could help you with"—Violet gestured to Phoebe's pocket—"your post. Like a quid pro quo arrangement. I'd feel less bad about you helping me. I know we talked about it before, but maybe you've had a chance to think. What do you say?"

Phoebe stared down at her shoes and fiddled with a piece of tinsel. "Only if you've got time. You shouldn't have to help me. It's a bit embarrassing."

"To be honest, helping you with your post gives me an excuse to see you again."

Phoebe reached for Violet's hand. "You don't need an excuse."

Violet feared that her heart might burst, it felt so full. How she wanted to draw Phoebe's hand to her lips and kiss it and press it against her chest and say *Everything in me, every part of me, wants you*. It took all of Violet's composure to say, "How about Sunday, then? We could maybe even make a day of it. You could, if it suited, bring your post, and we can blitz that first and then have some lunch. We could order a takeaway on Jack." They both smiled at their shared memory. "And then we can tackle my mountain of boxes. Deal?"

Phoebe squeezed Violet's hand tighter. "Deal."

"Would ten thirty suit?"

"Perfect. And I can see my hat. I'm so excited. Actually, I have an idea—why don't I collect the costumes at the same time. Or better still, you could come back here with me when we're done, and then you could stay for our drag night. You'd love it, I promise."

"That's what Dee said."

"And she's right. You don't have to decide now."

"Well said, Pheebs," Dee said, returning from the back. "I'm always right." Dee tossed Phoebe a roll of tape.

"Anyway, *big ears*." Phoebe twirled the tape round her wrist. "I'm thinking of collecting our costumes from the Emporium on Sunday."

"Great."

Violet shifted on the spot. This was her time to mention the fur to Dee, wasn't it. "Actually, Dee," Violet said, with apology heavy in her tone, "I wanted to let you know that unfortunately the fur you chose isn't available. I hadn't realised at the time that it wasn't for rent."

"Oh, that's a shame."

"But, on the theme of Freddie Mercury, I have white trousers, and I can add golden trim down the side. And then we have a crown and even a fur-trimmed cape. It could work."

"*Nice*. I'm all over that, Violet." Dee grabbed the microphone stand and struck a Freddie pose.

Violet laughed. An enormous sense of relief washed over her. "I'll try to get it ready for Sunday."

Dee replaced the mic on the stage. "No worries. In your own

time." She glanced about the room, and her attention eventually settled upon the naked tree. "Which is clearly how you pair are approaching the decorating."

"It'll be done in a blink. *And* we've got fake snow." Phoebe beamed with evident pride. Violet handed her the can. "Snow first?"

"Yep." Violet gathered together armfuls of tinsel. "Go for it—you can never have too much."

"I'm so excited. My plan is to add the lights next, then the tinsel and the baubles, then the beautiful ribbons tied to the tips. How does that sound to you?"

"Perfect."

"And not forgetting…our star." Phoebe looked so happy that even the brightest of stars anywhere in the universe couldn't have shined brighter.

"Yes, the star." Wherever it had come from. Not that Violet didn't have her suspicions.

## Chapter Fourteen

Ever-growing fear and worry continued to stalk Violet's sleep, emerging from the shadows as nightmarish phantoms of the realities she could not yet face.

*Bastard shop! I hate you!* Carl screamed into the ether of her fitful dream.

Paralyzed with fear, all Violet could do was watch as Carl prowled around the shop like a captive animal frustrated by its cage. Please don't let him see her. Please don't. It was too late to run. It was too late to hide.

He was staring wild-eyed and casting sharp erratic glances about the room. The sweat on his forehead glistened against his bleached skin. He looked somewhere between dead and alive. Why was he here? Had he come for his letter?

He began to pull at the boxes, dislodging them and pushing them into the centre of the shop. He turned them upside down, shaking the contents and the life out of them. Where did the anger in him come from? Was he born angry or made angry? Or both?

His letter was by the till. Why couldn't he see it? If she shouted he would see *her*.

He stood stiff and stared up to the ceiling. It wasn't just anger in him—behind his eyes was unmistakable fear. *I'm selling this place. What do you think of that then? Hey! Hey! I know you can hear me!* He grabbed a drumstick and raised it to the ceiling. *You don't frighten me.*

Who was he talking to? Carl turned sharply towards the door to the flat. Was he trying to find her? She needed to hide. Could she make it to the dressing room? He then looked over his shoulder directly at her. She closed her eyes. It was too late. Time was up. Would he do as he had always clearly wanted to and hurt her, blame her with blows for arriving unwanted in his life? He'd had to share his space, his air, his name with her. Violet waited for the pain. Nothing. There was nothing more terrifying than nothing. Could she look? Dare she?

Violet opened her eyes and stared into the half-light of her room. Her fingers ached with her tight grip on her bedsheets. All was quiet. It was just another bad dream. Nothing more. She turned over and pulled up her blanket under her chin. She couldn't bring herself to close her eyes. Carl was coming for his letter, and that was not a dream.

A soft creak on the landing drew her attention to beyond her nightmare and her room to thoughts of Vi. "Is that you?" Had Vi made that star for Phoebe and slipped it unnoticed into the box at the very time Violet had doubted she was there? How many more instances did she need to counter any doubt? No, she would choose to believe in her. She *needed* to believe in her. And what had Phoebe said about being pretty certain about Violet's sexuality without actually knowing for sure? She had said she knew by how Violet made her feel. Surely feeling was an equal sense to seeing? Violet could *feel* her great-great-grandmother's presence, and she would not question that any more. Vi was with her. She was certain.

Violet sat up and checked the time on her phone. Seven o'clock. She had a busy day ahead, and she should probably rally and get her thoughts in order. Wait. Phoebe? Her heart raced at the unopened message from Phoebe, sent late last night. Opening it up, she smiled at the image of the Christmas tree in pride of place on the stage, resplendent in lights and colour and adorning The Banana with festive magic. The accompanying message read: *The star of Saturday night. Sending thanks, from Phoebe and the tree xx*

Violet quickly replied with the image of a thumbs-up and a star and a heart. She finished her message with, *See you later!*

As she returned her phone to the bedside table, she caught sight of the brochure nestled next to her lamp. She studied the image of Vi and Robert on the front. "You're so glamorous, Vi." The magnificent tree to Robert's side had inspired Phoebe so much. Violet brought the image up close. "Did you make that star too?" Grabbing her phone, she climbed out of bed and slipped on her dressing gown and slippers. There was someone else who deserved Phoebe's thanks.

She was just about to push at the door to the spare room when she stopped and knocked instead. This wasn't the spare room. This was Vi's room. "It's me. Can I come in?" She waited. "So, I have a message for you, well for us, I suppose, from Phoebe." Violet inched the door open and stepped inside. She looked about the space. The stool was in place, and the wardrobe was closed, just as Violet had left it. Speaking in the direction of the dressing table, Violet said, "Shall I read it to you?" Violet waited. She cleared her throat and read out the text, adding, "Phoebe has taken a photo of the tree we decorated. Can you see your star?" Violet moved to the dressing table and turned her phone with the screen outwards. A glisten from the table's surface caught her eye. Violet swallowed. She knew what it was in an instant. She ran her finger through the sparkling golden dust. Glitter fit for a star. Tears of relief flooded through her, washing away any stubborn trace of doubt.

Violet's voice wavered as she managed to say, "So, thank you from Phoebe, the tree, and…me." She wiped at her eyes with her dressing gown sleeve. "Anyway, I must get ready for today. Phoebe's coming round, and we're sorting her post, and then I need to start going through the boxes and the drawers. We have to pack up. Me and you. Please understand, I have no choice. Carl's coming back any day." Violet's dream rushed up to her, and she reached for the table and took a seat on the stool. The image of Carl screaming and raising a drumstick to the ceiling struck her like a thump to her chest. It was like he was demented by something or someone. It couldn't be. Could it? "He was pointing to you, wasn't he? In my dream. It was you he was angry with. Did you haunt him, Vi? I mean, in real life. Did you try to make him leave? Did you do that for me? Have you been watching over me all these years? That's why I feel safest here, isn't it? Because of you." Had Vi been protecting and loving her all these years without her knowing it?

"Can I tell you something? Personal, about me? I like her. Phoebe, I mean. I think she likes me too. At least, Mr. Duke says she's taken with me, and I can feel that she is." Violet pressed her hand to her heart. "In here. I can't stop thinking about her. She steals my breath with her smile, and from the moment she leaves, I can't wait to see her again. Anyway, I just wanted you to know. You are my family, and you're all I've got." Violet waited for the reply. She would always wait, just in case.

She eventually stood and moved to the door. "You'll tell me when you're ready, won't you? Why you're making yourself known to me now." And with that Violet left the room, leaving the door just ajar.

In no time, she had breakfasted, showered, dressed, and arrived down into the shop with a determined excitement in her step. She flicked on the lights and smiled at the sight of the costume for Mr. Duke laid out on the counter. She'd spent the last few evenings working on it. She knew he would love it and imagined him performing his heart out. She could see him adorned with his crown and wearing the royal cape about his shoulders with effortless swagger. His sharp white vest complemented by his white trousers with the yellow stripe down the leg was just perfect for evoking all things Freddie. She couldn't wait for Phoebe to see it. But that wasn't all.

Violet went to the dressing room where she had hung up the costumes for The Banana. It wasn't just Freddie's outfit Violet had managed to finish—it was Emmeline's hat as well. She lifted it from the hook and inspected it one final time. A rummage in the shop's hat collection had produced a summer boater that was an even better match for the woman's hat in the image they had both admired. The bloom of flowers over its crown was just beautiful and like springtime itself in the darkness of winter.

"So what do you think? Have we got it right?" Even more than ever, Violet could sense that Vi was there with her, so much so the atmosphere felt heady with her presence. "I promised you I wouldn't use your hat. I will never break my promises to you." Violet waited. Maybe this time Vi would reply. But no. Violet returned her attention to the hat and brushed her thumb over the flowers. "It means so much to me that Phoebe is pleased with it. I want her to feel happy. She's been so sad, you see." They'd both been so sad. Violet pressed the hat momentarily against her and felt everything it stood for so keenly. The phrase *deeds not words* fell unexpectedly from her lips. Something made her turn towards the door and to the box of decorations she had taken to The Banana. Everything had been used for their tree with the exception of the lights, and now she couldn't quite believe what she thought she was seeing.

"They're lit." Violet set the hat carefully back on its hook, took a cautious move to the box, and stared down in disbelief at the shimmer of colour that greeted her. She should have been freaked out, but she wasn't. More than anything, she was curious. "Are you telling me we should decorate the Emporium? We don't have a tree. Uncle Walter always bought a real one. I could make one. That's it. Let's do a window display. It makes sense. And I know Phoebe would love it. One last act from the Emporium."

❖

"How beautiful." Phoebe stood on the street outside the Emporium and stared in delighted wonder at the large sparkling golden star suspended just above the top of a hand-crafted Christmas tree.

With her face inches from the window so as not to miss a single detail, Phoebe could just make out that the tree had been made of two identical designs fashioned from painted card and slipped together to form the three-dimensional shape. Delicately painted images of teardrop-shaped baubles adorned the tree in such an inspired way, and elegantly looped Christmas tree lights completed the quite magical creation.

Phoebe stood back a little to take in the whole display in one admiring look. A flurry of paper snowflakes fixed with cotton wool to the glass evoked a wintry snow shower and was just so clever. *Violet* was so clever. The Emporium's window had become in every way a magical snow globe.

Phoebe's heart skipped a beat at the glimpse of Violet through the window. She was coming in and out of view, lifting and reaching for the boxes at the back of the shop. She'd obviously decided to make a start. Phoebe took a deep breath. There was no more time for dilly-dallying. She had promised to help Violet, and she would not let her down.

She knocked on the shop door as she stepped inside. The bell gave a welcoming ding. "Hey, Violet, it's me."

"Hey." Violet brushed dust off her jeans. "I should wear an apron, really. It's quite dusty back there." Violet gave a frown of annoyance at clearly not thinking of it sooner. She was so cute.

Phoebe pulled off her bag and looped it over the dressing room chair. She then shrugged off her coat and rested it across the seat. "You have a new display." Phoebe looked over at the window. The tree looked just as good, if not better, from inside the shop.

"Yes. I saw you looking, and I was hoping that you would like it."

"Like it?"

Violet's face dropped. "You don't?"

"Violet, I don't like it. I *love* it. I only wish I had the smallest bit of your imagination."

Violet pushed her hands into the pockets of her jeans and gave a small shrug. "It was nothing really. I had all I needed already in the shop. In truth, I only decided to do it first thing, so I had to pull it together quite quickly. Considering, I'm pretty pleased with it. Although I think the paint will still be wet in places. Oh well."

"Seriously, you did it in a couple of hours? It would take me two weeks to just do the star."

Violet laughed. "No, it wouldn't—don't be silly."

"Er, yes it would. Have you forgotten the ribbon flowers already?"

Violet beamed a smile. "Speaking of which, close your eyes."

"Emmeline's hat?" Phoebe closed her eyes. She had been picturing herself wearing it with such pride. Only last night she had dreamed of being in the march alongside those brave women from the photo. She had woken herself up shouting out, "Votes for women!" Judging by the curious look she got from Dee at the breakfast table, she had probably woken them both up. It was certainly no coincidence that Dee then mentioned that she'd put something together for Violet and could she take it to her. "Don't let me forget to give you something from Dee. It's in my bag."

Phoebe felt Violet return to her side. "I've done Mr. Duke's outfit too."

Phoebe opened her eyes. "Have you?"

Violet held Emmeline's hat behind her back. "Yep. This first, though."

"I can't tell you how excited I am. I actually dreamed about wearing this last night."

"Really? I dream quite a lot too. Mine are mostly stress dreams." Violet drifted off for a moment.

Was Violet stressed about the stocktake? Or was she finding managing the shop harder than she was willing to let on? "Don't worry—we'll totally blitz the stocktake."

Violet came back to her in an instant from wherever her thoughts had taken her. "Absolutely. Your hat for the ball, madam." Violet bowed with a flourish and presented Phoebe with the flower covered boater. "It's a slightly different hat than before, but I think it works really well."

"You never found it?"

Violet looked taken aback. "No. I mean, yes, I found it. I prefer this one."

"Me too." The hat was gorgeous. "Can I try it on in the mirror?"

"Be my guest."

Phoebe rushed to the dressing room. She placed the hat with great care upon her head and looked in the mirror. She recognised herself and didn't recognise herself at the same time. The strangest of feelings of hurt and distress mingled with fierce determination rushed at her. She took the hat off.

Violet came quickly over to her. "Is everything okay? I did check that there were no stray staple ends sticking through, but I might have missed one."

"The hat's perfect. It's just when I put the hat on, I felt really weird."

"Bad weird?"

"Kind of, more *strange* weird. I think I've been imagining wearing it too much, so much so it actually felt like I'd worn it before when I put it on. I had all of these odd feelings."

"If it doesn't feel right, you don't have to wear it. We can find another hat or another costume, for that matter."

"No. I want to wear it. I love my costume." Phoebe took a deep breath. She was being oversensitive. *Come on, Frink, get a grip.* She placed the hat back on her head and braced herself for the strange sensations to return. They didn't. Instead, all she felt was properly chuffed and grateful. "You've done an amazing job. Thank you." She reached forward and hugged Violet, knocking the hat in the process. Violet reached up and caught it just in time. Her chest briefly pressed against Phoebe's with the action. Everything in Phoebe fluttered deep inside her at the sensation of Violet's soft breasts pressing against hers. Violet blushed in turn.

"Sorry, I didn't mean to…" Violet looked down. It was obvious she was hoping the floor would open up and swallow her.

"No, I'm sorry, I shouldn't just randomly hug you."

"I don't mind." Violet gave that same shy sweet smile that Phoebe loved.

"No?" Violet shook her head. They held each other's gaze, and all that once fluttered was swept up and submerged in a rushing wave of intense arousal. Would it be too much if she reached for Violet and held her again? Before she had chance to decide, Violet looked away. Was she drowning in intoxicating sensation too? Did it feel overwhelming in a wonderful way? *Please let that be the case.*

With newly flushed cheeks, Violet rested Emmeline's hat on top of Phoebe's coat. It seemed to take several attempts for her to catch her breath and speak. "So, now for Mr. Duke's outfit. I'm hoping it will shout Freddie Mercury to you."

"Oh, and here. This is for you. Dee told me to tell you it was from Mr. Duke. And that if you made it over tonight, you might want to wear it." Phoebe opened her bag, pulled out a small drawstring sack, and handed it to a curious Violet. Phoebe spotted her pile of post and quickly closed her bag. Maybe today wasn't the day after all. Maybe she didn't ever have to open it. Maybe… "Oh, Violet."

Violet had slipped on the waistcoat from the other day and was trying it on in the mirror.

"It suits you so much. Although maybe try it with your jumper off."

Violet laughed. "That's what Mr. Duke said too." She then inspected further inside the sack. "There's also a black tie and a moustache. It's different from the one I tried on at The Banana."

"Clearly chosen just for you. Let me help you." Phoebe gently released Violet's waistcoat from her shoulders and watched Violet wriggle out of her jumper. She hadn't intended for her eyes to follow every curve Violet's shirt clung to. Luckily Violet hadn't noticed. "Okay. Waistcoat." Phoebe lifted it in the air as Violet dipped her arms inside once more. "And tie." Phoebe lifted the tie from the sack, looped it under Violet's collar, and let it dangle loose against her shirt front. "And then the finishing touch." Phoebe held out her palm, and Violet dutifully dropped the moustache into it. "Oh, wow. A mini circus master handlebar moustache. I love the curls at the end."

"I love them too. It's fun and theatrical, isn't it."

"Camp gorgeousness. Hold still." She peeled off the backing tape and lightly placed the soft black material across Violet's upper lip, brushing it gently with her thumb to secure it in place. Violet looked so hot. "You're not safe." Phoebe gave a mischievous laugh. Violet looked horrified. "Oh no, Violet, I didn't mean you wouldn't be safe wearing it. I mean you wouldn't be *safe* wearing it. Because everyone will fall for you." She was gibbering like a fool. *Shut up.*

Violet's smile returned. She looked at herself in the mirror. But then she frowned. *Please don't let her comment have put Violet off.* Violet stepped out of the dressing room, reached up to the shelf above the formal dress suits, and brought down a trilby hat. As if she wore it all the time, she effortlessly put it on.

"There," Violet said. "Outfit complete."

Phoebe stood with Violet in the dressing room and looked back at her in the mirror. "You look amazing." They were standing just inches from each other.

Violet turned to Phoebe. "Do you think it would be okay for tonight? Am I going to stand out?"

"You will both stand out in a very hot way, and blend in, in a *You're in the right place* way. If that makes sense. So does that mean you're coming with me later?" *Please say yes.*

"Yes. I'm more than a bit nervous, though."

"I get that. But I promise, I wouldn't suggest you would enjoy it if I didn't think you would. I care too much about you to do that to you."

Violet's eyes filled with tears. All Phoebe wanted to do was hold Violet tightly in her arms and not let go. But it was so difficult to know for certain what Violet was thinking. From the warmth and delight behind the smile that often greeted Phoebe, it was clear Violet loved being with her. But Violet's natural shyness made her hard to read, and it was even harder to know whether Violet wanted more when Phoebe wanted so much more herself. It was one thing Violet confessing to her that she was a lesbian, but another thing to assume that she wanted her.

Violet looked for all the world like she wanted to say something in reply, but it was like she doubted herself and instead turned away towards the counter. "It's really kind of Mr. Duke to think of me. I really hope he'll like his outfit. I've laid it out for you to see." She moved from the dressing room and, at the same time, peeled off her moustache, slipped off her waistcoat, and rested them on her stool along with the trilby hat.

"What do you think?" Violet then lifted a pair of white trousers with a trim of gold edging in the air. They were so Freddie Mercury. They were perfect.

Joining Violet at her side, Phoebe smoothed her hand along the trouser leg. "I love them! They're amazing. And look at the cape and crown. Although, I worry that you may be creating something uncontrollable." They both laughed. "I wouldn't put it past Mr. Duke to make his entrance to the bar accompanied by a festive fanfare of royal trumpets. You must be so pleased with the trousers."

"Yep. Thank goodness for Wonder-Web and leftover yellow ribbon from an Easter bonnet."

"You're so resourceful."

"I'm also good at making tea. Want one?" Violet couldn't have changed the subject quicker. She carried Mr. Duke's outfit across to the dressing room and hung it up with the other items for the ball.

"Do I compliment you too much?"

"You risk making me big-headed." She paused and cast a quick glance at Phoebe's bag. She then carried on across the room towards the flat. She stopped at the bottom of the stairs. "Bring your post with you if you'd like to. No pressure, of course. Only if you want. See you up there." Violet disappeared upstairs.

Phoebe looked across to the chair. Her gaze drifted to Emmeline's hat. What would Emmeline Pankhurst think of her not able to face her future or even her post? She had sacrificed so much for young women just like her. At the sound of the kettle boiling, Phoebe looked back at the stairs to the flat. What would Violet think of her? *Come on, Frink. With Violet's help you can do this.*

Phoebe grabbed her bag, took a deep breath, and headed upstairs.

"Hey." Violet was standing at the small kitchen table, finishing pouring tea from the pot. "Grab your mug, and I'll bring the biccies. I thought we could go in my room. It's comfier than here."

"Great idea. Thanks."

Violet led the way and gestured for Phoebe to join her on her bed.

Phoebe placed her mug next to Violet's on the bedside table and unzipped her bag. "It's mostly uni stuff. And some banking and student loan things. I've got quite a few emails as well. I can't seem to face any of it. I sound so pathetic."

Violet gave a small shrug. "You sound human."

"I'm not even sure where to start."

"May I?" Violet pulled Phoebe's bag towards her, dug inside, and pulled out the letters. Phoebe looked on as Violet divided the post into smaller piles by sender. And then she organised the small piles into chronological order. It took no time at all. Already it seemed less overwhelming. When Violet had finished that stage, she reached across for her tea and took a couple of considered sips. "When I do a window display, I start with the big picture. I have a pretty good idea of what I want from the end product. With this, our end product is for you to feel on top of the things that are important to you. Believe me when I tell you—I know how hard that is and this afternoon you will be helping me with pretty much the same thing."

Phoebe nodded and swallowed down an awful sense of sickness and dread. Thoughts these last few weeks of what the letters would contain had grown in her imagination to become a frightening monster fed by her fear.

Violet carefully inched open the first envelope. She unfolded the letter and Phoebe watched her eyes scan the lines of text. "Shall I paraphrase?"

"Yes. Is it that awful?"

"No. Further to your chat with your course tutor, Dr. Lowe, they've made a note of your request to take a break from your studies. They've offered you counselling appointments. They ask that you keep in touch and let them know your decision by the end of this term."

Phoebe braced herself at the sight of the next letter.

Violet opened it in the same calm and purposeful way. Except this time, she raised her eyebrows and stared up at her. It was bad news wasn't it? Violet smiled. "Did you take some exams before you left?"

"They're constantly testing us. So a couple, yes. Why? I've failed, haven't I."

"Far from it. You aced them." Violet handed her the letter.

Phoebe stared down at the page. It was hard to take in what she was seeing. Even though her results confirmed in writing that she was good enough, somehow it didn't feel like that inside. Intelligence was one thing, but courage was another.

The remaining letters were administrative in detail and understanding in tone.

"It looks to me that everything has been put on hold for you," Violet said. "I reckon they see this a lot. I bet it'll be the caring intelligent doctors who initially doubt themselves and who go on with the right support to be proper fab. The arrogant ones who are in it for the money and kudos probably don't give things a minute's thought, which is frightening."

"Even with the break I've taken, I still don't know what to do."

"You've still got this month to decide."

"I guess."

"Do you want to do the emails from them?"

She'd had enough for now. "I think I should try to sort them myself." She reached for Violet's hand and gave it a squeeze. "Thank you."

Violet smiled, but then her expression fell a little. "Can I ask, if you decide not to continue, would you consider another course at the city's uni?"

"I hadn't thought about it. I had my heart set on medicine." She couldn't promise Violet she would even stay in the city, much as she wanted to.

"You can always take a year out. Work at The Banana and see how you feel then." Violet's eyes carried a kind of hopeful plea in them.

"I need to tell you about something. I don't think Dee would mind, as it's you. But maybe don't tell anyone else."

"I'm not sure who I'd tell. What is it?"

"The Banana's struggling financially. Dee went for a loan recently. Well, actually, Mr. Duke went for the loan, and the short of it is, he was declined. Dee hasn't exactly said how much cash The Banana has in reserve, but she's begun to talk about closing during the week, and I worry that it won't be long before The Banana closes for good."

"I'm sorry."

"So, if you need an assistant here…actually make that two, I know just the people."

Violet looked taken aback by her suggestion.

"I was kidding. You'd get no work done with us pair prancing around in your costumes all the time." They both laughed, although without the soul of laughter.

Violet took a deep and noticeably shaky breath. "I think we need a takeaway treat. How about pizza on Jack?"

"Actually, I'd prefer mine on a thin crust." This time when they laughed it felt real again. Even though it had been tough facing what she had been putting off, there was no question her shoulders felt a little lighter thanks to Violet.

"I'll get it ordered. Any preference?"

"Anything veggie would do me."

"Okay, I'm on it." Violet dialled the number and wandered onto the landing to make the call.

Phoebe took a swig of her cold tea and winced. As she went to place the mug back onto the side table, she caught sight of Vi's postcard from Harry. She lifted it carefully and stared at the image of Emmeline. How proud her family must have been of her. Imagine being one of her descendants. What an inheritance that would be. In fact, how proud Violet must feel to come from a line of Unwins of Unwin's Emporium. She knew so little of her own family history. What would her descendants think of her? Phoebe Frink the dropout, of course.

❖

"I once made a crocodile's head out of a pizza box." Violet flapped the cardboard lid and made a roaring noise.

Phoebe giggled. "Why am I not surprised? Can you show me?"

"Seriously?"

"Absolutely. I'm intrigued."

"Okay. Why not. I'll just get a pair of scissors." Violet scrambled from the floor and went to the counter.

Phoebe lay back on her side with her head propped on one elbow. Cushions were scattered about her on the shop floor. The pizza had taken no time at all to arrive. They had raced each other from the flat to see who would be first to the door to greet the delivery man. Phoebe suspected that Violet had let her win. They were so hungry that they didn't make it back upstairs before the boxes were open and their contents devoured.

Phoebe couldn't have felt more contented in that moment. Her tummy was full of pizza, and her heart was full of all things Violet. She watched, intrigued, as Violet took a moment to choose just the right pair of scissors from her craft box. She returned to her with an impish smile and eyes that shone with pleasure. Was she the first person to see Violet make her crocodile?

"Now then." Violet lifted the box and inspected it. "First the jaw and mouth." Working from the back of the box forward, Violet trimmed down the side edges to create a triangular shape, taking care to leave a blunt front edge. Then she bent the sides in to reinstate the edges and proceeded to cut out triangles for the impression of teeth along the bottom sides of the box. She then pushed the bottom edges outwards a little so that when the box closed, the lower jaw protruded, mirroring the croc's overbite.

"See how I've misspent my days?" Violet gave an embarrassed smile as she worked.

"I misspent mine trying to fit in and then trying not to." Phoebe released a sigh. "At least you know how to make a crocodile. And, for that matter, a beautiful star." Phoebe gazed over to the tree in the window, expecting to see the lights on, but they were off. Odd. They must be on a timer.

"Okay. Finishing touches." Violet dipped her finger in the residue of tomato paste and dabbed two eyes in the centre position at the back of the box. She then cut up a stray black olive and used each half for the croc's pupils. She smeared a bit more paste to redden the gumline. "What do you think—a Christmas Crocker."

Standing and brushing at her jeans, Phoebe laughed and said, "That's terrible."

"Talking of terrible," Violet said, making her way over to the boxes stacked at the back of the shop, "I never thought I'd find it so hard to sort through a pile of cardboard."

"Someone very wise said to me that's it's only human to feel overwhelmed." It was her turn to provide Violet with the perspective that was almost impossible to find alone. "Just think of all the free space you'll have to display more costumes or even for another changing room?"

"Uh-huh. Possibly." Violet couldn't have sounded less enthusiastic.

"So, tell me what you'd like me to do."

"I was thinking maybe we could have a go at sorting them into keep, recycle, bin. I've made a start. How does that sound?"

"It sounds like a plan."

A smile returned to Violet's face. "Thanks."

Without hesitation, Phoebe hugged Violet. "We've got this." Violet held her tighter in response. It felt so natural and so wonderful to be held in Violet's arms. If she never let go, it would be too soon. But there was work to be done, and Violet needed her.

True to her word, together they made short work of the cardboard mountain. Only the final few tucked against the back wall remained. Most boxes they inspected were in fact empty boxes within empty boxes. Violet seemed surprised but nonetheless relieved. Some contained packing material, which Violet gathered together in an orderly manner into one box. A couple of the boxes contained redundant brochures and spare order forms for companies that hadn't existed for decades.

At no point did Violet add anything to any list, which was sort of unusual for a stocktake. But then it made sense that Violet only wanted to list the items she intended to keep.

Violet stamped yet another box flat and set it aside for recycling. Releasing a satisfied sigh and stretching, she asked, "Can I get you a drink? I've got some orange juice, if you fancy?"

"I'd love one. Thank you."

"Great. I won't be a sec."

"I'll carry on."

"You can take a break, you know."

"We're so close to finishing. Plus I'm finding all the stamping on cardboard therapeutic."

Violet laughed. "Me too. I'm enjoying it a bit too much." And with that Violet made her way upstairs. If Phoebe was not mistaken, Violet seemed to have a new spring in her step.

The thought that she might have helped Violet filled her heart with pride and joy. "Right. Last few boxes, here I come."

The remaining boxes were noticeably more fragile and gave the impression that if they were lifted, they would collapse in her arms. Phoebe bent down to them and explored them where they sat, all but hidden in the shadows of the shop. It made Phoebe wonder how old they were and when the last time was that someone peered inside. Unbelievably, the first box contained a beautiful black hat, a cool twist on a trilby, and white formal dress gloves, which together caused Phoebe to gasp with delight. Why wasn't the hat in a hat box? She lifted it free. It was so silky and delicate. The light from the window somehow found the black ribbon around the hat's rim, causing it to shine. The neatly tied deep purple bow at the front lent a luxurious finish to the hat's androgynous appeal. Just holding it made Phoebe feel refined. The accompanying soft cotton gloves were smaller than she would have expected for male attire. She resisted the temptation to put them on. Violet would no doubt be as excited as her to have found these and would wish to inventory them and keep them safe. Phoebe placed the hat and gloves gently on the counter. What a glamorous find.

The second box contained a variety of leaflets and brochures. Phoebe recognised a small stack of the Christmas brochure with Violet and Robert Unwin on the cover. Just as before, she found it difficult to take her eyes off Mrs. Violet Unwin. She was as entrancing as her Violet. Her Violet? When did Violet become hers? Phoebe looked towards the stairs. A flashback to them racing down the steep steps like fools for the pizza delivery made her smile. How she loved being foolish with Violet. This wasn't getting the boxes finished.

She returned her attention to the various leaflets and brochures, which seemed to span the era 1900 to about 1914. Did promotion pause when Robert went to war? Had Vi waited by the window for his return? Or was it Harry she worried for? How history kept its secrets tight-lipped.

The label on the third box caught her eye. On closer inspection, it became clear that it was a packing list for a variety of boots and shoes. It was dated 1st February 1908. The shoe company's gilded logo was really elaborate and distinctive. Phoebe carefully tilted the box towards her. The emblem read: *Leicester Co-operative Boot & Shoe Manufacturing Society Limited. Established 1886. Equity Works Trade Mark.* The image of a sun formed the background for a set of cones in the shape of seahorse tails. Each cone was topped with an abundance of what looked like fruit. Phoebe expected to find shoes inside the box, but instead the box was empty except for a large folded sheet of paper covering the base. A strong smell of ink and mustiness greeted her. She unpeeled the paper, which had shaped itself over time to become as much a part of the box as the box itself.

With the utmost care, Phoebe unfolded the paper. In bold capital letters, the resulting poster-sized sheet read: VOTES FOR WOMEN. READ OUR PAPER. 1d WEEKLY.

Chills prickled across Phoebe's skin. At the same time, Violet returned and set down their drinks on the counter.

"I've found something amazing," Phoebe said, "at the bottom of a box with the label *Equity Works*."

Violet moved to Phoebe's side and stared at the newspaper advert with her mouth slightly agape. "I've heard of that name before. I'm pretty sure that the local suffragette hero Alice Hawkins worked for them. Equity shoes were one of the first co-operatives with an active trade union in place."

"That sounds cool."

"It was. It was also closely linked with the Women's Social and Political Union. The suffragettes."

"That explains the paper, then. It doesn't explain what it's doing in your shop."

"There's definitely a connection between the suffragettes and Unwin's Emporium. And the connection seems to be Vi."

"That's so intriguing, Violet. All of this is just amazing."

Violet nodded. "We have more questions than answers, though."

"That's what makes it so enticing. The unknown begs to be discovered. Have you seen the hat and gloves? They were in the first box. Oh, and some more promotional shop brochures from before the First World War are in the second box."

"Really? Wow. Thanks for sorting all this." Violet raised her eyebrows in the direction of the hat. "It's unusual, isn't it."

"Try it on."

Violet hesitated.

"Go on. Here." Phoebe placed the hat on Violet's head. "Seriously, if I didn't know better, I would say it had been made for you. It's like it was waiting for you to find it."

"You found it."

"You know what I mean. Wear it tonight. For me."

Violet's cheeks flushed as she removed the hat and placed it with the items Mr. Duke had lent her. "Talking of tonight, we'd best get ourselves together." She reached for their drinks. She handed one to Phoebe and raised hers in the air. "Cheers for helping me."

"Cheers for helping me." They clinked glasses. It had been an amazing day. And they still had the evening ahead of them.

"Oh, wait. There's one more. It looks a bit worse for wear." As Phoebe lifted the last small box, dented and all but forgotten, something slid within it. "Ooh, intriguing." The last thing she expected to find as she peered inside was a small red leather jewellery box nestled in some light blue tissue paper.

"Violet."

"What?"

"Look." Phoebe lifted the jewellery box free. Holding her breath, she opened its lid. The first thing she saw was the light sparkling from gemstones. "No way. Can you see? It's a brooch in the shape of a flower set on a long pin. The flower has this amazing blue stone at its centre surrounded by glasslike jewels. It's stunning." Phoebe held out the open jewellery box towards Violet. "Oh my God, I feel sick. When I first saw the last cardboard box, for some reason I thought it was empty. I was a heartbeat away from stamping on it."

Violet took the jewellery box from Phoebe and blinked into it. It didn't look like she was breathing. She glanced at the back wall, now newly empty of the boxes that had hidden it for decades. "I can't believe such a precious thing was there all along."

Phoebe stood close at Violet's side. "You don't suppose the stones are real, do you?"

"Well, the pin is tarnished a little, so I guess it might be made of silver or at least plated. There's a definite possibility that the blue stone is sapphire and the glasslike stones—"

"Diamonds?"

"Yes."

"That's incredible. And the jewellery box is so beautiful too."

Violet carefully moved aside the advertising poster and the hat and gloves and rested the jewellery box on the counter. She eased the pin free from the cotton wool pad it rested on and held it in the palm of her hand. It looked like it might fly away. Violet cupped it safe and turned it over. "It has an inscription."

Phoebe's shoulder brushed against Violet's. "Can you read it?"

"Just. *For Vi, Always and always facing toward the light. H. 1911.*"

"The local suffragette motto from the banner." Phoebe glanced up to the ceiling. She nervously giggled as she said, "I was waiting for the thud. I remember that's what triggered it last time."

Violet blushed. "No thud this time."

She didn't seem entirely certain. She recalled Dee's advice not to frighten Violet so returned her attention to the inscription. "Could the *H* be Harry from the postcard?"

"It's possible." Violet returned the brooch to the safety of its box. "I remember from school that people thought it was just women who supported the suffragettes, but it wasn't. It was their husbands and families too. The web page with the image of the local suffragettes marching pointed out that when someone heckled Alice Hawkins at one of her rallies, saying something like *Go back to your family*, Alice's reply was that her family were right there with her."

"That's so cool. Although, awkwardly, Harry wasn't Vi's husband, was he?"

"No. The shop paperwork I've seen for this period clearly records Mr. Robert and Mrs. Violet Unwin."

"So, what do you do when you are given something that you don't want someone else to find?"

"You hide it. Although in boxes at the back of the shop is pretty risky. Robert could have found it or thrown it out, like we nearly did."

"Maybe she thought hiding it in plain sight was the best option. She was sort of right."

"She certainly had no way of knowing who would find it."

"But then I guess she couldn't exactly hand it down to her children. Who would she say Harry was? It seems like she left it to fate. What will you do with it?"

"Technically, it's the property of the shop and therefore belongs to Uncle Walter. I'll have to hand it over. I guess via Carl..."

Phoebe reached for Violet's arm. "*No*, don't give it to him. If it were me, I'd keep it. I think Vi would want you to have it."

Violet seemed to pause and it looked like she was listening, but not to Phoebe. She then shook her head, "I have no choice but to hand it over."

"Okay. I understand—well, I don't understand, but I respect your decision."

Violet placed the brooch out of sight in the drawer under the till. "Anyway, we need to get ready."

Violet frowned at the waistcoat on her stool. "Do you think my jeans and this shirt will work with the items Mr. Duke lent me?"

"I think he's given you them. And yes, they're perfect." She took a deep breath and with a courage that surprised her she added, "*You're perfect.*"

Violet looked at her and blushed, yet she didn't turn away. Instead, she said, "Mr. Duke…he mentioned you were quite taken with me."

Phoebe slipped her hand into Violet's. "I'm more than taken with you. I'm my happiest when I'm with you."

"Me too." The Christmas tree lights flickered on and caused them both to turn to the window. They stared at the magical display, lit as if just for them.

Without another moment lost, Phoebe leaned forward and kissed Violet on her cheek. Before she could tell Violet how beautiful she was, Violet placed the most tender of kisses on Phoebe's lips.

It wasn't Phoebe's first kiss, but if she never kissed anyone again, with the exquisite sensation of Violet's lips to hers, she knew she had experienced what a real kiss was. A kiss made of complete trust and unguarded desire. An infinite kiss that began at her lips and travelled through every atom of her being. A kiss which blocked out the world and united their hearts as one.

"Was that okay?" Violet asked, with a tone of the most endearing uncertainty. Her pupils were dilated, dark as a starless sky, and her lips were full, parted with their kiss and the promise of the kisses they were yet to share.

"More than okay." Phoebe kissed Violet with equal tenderness and equal need. Violet's body was so wonderfully familiar and fitted hers just perfectly.

When they eventually paused to take a moment, it was no surprise to Phoebe when Violet said, "This is going to sound a bit out there, but it feels like I've kissed you before. Even though you're the first person I've ever kissed. It feels so right, doesn't it? Like your lips were meant for mine."

Phoebe placed her palm to Violet's flushed cheek. "Everything about us feels right. It always has."

## Chapter Fifteen

How was this her life? When did she start walking across the city dressed in drag holding the hand of the coolest girl ever—unbelievably, a girl she had just spent the last hour kissing? She had thought there was nothing she couldn't imagine. Victory on the burning wastelands of war, kingdoms falling to brave assassins intent on a just revenge, daring explorers risking everything to be history's first. But nothing could have prepared her for the all-consuming mind-blowing impact of her first kiss. It was not just the breathtaking thrill that rippled through her body at Phoebe's touch. No, it was a signal thrown out to the universe and the never-thought-possible pulse of life in response. Her fantasies in comparison were mere imitations of life, but that kiss was what it felt like to be alive. It was so incredible it was difficult to believe it was real. What was going on?

Things like this didn't happen to her, for she was Violet Unwin, and up until three weeks ago she had felt utterly invisible.

"Violet?" Phoebe squeezed her hand. "You okay?"

They had paused at the door of The Banana.

"I'm fine. It's just, erm, all a bit new."

"You'll be okay, I promise. You can sit with me at the bar. Other than to serve customers, I won't leave your side until you find your feet."

"Thanks."

"And Violet…just so you know, it means the world to me that you're here." Phoebe gave Violet a quick kiss before leading her inside.

Gesturing to the costumes for the ball they had carried over from the Emporium, Phoebe then said, "Let's take these to Dee's office to keep them safe, and then we can head up to my room. I need to change for my shift."

"Okay."

"Miss Violet Unwin," Dee said, as they arrived at her office. "Welcome back to The Banana. You look great, by the way." Dee nodded to Violet's moustache. "Handsome bugger."

Violet's cheeks burned. "Thank you, and thank you for your gift."

"My pleasure. And I'm hoping that's *my* gift." Dee pulled at the edge of a bag and peeked inside. "Oh my God, it's my crown...and is that my cape?" Dee inched out the fur-trimmed cape and wrapped it around her shoulders. "Step aside please—Her Majesty, soon to be His Majesty, is in residence. What do you think, Violet? Does it suit me?"

Violet nodded. "Yes. Very much."

"Suits you a little bit too much, if you ask me." Phoebe placed the costumes next to Dee's desk.

"Pretty sure we didn't ask you, Frinky Boots." Dee gave Phoebe a look. "Now scram, the pair of you. The bar opens in half an hour."

"Let's go to my room before I get myself in any more trouble." Phoebe slipped her hand into Violet's. "You can see my stars."

"I guess you've seen mine." They both giggled.

Phoebe wasn't kidding when she said she'd painted her room black. Even her light switch and door handle had been muted of all colour or shine.

"It's shocking, isn't it." Phoebe looked about her.

"It's...unique."

"That's one way of putting it. I don't really know what I was thinking when I did it. Actually, I wasn't thinking. I was mainly hurting." Phoebe went to her wardrobe and pulled out a change of clothes. At the same time, she pushed a stray boot or two back into place. She gave a heavy sigh as she closed the wardrobe door.

Violet hated the thought of Phoebe in such distress. "Are you hurting the same? Sorry, you don't have to answer."

Phoebe stood still and looked down. "I think I'm becoming a bit more comfortable with how uncomfortable and uncertain life is. I think expecting certainty has hurt me the most. When I have my crap days, I try to remember that the world is far from perfect. When it works, I feel less pressure."

"That's a good plan. I'll try it too."

Phoebe looked up straight into Violet's eyes. "And there are fewer crap days since…since I met you."

Violet's heart swelled with the thought that she had mattered to someone, and that someone was Phoebe.

"I'm so thankful I met you, Violet." Without another word, Phoebe pulled off her jumper and stepped out of her jeans.

Violet didn't quite know where to look. Everything in her wanted to drink in each detail and quench her aching need at the sight of her. But how did she know if that would be okay? She'd seen Phoebe's body before, dancing around in Kylie's skimpy shorts. But this was different. *They* were different. She politely turned away and stared up to the ceiling and to the stars puncturing light through the darkness. "I love your stars." Violet glanced at Phoebe, who was buttoning a black shirt and gazing up at the ceiling with her.

"I'm thinking of adding a crescent moon."

Violet gave a distracted, "Yeah, that would be good." She tried her best not to look at Phoebe's bare legs, but they were just so beautiful.

She caught Phoebe's eye. Violet quickly looked down, embarrassed, and mumbled, "I'm sorry. I didn't mean to…stare at you."

Phoebe pulled on her jeans. "Sit with me a second."

Violet joined Phoebe on her bed. She tucked a pillow into her lap. She still couldn't bring herself to look at her. For surely she would give away with her eyes how much she wanted Phoebe.

"FYI, if I wasn't quite ready for you to see me in my undies, I would have changed in the bathroom. To be honest, if you hadn't checked me out, I would have worried that you weren't in the same place that I am. I want you to be curious about me. It's normal and natural. I'm curious about you."

Violet looked up. Phoebe rested her hand on Violet's knee.

Violet's heart was thumping so hard in her chest that it actually hurt. Would Phoebe's curiosity end in disappointment? "There's not much to be curious about. I'm small and skinny." Violet shrugged. "It's just how I am."

"I love how you are."

"You do?"

Phoebe nodded. "I'm excited by the thought of us."

Did Phoebe think Violet knew more than she did? About sex? About love? "I don't know what to expect. I have no clue about any of this."

"Me neither."

"You haven't had girlfriends before?"

"Nope. I've a string of drunken snogs to my name. It's never gone beyond that. I wasn't deliberately saving myself as such. Somehow, I knew I should feel more. And with you, I do. I feel so, so much more. Even though we've only known each other a short while and it's just the very beginning."

If Phoebe was wondering about her future and whether she would even be around in the city for much longer, she didn't seem to be giving that thought much headspace. It seemed to be her heart that was being given room to breathe and live. And it felt like her own heart was taking a full breath for the very first time.

"I'm not scared about what's happening." Violet shook her head. "I just can't quite believe it." They shared a smile that spoke of wonder.

"I actually think I *would* be a bit scared, but I'm not because it's you."

Phoebe obviously had complete trust in her. What would she think when she found out she'd been lying to her about the shop? "I don't want to mess things up."

"You're talking to the queen of messing things up. Let's just take things as we find them. And at a pace that feels right for us both."

Violet put her hand over Phoebe's hand resting on her leg. "I loved kissing you. *Really* loved it."

"Me too."

Depeche Mode's "Personal Jesus" blasted out from the bar below.

Phoebe looked genuinely cross. "How can she know the *perfect* time to disturb us?"

Violet laughed. "The timing could be better."

Phoebe looked at her watch. "Oh, it's nearly half-past five. Fair enough, I suppose." Phoebe took a deep breath. "So, are you ready for Sundays Are a Drag?"

She was anything but ready. "Yep."

Phoebe held out her hand and gently eased Violet from the bed. "I'm right by your side. Always."

True to her word, Phoebe held Violet's hand all the way to the bar and only let go of it to fetch her a stool. And as promised, she positioned it at the end of the bar, so Violet would have her right by her side.

"Okay, so this is normally Reggie the Regular's spot on a Sunday night." Phoebe patted the stool for Violet to take her place. "She never misses it. She's a huge Mr. Duke fan. I mean *serious* adoration. She's lovely, and there's always some fun mini drama going on in her life. It was an invasion of moths the other day. I can never tell whether she knows how funny she is, so I tend to keep a straight face, just in case."

"Got it." Violet smiled. It was clear how much affection Phoebe had for The Banana and its patrons.

Phoebe bent behind the bar, and the lights above the optics came on. She placed beer mats along the length of the counter. "They never use them. Tell a lie—they get *thrown* quite a lot."

Violet laughed.

"Okay, it looks like Dee's hooked up the kegs. I'll just empty the dishwasher."

"Can I help?"

"Nope. You are our guest."

"That'll be great—thanks, Violet." Dee strolled towards them from the direction of her office and threw her a bag of lemons. "Slice them thin as you can. Don't look at me like that, Frinky Boots. Violet's part of our crew now. No?" Dee's eyes shone with a knowing glint.

"Yes, but you can't expect Violet to work."

"I didn't expect anything. Violet offered. And we're not exactly talking a shift, Pheebs."

"I don't mind." Violet slipped from the stool. "I'd rather help you out."

Dee nodded at Violet and said, "There you go." Although the point was clearly aimed at Phoebe.

Phoebe put her hands on her hips and looked directly at Dee. "Oh my God, you're shameless."

Dee put her hands on her hips in reply. "*Oh my God*, and that is news to you in what way?"

Phoebe let out an exasperated sigh. "If I didn't like you so much…"

"Not my fault either. Zip it. Refill." Dee tapped on the ice bin. "And brace yourself, I'm letting them in." With that final word on the matter, she made for the entrance. As bosses went, Dee certainly *bossed* it.

There was nothing about this moment that Violet felt in charge of as nerves fluttered in her stomach. She concentrated on slicing each lemon to translucent states of thinness.

"Remember, I'm right here." Phoebe rested her hand over hers. Violet looked up into the reassurance of Phoebe's warm smile.

"Phoebe, love. What a day I've had." A woman all bundled up in layers of clothing climbed up on the stool Violet had just vacated. She wrestled with her scarf as if it was strangling her. It looked like she'd endured a storm, even though the winter evening was still and dry. "You're never going to guess what's happened." The woman picked up a slice of lemon from the pile Violet had cut. She bit into it and winced. "Lunatic in the flat above me went away for the weekend. Only left the kitchen tap on. I woke up this morning floating in my pyjamas."

Violet held in the urge to laugh. Phoebe kept a neutral expression. She was the very definition of a professional bartender or, for that matter, a doctor in the making. "That's terrible, Reg. I hope you've been able to get it sorted."

"The housing officer came first thing, in all fairness. She says she'll get on to the insurer for me. But honestly, Phoebe love, I've got underwear older than she is, so I'm holding out little hope that it will get sorted soon. And when the firemen turned up, she was quite the distraction, randy sods. If I had one mention of greasy poles, I had too many."

Phoebe bit at her lip. "Your usual?"

"Make it a large one."

Phoebe dutifully prepared a double measure of white wine and topped it up with soda water finished with a slice of perfectly cut lemon. She placed it in front of Reggie. "There you go. Easy on the spritz, just how you like it."

"Thank you, Phoebe love. You're a little smasher."

Despite Violet's best efforts to blend into the background of the bar, Reggie's gaze had fallen upon her. Reggie took another slice of lemon. This time she ate it slowly. "You're new," she said in a tone that implied *I could eat you in one bite.*

"Reg, this is Violet." Phoebe looked so proud, and Violet in turn couldn't have felt more wanted.

Reg cupped her hand to her ear. "Who?"

"I'm Violet. Pleased to meet you." Violet gave a nervous smile.

"Pleased to meet you too, Valiant."

Valiant? "Oh no, it's—"

"Yes, that's right, Reg. Valiant Unwin." Dee hung her arm over Reg's shoulder and looked directly at Violet. She was nodding and smiling. "Perfect, in fact."

Valiant Unwin. As nicknames went, Violet had to admit it was kind of cool, even though she felt anything but valiant. Was Dee taking the piss out of her? But that didn't seem like something Dee would do to her.

"Is Mr. Duke making an appearance tonight?" Reg looked at Dee as if her life depended on her answer.

"You bet. He'll see *you* later. Oh, here come the other acts we've got on tonight, Reg, and who I'll be sharing the stage with. You'll note I didn't say limelight." Dee waved to her two fellow performers. One was carrying a tan plumber's bag over their shoulder and the other, dressed in a silver sequinned jumpsuit, wheeled a small suitcase. They both waved back as they made their way across the room to the stage.

Dee then turned to Phoebe. "I'll be in my office getting ready. Shout if you need me."

"Will do."

"And enjoy tonight, Valiant Unwin."

"Thanks, Dee." Violet watched Dee stride away, and with every step and swagger begin the transformation into Mr. Duke.

Phoebe slipped her arm around Violet. "The name Valiant suits you."

"Dee was just joking."

"I don't think she was. I think you have been assigned your bold name."

"Bold name?"

"It's how I describe the idea of having a persona we can slide into now and then. You know, when we need to be someone maybe braver or more carefree than we feel in that moment. Performers use bold names all the time, if you think about it—their stage names or alter egos. Take Beyoncé, for example, she has Sasha Fierce. And Dee, of course, has Mr. Duke. Although this may become His Majesty or His Royal Highness. It's only a matter of time." They shared a smile. Violet then followed Phoebe's gaze across to the stage and to the drag artists unpacking the equipment for their act. "Many drag kings choose a persona name that brings everything together for them. Sometimes the name can be comedy camp and other times a little more insightful, or even cleverly both together. Do you see the performer in the white T-shirt and blue dungarees?"

"Yeah. I love the grease spot on their cheek."

"That's Handy Man Joe—*J-O-E*. Offstage, that's Jo, no *E*. They do local odd jobs and they're a really popular and trusted tradesperson. But tonight, Handy Man Joe will be offering a different type of plumbing service."

Violet laughed.

"And next to Handy Man Joe, that's Elvis the Pelvis, Mr. Duke's main competition. Not that he'll admit it. Let's just say, snake hips."

Reggie wagged her finger at Violet. "Not a patch on my Mr. Duke."

Phoebe nodded. "Absolutely, Reg. One moment, I just need to serve this customer."

Phoebe moved to deal with the customer a little further down the bar. Reggie was staring at Violet, and at the same time sucking on her straw. "Will you be performing tonight?"

"Me? No. I'm just having fun with the outfit." Violet pressed at her moustache. "I work at Unwin's Emporium. The costume shop." Would that be the last time she would say that?

"I know it well. I used to go there as a little girl for my party costumes. Odd little place. Always seems to have been there."

"It opened in 1898."

"Lots of history to it, then."

"Yes. Lots." Reggie had no idea how much. It felt strange to be away from it. She thought of Vi in her room and her heart ached. It struck her that she couldn't remember the last time she spent an evening away from the Emporium. Her holidays from school she'd spent helping in the shop. They were the best holidays ever. It didn't occur to her that going *away* on holiday was an option. Her uncle and aunt seemed to have days away but returned by the evening. Her aunt would holiday with her sister. And sometimes Carl would go with her uncle for a bonding trip which Carl always returned from in a sulk. The Emporium had been her work and her rest. It was everything.

"You two okay?" Phoebe returned to Violet's side.

"Yep, all good here," Violet said, mustering a smile.

Reggie gave a thumbs-up.

"Cool. Where was I? Oh yes, so offstage, Elvis the Pelvis is Lucy the accountant."

"Really? I love that." Violet had always loved to dress up. But it had felt like a guilty secret. The thought that others were openly exploring and enjoying their full self or another aspect of themselves or being someone completely different was just incredible.

"It's cool, isn't it. Lucy is the first to say that she embraces all that unapologetic masculine ego and energy and explodes it on stage. It's totally her release. And honestly the girls in the audience literally scream at her. They adore the fearless confidence she brings to her act."

Phoebe's face lit up in admiration as she spoke. Could Violet ever be fearless? But then maybe she could, for she was here tonight facing her fear of an ever-growing crowd of strangers.

"It's going to get busy," Phoebe said. "Sorry."

"Go do your thing. I'm fine."

Phoebe kissed Violet on the cheek. With her face still pressed to hers, she said, "Thank you for being here." And that was pretty much the last thing she said for the next two hours. To say it was full-on was an understatement.

Every now and then, Mr. Duke would appear from his office and lend a hand to help Phoebe catch up with the drinks orders. "We've got this, Frinky Boots," he would say each time. It made Violet wonder if Frinky Boots was Phoebe's bold name. Maybe Reg would know?

Reg had not moved from her stool the entire evening. She seemed to be content to just take everything in. What she didn't know was probably not worth knowing. And what she hadn't seen was probably not worth seeing.

"Can I ask you a question?"

"If it's about my age, Valiant love, I've scratched it off my library card for a reason."

"Oh no, it's not that. It's just I was wondering, Dee calls Phoebe *Frinky Boots*. Do you happen to know if that's her bold name?"

Reg screwed her face and cupped her palm to her ear. "Her what?"

"Her bold name. Like a name to use when you want to be a bit braver or even someone else."

"Oh. Got you. Like my neighbour downstairs when she's trying to avoid the bailiffs. Between me and you, she's never been Mrs. Smith."

Violet suppressed the urge to laugh. "Sort of."

"All I know is that it rhymes with *Kinky Boots*."

"What does?"

"Her surname, love. She's Phoebe Frink." Reg gripped Violet's arm. "I think it's about to begin."

Frink? Where had she heard that name before?

A trumpet fanfare came through the speakers. A royal fanfare. Violet and Phoebe looked to each other at the same time as the lights dimmed.

Handy Man Joe stepped up to the microphone. "Be upstanding for His Majesty, Mr. Duke."

The crowd parted and an ermine caped, becrowned figure, strode on to the stage. Phoebe moved to Violet and held her hand.

"Someone couldn't wait to wear their outfit for the ball," Phoebe said, smiling.

Even Violet couldn't quite have imagined how perfect it would be for him.

Mr. Duke pressed his moustached lip to the microphone, at the same time slipping the stand against his inner thigh. The crowd fell into mesmerised silence.

Mr. Duke raised his hand in the air and called out, "Ayyyyy-oh."

The crowd replied in instant union, "Ayyyyy-oh."

It was on. The evening of hip thrusts, of leaning into the baying crowd and sending them wild, of blowing lingering kisses, and of leaving everything out there on the stage had begun. Violet had stood holding Phoebe's hand tightly in amazed wonder. When did this become her life?

❖

"Vi? Are you awake?" Violet slowly pushed the door to Vi's room open. "I'm sorry. I know it's late. Can I come in?" Violet waited. "I've had the most incredible night. Well, day really. Phoebe and Mr. Duke have just walked me home. I've been at The Banana Bar. I'm not sure my feet touched the ground all the way back here." Violet placed her hand to her chest. "My heart is racing. I wanted to tell you about it. I've so much to share with you, in fact, that I won't sleep without talking to you. Would that be okay?"

Violet stepped into the room. The light from the landing lit the space just enough without needing to put on the main light. Violet made her way to the dressing table and sat on the stool. She looked at herself in the mirror and rested her hand to her face. Valiant Unwin stared back at her.

"This is my drag king look. Do you like it?" Violet listened for a whole minute. Nothing. She gave a sigh and pulled off her hat and placed it on the table. "Phoebe and Mr. Duke like it." She looked in the mirror again. "I know I look different, but it's still me. I've got a bold name now, would you believe? Valiant Unwin. For when I need to feel a bit more confident. I won't need it all the time. I'm still Violet." She peeled off the moustache and slipped it into the top pocket of her shirt. She took a last look at herself again. This time, her face seemed to blur at the edges.

"Vi?" Violet touched the mirror to the face looking back at her. "Hi. It's me. Were you with Phoebe and me this afternoon? I mean, it's okay if you were. I thought you might have been because of the tree lights. You see, I know they don't have a timer. Anyway, thank you for putting them on for Phoebe." Violet looked away from the mirror. "I think I might be falling in love with her, Vi. We kissed." Violet looked up. "But then you probably know that. We feel right together. It was like I had kissed her before. That makes no sense, does it. And, what's more, she might not even be staying in the city. I don't know what will happen to us if she leaves. I risk getting hurt, don't I? But then nothing about *not* being with Phoebe feels right either. So much is unknown for me. It feels like too much." Violet stared at the face looking back at her. "There's something else. We found a piece of jewellery in the storage boxes today. It was a brooch in the design of a flower made up of gemstones. It was extraordinary. Do you know anything about it? It's just, there was an inscription on it." Violet closed her eyes and she could see the words so clearly. *For Vi, Always and always facing toward the light. H. 1911.*

Violet opened her eyes and the face in the mirror was hers once more. "Vi? Are you here?" Why would she leave her now? Or was she still with her? "So do you recognise it? Phoebe wondered whether the *H* was Harry from the postcard. Do you remember the card? It was addressed to you. I'll get it for you. One sec."

With a peculiar impulse to hurry, Violet went to her room and switched on the light. She stopped short at the sight of the brooch resting on her bedside table. There was no doubt in her mind that she had left it in the drawer under the till. She gathered the brooch with the postcard and the brochure and brought them with her, back into Vi's room. She then carefully laid them out onto the dressing table. She sat on the stool and stared down at them.

"Why did you put the brooch in my room? It was safe in the drawer. If you're trying to tell me to keep it, I can't. It belongs to Uncle Walter. Everything does. I have to hand it over to Carl." Violet looked up into the mirror again. "I've no choice…" Hold on. In the reflection she could see that the wardrobe door was open. It was shut, wasn't it, when she first came in? She was sure it was. She turned around in her seat. Through the gap, she could see the hat in place on the shelf and the soft brown fur of the arm of Vi's coat hanging up. Her thoughts strayed to the bail form tucked in its pocket. Her heart caught in her chest, and her mouth turned dust dry. *Frink.* That's how she recognised Phoebe's name. Of course it was. She scrambled from her seat and went to the coat to fetch out the form. She laid it out on the table and read aloud the words, which now carried with them a whole new sense of importance.

"*Take notice that you Miss Harriet Frink are bound in the sum of two pounds to appear at the Westminster Police Court.*"

Miss Harriet *Frink*. Could she be related to Phoebe? Or was it a coincidence? But surely too much of a coincidence?

"Who is Harriet Frink, Vi? I know I keep asking you. I sense it's really important that I find out. I think you want me to find out. So please help me." Tiredness pressed upon her so much that she feared she would fall asleep where she sat. "I need to go to bed. I'll leave these here for now. Night-night."

Violet left Vi's room, leaving the door ajar. She slipped off her waistcoat, unlooped her tie from under her shirt, and collapsed on top of the bed. With the last dregs of energy, she dug into the pocket of her jeans and composed a text for Phoebe.

*Hey. Sorry to send this so late. Had the best day with you. Thank you. Can we meet tomorrow? There's something I want to show you. X*
She pressed send, not expecting a reply until morning. The bleep that followed made her jump.
*Hey. Can't sleep? Me neither. Thinking of you. Yes to tomorrow. How about a walk? I could even beg the night off work. We could meet at The Clock Tower at five thirty and see the tree lights? What do you think? X*
Violet took no time to reply. *Yes. Fab. Can't wait to see you. X*
Phoebe's reply of a single red heart was the perfect ending to an incredible and amazing day.

## Chapter Sixteen

It never ceased to amaze Phoebe how quickly things could change. One minute she had been a doctor in the making, and the next she was pulling pints in a drag bar. One minute she was lonely and confused, and the next she had found the tentative beginnings of something wonderful with a person with whom she just might allow herself to dare to glimpse the faintest glimmer of hope.

Hope.

She had got so cross with the notion of hope hanging around when it had no business to stay. It had felt like it was mocking her and making her feel weak for not having the strength to rally, dust herself down, and carry on. Fortunately, she had come to understand that the world carried on, regardless. She had simply closed her eyes and held on as best she could, adrift on fate's current, which it seemed had carried her to Violet.

Phoebe looked up at the large clock face. It read twenty-five minutes past five. Violet would be here with her at the Clock Tower any minute. What had Violet wanted to show her? The question had intrigued her all day. Had Violet found another piece of jewellery tucked away somewhere? Had she discovered more about Vi? Or was it something else? It couldn't be anything related to her. Could it? No. Why did she always assume everything was her fault or her mistake or her failure? But she *was* a failure. Wait. *Stop.* What was she doing? Ruminating again. How easily these negative thoughts returned. She'd been so engrossed lately with the costumes and Violet that she'd had mercifully no time to dwell upon internal chunters that insisted on reminding her of how crap she was. *Be in the moment, Frink.* What would she be doing if Violet was at her side? They would be looking at the tree together, wouldn't they?

She urged herself to concentrate on the huge Christmas tree, resplendent beside the Clock Tower. When she last stood staring up at this tree, it was dangling from a crane, trussed up and bare for all to see. And now you would not guess at the indignity it had suffered, witnessing it utterly transformed with metres upon metres of garlands of lights sparkling in the prism of brightly coloured baubles. At the very top of the tree was an illuminated star. It was impressive. But it could not compare with the star that Violet had made for her. Nothing seemed to compare with Violet.

Could it really be only a few weeks since they had first met? But since that first meeting, they had spent nearly every day together. With each day that finished, they arranged the next and the next, forming an invisible link that had bonded them from that first day and grown stronger and stronger until their first kiss. There was a strange urgency to them but not in a panicked way—more in a *this is right* way. This was the right path for her. She had found the person she was destined to meet. Had Violet felt that too? Was she hurrying to her now, in fact? And not because she didn't want to be late, but because there was no time to waste when you'd found your future?

The bell rang out to mark the half hour, and before the final note, Violet was at Phoebe's side holding two cones loaded with scoops of chocolate ice cream.

"I thought I was going to be late," Violet said, through gulps of ragged breath. "I had this spur-of-the-moment notion that I would buy us an ice cream. For some reason, I hadn't thought about the queue. And then I had no idea how to run with two ice creams."

They both laughed. Phoebe could sense the curiosity of those around them. Not that she cared. Instead, she placed a quick thank-you kiss upon Violet's cold flushed cheek. "Hi."

Violet looked back at her with eyes that glistened with fun and unmistakable happiness. "Hi. Oh, here, before it melts."

"Thank you so much. I love that you've bought us ice creams in December. Very cool, in all senses."

Violet giggled as she licked at the drips of ice cream that ran along the edge of her hand. Phoebe found it hard to draw her attention away from Violet's mouth and her bright red lips, plump with cold and smudged in chocolate.

Phoebe mustered concentration and proceeded to match Violet lick for lick. In no time the ice creams were just a sticky joyful memory.

"They've done a great job with the tree." Violet stood with her head tipped back, taking in every last detail. Phoebe slipped her hand into Violet's, and they stood together with their sides pressed close.

"It's not bad." Phoebe gave a shrug. "Not as good as yours, though. It's lovely to see you, by the way."

"You too." It looked for all the world as if Violet wanted to kiss her almost as much as Phoebe wanted to embrace her and hold her tight.

"I've been very intrigued by your text," Phoebe said with a broad smile. "What do you want to show me?"

Phoebe watched Violet take a deep breath in response. What did that mean? *Oh my God, please don't let it be something bad.*

"Okay, brace yourself for something a bit…" Violet frowned.

Phoebe held her breath. A bit what?

"How do I put it…of a coincidence. As in, I don't quite know what to make of it."

"Now I'm even more intrigued."

"Tell you what, let's take a seat for a sec." Violet led Phoebe to a nearby bench, and they sat huddled up together. "You know I said I've been dreaming a lot recently?"

"Yes."

"You remember the fur coat that Dee wanted to rent for Mr. Duke?"

"Uh-huh."

"Well, in my dream, Mr. Burrows…" Violet stopped herself short. She looked momentarily uncomfortable. "He's just a man who visited the shop recently. Anyway, in my dream, he was searching through the pockets of the fur coat."

Phoebe nodded. "Strange."

"It gets stranger. You see, I remembered the dream, and out of curiosity I checked the pockets of the coat. I honestly thought I wouldn't find anything. But I did."

"No way. Really? What was it?"

"A bail form from The Metropolitan Police. The date on it wasn't clear—maybe 1907 or 1909."

"That's incredible."

"I know. And there's something else about the form I need to show you. It's just, it felt too precious to bring it with me. Had I thought, I could have taken a photo of it, but now I have an even better idea. Follow me."

"Ooh, where are we going?"

Violet held out her hand for Phoebe. "To what was the headquarters of our local suffragettes. Fourteen Bowling Green Street."

"Okay, that's seriously awesome." Everything about being with Violet was seriously awesome.

They were soon swept up in the excitement of the city streets illuminated by colourful Christmas decorations, and heady with the festive anticipation spilling out from pubs and shops along the way. Before they knew it, they had turned the corner into Bowling Green Street. Phoebe spotted the round wedding cake shaped majesty of Hansom Hall coming into view at the far end. Her thoughts turned in an instant to the image of the Hall as the backdrop for the photo of the marching women. It was as if with every step they were travelling back in time.

Violet eventually stopped next to an information board. Phoebe had passed it many times and now wondered why she'd never thought to read it. How much she must miss each day.

Violet lit the torch on her phone and shone it onto the surface of the board.

With excitement thrilling through her, Phoebe immediately recognised images from the city's history website. She pressed her finger to the photo of the proud women carrying their banner and poised to take their message—*Always and always facing toward the light*—to the people of Leicester. "They never cease to enthral me."

"Me too. But this is what I want to show you." Violet focused her light upon the photograph of a bail form. "It was served upon Alice Hawkins. However, it's pretty much, give or take, the same form as the one I found in the fur coat." Violet looked at her. "With the notable exception of the name."

"Whose name is on your form?"

Violet took a small intake of breath. "Harriet Frink."

*What?* "Did you say *Frink*? That's my name."

"I know. Reg told me at The Banana. It took me a little while to make the link."

"*Harriet Frink*. That's kind of freaky. Do you think she's related to me? I mean, it's not exactly a common name, is it?" Phoebe stared back at Alice's form. "What does that say? It's hard to read." Phoebe ran her finger under the line that began *To answer the charge of*...

Violet leaned closer to the board and read aloud, "Disorderly conduct and resisting police."

Phoebe looked at Violet. "Is that what it said on Harriet's form too?"

"Yes, I'm pretty sure it did."

"Did Harriet get arrested with Alice Hawkins?"

Violet frowned. "I don't know. We'd be guessing. So, possibly, possibly not. Many brave women were doing many brave things—some alone and some as a group. All incredible, though."

Phoebe couldn't find the words to express how peculiar it all felt. It was the weirdest sensation of familiar and strange at the same time. Could it really be that she had a relative who was a suffragette, breaking laws and risking everything for women to have the vote? How incredible that would be. Phoebe's gaze fell once more upon the photo of the marching women, settling upon the suffragette with the bow tie and the hat she had so admired.

"And that's not all." Violet's tone was tentative and heavy with whatever she was about to say. Phoebe's nervousness returned.

"Phoebe, the fur coat belonged to Vi."

What? "It *did*? I don't understand. What was Harriet's form doing in the pocket of your great-great-grandma's coat? Unless they knew each other, of course. Although that still doesn't explain what it's doing there."

"It's a bit of a mystery, isn't it?"

"How freaky would it be if Harriet was related to me and Harriet and Vi actually knew each other?"

"Seriously freaky. They might even have hung out here together." Violet gestured to the red brick building across the street from where they stood. "In the suffragette headquarters."

Phoebe compared the picture of the headquarters displayed on the board with the actual building, triggering goosebumps along her body.

It was the same Victorian terrace with a shop window. The difference was that instead of selling vapes, the 1911 building had the sign VOTES FOR WOMEN across its front.

Violet pointed again to the board. "It says here that on the night of the census of April 1911, women stayed over at the headquarters." Violet carefully read the exact words, "*Refusing to be counted in protest at their continuing lack of a parliamentary vote.* Imagine that. They were so determined, weren't they?"

Phoebe shook her head. "I can't imagine being so brave."

Violet frowned a little. "I don't think in the moment you know that you *are* being brave."

"But you'd know what you were risking."

"I guess so. But then, maybe the risk to their equality and freedom by doing nothing was far greater."

Of course, the heart of the suffragette cause. Every day, Violet impressed her more. Phoebe slipped her hand into Violet's. "Can we go back to your place? Get some fish and chips on the way maybe? I can see Harriet's form, and we could spend the evening together."

"I'd love that."

"Me too." The thought filled Phoebe with even more joy than she had ever thought possible.

❖

Violet lay contentedly on her bed, staring up at the stars on her ceiling. She'd tucked one hand behind her head and the other rested on her stomach full of fish and chips and laughter. She could hear Phoebe in the bathroom singing Kylie's "Spinning Around" and guessed she was probably doing the moves as well. The thought made her smile. Everything about Phoebe made her smile.

After a moment, the singing stopped, and the bathroom door opened.

"Violet."

Violet sat up and glanced in the direction of Phoebe's voice. Phoebe was standing in the hallway staring into Vi's room. "You okay? Are you ready to see Harriet's form?"

"Yes." Phoebe's mildly alarmed expression didn't make her *yes* that convincing. "The dressing table stool has fallen over again. I didn't hear it this time." Phoebe looked across at Violet. "Did you?"

"Nope."

"I'll pick it up for you."

Violet heard the flick of the light switch. "No. It's okay." The thought of Phoebe alone in Vi's room filled her with panic. She wasn't quite sure why. "I'll do it."

Violet scrambled from her bed and made for the stool, only to find Phoebe bending down in front of it and picking something free from its base.

"There's something stuck to the bottom of the seat. It looks like the back of an envelope."

Violet stood beside Phoebe in a state of complete amazement.

"There we go. Got it." Phoebe turned the sealed envelope over and found a blank front. Gently, she pinched at its edges. "It feels like there might be something in it."

"Do you think you can open it?"

"I'll try. Although I'm scared to rip it in case I tear its contents." Surprisingly, the seal gave way as if it had been newly licked and not yet set. Phoebe inched out a black-and-white photograph and held it in front of them.

Violet placed her hand over her mouth at the sight of two women smiling at the camera, standing arm in arm. The one on the left was dressed in a smart trouser suit with a tie, hat, and spats-style shoes. The other wore an ankle-length full skirt accompanied with a pretty floral blouse. A cardigan was draped over her shoulders, and her arm was tucked affectionately around the other woman's. They gave the viewer the sense that they had made each other laugh just as the photographer had called their names, and they had glanced over as the shutter clicked with the joke still lingering in their eyes.

"Violet, isn't that Vi?" Phoebe looked up at her with eyes wide with wonder.

"Yes. And I recognise the woman standing with her too." Violet pulled her phone from her pocket and brought up the now so familiar image of the marching women. "It's her." Violet pointed to the screen. "I'm certain of it."

"Oh my God, you're right. It's the woman with the bow tie."

Phoebe looked back at the photo of the two women. "And that symbol, can you see? The one with the cones, on the building behind them. That's the same one as on the box we found in the shop."

"Yes, you're right. Equity Shoes. I'm wondering now if they were suppliers to the Emporium. I mean, the box certainly suggests it. I'll check our records. Is there anything on the back of the photo?"

Phoebe turned the photo over. Her eyebrows rose and she swallowed several times. She looked at Violet. "There's a faint line of writing. I can read it. *You and me, girl, impressing Sylvia P in style. Yours ever, Harry. Summer 1907.* Hold on, we thought Harry was a man." Phoebe's expression drifted off as if her thoughts had travelled to a place where everything made sense. A place of revelation. "When all along, Harry was a woman."

Violet nodded. "And what if"—she reached for Harriet's bail form resting on the dressing table alongside the brochure, postcard, and jewellery box—"Harry is short for—"

"Harriet." Phoebe stared at the form in total wonder. "Harriet *Frink*. I still can't quite take it in." Phoebe took a seat on the stool. Would she look in the mirror as Violet did? Would she see someone other than her?

Instead, Phoebe's attention fell from the form to the other items in turn eventually settling on the jewellery box. "It's an amazing collection from your great-great-grandmother's time."

"Yes. It's quite incredible." Could she tell Phoebe that she'd mysteriously discovered the brooch in her room even though they both knew she'd put it in the drawer? But then how much could she say before she frightened Phoebe away?

"Although…" Phoebe said, her forehead furrowing to a frown.

"What?"

"I'm a bit puzzled. Why would Vi have so many things related to Harriet, either belonging to her or from her?"

Violet shrugged. "They were both suffragettes. Or at the very least, Vi was a supporter of their cause. I'm pretty sure the *Sylvia P* mentioned on the back of the photo is Sylvia Pankhurst, the daughter of Emmeline."

"That's amazing, isn't it?"

"It's thrilling. So, it's possible they were in and out of each other's houses. They were close friends who shared a common cause. Emotions can run high."

"Maybe. Although, what about the brooch? We originally reckoned it was a gift from Harry to Vi. The only reason you'd give something so valuable to someone is if you cared for them. I mean *really* cared for them. And then the note on the back of the photo ends *Yours ever*. I mean, those are quite passionate words."

Violet waited a moment to see if she could feel Vi's presence. What must she think of their speculation? Or was this her way of telling Violet about Harriet? Knocking the stool over until the envelope was found? Hoping they would find the clues about the place? After a moment, she said, "It's possible there was more to it."

"I like to think they loved each other," Phoebe said, her gaze resting on Violet.

Would she add *like us*? Violet held her breath for a second. No, of course not. It was too soon. But then nothing about them felt too soon. It felt wonderful.

"I can't wait to do some research to see if I can trace Harriet in my family line. I'm so intrigued to find out."

"Definitely."

"Can I come over Wednesday afternoon? We could look online together. I could even beg the evening off work. I'm sorry, I'm sounding so pathetic, aren't I? Constantly asking to be with you."

"*No.* Remember, I asked to see you today. It's not just you. I count the hours until I can see you again. Not literally, obviously." They chuckled.

"Dee won't start to worry about me for another hour. I could make us a tea?"

"I'll do it. You're my guest. Make yourself comfy in my room if you want."

Phoebe's eyes shone with excitement. "Okay. See you in there."

"Yep." Violet made for the kitchen. She couldn't make the tea quickly enough. She glanced back at Phoebe one last time to find that she was staring at the photo of Harry once more. Violet knew what it was to hope that the woman in a photograph was part of you and to look for yourself in her. What would Wednesday bring? And how many more revelations did Vi have in mind?

## Chapter Seventeen

Violet had yawned her way through Tuesday. Phoebe had eventually left just before midnight and then only after a grumpy call from Dee telling her off for not sending a text. "I know you just want to be with Violet. We've all been there, Pheebs. Goodness only knows I had to be crowbarred off Suzie. But don't be that thoughtless plonker who worries others. Got it?" Phoebe had apologised profusely. Violet had wondered what it had been like the next morning over breakfast at The Banana. But she knew in her heart that Dee would get it. More than anyone, Dee seemed to understand what it meant that they had found each other. Violet couldn't have valued that more.

Thankfully, it had been quiet in the shop with customers mainly calling in to return items. Only one visitor, Lois Lane, aka Mrs. Allen, had needed Violet's particular assistance. Mr. Allen had been watching the women's football on the television. It had piqued his interest. Mrs. Allen had called in just on the off-chance that Unwin's Emporium might stock a referee's costume.

"What would I do without you?" Mrs. Allen said on leaving. Violet had smiled and wished her a good day. There wasn't another costume shop in the city. So what Mrs. Allen would do, she really didn't know. If Mrs. Allen had wanted to order online, then she would have done. What she wanted was the personal touch. A confidant. It was one of the things Violet liked most about her job and one of the many things she would miss.

That said, it was a relief when five o'clock came and she could close the door.

As she turned the key in the lock, her phone buzzed in her pocket.

Pulling her phone free, she could see it was a message from Phoebe. *Hey, been thinking of you. Hope your day has been good? xx.*

Violet's heart raced. Texting her reply, she made her way to the stool behind the counter. She pulled up short with a cry of pain. Her leg had caught on an open drawer from the cabinet. Curiously, it was the same drawer which had surprised her before by opening seemingly of its own accord—not that Violet blamed the drawer. Rubbing furiously at her shin, she cast an angry glance to the ceiling. "Seriously, Vi. You couldn't just leave whatever paperwork from this drawer you need to show me on the counter? I mean, you move hats, open locked doors, and fiddle with Christmas tree lights. And that's just some of the stuff I'm aware of. Busting my leg won't help us." Violet collapsed onto the stool with a sigh. "No one can help us."

Her phone buzzed in her hand. *One, two, three, four...that's me counting the hours 'til tomorrow* :) *P xx*

A sickening wave of guilt rolled in Violet's stomach. "I need to tell Phoebe, don't I? About this place. But how do I tell her that in a few weeks the Emporium will be no more? Our special space will be gone. I should have told her from the start. She'll think I'm weird for not saying anything. And she's shared so much with me. What happens if she doesn't want to see me again?" Violet looked over to the window at the lights on the tree, twinkling their colours against the glass pane.

The words *Always and always facing toward the light* played on her lips. "What happens if I can't see the light?" Her shin ached, and she pressed her hand against it.

She texted Phoebe, *Hey, day been quiet. How about you? xx*

Phoebe's reply came back instantly. *Overslept, had a walk, helped Dee—still a bit pissed off with me—restock. Just about to start my shift. You okay? xx*

What could she say? *Yep. A bit tired, that's all. Five, six, seven...* She added a heart and pressed send.

Phoebe's immediate reply of *Dirty stop up* :) made her briefly smile. Why hadn't she told Phoebe? And why hadn't she come up with a plan for her life after the Emporium? She knew why. If she told Phoebe, it would be real. And...Violet's eyes smarted...there was no life for her after the Emporium. How could there be?

A creak from above made her look to the ceiling once more. Her thoughts turned to Vi's room and to the objects laid out on the dressing table. She called to mind the image of Harry dressed sharply in her suit. What would she think of Violet if they met? A feisty suffragette not afraid to break the law for what she believed was right would surely think Violet was being pathetic. Did Vi think that too?

"I'm not weak, you know. I just don't know what to do." She looked down at the floor only to find her attention caught by the open drawer.

She carefully slipped from the stool. With a slight wince, she bent down and lifted the entire contents from the drawer and dropped the papers onto the counter. Fanning them out, she found nothing that caused her to question what she was seeing. It was just a collection of completed order forms for miscellaneous stock and receipts from costume hires. There was no sign of Equity Shoes or mention of a Harriet Frink. Maybe it wasn't this drawer.

Violet bent to the drawer labelled 1919–1925. It was locked, wasn't it? But then, if the past few weeks had shown her anything, it was that rules of reason did not always apply. Her heart quickened as she pulled at the drawer and felt it give way and slide open. A careful rifle through it revealed similar contents. The paperwork clearly showed that Robert and Vi were still the proprietors of Unwin's Emporium. The only notable item was the Christmas brochure for the year 1919. This time, Vi and Robert were standing together by the Christmas tree. Vi held a baby in her arms, and a young boy, no more than five or six, was gripping her skirt. Robert held a protective arm around Vi's waist. They looked tired but proud. The heading read: *From Our Family to Yours, Wishing Our Customers the Most Wonderful of Festive Seasons.*

Violet brought the brochure out of the drawer and placed it on the counter. What about Harry? Were she and Vi still in touch?

"Were you happy, Vi?" Violet waited. Nothing. She stared down at the open drawers. If only their contents could tell her more. Hold on. Was she imagining it, or was the 1900–1914 drawer shallower than 1919–1925? The latter seemed to hold much more.

Violet bent down and reached into the far recesses of the empty drawer. Her fingers pressed against the wooden sides and then to her surprise they touched upon a piece of material that did not come away when she tugged at it. It seemed to have got itself wedged somehow.

Violet lay down on her side, lit the torch on her phone, and shone it into the wooden box. A piece of purple satiny material caught the light.

It was trapped between the left-hand side and the base of the drawer. Violet knocked on the base, which sounded surprisingly hollow. She repeated the action on the drawer next to it, which gave a duller sound. It couldn't be a false bottom, could it? What if she damaged the drawer by trying to push it? But then what if…

Violet stood and stared at the drawer. "Vi. I need you to tell me if I should try to force the bottom." Immediately, the front door handle rattled and the bell struck once. Violet stood petrified. She had expected nothing. *Don't be frightened, don't be frightened*, she repeated over and over. Violet took a deep breath. "Okay. If I break it, I'm blaming you. Deal?" This time Violet didn't wait for a response. She knelt in front of the drawer and pulled the sleeve of her jumper over the heel of her palm. If she hit the wood too hard, it would hurt her hand before it hurt the drawer. That was her reasoning, at least. She banged at the base gently at first. It did not move. She would need to hit it harder. With her eyes closed and lips pressed together, she gave a single sharp and firm bang on the base near the front of the drawer. To her surprise and relief, it gave way.

She shone the torch of her phone into the drawer once more. The purple material that had poked through had been wrapped into a ball. Violet lifted it away and sat on the floor with her back to the cabinet. With the utmost care, she unwrapped the material and fed it through her fingers, letting it unravel to form a long cut of purple satin. It took no deciphering to know in an instant what it was. This was a suffragette's sash. It was only when she'd unwrapped all but the last section that she stopped, and her breath caught. "You *were* a suffragette and not just Harriet." Violet stared in wonder at the finely embroidered white thread spelling out the initials *V. U.* "In my heart, I knew you were. I feel your strength, you see. Your courage. I want you to know that."

Unwrapping the last length of the sash revealed a slim navy-blue leather box. Violet couldn't quite believe what she was seeing. Protected for decades in the embrace of Vi's sash and shaded from the damage of light and the intrusion of foreign eyes, the box was in immaculate condition.

"Is this another piece of jewellery? Are you okay for me to open it?" This time Vi's answer appeared to be silence. "I'll be careful."

With as much care that she could possibly take, Violet opened the box.

One thing for sure, it was not jewellery. Far, far, from it. "It's a medal." Displayed on a bed of green felt, a short strip of webbing in purple, white, and green was held between two metal clips. The engraving on the top clip read *For Valour*. Hanging from the bottom clip was a coin-like shape inscribed with the words *Hunger Strike*.

Violet's awestruck gaze fell upon the underside of the lid. Emblazoned in gold on a pillow of cream satin were the words Violet knew in that instant she would never forget: *Presented to Harriet Frink by the Women's Social & Political Union in recognition of a gallant action, whereby through endurance to the last extremity of hunger and hardship a great principle of political justice was vindicated.*

Violet couldn't even begin to imagine the suffering Harry had endured. Was her imprisonment related to her bail form? Or was she a repeat offender and this medal was for something else? Something defiant, no doubt.

"How proud you must have been of her, Vi." Did Vi escape arrest?

What would Phoebe think when she knew? More than anything, Violet hoped that Harriet was related to Phoebe, so that Phoebe could feel proud too.

Violet closed the lid on the box. Above everything, she must keep this safe. As she stood with the sash and box held tightly in her grasp, she glimpsed a note slipping onto the floor. It must have been underneath the box. Placing the sash and box onto the counter, she bent to pick up the note.

She blushed at the words intended for another's gaze—for another Violet.

*I hungered for you, Mrs. Violet Unwin.*

## Chapter Eighteen

*Why didn't you tell us before?* The memory of her mother's words played over and over, drowning out the pleasure and excitement Phoebe always cherished on her walk through the city streets to Violet. Every trick Phoebe had learned to escape these thoughts didn't seem to be working. How many shades of green could she see in the trees? How many pigeons could she count? How many shoppers were wearing boots?

The last thing Phoebe had expected when she woke that morning was for her parents to turn up at The Banana out of the blue. In fact, her day had begun full of excitement. She had chewed Dee's ears off over breakfast about whether or not Harriet would turn out to be related to her, and what were the chances of Harriet's bail form being in Vi's fur coat? Dee had listened quietly, only commenting once to caution her not to be disappointed if there was no Harriet connection. Phoebe had even completed chores with minimal moaning. When the doorbell went, she didn't even need Dee to say *It's your turn* for her to race to open it. And then the excitement stopped. Everything stopped as reality arrived on her doorstep unannounced.

She should have guessed this day would come. Her phone calls home had become far less frequent this term and she had been continually evasive about her plans for Christmas. She knew that once she actually went home and saw her parents, she could not look them in the eye and lie. The game would be up.

Thank God for Dee who was lovely with them. "Perfect timing," she had declared without showing a moment's surprise at their arrival. "Why don't we all have a seat at the kitchen table. I've just boiled the kettle." She hadn't. She'd just downed a full fat Coke and a paracetamol. And in what way was it perfect timing? There would never be a perfect time.

Phoebe couldn't say a word. Dee had stepped into the silence and explained that Phoebe was taking time out from her studies to catch her breath and regroup. She had added in a firm, yet kind, way that this was a perfectly sensible thing to do. She then confirmed that the university were fine with it and were keeping in touch with her, and Phoebe was welcome to stay at The Banana for as long as she needed. She'd then given Phoebe a kick under the table. "Isn't that so, Pheebs?" Phoebe had nodded, managing to mumble, "I'm sorry." Her mum had pressed her hand to hers. "Why didn't you tell us before?"

❖

Phoebe arrived at the door of the Emporium almost without realising. She glanced back from where she'd come to see what chaos she had no doubt caused by crossing the roads without looking. Thankfully no cyclists were raising their fists at her this time.

"Hey." Phoebe turned at Violet's voice to find her standing in the doorway, smiling. Her smile soon faded to a look of concern. "You okay?"

"To be honest, I don't know."

"That's all right. Come in out of the cold." Violet tugged lightly at the sleeve of Phoebe's coat, encouraging her inside. "Sometimes it's difficult to know how you feel, isn't it?"

Phoebe slipped her arms around Violet's waist and kissed her. She wouldn't say *I missed you* because she feared sounding too needy. But she hoped her tight embrace would say it for her.

Violet whispered in her ear, "I missed you too," before she tucked her hand into Phoebe's and led her upstairs to the comfort of her room.

It was so good to be back in Violet's space and to be amongst the things Violet treasured. It had been hard to leave Violet on Monday night. Everything in Phoebe wanted to stay and kiss her yet more and hold her ever closer. Every now and then, Violet had paused from their kissing and looked at her with flushed cheeks and eyes full of wonder and need. That had only made Phoebe want her more. It was like they were beginning a magical journey together, and every kiss, every tentative touch, made them ever more curious as to where this adventure would lead. If Dee had not rung, she wasn't sure that either of them would have wanted their explorations to stop.

"I love being here with you," Phoebe said, dropping her bag onto the floor before pulling off her coat and hanging it from the door handle of Violet's wardrobe.

"Me too." Violet collapsed onto her bed with her arms out wide. "I wish more than anything we could stay here forever."

Phoebe clambered over Violet, causing her to giggle. Eventually, she found her place amongst the soft blankets and plump cushions, settling to sit with her back against the wall. "Deffo. Although can we go out for ice cream every now and then?"

Violet rearranged herself to rest her head in Phoebe's lap. "Absolutely, emergency rations." They smiled together. But Phoebe couldn't quite find it in her heart to laugh. The emotions of the morning had left her bruised and sore. She took several deep breaths attempting to rally herself and hoping that she wouldn't bring the mood down. Today was meant to be exciting and about discoveries and maybe more. *Come on, Frink.*

"Tell me to mind my own business," Violet said, looking up at her, "but has something happened?"

Phoebe took a deep breath in. Just recalling the last few hours asked her to be stronger than she felt capable of. "My parents turned up at The Banana this morning. Completely out of the blue. They'd gone to my halls and been told by another student that I wasn't there any more and that they could find me at The Banana."

Violet sat up and reached for Phoebe's hand and held it tight. "No way. I'm so sorry, Phoebe. You'd think they would have messaged you to say they were coming."

"They wanted to surprise me. Well, they did that for sure. I knew at some point I'd have to face them. I just wasn't prepared for it to be today. Thank God, Dee was there. Otherwise…" Phoebe shrugged.

"You'd have handled it."

Phoebe shook her head. "I couldn't even bring myself to speak. I just sat there at the kitchen table saying nothing, like a right lemon. My mum asked me several times if everything was okay. It took Dee to explain about uni and about me being at The Banana. She was brilliant with them. With us all."

"Were your parents okay with the news?" Violet couldn't have sounded more concerned.

"I don't know really. My dad didn't say much. He just mainly looked a bit embarrassed. My mum, on the other hand, looked utterly bewildered. And then, after a few moments, she said that she and my dad had been wondering for some time if something was wrong, if maybe I had a boyfriend who'd become a distraction. And I kept thinking—but you never really pressed me on any of this. The closest you came to asking how I was, was to say *I can only imagine how well you're doing.* But there was never a pause for me to say that no, I wasn't doing well."

Violet's grip on her hand never wavered.

"I sat there at Dee's kitchen table, watching my mum fiddling with her mug of tea that had long gone cold, and all I could think was *You never really wanted to know, did you? You didn't want anything to change. You didn't want* me *to change.* And that was that—something burst in me, and I told them everything. All the things I'd felt but never said just came spilling out. That I found being the perfect daughter for them really hard and a constant worry that I would let them down. I remembered Dee saying something before about how you can fear failure so much that it becomes self-fulfilling. I told them that too."

Violet shifted a little. "What did they say?"

"Nothing at first. They looked completely shell-shocked. I just carried on, regardless. Dee was trying to catch my eye, but I ignored her. I knew I was upsetting them, but I couldn't stop talking. I told them that I loved them, but they needed to understand that I had changed. I was no longer their little girl. And that going forward I would be doing things on my own terms. Setting my own goals that may or may not coincide with theirs for me."

"That's incredibly brave."

"And then without pausing for breath I told them that, yes, I had met someone and how important they were to me and in no way a distraction and every way a life saver. I looked them in the eye and said her name is Violet Unwin, and she is the most magical, incredible human being on this planet. Because you are."

Violet's cheeks flushed pink. "I think you're a bit biased."

"I'm more than *a bit* lucky to have met you, more like. Do you know what else I kept thinking about? The marching women. Harriet marching in her bow tie with that defiant look about her. Those brave women have fired something up in me. And I like it."

"I like it too. Totally kick-ass." They shared the broadest of smiles. Then, speaking a little more hesitantly, Violet asked, "What did your parents say when you told them about me?"

"That's the funny thing. I was expecting to have to explain myself or defend us. But they seemed almost relieved—like a girl would be less trouble than a boy who would get me pregnant and steer me away from my career. I could tell my mum wanted to ask more about you, but she kept it in. At least for now. Don't be surprised if you get an invite at Christmas. You don't have to come, of course."

"I'll come. Only if you want me to."

"I do." Phoebe lifted Violet's hand to her mouth and kissed it.

"How did you leave things with them? Are they still in town?"

"We left things sort of okay, considering. I think they were still taking everything in. They've gone up north to visit friends. I was on the way. I wasn't the destination. But they said they'd call in again on the way home on Friday morning for us to chat more, which is something. And actually, on a positive note, I did remember to ask my dad if he knew anything about the Frink family line. I thought it would lighten the mood."

"Ooh, good thinking."

"Given everything, it wasn't exactly the best time to talk about it, so I didn't go into details about why I was asking. I just said casually that I had been wondering. He was only able to go back to his grandfather, Frank Frink. But at least it was more than I knew."

"That's brill." Violet gave her the warmest of encouraging smiles. "I reckon you've enough info to begin an online search."

"I hope so. I can't tell you how close I came to looking up Harriet last night."

"I'm amazed you didn't. I'd be really tempted. In fact, I've something to show you…" Violet hesitated and then gave a small shake of her head. "It can wait, though. You've had such a full-on morning. Have you eaten? Do you want me to make you something?"

"I'm not hungry, to be honest. But I'm gagging for a tea."

Violet gave a thumbs-up. "One builder's brew coming up."

"Thanks. And thanks for listening."

"Always. I think it's good you've spoken to your mum and dad. As stressful as it was, I reckon it will help."

"Yes, you're probably right. I'd been dreading something like this morning happening, and now that it has, I feel kind of numb but sort of relieved as well."

"I bet." Violet's thoughts seemed to drift away, only to quickly return at the growl of a motorbike passing on the street outside. "Won't be a mo."

With Violet making tea in the kitchen and with the sound of the kettle boiling in the background, Phoebe reached for her bag and pulled out a page of notes, along with her laptop. She called through to Violet, "I can't wait any longer to find out about Harriet, so I'm signing up for a free trial on one of those genealogy websites."

Violet shouted in reply. "Sounds like a plan to me."

By the time Violet returned to her room, Phoebe had signed up and was working her way through the rudiments of a family tree built of three generations of Frinks.

Having placed their tea on her side table, Violet tucked herself up on the bed next to Phoebe.

Phoebe turned the laptop to face them both. She placed her finger by her own blank photo and name. "You start with you and then work your way back through the generations. I've skipped my mum and dad and gone straight to my paternal grandfather, Grandpa Pete, tracing the line of the Frink surname to as far back as I can where I have some facts."

"Makes total sense."

"Except now I'm a bit stumped as I keep reaching dead ends."

"I wonder…let's try something different. How about searching for *Harriet Frink* in the UK Census Collection instead. It might just tell us a bit more based on address. We could start by putting in Leicester 1911. There's a strong possibility that Harriet was living in the city at the time of the 1911 census. We know she was an active suffragette around this time."

"Yes, that's a brilliant idea."

"Oh, and add in *shoemaker* as a keyword. You never know. We've seen there's some link to Equity Shoes. Alice Hawkins worked there, so why not Harriet?"

"Okay. Oh my God, Violet. What if it finds her?"

Violet gave Phoebe's hand a squeeze. "Fingers crossed."

Phoebe edited the page and added the speculated details of Harriet's life. She closed her eyes as she clicked on the search button. She reopened them at Violet's surprised, "No way."

Phoebe stared at the form summarising the 1911 England census information. She couldn't quite take in what she was seeing.

*Name:* Harriet Frink
*Age:* 27
*Born in:* 1884
*Relation to Head:* Visitor
*Gender:* Female
*Birthplace:* Leicester, England
*Address:* Unwin's Emporium, Duke Street, Leicester
*Marital Status:* Single
*Occupation:* Boot & shoe machinist
*Household members:* Robert Unwin 30 Violet Unwin 28

Violet was leaning into the screen with her mouth agape. "Harriet was recorded *here* on the night of the 1911 census as a *visitor*."

"That suggests she didn't live here at the time—otherwise she would surely be recorded as a household member."

"Yes, that would be my guess too."

"And look, Violet, it says she was single at the time. I never got the feeling that she would be married. Not the Harry in that photo. Not Vi's Harry."

Violet frowned as she stared at the screen. "What was Harry doing here that night? Surely with everything we know about her, she would have wanted to disrupt the census and be at the headquarters to avoid being counted."

"Maybe she didn't want to cause trouble, having been arrested before."

"No. Trust me, Harry would want to protest to the full. I need to show you something." Violet scrambled from the bed. "Follow me."

Phoebe followed Violet across the hall and into Vi's room.

"Here. I found it yesterday evening just after closing. Do you remember me telling you about the drawer that kept opening?"

"Yes."

"It has a false bottom."

"Oh my God, that's really intriguing."

"I found this hidden away within it." Violet gestured to a navy leather box resting on the dressing table amongst Violet's collection of precious objects related to Vi. "I thought it was more jewellery at first. But then I looked inside and found this." Violet gently opened the box. "It's a medal. And not just any medal."

Phoebe struggled to catch her breath at the sight of the words engraved on the metal clips—*For Valour* and *Hunger Strike*.

"Maybe take a seat." Violet pulled out the dressing table stool.

"It's awarded to Harriet. *For recognition of a gallant action.* She was incredible, wasn't she?"

Violet nodded. "And the medal's not all that was hidden. I found a suffragette's sash with Vi's initials embroidered on it." Cradled in Violet's hand, the purple material caught the light and shone its colours and its symbol of defiance into the room.

"Oh, Violet, that's awesome. You know for certain now that Vi was a suffragette. You must be so chuffed."

Visibly choked, Violet said, "I just feel so proud."

Phoebe reached for Violet's hand. "You should be. And I'm not a bit surprised that an ancestor of yours, your namesake, was gutsy and principled and cared about women's rights and their visibility. Because that's you in spades—an awesome human being."

Violet broke down in tears.

"Oh no, I'm so sorry. I didn't mean to upset you. That's all I've done all day is upset people." Phoebe reached for Violet and held her.

"I'm okay. I promise." Violet wiped her eyes with her sleeve. "Just don't be nice to me for a bit."

"Deal." Phoebe brushed Violet's fringe from her tear-reddened eyes. "You don't look beautiful at all. And as for your lips, not kissable. No way." They giggled together, and then Violet's expression became full of thought.

"Actually," Violet said, looking back to her bedroom beyond the hall. "Do you mind if I use your notes to check something?"

"Not at all. Go ahead. I've left the webpage open. My laptop password is *Frinkyboots1!*."

"Perfect. I won't be a sec."

"Fine, bugger off then." Phoebe giggled, taking her seat once more on the stool.

"Rude." Violet headed back into her room, leaving Phoebe in the company of the bravest of the brave. She brushed her fingertips lightly over the name *Harriet Frink* printed in the finery of gold fit for the heroic. This award must have meant so much to Harry. Did she wear the medal often? When she marched, maybe?

She couldn't draw her eyes away from it. It held the strangest magnetism, absorbing her more and more in its spell until her curiosity was such that she eased it out of its box and rested it flat in her palm. Why did it feel like she'd held it before? Without thinking, she lifted the medal and pressed it to her heart. She looked up to the dressing table mirror to admire how the medal might look against her. Her breath caught, and she gasped in surprise. For a heart-stopping fleeting second, she saw someone reflected in the mirror standing behind her. She was certain of it. When she focused upon them, they disappeared.

Phoebe turned in her seat and looked about the room. "I'm putting it back now," she said into the space.

Violet called out, "Do you mean the medal? That's fine. I'm nearly done here."

"Uh-huh, great," Phoebe replied, feeling like a jewel thief caught in the act. Securing the medal back into its box, she closed the lid. "There," she said, in almost a whisper. "No harm done."

Was that the presence that Violet seemed not to be bothered by standing right there with her? If this was Vi's room, was that Vi? Speaking softly, she said, "I'm Phoebe. Violet's…friend." Phoebe felt nervous but not scared. It was the sort of feeling she imagined you might get when you met the parents of someone you liked. You want them to like you, no, to approve of you. Vi was a brave suffragette to be respected and admired. What would she think of her? What would Harry think of her? Would she be curious too that they shared the same surname?

The photograph of Vi and Harry standing arm in arm caught her attention. Sliding it towards her, she felt herself smile with them at the sight of their proud and happy faces. "I wish we'd met. Me and Violet and you and Vi. You pair would have loved it at The Banana. I just know you would."

"I can see Harry trying to get free drinks."

Phoebe looked up at Violet's voice to find her standing in the doorway wearing a broad smile and holding Phoebe's open laptop.

"Yeah." Phoebe chuckled. "And Dee not having a bar of it."

"Until Harry says *What about family discounts?*"

Phoebe swallowed. "What do you mean?"

Taking a deep breath, Violet struggled a little to say, "Phoebe, Harry belongs to you. By my reckoning, she's your great-great-great-aunt."

"You found out for certain?" Phoebe was frightened to trust that it could be true. She simply could not bear to find it was a mistake.

"Yep. I'll show you." Violet moved to the dressing room table. "Can you move Vi's things a little?" Phoebe made space for Violet to place the laptop on the table in front of them. The page Violet had brought up showed the title 1891 England Census for Harriet Frink. A handwritten form with bewildering rows of individual entries for each resident, and organised by street address, filled the screen.

With an expression of determined concentration, Violet explained, "The moment I saw just how much information the enumerator records for a census, I knew we had a chance of linking you back to Harriet. The key information it gives us is the list of *everyone* at a particular address on the date of the census, including their age and occupation and their relationship to the head of the family. So, with the help of your notes, since I knew Grandpa Peter was born in 1940 in Nottingham and had an older brother Roy, I began by searching for his dad, Frank Frink, in the 1939 England and Wales Register. I found Frank recorded at an address in Nottingham with his wife Ann and, vitally, their son Roy listed with them, aged two. It gave Frank's age as thirty-five and his occupation as a hosiery knitter."

A chill of amazement flowed through Phoebe's body. "This is so cool, Violet."

"We also struck lucky. An older man and woman were also recorded as living with Frank's family—Arthur Frink aged sixty, and Lila Frink aged fifty-nine. Sounds like your great-great-grandparents. This register didn't record who was head of the family, so it could be that either Frank was living with his parents, or they were living with him. The search brought up no other individuals with the surname Frink. You have a really unusual surname. It's helping us so much now."

"Good to know my quirky name has its uses other than making me a target for teasing. Anyway, okay, so that's the position in 1939. Got it."

"Now, Harry, we know from the 1911 census, was born in 1884—five years after Arthur."

"Then she could be Arthur's younger sister?"

"Yes. That's what I wondered. We also know from the 1911 census that Harry was born in Leicester. This time I searched for Harriet Frink, Leicester, in the 1891 England Census. Again, only one record came up for the Frink surname. Thankfully, this particular census recorded the relation to head of family."

Even though Violet had told her that she *was* related to Harry, Phoebe found herself holding her breath.

"Here"—Violet placed her finger to the screen—"George Frink is head of family and then"—Violet dragged her finger down past George's wife Eliza to *Arthur Frink*. "Arthur is recorded as their son aged twelve, which fits with the age that Arthur would have been. And below Arthur is *Harriet Frink* listed as their—"

"Daughter. Aged seven."

"When I double-checked for any Frinks in Nottingham at this time, no records came up. Which convinced me further that we have found Harry and traced her back to you."

Phoebe slipped her arm around Violet's waist and pulled her close. "Thank you for finding her for me."

Violet leaned down and kissed Phoebe's lips with such tenderness that it made Phoebe's heart ache.

"My pleasure," Violet said, smiling. "I'm so pleased she's yours."

"Me too." Phoebe still couldn't quite believe it. It was almost just too awesome. "And I love the idea that she made boots for her job." Phoebe shook her head and chuckled. "Maybe that explains my obsession with them."

"Why not? It's definitely possible. You have her genes. You could even say you are her. After all, her blood runs through you."

Phoebe reached over the laptop to bring the photo of Harry and Vi towards them. She shook her head. "She is so much more than me, though. She went to prison for what she believed in. She even endured a hunger strike, for God's sake. I flake at the slightest pressure." Phoebe fought back tears. "I am a worthless dropout."

Violet bent down at her side. "*No.*"

"Everyone thinks it."

"Who is everyone?"

"My parents. The uni teachers."

"Have they said that? Any of them?"

"My parents didn't have to say anything."

"From what you told me, they were left confused more than anything. And I don't blame you for being cross at them at the pressure they have intentionally or unintentionally put on you. And good for you for sticking up for yourself with them. Now you need to keep doing it more generally and start believing in yourself."

"I don't know how to."

"Then maybe channel Harry. Let the spirit of her shine out in you. Use her strength and borrow it for a while. Draw upon it when you don't feel so strong."

"I *do* feel really connected to her. Whenever I wear the suffragette costume, I have the strangest sensations. It's like I am experiencing their passion and defiance. I now wonder if I am sensing Harry's feelings. Is that even possible?"

"Yes, why not? You know what you feel, after all. No one can tell you otherwise." Violet's gaze drifted over Vi's objects laid out on the table. "I can feel Vi with me, particularly when I'm upset. It helps. *She* helps me."

"I get that. If Harry is with me, then it explains why I was certain I recognised Emmeline as if we had met. Because in effect we have. And Vi, I know her in my heart. This is going to sound unbelievable, but it's like I've loved her. Like properly loved her."

"Funny you should say that." Violet turned to the wardrobe. Opening it, she reached inside the pocket of Vi's fur coat and pulled out a small note. Then she closed the laptop lid and placed the note on top of it. "I found it with the medal and Vi's sash. It's such a private thing that I wanted it away from view, so the fur seemed perfect."

"Yes." Phoebe took Violet's hand as she read the words that sent shivers right through her. *I hungered for you, Mrs. Violet Unwin.* "I was right, then. They did love each other."

"Harry certainly felt passionately about Vi. We know that much."

"Just like I feel passionately for you," Phoebe said, feeling herself blush. "It's like we're fated to be together."

Violet nodded, and with the most adorable of expressions said, "I'm certain you're meant to be mine."

Phoebe swallowed down the emotions rising in her throat. She would embarrass herself to let the sentiment of the moment spill over into tears. Eventually she managed to ask, "You don't suppose Vi and Harry have brought us together somehow? I've lived in Cornwall all my life. There are medical schools all over the country. And yet not once did I question why I had chosen Leicester to study and to make my home. When my dad told me about Frank and his connection with the Midlands, it was the first I'd heard of it. Surely it's much more than a homing instinct?"

"It's hard to believe it's just that."

"Do you think it's possible they've done this so *they* can be reunited? You hear of spirits separated by an incident and not able to rest until they find each other again or achieve peace somehow. Could that be going on here?"

Violet turned sharply to the hallway. She stared into the emptiness for a moment before looking back. Phoebe wondered what Violet thought she'd seen or heard. Vi?

"Even if they didn't actively bring us together," Violet said, "then just you and me falling for each other here in the Emporium would surely resonate with them and be enough perhaps to trigger something. When you mentioned an incident separating them, were you thinking the War or a fallout or…hold on. Phoebe, *the postcard*."

"Oh my God, of course." Phoebe reached for the postcard and placed it next to Harry's note. She reread aloud the words once more. *"Vi. Just for one night I needed to be invisible. I thought, no, I hoped you of all people, would understand. Harry.* She was certainly cross with Vi. You can hear her exasperation coming through."

Violet nodded and then frowned. "Why did Harry want to be invisible? And how had Vi not understood? What on earth went on that night?"

A loud and insistent banging on the shop door caused them both to jump. Phoebe placed her hand to her heart. Violet went deathly pale.

"Violet! Open the fucking door. Every time! Violet!"

"It's Carl." The concern in Violet's voice was clear to hear.

It was heartbreaking to see her standing there, suddenly rigid with terror. How dare he do that to her.

"I'll go," Phoebe said. "It's okay. You wait here."

"No, I can't let you go."

"Let's go together, then. Why is he always so cross?"

"He just is." Violet took a deep shaky breath and made her way downstairs. Phoebe followed close behind.

"I know you're in there, Violet." Carl banged his fist against the door. "How many times do I have to tell you about that damn snib. Thank God it's the end of this…shit."

What was Carl talking about? What was it the end of?

Violet grabbed Phoebe's hand. "Let's hide. Here in the dressing room."

"Why? What's going on?"

Violet tugged Phoebe inside and drew the curtain across.

Carl continued shouting, "And I know the solicitors have written. Are you ignoring me? You can't hide from me forever. Violet!" Carl all but shook the door off its hinges. The glass rattled in its frame, and the bell rang out with each shake, almost as if crying in pain.

Violet bowed her head, and with her eyes closed and holding Phoebe's hand tightly in hers, she began to repeat the words, "Always and always facing toward the light. Say it with me. Please."

"Okay. If you think it will help." How on earth could it help? It wouldn't make him go away, would it? Pushing her puzzlement aside, Phoebe squeezed her eyes shut and spoke the words in time with Violet. She would do anything for her. Anything at all.

Their words became a chant and then merely a sound, and then there was a weird silence that was neither quiet nor still. Phoebe shivered as a cold that felt like a winter morning's mist swept in, shrouding and absorbing them into vapours of nothing.

And then the banging returned. It could be heard in the distant background at first, and then it became more insistent and louder and louder. As the last elements of her thoughts dissolved, all Phoebe could grasp were the words *Make it stop*.

"Make it stop, Vi." Harry pressed her hands to her ears at the insistent knocking on the door. What she really meant was make this whole moment go away. She didn't want to be here. Not tonight of all nights.

"I can't, Harry. It's the enumerator. He can see from the lights that we're in. I must answer the door." Vi moved from the counter, and Harry grasped her sleeve.

"Why?"

"Because I have no choice. You know that." Vi looked to the stairs that led to the flat. She lowered her voice. "What would Robert say?"

"He'd understand. And as for choice, it is ours to make."

"Then I choose not to rock the boat. For he wouldn't understand. If anything, it would be proof to him that you are trouble in my life."

"Is that what you think?"

"It is what he thinks."

"And is what he thinks all that matters now?"

"Right now, Harry, yes. Because if I don't answer the door, he will."

"Then what am I going to do? I told you I wouldn't be counted. That if women didn't count in the eyes of the government, then we would not be counted."

"And you know I agree."

"Then why didn't you come to the headquarters tonight and hide there with me?"

"I said I would try, not that I definitely could."

"But you knew how much it meant to me. For one night I wanted to be invisible. I wanted to be there with you." Was it too much to ask? Lately everything had felt too much as Robert's grasp upon Vi got tighter and tighter. Vi had said only yesterday that he had suggested that the suffragettes' cause had gone too far. That he needed her in his shop. And there was nothing she could do. Vi belonged to Robert and not to her.

"Vi," Robert called down from the top of the stairs, "is someone with you? Violet? Are you there? Will you please answer the door before that wretched fellow knocks it down. He is in every way a man possessed like the devil."

Harry held Vi by both hands. "No, please, Vi."

"Let's hide, then. In the dressing room."

"How's that going to work?"

"I don't know what else to do." Vi rushed to the dressing room. Harry looked to the stairs and to the sound of Robert groaning and making his way down. They were going to get caught. Harry dug into her pocket and pulled out the precious box she'd carried around with her for days. She knew that Vi would love the brooch made just for her. She'd be saving for months on end to afford it. She'd meant to give it to Vi that night. When they were alone. Now they were anything but alone. What would Robert say if he saw the box? Why would he see the box? But what if he did? In a panic, and with Robert descending ever closer, and the enumerator's shadow looming black at the door, Harry lifted the lid of a cardboard storage box and tucked the precious jewellery out of sight. She could tell Vi where to find it when they were alone again.

Then she ran for her life to the dressing room, just closing the curtain as Robert stepped down the last stair into the shop. Vi clasped Harry's hands in hers and fixed her eyes shut. Harry could make out that she was mouthing Always and always facing toward the light *over and over*. But how would it help? It wouldn't make any of it go away. Harry closed her eyes. Make it go away…

"Phoebe? Phoebe? Hey." Phoebe opened her eyes at the sensation of her hands being squeezed. Violet's smile was such a welcome sight. The curtain had been drawn back. "He's gone. For now, at least."

Had Violet just experienced what she had? Had she dissolved into a mist of nothing? Had she become Vi as Phoebe had become Harry? Had she seen and felt what she had? "I know what happened that night."

Violet visibly tensed. What did that mean? Did she know too?

"And I know about the brooch."

And then Violet double blinked. "You do?"

So, Violet hadn't gone back in time with her. Or had she as Vi not seen Harry hide the brooch away? "Just then, it all went a bit odd, didn't it?"

Violet nodded. "I'm sorry about Carl."

"I meant in the dressing room. Call me bonkers, but I swear it was like I was Harry and went back to the very moment of the drama that the postcard refers to. *I* spoke the words on the postcard. The man collecting details for the census was banging at the door. That door." Phoebe made her way over to the shop's entrance and pressed her hand flat where Carl had banged and banged upon the wood. "I was *there*. And I, well Harry, had got trapped coming to the Emporium to look for Vi. Harry had wanted to spend the night in the WSPU headquarters.

She'd wanted Vi to be there with her. She said she'd thought Vi would understand."

Violet didn't say anything. Had Carl's arrival been a bit too much for her, as her parents were for Phoebe earlier that day?

But Phoebe was determined to talk about what happened and for the moment of realisation not to be lost back into the white mist from which it had come. "Harry had the brooch with her. I held it in my hand. She panicked and hid it in the box we found. The intention was to tell Vi about it when they were alone again." Phoebe returned to her place where Violet sat cross-legged on the dressing room floor. "I worry that Vi didn't find it. And more than that, I worry what that means."

"You think they didn't see each other again after that night?"

"I don't know. You woke me from where I'd gone, and I didn't see what happened."

"Me neither. I *was* there with you in the Emporium that night. It hurt that you were so cross with me." Violet bit at her lip.

Phoebe reached for her hands and held them tight. "*I'm* not."

"I had a dream, a few weeks back now. I didn't know at the time what it meant. I was upset and crying over something I was reading. I was dressed in this full skirt with flowers sewn on it. I made it wet with my tears. It was the postcard from Harry scolding Vi about that night. I'm certain of it."

"It's like you have her memories in you."

"I wish they were happier. For Vi."

"She'd be happy we found each other if what we believe might be true."

"There's nothing to suggest it isn't. Come on." Violet stood and glanced at the door before leaving the dressing room and heading upstairs.

Phoebe sat for a moment more, letting things sink in. Was she imagining everything that was happening here in the Emporium? But then everything about Violet was real and wonderful. She wanted her time here with Violet to be forever. Phoebe stood and, just like Violet, glanced at the door one last time. What had Carl meant when he said it was the end? And why did she know instinctively not to ask Violet?

When Phoebe went back upstairs, she found Violet in the kitchen tipping fish fingers onto a foil covered tray. She looked so much better than a few moments ago, for all the colour had now returned to her cheeks.

"I figured we need some comfort food. My go-to is a fish finger sandwich." Violet looked up at her and smiled. "What say you?"

"I'd say how did you know that was my favourite?"

"All my own intuitive genius, and nothing to do with Vi." They chuckled.

"I'm just going to check if I can see what happened to Harriet."

"Okay. See you in a mo."

Phoebe went into Vi's room and collected the laptop, taking care to place the note and the postcard safely with the other objects. She would leave it to Violet to return the note to Vi's fur coat. As she moved to leave, she paused and found herself looking back at Vi's dressing table. The words "I'm not cross with you" tumbled from her lips.

She turned away and headed to Violet's room. Violet had needed to hear those words, and Harry must have known that so did Vi. The cruelty of those decades that followed if there was so much unsaid and unresolved. "What happened to you, Harry?"

Perched on Violet's bed, Phoebe brought up the genealogy site and searched the UK census collection for any sign of Harriet and drew a blank with the 1921 census. And then she checked the marriage registers followed, with her breath held, by the death registers. Nothing. She would ask Violet to check for Harry too. But in her heart she knew they wouldn't find her. Maybe it wasn't just for one night she'd wanted to be invisible. Phoebe brought up the city's history website and the image of the marching women. She stared at the date, and said to herself, "May 1911." Had she wanted Vi by her side marching with her, and she was stopped from being there? Did Robert break them up for good following that night? "You look so brave, despite everything. I am proud to be yours. I want you to know I have found Violet, and she's everything to me."

"Here you go. Our food won't be long." Violet placed a juice on the side table and removed two cold mugs of tea.

How much had Violet heard? "Thanks. I'd best text Dee and let her know I haven't forgotten to go home tonight."

"You don't have to."

"Yeah, right, she would kill me."

"No. I meant you don't have to go back to The Banana tonight. If you wanted you could stay here—"

"Yes."

"With me."

"You had me at *no*." They laughed. The oven timer buzzed.

"We could watch a film." Violet said it in such a way that suggested the last thing she wanted to do was watch a film.

"Uh-huh."

The oven timer kept buzzing. Not that Violet seemed to notice.

## Chapter Nineteen

"Remind me not to go shopping on a Friday lunchtime again." Dee dropped a bag of groceries on the kitchen counter. "Barely escaped with my life. Anyway. Good news, bad news. Which do you want first?"

Phoebe paused from refreshing the messages on her phone. She'd sent Violet a text earlier and was waiting on her reply. It was more than possible that Violet was dealing with a particularly tricky customer or was caught up in an errand in town. Just because it wasn't like her not to reply pretty much straight away, it didn't mean there was anything wrong. "Erm. Bad news, I suppose. Get it out of the way."

"Fair enough. Brace yourself then, kiddo—Rice Krispies have gone up out of our price range."

"You're kidding me."

"'Fraid not. Sad day." Dee began to unpack her shopping, which included a bag of apples. Tipping them into a bowl, she added, "They wanted to charge me a whole pound more just for the Kellogg's name."

"That's terrible. And the alternatives are just not the same." Even though Phoebe knew this was a First World problem, it was nonetheless ridiculously depressing. "Now I definitely need the good news."

"Rice Krispies have gone up out of our price range." A smile flickered in Dee's eyes despite her otherwise deadpan expression.

"That's just mean."

"That's just lucky for me." Dee selected an apple, rubbed it to a rosy shine on her jumper, and took a large unapologetic bite. "A snap, crackle, and pop-free breakfast time, here we come."

Phoebe shook her head. "You're unbelievable."

"Thank you. It is not without effort." Speaking in between crunchy mouthfuls, she then added, "How did it go this morning with your mum and dad? Are you still in the will?"

"Yup."

"Good to hear. Am I in the will?"

Phoebe had returned her attention to her phone and the hope of a message from Violet. "Yup."

"Are you even listening to me?"

"Yup." Still no message. There was, however, a new email from her tutor. Phoebe held her breath as she opened it and read the first line.

*Dear Phoebe,*

*Thank you for your message. Wonderful news regarding your decision to recommence your studies. Please make an appointment with Wendy in the office to arrange a time for us to meet to discuss this further. Best wishes, Annie Lowe (Dr.)*

Phoebe released an excited gasp.

"Don't tell me young Violet is making yet another amorous suggestion."

"They've accepted me back. The university. At least, I think so."

Dee stopped eating midbite. The broadest of smiles spread across her face.

"I've got to make an appointment to chat about it. But you wouldn't call it wonderful news, would you, if you didn't want someone?"

"Generally speaking, no. Although when *I* say *wonderful news*, hit or miss whether I mean it. Is your tutor a sarcastic so-and-so?"

Phoebe laughed. "No."

"Well then, you're back in, kiddo. Good for you. They're lucky to have you, Dr. Frinky Boots." Dee threw her apple core towards the bin and missed. "Oh well."

"You're not going to pick it up?"

"Nah, I know it will irritate you really quickly, and you'll pick it up."

"That's called taking advantage."

"That's called *reading the room*. Remember I'm first in line for Botox on the NHS. Before you say that's a private procedure, we all know it's who you know."

"It doesn't work like that."

"This is about the Rice Krispies, isn't it? Damn, you're a good negotiator."

Phoebe laughed. "I don't know why I'm laughing. I get the feeling you're serious."

"Me? Serious? Never. Although anything you can do about these laughter lines..." Dee pulled at the edges of her eyes. "I'll leave it with you. No pressure."

"Uh-huh."

Smiling, Dee took a seat at the table. And then her expression fell a little. "Talking of pressure, your decision to go back to med school, it was *your* decision, wasn't it?"

"How do you mean?"

"Well, we both know that your mum and dad have hopes for you. And total respect to you for setting out your boundaries with them, but I get that you might still feel some obligation..."

Phoebe shook her head. "It's my choice. One hundred percent. It had nothing to do with my parents. They surprised me when we chatted today by how sorry they were. I genuinely think they thought their ambition for me and unquestioning confidence in my abilities were good things. And I guess I didn't actually let on to them that I felt pressure. But, anyway, I could tell they'd discussed things a lot between them since the other day, and they both made a point of saying in their own way that they wanted things to be more open between us going forward. My mum even mentioned that medicine was just one of many options. I know what it would have taken for her to say that."

"Good for her."

Phoebe nodded. "Perhaps it would have been kind of me to tell them this morning that I had already decided to go back to uni. But until I heard back from my course tutor, I didn't know if they would want me. So I didn't feel I could tell anyone, not even you and Violet."

"I get that. Would I be right in thinking, then, that your decision had something to do with the beautiful Violet?"

Phoebe nodded. "And Harry. When I found out about her and that she was my great-great-great-aunt, at first, I felt inadequate. Like I was letting her down almost. She'd gone through so much to fight for women's rights, and here I was just giving up. And then Violet said that in those moments when I didn't feel worthy or strong I could channel Harry. Borrow a bit of her confidence."

"Wise words."

"I knew in my heart that if Harry was in my place, she would go back to her studies despite any fear she might have. I just know she would."

"And I *just know* that one day some young Frink will channel *you* and draw on your courage. I couldn't be more impressed, Pheebs."

"Thank you. And thank you for everything you have done for me. Taking me in. Putting up with my moods and my crapness."

"Ditto, kiddo."

"And being there for me. Helping me to find Violet."

An unusual tenderness in Dee's expression softened the edges of her features. "I can hear Suzie saying that Violet was there waiting for you all along." She gave a small sigh and stood. "She was such a hopeless romantic."

"I'm sorry, Dee. I know how much you miss her."

Dee picked up the apple core and deposited it in the bin. "She's in my thoughts when I wake and when I fall to sleep. A day doesn't go by that I don't think of her. I never once regretted loving Suzie, though. And even knowing what I know, I would do it all again. Over and over."

What could Phoebe say to that?

Dee packed away the last of her shopping and moved to leave.

"Can I stay at The Banana? Rather than go back to halls when I begin my studies again."

"You want to stay here? It's not exactly the quietest of places."

"Neither are halls. I'll use the library, and I can always ask Violet if I can study at hers if I need to. And I'd like to try to keep working my shifts if that's possible. What do you say?"

"Look, Pheebs, we must face facts that I have no idea how long The Banana will be able to keep going. I can't promise anything permanent."

"I know. And I'll do everything I can to help."

"You're going to have your hands full with your studying. And you'll want to save some time for Violet."

"I will. Please, Dee."

Dee nodded. "You know the answer is yes."

Phoebe rushed up to Dee and hugged her. "Thank you."

"Yeah, yeah, whatever."

"I can't wait to tell Violet about uni." She also couldn't wait to check to see if Violet was okay. Her news offered the perfect excuse to call round.

"And I can't wait for you to let go of me," Dee said, politely untangling herself from Phoebe's hug.

Phoebe released her hold. "Sorry."

"Are you still here?"

"I'm gone. Bye! Thanks again!" Phoebe grabbed her bag, coat, and two apples and headed for the Emporium. She didn't have to look back to know that Dee was smiling.

Harry wouldn't worry what people would think of her running through the streets to be with *her* Violet. So neither would she. Who cared? Not Phoebe Frink, no way.

"Violet?" Phoebe called out, at the same time catching her breath. "Hey, it's me." The door to the Emporium was open, and as she first stepped inside Phoebe assumed that the two men pulling the clothes from the rails were customers choosing costumes. That assumption was short-lived at the sight of the dismantled Christmas window display. "What's going on?"

Phoebe rushed over to the windowsill and to the tree all tangled in its lights, which flickered on and off as if gasping for life. The painted branches of green card were battered and bruised. What on earth had happened here?

"Oh no." Phoebe reached to the floor and lifted the large gold star which had once hung so proudly for all to see and was now indelibly defaced with a dusty shoe print. "Have *you* done this?" Phoebe asked the two men. She was furious. One of them glanced across at her and just as quickly looked away. "Excuse me—I'm speaking to you. What *exactly* are you doing here?" She knew her question was in every way an accusation rather than an enquiry.

Without looking at her, the man replied, "Our job, love. That's what I've been trying to tell the young lady all morning."

The young lady? "Where's Violet Unwin?"

The man looked up to the ceiling and shrugged.

Phoebe raced up the stairs. An awful sick feeling of dread lay heavy in the pit of her stomach.

Phoebe soon discovered Violet pacing up and down in Vi's room. Utterly consumed with distress and agitation, Violet seemed completely oblivious to Phoebe's presence.

Her brave beautiful Violet. It was utterly devastating and just heartbreaking to see her in such a state. So much so, that Phoebe found she couldn't move as she watched in horror as Violet pressed her hand to her forehead and knocked her palm against it repeatedly. "I don't know what to do. It's sold. I can't stop them. They won't leave. We've lost this place. It's sold. I can't save us, Vi. I don't know what to do. It's sold. What do I do?" Violet eventually slumped onto the dressing table stool and laid her head on the table and sobbed.

*Come on, Frink.* Phoebe took a deep breath, made her way cautiously towards Violet, and rested her hand softly upon her back.

"Violet. It's me."

Violet sat up with a start.

"Sorry, I didn't mean to startle you." Violet looked back at her with an expression of someone who had lost trust in everything and everyone. "What's going on?"

Violet stood and looked beyond Phoebe to the hallway. Her whole body was rigid with fear and trauma.

She looked back to Phoebe with her complexion paler and bleaker than the moon. "How long have you been here?" Even her voice was newly hollow and empty of the warmth that Phoebe loved to hear.

"Not long. You kept saying, a moment ago, *It's sold.* Did you mean the Emporium?"

"You saw me?" Violet looked completely mortified.

"Like I said, I've not been here long. Don't be embarrassed. I talk to myself all the time—"

"Can you leave?"

What? "No, Violet." Phoebe went to reach for Violet, but she stepped away.

"Please, leave."

"I want to help you."

"There's no help for me. There's nothing anyone can do. So please, just leave." Violet sat back on the stool, held her hands over her face, and sobbed.

Phoebe had no idea what to do. "Violet." If Violet heard, she did not reply. Nothing in Phoebe wanted to leave, but Violet couldn't have made it clearer that she was not welcome.

Phoebe made her way downstairs and past the men who were now shoving the costumes into bin bags. She couldn't bear to watch them crush the Christmas display into a refuse sack. "What will happen to everything?"

The man who had spoken to her earlier gave a shrug. "The buyer doesn't want them. We've just been told to pack everything up in bags. Is she all right?" The man jutted his chin to the stairs.

Phoebe said blankly, "No."

"She *was* told about the sale, your friend." Then the man turned away and continued ramming the costumes into bags.

Why hadn't Violet said something? Why hadn't she trusted her enough to tell her when they'd shared so much?

Phoebe closed the shop door behind her. The street did not need to see the destruction and heartbreak within.

She couldn't remember her walk back to The Banana or recall her first words to Dee when she arrived at the counter of the bar.

"What do you mean, something's happened at the Emporium? *Phoebe.*" Dee clicked her fingers under Phoebe's nose.

"It's been sold, Dee. There are two men there taking everything down and shoving it into bags. All the beautiful costumes are being treated like rags to be discarded. And Violet had done this amazing Christmas display and they just tore it down. It was…awful."

"Oh my God." Dee came from behind the bar and pulled off the apron she wore around her middle when changing the barrels. "Where was Violet?"

"Upstairs in the flat."

"She wasn't stopping them?"

Phoebe shook her head. "She wasn't coping so well." Dee didn't need the details. She would not betray Violet's trust, even if Violet might already feel betrayed by Phoebe witnessing something that was meant to be private. "It was like she didn't know the shop was being sold. Let alone that the sale had gone through. It seemed like the most terrible shock to her. But the man in the shop said that Violet did know about the sale. If that's right, then why didn't she say anything to us, to me?"

"She would have had her reasons, Pheebs. So why are you here and not there helping her?"

"She sent me away."

"And, what, you just went and left her there with those men?"

"You say that like I had a choice."

"We always have a choice. And now's the time to learn the first lesson of loving a woman. Don't listen to *what* she says—listen to the way she says it."

"She was upset. Everything was too much for her. Me being there was too much for her."

"Were those her actual words?"

What had Violet said? "She just asked me to leave. Oh God. I should have just left the room and not the shop, shouldn't I? I could have given her space without leaving. I should have stayed and sent those men away." How could she have been so stupid? "I have to go back."

"Yes, go straight away to Violet. I'll follow. I just need to make a quick phone call. And Phoebe—don't take any shit from those fellas. I won't be long."

"Thanks, Dee." Phoebe ran without stopping all the way back to the Emporium and to Violet. With every step she thought: What would Harry do? *Come on, Frink.* Remember who you are. You have Harriet Frink's blood running through you. You are the descendant of women who *will* be heard, who *will* be seen, who *will* be counted and who will take *no shit*.

❖

Numb to the men working around her, busy dismantling her life, Violet stared at the counter and at the surface of darker varnish in the shape of the vintage National. The haunting footprint was the only reminder left of the pride of place the till held for all those years at the Emporium. It had been carried out earlier that day with a dust sheet thrown over it. Images of a hooded prisoner had come crushing into Violet's mind. And there was nothing she could do to save it from its uncertain fate.

Nausea then pressed at Violet's throat at the sight of that day's post lying on the doormat. She couldn't even face leafing through it. Just the sight of her name alongside Unwin's Emporium was too much to bear. For she was no longer Violet Unwin of Unwin's Emporium. She was Violet Unwin of nowhere. She picked up the post and dropped it on the edge of the cabinet. The word *Sold* printed in red on a white label and stuck to its top were so final. It might as well have said

*End*. Carl knew how much Violet loved these drawers. To sell them without a moment's regard for her felt like a defining act of cruelty from the cruellest of men. Not caring whether she had emptied them of their precious contents epitomised how little respect he had for the Emporium and the history that had made it such a special and unique place. With no regard for the past, he would always be a shallow man with no depth to him for the roots of love and integrity to grow. She would pity him if she didn't loathe him so much.

Not long after she had sent Phoebe away, Carl arrived to check on progress, looking flushed and sweaty. In many ways it was good that Violet had cried out every tear by the time he showed up. She would not give him the pleasure of seeing her upset.

"What are you looking at?" Carl stepped towards her and brought his face a few inches from hers. His aftershave choked her throat. "Well?"

Violet leaned away from him as she dared to ask, "Why didn't you tell me the sale had gone through and the shop needed to be cleared by today? I haven't had the chance to empty the drawers."

"Why didn't *you* let me in the other day? I came here specifically to tell you. You brought this on yourself."

"You gave me a month. Mr. Burrows said I had until the end of December."

"Do yourself a favour and just accept it's over. You lose. I win." His face was now so close she could feel his breath on her. "I win," he repeated, this time looking up at the ceiling.

Suddenly, the door burst open and the bell rang out. Carl went ashen and all but gave himself whiplash as he jolted his head to see who had arrived.

It took all of Violet's strength not to cry at the sight of Phoebe striding towards them.

"Get away from her." Phoebe shooed at him like he was a wasp bothering them at a picnic. Carl laughed. "You pathetic bully. This is from Harry." Then Phoebe gave Carl an enormous shove at his shoulder, causing him to stagger. He didn't laugh that time. The doorbell rang out again. Twice. Everyone turned in puzzlement, for this time there was no one at the open door.

Phoebe took Violet's hand and whispered. "I'm so sorry I left you. I'll never leave you again."

How could Phoebe even bear to talk to her? She'd kept the biggest thing in her life from her as if Violet had deemed her not worthy of sharing it with. "You're not cross with me?"

"*No.* A little confused maybe, but not cross. Never."

Carl looked at their hands entwined and scoffed at Violet. "I might have known—freak."

A rage like a storm front built up in Violet, and she clenched her fist. How she wanted to hit him and knock him down and shut him up for good. She would do it for Phoebe and herself, but moreover she would do it for Vi.

He tapped at her fist. "Go on. I dare you."

If she hit him, he would win—Violet wouldn't give him that satisfaction. As it happened Phoebe saved her the trouble as she stamped on his foot with such force that it crumpled the toe of his shoe and wrecked his suede loafers for good.

"Look, mate, are you going to pay us or what?" The men who had looked on had clearly seen enough and wanted out of the drama.

Carl all but foamed at the mouth as he gripped his foot in pain. He shouted back at the men, "I will pay you when I'm ready to." Mercifully, his phone then rang and he hobbled away to a corner to answer it.

Violet felt Phoebe's hand grip hers ever more tightly. She obviously knew, like Violet, that this battle was far from over. But this was not Phoebe's battle. It was hers. What right had she to expect Phoebe to endure this?

"You'd better go, Phoebe," Violet said. "I don't want him to hurt you."

"Never. Always and always facing toward the light. Remember?"

Violet nodded. She would never forget those words or what they stood for—courage.

"You can collect the drawers today," Carl growled at the caller. "Yes, whatever. What? *No.* It's nothing to do with Violet. Look, take it or leave it…Fine. Bring cash." And then Carl ended the call and rolled up his sleeves.

"I think you'll find it's everything to do with Violet." Mr. Duke stood in the doorway wearing a razor-thin moustache and dressed in jeans and a denim jacket, accompanied by an expression that said *Just you fucking try.*

Carl laughed. "The whole circus is in town, eh? Who are you—

the ringleader of this freak show? Oh no, wait, I know you from that drag bar. The home of the freaks." Carl turned to the men, no doubt expecting them to laugh with him. Instead, they just stood in silence, looking uncomfortable.

Mr. Duke moved into the centre of the room. He turned briefly to Violet and asked, "You okay, Valiant?"

Violet nodded.

"Great stuff. Pheebs—all good?"

"Yes." Phoebe gestured towards Carl. "You should see the other guy."

Mr. Duke smiled and then made a point of looking Carl up and down, pausing at his crotch. "Yeah, I'd rather not."

Violet didn't know much about men. But one thing she did know was how sensitive they were about their manhood. Clearly Mr. Duke didn't have reconciliation on his mind. Carl visibly puffed up his chest.

Violet resisted the urge to close her eyes.

Carl hissed, "Like I'd come near you with a bargepole, you weirdo."

"Devastating news. Still, I'll get over it. In the meantime, why don't you take a hike, you pointless fuckwit, and crawl back under the stone from where you came."

Carl moved to Mr. Duke in a way that wasn't going to end well. "You—"

"And don't let *me* stop you from fucking off." Handy Man Joe, dressed in his full stage costume, arrived, clearly poised to do so much more than entertain. He stood his ground between Mr. Duke and Carl. At the same time, he patted a wrench against his palm. Plumbing clearly wasn't on his mind.

"You're making a fool of yourself, Carl." One of the removal men nudged his mate to leave. "You won't win this one."

"*What?*" Carl gave an indignant gasp. "They're not *real* men."

"That's right," Joe said. "We're so much more."

"You better pay us, Unwin. We know where to find you." And with that the two men pushed past Carl and left.

Carl gave a petulant kick at a bin bag of costumes. "Good riddance to it all. Get rid of this crap, Violet, and be out by midnight." Still hobbling, he made for the door. He cast a last hateful look at Violet, who simply shrugged in reply. If this was the last time she ever saw her cousin—and please say it was—then she would not give him the memory of her cowering.

"Missing you already," Mr. Duke said, waving.

Carl grabbed the door and stepped outside, slamming it shut with all his might. Rather, he tried, but instead the door closed softly, and Carl was left to storm off like the pathetic man-child he was.

"Thank God he's gone. I don't know what I would have done without you guys." Violet shook her head.

"Bullies are all the same," Joe said. "When push comes to shove, they scuttle away like the cockroaches they are. Come here." Joe gave Violet the tightest of bear hugs. "There's nothing on you wee girl. Phoebe, you need to bake more of those scones of yours for your Violet."

"What's Violet ever done to you, Joe?" Mr. Duke quipped.

Phoebe folded her arms. "I'm choosing to ignore that because you have been especially brave."

"To be honest, I was shitting myself, Pheebs." Mr. Duke peeled off his moustache and Dee returned in his place. "He's a big bugger, isn't he? Still, fake it till you make it, that's what I say. Although, given that you're a doctor in the making, maybe don't fake it on the job. Right, we need a drink and a plan. I'm going to pop out and get some beers."

"I'm off too," Joe said, wiping the oil smudge from his cheek and returning seamlessly to Jo. Slipping their spanner into the bib of their dungarees, Jo added, "But I'm about all evening if you need me and my van for anything."

"Thanks, Jo," Phoebe said. "You're a star."

Jo raised their hand to signal goodbye and followed Dee out.

Violet stared after them. "Dee's still determined to get you not to give up on your studies, isn't she."

Phoebe slipped her arm around Violet's waist. "Actually, I have news about that. But it can wait."

"No, tell me. Please."

"Are you sure now's a good time?" Phoebe looked concerned.

Violet looked about her at the chaotic scene and sighed. There was a funny certainty about finding yourself immersed in a state of chaos. Somehow, it was the threat of it that was worse. What was done was done, and there was no undoing it. "I'm sure."

"Okay. But then you need to tell me what's going on. Deal?"

Violet nodded. "Let's go to my room."

Hand in hand, they made their way to Violet's room and settled themselves on her bed. Phoebe couldn't have held Violet closer or squeezed her any tighter.

"I couldn't bear it if he'd hurt you." Phoebe followed these heartfelt words with a kiss that spoke of her promise never to leave Violet again.

It was an embrace that made Violet feel so safe and reassured in a way she'd simply never felt before. "Thank you for coming back to me."

"I'm not going anywhere. In fact, that's sort of my news." Phoebe brushed her thumb lightly over Violet's warm and tingling cheek. "I've decided to continue my studies."

"Oh, Phoebe, that's awesome." Relief flooded Violet's whole body as she hugged Phoebe against her and whispered in her ear, "I'm so proud of you."

"I'll be channelling Harry when I feel wobbly."

"Good plan. And I am here for you—always."

"And I am here for *you* too. If I'm honest, I hoped that you knew that already."

"I do."

"Then…" Phoebe hesitated. "Why didn't you tell me about the Emporium closing? Dee reckoned you would have had your reasons for not telling anyone, not even me. Is she right? Because, to be honest, I'm struggling to imagine what they might be."

The best and only way Violet knew to answer Phoebe was to tell her the truth. "If I told you, then it would be real. I couldn't cope with *real*. I know that sounds weak—"

"*No.* I understand more than anyone what it feels like not to be able to cope with reality. You know that. I wouldn't be where I am right now without your help. I wish you had let me help you in the same way."

"I couldn't. I didn't think there was help for me. All I know is the Emporium. All I *am* is the Emporium. Without the Emporium, I'm nothing. And why would you be with someone who is nothing? Has nothing? And not only that, but you loved it here so much. How could I tell you that you were losing it? We were losing it?"

"Is that why you sent me away?"

Could she tell Phoebe the real reason? That when Phoebe had caught her talking to Vi, she thought she'd seen in Phoebe's expression the same look that people sometimes used to give her. "I saw it in your eyes. When you found me."

"I don't understand. You saw what?"

"Like I was something weird."

"*No.* Oh my God, Violet, *no.* I was just confused and really concerned about you, that's all, I promise." Phoebe held Violet in a tight embrace. "Clever, brave, independent, talented, sensitive, wise, and beautiful inside and out—that's what I see when I look at you."

"Really?"

"Yes, I swear."

"I worried that you would think there was something wrong with me and that I was mad for talking to Vi. You see"—tears pushed and bullied, gathering and thickening at Violet's throat—"I'm frightened that I'm like my mum, who struggled with her mental health." Violet swallowed and swallowed as the deepest sadness threatened to overwhelm her. "And she didn't make it."

Phoebe held Violet ever closer, pressing her heart to hers. "Well, if you are mad," Phoebe said in a voice thick with emotion, "then I'm mad too. Because *I've* spoken to Vi and to Harry. I believe in their existence alongside us. You know I do. And, what's more, I hear Dee talking to her wife Suzie as if she is right there with her, helping her through—because she is. Who is anyone to tell us who is real to us and who can and cannot help us in our lives? No one. Got it?"

"Got it."

"Good."

"I'm so thankful for you."

"And I am thankful for you." Phoebe kissed Violet once again, this time with such tenderness and feeling that it was less a kiss and more an expression of her conviction of how much Violet meant to her. By how complete Phoebe's kiss had made her feel, Violet could only imagine that she meant *everything* to her.

Violet knew she would never forget that kiss and that it would stay in her heart forever.

She took a deep breath to calm herself and to find her balance again. A chuckle bubbled to the surface. "And I just want to say that you were totally kick-ass. I loved it when you stamped on Carl's foot."

"Me too. I'd do it again right now if he came back."

"I don't doubt it." They laughed, only to stop short at the sound of a loud knock on the shop door. "I'll go. I'm not intimated by him any more."

"*We'll* go. He's got some nerve, daring to show his face again." Phoebe scrambled from the bed, and with the demeanour of someone who would take no prisoners she ran downstairs.

When Violet caught up with her, she heard a familiar voice ask, "Is Miss Violet Unwin in, please? Can you tell her it's Mr. Burrows."

Mr. Burrows? Violet joined Phoebe at the door. "Mr. Burrows. Hi. Please come in. How can I help you?"

Mr. Burrows gave her the warmest of smiles as he stepped inside. "I rather hope that it's how I can help *you*, young lady. On the explicit instruction of my wife, after I felt compelled to tell her about my visit to this wonderful place, I have purchased your vintage cabinet of drawers. I want you to have it."

"You've done that for me?"

"Yes. Too often people get separated from the things that are rightly theirs. It seems to me that you have suffered your fair share of injustice. At least, in this small way, I can perhaps prevent another unkindness being done to you. And here. You keep this cash." Mr. Burrows handed Violet an envelope. "And if Mr. Carl Unwin has a problem with it, then he is more than welcome to talk to my wife." Mr. Burrows gave a defiant nod. "Good evening, then." He shook Violet firmly by the hand. "You have my very best wishes." With that Mr. Burrows left.

Violet tried to process the enormity of what had just happened. But what on earth would she do with the cabinet? For that matter, what on earth was she going to do?

"Wow, what a sweet guy," Phoebe said, smiling at Violet.

"Yes, he is. Except I don't really know what I'm going to do with his gift. I don't even have a place organised for me to go to, let alone—"

Before she had chance to finish her sentence, Phoebe leaped in. "You can stay with me. You see, I'm not going back to halls. And we can always store the cabinet at The Banana. I know Dee won't mind on either count. Jo has offered to help us with their van. I'm sure we can rally the Friday night regulars to give us a hand to move you in. Come to think of it, I reckon the cabinet would fit in the Saloon Bar." The strangest of expressions came over Phoebe's face. "Wait a minute…it could work. It could actually work."

"What could?"

"I need to talk to Dee when she comes back with the beers." Phoebe squeezed Violet's hands. "But I think I might have a plan. A bloomin' marvellous one, at that."

A plan? Violet's life was a pile of bin liners and a cabinet of drawers. The place and the very existence she loved and that had kept her safe were gone. She didn't need a plan. She needed a miracle. But then fate had brought Phoebe to her, and surely that was a miracle in itself. So maybe it wasn't a miraculous act she needed, but just a little faith in that which was meant to be.

❖

"I can see it now. Our name in lights. Unwin's Emporium at The Banana Bar." Dee stood amongst the chaos of bin bags in the middle of the shop staring up at an imaginary sign and gesturing in the air as she suggested how the branding for their shared business space could work. "And your dedicated zone, once occupied by the oh-so decadent Saloon Bar, will blow your mind." Adopting the tone of an estate agent, Dee then added, "The large room has retained all its original Victorian features from ceiling rose to gothic stained-glass windows to decorative tiled flooring. It's perfect for you, kiddo, and all yours for you to make your own. How does that sound to you, my new partner in crime?" Dee looked the most excited and happiest Phoebe had ever seen. And Violet kept blinking and blushing and smiling and looking at Phoebe as if she couldn't quite believe what was happening.

No sooner had Dee arrived back at the shop, with beer bottles clinking in her carrier bag, than Phoebe had spilled out, in one excited breath, her idea of Unwin's Emporium finding its new home at The Banana. "It's a successful business that can hold its own. It would be amazing, and there's so much synergy between the businesses. This was where you found Mr. Duke, and it can be where other Mr. Dukes can be created right at the heart of everything."

Dee had needed no persuading. She straight away asked, "How does that sound to you, Violet? I'd make the rent affordable. Is that something you might consider? No problem, if not. We'll still do everything we can to help you, whatever you decide."

"Deffo," Phoebe chipped in, quickly adding, "and tell me to bugger off if I'm speaking out of turn or getting ahead of myself."

Violet had stood in silence, with an expression of both intrigue and wonder, while she listened to Phoebe's idea. When she eventually spoke, she simply said, "I'm in." They all squealed, even if Dee denied that the loudest scream of delight was hers. The beers were cracked open in celebration, and the cheap fizzy booze had never tasted so good.

"Obviously, the sign needn't be in lights…" Dee held her hand suspended in the air, like her thoughts.

"No, lights are perfect." Violet nodded. "And let's keep the original shape somehow. You've worked so hard to establish your brand, and you don't want to lose that. Perhaps the smiling banana could have a bow tie and top hat? Except at Christmas time, of course." Violet stared up at the imagined sign as she spoke, as if it hung above them and was not merely floating in the ether of their collective hopes and dreams. "I think it could be great. Thank you so much."

"Just great?" Dee frowned a little and dropped her hand to her hip. "The Banana Bar and Unwin's Emporium joining forces to create a business is not just great. Oh, no sirree. It's just *genius*, that's what it is. It's a triumph, it's…*inspired*."

"And it makes loads of sense. Like it's meant to be," Phoebe said, smiling at Violet. "After all, you said it yourself that you are the Emporium. It's *you*, Violet. It goes where you go."

Phoebe took Violet's hand. "You are the natural inheritor of Unwin's Emporium wherever it is located. You are the heir to its future."

Violet took an unsteady emotional breath. "*We* are. Us three."

Sniffing back a tear that she would deny if challenged, Dee raised her beer in the air. "To Unwin's Emporium at The Banana Bar."

"Oh no—wait." Violet's face dropped to an expression of worry. The room went deathly silent. "There's no way Carl will let me have the name Unwin's Emporium."

"But he hates the shop," Phoebe said, looking at Dee and back to Violet. "Doesn't he?"

"He hates me more. He wouldn't give me anything if he thought I wanted it."

"Why does he hate you so much?" How could anyone harbour such animosity? And towards Violet, of all people. "You've done nothing to him."

"Let's just say it's complicated. But I think a lot of Carl's anger towards me might have something to do with Uncle Walter." Violet looked at Dee, who stood listening without comment or judgement. "When Uncle Walter first took me in, he seemed pleased to have me. He loved that I loved the Emporium so much. We were like two peas in a pod. My aunt hated it and Carl resented me. Together they never stopped resenting me. Their mission seemed to be to separate us. And it has worked to this very day."

It was heartbreaking to hear Violet speak of the emotional neglect she had endured. If Carl was here, Phoebe would do far more than stamp on his shoe. And as for Violet's uncle, she would give him the almightiest of shakes to wake him up to what a wonderful person he turned his back on.

Dee gave a heavy sigh. "Let's face it, jealousy improves no one and is responsible for the most unforgivable behaviour. It eats away at people and leaves them a skeleton of themselves with the barest bones of humanity, just like Carl. Just a thought, though—Carl doesn't actually own the shop, does he? It belongs to Walter, doesn't it?"

"Technically, yes. But Carl and my aunt rule the roost, and they have blocked me from speaking to my uncle. They keep saying he's too sick and I'm not to trouble him. We'd never get to ask Walter himself."

"And you believe them about him being ill?" Dee asked, with a note of scepticism to her question.

"I don't know what to think. When he was here, Uncle Walter gave in to them. So even if he isn't as ill as they are making out, why would he overrule them now?"

"Because he doesn't love his wife and hates his son and no doubt misses his shop and his niece and his customers, and one regular in particular."

"Uh-huh. Let me guess who that could be." Phoebe laughed and then stopped laughing. "You're serious."

"Cover your ears, Violet. Do you remember, Pheebs, when I told you that not every person who proposed to me was single."

Oh my God. *No way.* Walter had a thing for you?"

"You could sound less surprised, thank you very much. Although admittedly it was more a proposition than a proposal."

Violet nodded. "Makes sense. I would love to have served you, but he always insisted it must be him."

"Don't get me wrong"—Dee shook her head—"I enjoyed the personal attention, and I'm really fond of Walter, just not in the same way that Walter is *really fond* of me. I let him down gently, of course, and I'd like to think he still considers me a good friend. In fact, I think it's time Walter and I caught up."

Violet shook her head. "They won't let you speak to him."

"We'll see. What's the name of the solicitors who carried out the sale on this place?"

"Erm...Sharp and Co., I think."

"Excellent..."

"My aunt is smart, so she'll recognise your voice."

"Mine, maybe. Phoebe Frink, the new hotshot PA ringing from Sharp and Co. and insisting to speak to Mr. Walter Unwin and Mr. Walter Unwin alone, not so much. What say you, Pheebs?"

"I say give me the number, and I'll make the call, and once he answers I'll hand over to you."

Violet gave a small shrug. "I suppose there's a chance it could work."

Phoebe held Violet loosely by both arms. "It *will* work."

"Okay." Violet took a deep breath. "I'll find you my uncle's number. Oh, that reminds me, if you do get through, can you tell Walter that I found an item of jewellery and ask what he would like me to do with it. It's a brooch in the shape of a flower. It's made up of gemstones. There's a real possibility they're sapphire and diamond."

"*No*, Violet." Phoebe placed her palm to Violet's cheek. "Vi would want you to have it. You know that."

"It doesn't belong to me."

"Of course." Dee effortlessly intervened. "Absolutely. I'll mention it. No problem."

"Thank you." With apology in her eyes, Violet held Phoebe's gaze and said, "I'm sorry. It's the right thing to do."

It wasn't the right thing, but Violet was too honest to see that. "Don't give him anything else, though. Promise me."

"I won't. I promise."

As Violet glanced down to retrieve her phone from her pocket, Dee shot Phoebe a look that unmistakably said *I have absolutely no intention of mentioning that*.

"Here you go." Violet showed Phoebe Walter's number, and Phoebe typed it into her phone and pressed dial. After just two rings, a woman answered.

"Good afternoon, this is the Unwin residence." Was this Violet's aunt? The woman's voice was utterly devoid of warmth.

"Hi." Phoebe cleared her throat. *Hi* was not the way Phoebe Frink the hotshot PA would begin her call. *Get into character, Frink.* "Good afternoon. My name is Phoebe Frink from…" Violet mouthed the words *Sharp and Co.* "Sharp and Co. Solicitors. Is Mr. Walter Unwin available, please?"

"May I ask what it regards?"

"It is a matter related to the sale of Unwin's Emporium."

"I see. Then the best person for you to speak to is my son Carl. He is handling everything on behalf of the family. Let me give you his number."

"*No.* I mean, there's no need. It is rather important that I speak directly with the owner of Unwin's Emporium, rather than"—*the arsehole*—"the go-between, so to speak."

Phoebe could sense some bristling in the silence at the other end of the phone. Maybe *go-between* wasn't the best choice of phrase, although better than the one she wanted to use.

"Mr. Unwin has been rather unwell recently, so I would prefer—"

"It won't take long. I promise." Phoebe could hear a man's voice in the background and Violet's aunt trying to send him away.

"Hello. This is Walter Unwin."

Walter?

"Hi. This is Phoebe Frink, and I am ringing on behalf of your niece Violet and your good friend Dee from The Banana. I know this sounds strange, but I need you to pretend that you are speaking to an employee of Sharp and Co."

"That does sound strange. I hope everything is okay?"

Which bit did Walter hope was okay? The bit where he emotionally neglected his young niece or the bit where he sold her livelihood from under her? "Sort of. Can I put Dee on to speak to you?"

"Yes, of course." Violet's aunt was clearly hovering, and Walter was doing his best to send her away. Phoebe couldn't tell whether he'd succeeded or not. She handed her phone to Dee.

"Walter. It's me, Dee."

Phoebe moved to Violet and held her close. They stood utterly fixated on Dee's every word and expression.

"Yes, it must be at least that long, perhaps longer. Congratulations on your retirement, and I'm sorry to hear that you've been under the weather...Yes, stress is a terrible thing...nothing that wonderful sea air won't sort I'm sure...yes...Look, I won't keep you long, it's just I have a favour to ask...Anything? That's very kind, Walter." Dee gave an unusually coquettish laugh, which made Phoebe and Violet chuckle. Dee scowled at them and shooed them away and then made for the relative privacy of the shop window. Phoebe could now only just make out the odd word or two and which included *wonderful*, *Violet will be so pleased*, and *have it sent to The Banana*. After a short while, Dee moved back towards them. "Yes, you too...Yes, you never forget the good times. Take care then, Walter."

"Did he say yes?" Violet held her hand over her mouth.

The widest of grins spread across Dee's face. "You bet, kiddo. You, me, and Dr. Frinky Boots, a formidable team to reckon with. Look out world, here we come."

"That's incredible. Thank you for helping me, Dee."

Dee gave a salute. "You're very welcome, Violet Unwin, of Unwin's Emporium at The Banana."

Violet bounced into Phoebe's arms. "I can't believe it."

Phoebe held Violet tightly. "I'm so pleased for you, Violet."

When Phoebe eventually let her go, Violet asked Dee, "Did Uncle Walter say anything else? What did he say about the brooch?"

"The brooch?"

"You did remember to ask him?"

Dee feigned offence. "Yes. Absolutely. Determined you should have it. One hundred percent."

"Really?"

"Couldn't be persuaded otherwise."

"There you go." Phoebe rubbed at Violet's shoulder.

"Okay." Violet didn't seem entirely convinced. "I don't suppose Uncle Walter mentioned me at all, did he? I wondered for a moment if he might ask to speak to me."

Phoebe held her breath. *Please, Dee, find the right words.* If anyone could, it was her.

Dee began, "You need to understand that your aunt was hovering like a mosquito in the background. It was difficult for Walter to speak freely."

Violet was visibly deflated, with her small frame bowing under the weight of her disappointment. "Of course. I understand."

"*But* it didn't stop Walter making it clear how proud he was of you. He didn't hesitate to agree to you carrying forward the Unwin's Emporium name."

"Really?" Violet looked at Phoebe, her eyes glistening with emotion.

"Yes, indeed," Dee continued. "It was clear he was chuffed to bits. And more than that, whenever he mentioned your name, his voice brightened with unmistakable love."

It somehow didn't matter whether Dee was telling the truth or not. What mattered was whether Violet chose to believe her. The tears rolling down her cheeks suggested she did.

"We could perhaps get in touch with him again when we're up and running," Violet suggested, "and invite him over."

"Absolutely. Let's do that. But for now, I've got to go back to *our* place and open for the Friday night crowd. I shall leave you in Dr. Frink's capable hands." Dee tucked a beer in each pocket of her jacket and turned for the door.

"Oh," Phoebe said, "will you ask a few of them if they could lend us a hand a little later to pack up. And could you tell Jo yes please to their offer of their van."

"Good thinking. Will do."

"Great. I'll stay and help Violet gather her things together."

"Good one, Pheebs. Laters, partner."

"Laters. Thanks again, Dee." Violet held out her hand and Dee shook it.

"My pleasure, treasure." As Dee left, the front doorbell rang out. Maybe Phoebe imagined it, but it sounded like a wedding peal of celebration and nothing like its usual shrill alarm. Violet was looking up at the ceiling to Vi's room. Her face was lit with the unmistakable glow of relief.

Phoebe's heart felt so full of joy. And not just for herself but for The Banana and most of all for her girl, the beautiful Violet Unwin, proprietor of Unwin's Emporium.

❖

Violet called to Phoebe from the top of the stairs, "I'll be with you in a moment."

"Okay. That's the last of the things down here. I have no idea how the cabinet fitted in the van. I've never seen Jo look so bewildered."

"It was a bit tight, wasn't it? I certainly owe Jo a huge pint."

"Deffo. Two, I reckon. They'll be back any time now for you and me and the remainder of your belongings."

"Great. I won't be a sec."

"No probs."

What did they say, teamwork makes the dream work? There was no way that Violet could even have dared to imagine this future full of such promise. She couldn't even have *dreamed* this when all she once had were nightmares that bled into her days and haunted her nights.

Even now, she would pinch herself just to check that this was real. But it was. For here was the solid banister and the stairs down which she'd raced Phoebe for their pizza delivery. And just there the little kitchen where she'd first made tea for Phoebe. And then her room… Violet made her way across the hall to the tiny space that had kept her safe for so long. It was empty of the rugs, the cushions, and her books. But it still somehow felt full of her and packed wall to wall with memories. Violet took a final seat on her bed, now stripped of its linen to its bare mattress. This would always be the place of her first night with Phoebe, where they lay in each other's arms looking up at the stars on the ceiling. The moment in time when Violet's world changed for good. Where there had once been fear, there was now trust. Where there had once been loneliness, there was now passion and life. For so many years she had believed she was fated to be alone. If only she had known as the little girl first sitting on this bed that she would be far from alone.

A bump from below made Violet look to the hallway. "Vi?"

"Sorry!" Phoebe shouted. "Just lost a fight with the broom. I'm fine, though. You okay?"

"Yep. Nearly done."

Violet stood outside Vi's room. She softly knocked on the door as she entered. "I'm coming in to collect the last of your belongings. Phoebe has made a safe space in her wardrobe for your coat and your precious things. Just to let you know we'll be leaving shortly. You'll love it at The Banana."

The wardrobe door was open, the hanger swung empty of Vi's fur coat, and the shelf was missing her hat. Violet stopped the hanger from moving and looked about the room. Where were they? She went to the box resting on the dressing table where she and Phoebe had earlier gathered the precious objects together. At first glance, they all seemed to be there. Vi's sash, the medal, the brochures, the postcard, even the bail form and passionate note from Harry, and the photo of them outside Equity Shoes. It was all there…wasn't it?

"Phoebe, have you seen Vi's fur coat and hat?"

"Nope. Are they not up there?"

"No. The wardrobe's empty."

"I'll have a look for them down here."

"Okay, thanks." Violet had the most awful growing sense that something wasn't right. "Vi?" She pulled out the dressing table stool and took her seat in front of the mirror. She stared into the glass. "Please." She stared and stared. "Vi." Nothing. Violet reached into the box, pulled out Vi's sash, and held it to her heart. "Please stay with me. I know you probably think that I have Phoebe and that Unwin's Emporium is safe and that I maybe don't need you any more, but I do. Please." Violet laid her head upon the dressing table. "Please."

"Violet." Phoebe placed her arm around her and kissed her cheek.

"She's gone, Phoebe."

"I can't feel Harry either. I didn't like to say."

"She's taken her coat and hat and left."

"A lady never leaves without her coat and hat." They shared a heartbroken smile. "I like to think Harry will be waiting for her on a street corner with a bunch of flowers or a glamorous gift."

*The brooch.* "Where's the brooch?" This time Violet methodically emptied the objects onto the table. "Can you see it?"

"No."

"We definitely put it in the box earlier, didn't we?"

"Yes, that's my memory too."

"Please don't say I've lost it."

"How can you have lost it?"

"I don't know." That was the awful thing about losing things—they were lost before you knew you'd lost them. It was already too late.

"I have a feeling it'll turn up, please don't worry. It's got itself packed away in another box somehow, or maybe Vi has taken it with her."

"Let's hope so."

"Deffo. Hold on. Violet, what's that photo?" Phoebe lifted the photograph free from where it rested face down alongside the other objects. She flipped it over and held the colour Polaroid between them.

Violet blinked and blinked at the image she never expected to see. "It's me."

In a gentle tone, Phoebe asked, "Could the woman with you be—"

"My mum." Violet recognised her mum immediately. All these years of the memory of her fading had led Violet to believe that her mum was lost to her for good. This photo was so much more than paper and chemicals—it was proof that she had been loved. Violet's tears dripped onto the bleached photo of a young Violet holding her mother's hand.

"That's so amazing. Vi found it for you." Phoebe wrapped her arm around Violet.

"How could she? Where was it all these years?"

"I reckon it was in the same magical place where all the invisible things belong. I like to think that nothing is truly lost but simply waiting to be seen." They stood in silent wonder staring at the photo. "You look like her. Just so beautiful, Violet."

The beep-beep of Jo's van approaching round the corner reminded them that their time in the Emporium, Duke Street, was now over.

Phoebe gathered herself together. "I know you don't want to leave, Violet…"

Violet wiped at her eyes with her sleeve. "It's okay, I'm okay, I promise. I'm ready. Ready to start our future." Violet reinforced her sentiment with a kiss upon Phoebe's lips. Then Violet gathered the belongings back into the box, taking care to tuck the photo of her mum safely inside. As Violet closed the bedroom door, she spoke into the room. "Thank you, Vi. Please know, I am taking you with me in my heart."

As the van drove away, with Phoebe and Violet and all the last of her belongings on board, Violet took one last look at the building she had called home. Who would live there next? And would they ever pause to wonder who had lived there before?

## Chapter Twenty

"Merry Christmas! And welcome to The Rebellion Hall," Phoebe said to the umpteenth person in the queue of excited revellers. "Do you have your ticket, please? I'm afraid we're fully booked and can't do walk-ins." Phoebe had expected the ball to be popular, but she hadn't fully prepared herself for it to be sold out with a waiting list of hopeful souls.

Word, it seemed, had got round in no time that a costume shop had been established in The Banana. Every drag king, drag queen, and Banana Bar regular—not to mention several of the Emporium's customers—had rushed to hire an outfit in time for the Christmas Ball.

"My God, Pheebs, our bartenders can barely cope." Mr. Duke pushed his way out onto the street and adjusted his crown. "If I didn't know better, I would say we were offering free drinks. We're not, are we?"

Phoebe laughed. "Your face! No."

"Right, phew. Thank God for Handy Man Joe and Elvis the Pelvis stepping in to bartend in between stints on stage. Speaking of additional bartenders, have you seen your Violet? I've scheduled her for the late shift. Live-in hazard. Sorry."

"No worries. We'll be on together, so that's fine. And yes, I last saw her in the loo making some final adjustments to Reggie's outfit. Oh, speak of the devils."

"Phoebe love, how Kylie moves an inch in these heels is beyond me." Reggie took a large suck on the straw bobbing in her highball glass. "I'm thinking now I should have accepted Valiant's offer to be Queen Elizabeth. But then, I thought, I don't want to upstage Mr. Duke in a competition of crowns. Not to mention, the wig looked like it required more neck strength than I can muster. Anyway, a few more spritzers and I feel sure I won't notice the gusset of these shorts forever creeping up my crack."

It took all of Phoebe's resolve not to burst into laughter. She dare not look at Violet for fear of laughing, when all she wanted to do was look at Violet.

Instead, mustering composure, Phoebe said, "You look wonderful, Reggie. The perfect rebel for our rebellion ball."

"Thank you. And you look just marvellous in that outfit. Such brave women. How they went on a hunger strike is quite incredible. I can barely go five minutes without a suck on a humbug, what with my low blood sugar. Speaking of which, when can we expect the buffet? And don't be fobbing me off with a frosty vol-au-vent."

"Come with me, Reg." Mr. Duke offered his arm, and Reg slipped hers in without missing a beat. "We'll get you first in the queue, international diva that you are."

"Mr. Duke, that would be an honour. And I hope I can include you on my dance card."

"I would be offended to find I was missed off. Give me a shout, Pheebs, if this crowd gets too excited."

"Will do. Have a lovely night, Reggie."

"I don't think she heard you." Violet smiled at Phoebe, and everything in her tingled.

Violet looked so handsome. Phoebe's thought—that she would be the one at the end of the evening who would kiss those lips, undo that tie, and ease the waistcoat off those shoulders—sent a thrill that trembled through her.

"I've got to, erm…tickets."

"I'll help. Next, please."

Working together, they got the queue down in no time. Only now and then was there a hold-up when one of Violet's customers wanted the low-down on the move from Duke Street. Mrs. Allen, dressed to impress as a football referee, expressed her relief that Unwin's Emporium had moved and not shut. Her affection for Violet couldn't have been clearer to see. There was general agreement that while nothing could replace the Duke Street shop, the new space held such promise for The Emporium's future. In fact, the buzz of excitement was palpable.

You could never predict how an evening would go. More than any other event at The Banana, The Rebellion Ball seemed to strike a chord with everyone. To see a roomful of people dancing, laughing, and celebrating courage, determination, and victory over the most formidable of obstacles was incredibly moving and left no one untouched. Some people came to the stage and just spoke emotionally, without any plan to do so, about their rebel hero.

Phoebe stood behind the bar with Violet at her side, serving customers and taking everything in. She never thought such happiness could exist.

"Hey, Valiant Unwin." Mr. Duke rested both hands on Violet's shoulders. "Now's your moment to ask your girl for the last dance."

"That would be great." Violet beamed an excited smile at Phoebe. "Thank you. Will you be okay?"

"I'm more than okay, thanks to you two." Mr. Duke's voice faltered. "And I will deny I said that. Now scoot."

Phoebe grabbed Violet's hand. "Come on." Phoebe led Violet onto the packed dance floor, finding a space by the stage under the lights of the Christmas tree. Holding each other close, they moved in time to the music's slow beat. It felt so, so good. Memories of their first kiss, so tentative and charged with feeling, came flooding back in a warm thrilling rush. And their first night…how the stars on Violet's bedroom ceiling shone upon them as their bodies gave up their deepest secrets to each other's touch. She felt Violet pull her yet closer and place her lips to her neck. In response, Phoebe pressed herself into Violet, as closer couldn't be too close, and the slightest separation, agony. She wanted to lose herself in Violet and never be found. Drown herself in Violet and never be rescued. Violet was hers, and she was Violet's. And the thought that this was just the beginning left her breathless with excitement of what was to come. She whispered in Violet's ear, "You're not safe."

Violet laughed. "Good."

Phoebe didn't notice anything but Violet in her arms. It wasn't until a weary Dee called over, "Switch off the lights when you eventually head up. Goodnight, you pair," that Phoebe came to and realised the music had stopped and the crowd dispersed.

Violet gave a contented stretch. She teased off her moustache and kissed Phoebe. "A tickle-free lip." She giggled. Looking at the stage, she said, "The tree's holding her own." Then, out of nowhere, her expression quickly changed from sleepy delight to a newly focused curiosity.

"What is it?" Phoebe followed Violet's gaze to a small box tied with a red Christmas bow that was lying under the tree.

"I recognise it," Violet said, not letting her gaze shift from it, as if afraid it might disappear if she looked away for a second.

Violet wasn't the only one who recognised the red leather box. Phoebe's heart pounded in her chest, and she reached for Violet's hand. "I think we've found the brooch. Before you ask, I didn't put it there, and I know you didn't either."

"Dee is the only other person who knows about it, but it can't possibly have had anything to do with her."

"It didn't. We know who put it there. We don't need common sense to work it out—we just need to listen to our hearts, and mine is telling me…"

"Telling you what?"

Phoebe knew what her heart was telling her. What Harry needed her to do. She gently lifted the box from under the tree. "Undo the ribbon with me?"

Clearly lost in an understandable daze, Violet gave a distracted, "Sure."

They undid the bow between them and then eased the lid open to stare in wonder once more at the breathtaking flower with its beautiful gemstones sparkling in the lights of the Christmas tree.

Lifting the brooch free, Phoebe unclipped the pin and slipped the thin metal into the buttonhole of Violet's waistcoat. She placed her palm flat to rest over the brooch, which in turn lay against Violet's heart. She had never felt more certain of what to say. "Always and always…"

Seamlessly, Violet joined in and said with her, "Facing toward the light."

"I give this to you with all my heart. It is yours. It's always been yours."

Pressing her hand to Phoebe's, Violet kissed her. It was a kiss that felt for all the world like it had waited many lifetimes to be given. "Thank you, I'll treasure it…forever."

Never had a moment felt so complete. "Let's go up."

"Yes."

Phoebe took a last look around the bar and dutifully turned off the lights. Violet held her hand and led the way up the first few steps.

"Wait. Violet, look."

They stood on the stairs and looked back at the tree, with the star in pride of place shining brightly and lit by an unearthly light invisible until that moment.

Violet whispered, "Happy Christmas, Phoebe Frink. I love you."

"Happy Christmas, my beautiful Violet Unwin. I love you too."

## About the Author

Anna is an English literature graduate with a passion for LGBT heritage. She has master's degrees in museum studies and the word and the visual imagination.

Anna's debut novel, *Highland Fling*, was a finalist in the 2018 Golden Crown Literary Society Awards. Her second novel, *Love's Portrait*, was a finalist in the 2019 Rainbow Awards and in the 2019 Foreword INDIES Book of the Year Awards. Her third novel, *Highland Whirl*, featured in Lambda Literary December's 2021 Most Anticipated LGBTQ+ Books. Her short story "Hooper Street" can be found in the BSB anthology *Girls Next Door*. Her poems have been published with Paradise Press and the University of Leicester's Centre for New Writing.

Find her at her website, www.annalarner.com, or on Facebook and Instagram: @anna.larner.writer.

# Books Available From Bold Strokes Books

**Coasting and Crashing** by Ana Hartnett. Life comes easy to Emma Wilson until Lake Palmer shows up at Alder University and derails her every plan. (978-1-63679-511-9)

**Every Beat of Her Heart** by KC Richardson. Piper and Gillian have their own fears about falling in love, but will they be able to overcome those feelings once they learn each other's secrets? (978-1-63679-515-7)

**Fire in the Sky** by Radclyffe and Julie Cannon. Two women from different worlds have nothing in common and every reason to wish they'd never met—except for the attraction neither can deny. (978-1-63679-561-4)

**Grave Consequences** by Sandra Barret. A decade after necromancy became licensed and legalized, can Tamar and Maddy overcome the lingering prejudice against their kind and their growing attraction to each other to uncover a plot that threatens both their lives? (978-1-63679-467-9)

**Haunted by Myth** by Barbara Ann Wright. When ghost-hunter Chloe seeks an answer to the current spectral epidemic, all clues point to one very famous face: Helen of Troy, whose motives are more complicated than history suggests and whose charms few can resist. (978-1-63679-461-7)

**Invisible** by Anna Larner. When medical school dropout Phoebe Frink falls for the shy costume shop assistant Violet Unwin, everything about their love feels certain, but can the same be said about their future? (978-1-63679-469-3)

**Like They Do in the Movies** by Nan Campbell. Celebrity gossip writer Fran Underhill becomes Chelsea Cartwright's personal assistant with the aim of taking the popular actress down, but neither of them anticipates the clash of their attraction. (978-1-63679-525-6)

**Limelight by Gun Brooke**. Liberty Bell and Palmer Elliston loathe each other. They clash every week on the hottest new TV show, until Liberty starts to sing and the impossible happens. (978-1-63679-192-0)

**Playing with Matches** by Georgia Beers. To help save Cori's store and help Liz survive her ex's wedding, they strike a deal: a fake relationship, but just for one week. There's no way this will turn into the real deal. (978-1-63679-507-2)

**The Memories of Marlie Rose** by Morgan Lee Miller. Broadway legend Marlie Rose undergoes a procedure to erase all of her unwanted memories, but as she starts regretting her decision, she discovers that the only person who could help is the love she's trying to forget. (978-1-63679-347-4)

**The Murders at Sugar Mill Farm** by Ronica Black. A serial killer is on the loose in southern Louisiana, and it's up to three women to solve the case while carefully dancing around feelings for each other. (978-1-63679-455-6)

**A Talent Ignited** by Suzanne Lenoir. When Evelyne is abducted and Annika believes she has been abandoned, they must risk everything to find each other again. (978-1-63679-483-9)

**All Things Beautiful** by Alaina Erdell. Casey Norford only planned to learn to paint like her mentor, Leighton Vaughn, not sleep with her. (978-1-63679-479-2)

**An Atlas to Forever** by Krystina Rivers. Can Atlas, a difficult dog Ellie inherits after the death of her best friend, help the busy hopeless romantic find forever love with commitment-phobic animal behaviorist Hayden Brandt? (978-1-63679-451-8)

**Bait and Witch** by Clifford Mae Henderson. When Zeddi gets an unexpected inheritance from her client Mags, she discovers that Mags served as high priestess to a dwindling coven of old witches—who are positive that Mags was murdered. Zeddi owes it to her to uncover the truth. (978-1-63679-535-5)

**Buried Secrets** by Sheri Lewis Wohl. Tuesday and Addie, along with Tuesday's dog, Tripper, struggle to solve a twenty-five-year-old mystery while searching for love and redemption along the way. (978-1-63679-396-2)

**Come Find Me in the Midnight Sun** by Bailey Bridgewater. In Alaska, disappearing is the easy part. When two men go missing, state trooper Louisa Linebach must solve the case, and when she thinks she's coming close, she's wrong. (978-1-63679-566-9)

**Death on the Water** by CJ Birch. The Ocean Summit's authorities have ruled a death on board its inaugural cruise as a suicide, but Claire suspects murder, and with the help of Assistant Cruise Director Moira, Claire conducts her own investigation. (978-1-63679-497-6)

**BOLDSTROKESBOOKS.COM**

Looking for your next great read?

Visit BOLDSTROKESBOOKS.COM
to browse our entire catalog of paperbacks, ebooks,
and audiobooks.

Want the first word on what's new?
Visit our website for event info,
author interviews, and blogs.

Subscribe to our free newsletter for sneak peeks,
new releases, plus first notice of promos
and daily bargains.

**SIGN UP AT**
BOLDSTROKESBOOKS.COM/signup

# Bold Strokes Books
Quality and Diversity in LGBTQ Literature

*Bold Strokes Books is an award-winning publisher
committed to quality and diversity in LGBTQ fiction.*

Milton Keynes UK
Ingram Content Group UK Ltd.
UKHW012140131223
434291UK00001B/85